I Don't Know
But I've Been Told

I Don't Know But I've Been Told

Raul Correa

HarperCollins*Publishers*

This is a work of fiction. Names, characters, places, and incidents either are the product of the author's imagination or are used fictitiously. Any resemblance to actual events, locales, organizations, or persons, living or dead, is entirely coincidental and beyond the intent of either the author or publisher.

HarperCollins books may be purchased for educational, business, or sales promotional use. For information, please write: Special Markets Department, HarperCollins Publishers Inc., 10 East 53rd Street, New York, NY 10022.

Printed on acid-free paper

The author would like to thank the corporation of Yaddo and the MacDowell colony.

FIRST EDITION

Designed by Nancy Singer Olaguera

Library of Congress Cataloging-in-Publication Data
Correa, Raul.
    I don't know but I've been told / by Raul Correa.—1st ed.
        p. cm.
    ISBN 0-06-019611-4
        1. Americans—Panama—Fiction. 2. Illegal arms transfers—Fiction. 3. Fort Bragg (N.C.)—Fiction. 4. Parachute troops—Fiction. 5. Young men—Fiction. I. Title.
PS3603.O683 I18 2002
813'.6—dc21

                                                          2001039438

02 03 04 05 06 ❖/RRD 10 9 8 7 6 5 4 3 2 1

. . . if I'd a knowed what a trouble it was to make a book I wouldn't a tackled it, and I ain't a going to no more.

Huckleberry Finn

I Don't Know
But I've Been Told

prologue

She Wrote Me a Letter

Dear Sergeant Cara Bebe

*I have begin this letter many times and it is Marta who writes
for me. We must steal   bar office for use of some type writer .
Misising You are missing from me you is what I am and feel
some days the all word on my back.   I have never forget you
but want you only remember me .No remember bar Le fleur
or this Colon, Panama . In the last week ther were all greek
sailors and russian sailors in bar le Fleur. I stay only in my
room up of stairs and make no money and boss mad. I only
happy and hurt when I remember you you remember me? I
want and happy you happen to me. I want to this North
Carolina with you.   you to make a change to Special forces
and come Panama for ever? what. baby face. I make i kiss
you now and i kiss you. Write me and LOVE, I miss you
totell me what to happen,   Paola.*

I have taken this old letter everywhere that matters. It was typed on
a sort of stiff onionskin and some words have been creased and
folded away. Lips form the words no longer on the page and if some
hard wind rose and tore the letter from my hands, I possess fingers
which would remember the rise and fall, the contour of that page
which has never lain flat.

Standing along the promenade in Brooklyn, NY, I'm holding my
old letter, my good thing, and thinking that in the pre-dawn it is
somehow wrong to be this close to the water and unable to hear it
being turned up by the working boats.

I work the tugs out of Staten Island: Macalister Nautical Towing, two weeks out and two weeks in. It's nice like that, put in half a month's work on the water then hit dry land a free man for the other half.

The guys on the tug like me, because I learned a long time ago that I am the guy who has to be quiet and work hard for a good long while before I start with the mouth.

We docked today around suppertime.

Most of my two weeks off the tug I walk the streets at night. I leave the apartment at 2:30 A.M. and get ready for it like those kids who go to camp: proper clothing, Wet-Naps. My letter comes with me, secured in a Ziploc bag, and placed in the middle of an old Signet paperback of *Huckleberry Finn*. I ride the trains up and down for a while. There are others—burnt faces, cleft heads, double and triple amputees, no noses, horror shows. It is natural for them to want to ride the subways, do errands, to go through the motions a few hours before everyone else. I doubt they have letters like mine.

In front of me on the subway home tonight was a man with one leg. His stump stuck out through the cut-off and soiled pant leg of a pair of knit dress slacks. It moved about like a blind kitten just left its mother.

His face was that of a black child star from an old TV show, though he could have been forty-five. He was turned so that he could see his reflection in the shiny metal below the placards. He pulled down an eyelid and stared at it in the metal. He pushed it and pulled on it, moving his face around, observing what he could make of himself. His fingers pried his teeth apart and he peered deep inside his own mouth.

Two Transit Authority workers dirty from a night in the tracks sat across from him, eating fish-on-a-bun. The one next to me pointed at the one-legged man with his sandwich, smiled, and said, "Money got better teeth than me." I nodded back, thinking how odd and kind of cool it is to refer to a one-legged man on the subway as "Money." It was quiet as the men continued to eat and Money rolled his head along his metal mirror.

"Hey, want to trade teeth," said the man after he finished his sandwich. His friend leaned across the aisle and thrust a dollar bill at the one-legged man, who snatched it up and made the face of a mean baby at the men who laughed, and it was then quiet again.

The men tried to sleep, but kept opening an eye to look at the one-legged man called Money. It seemed like they were winking at him. After the 42nd Street stop, Money leapt to his foot—he had no crutches—and began to whirl around on his leg, faster and faster, until his arms were out straight at shoulder height and he looked like one of those green helicopters that fall from maple trees.

"Look, look, he's going somewhere," and "Yeah, buddy. Money taking off" was what the men said, as they sat up to watch him spin fast on one leg.

In one fluid motion the one-legged man stopped short and swooped down, sticking his nose flat against his reflection in the metal. It looked to me as if two one-legged men had flown into each other.

"Yeah, he's going somewhere."

"Going."

Sometimes I go to the twenty-four-hour pool halls, any of them, and watch the teenage Chinese gangsters with the best hair and the best girlfriends. I have to be careful, but I love all the Chinese because they always look like they are in a foreign movie.

I get off by the water and the cobblestone all the way downtown thinking that I'll find a cat or a dog or a lost refugee boat woman. Something.

Never lost my night vision, recon hearing, and once and a while something will flare up and burn right in front of me all red and crackling against the back-lit and milky gray New York morning: a trucker with Wyoming plates leaning out of his cab to give a hooker a hand up while a morning's red light worth of traffic clap their hands and toot their horns, and he takes a bow. The back of the Broadway–Nassau Street station, where the homeless fuck and buck until the trains run regular. Their sounds, they are like chants that escape from the throat before the tongue can whip them into words.

I have crouched at the stairs that lead into the station, and sent back down the sounds their lovemaking sends up. Singing. It was as if we sang together until the trains ran regular.

My letter and *Huckleberry Finn* are always running in my head, and even when I sleep the two are being read by me always, over and over.

Underneath whatever present thought I may be having, the book and the letter are being gone through, carefully. They never stop. I must only concentrate for a second or maybe two, and then I find my place in the book, the letter. I have done this for fifteen years and many times I have laughed out loud or fought back tears because some special part of them has sought my attention. It has happened in the middle of sex, a fight, a ride on the subway, or just walking down the street. That funny shit Jim says to Huck about the Duke and the Dauphin, Paola hiding upstairs from the sailors that I know she had to service, and sometimes a sweet stretch of words would come up to calm me at just the right time.

Next we slid into the river and had a swim, so as to freshen up and cool off; then we set down on the sandy bottom where the water was about knee-deep, and watched the daylight come. Not a sound any-wheres—perfectly still—just like the whole world was asleep, only sometimes the bullfrogs a-cluttering, maybe.

Like that.

I want and happy you happen to me.

Like that, too.

The first week off the tug begins like good magic. It's like just getting out of prison or the Army, or like putting your feet in the middle of some strange place where you don't understand the language. It's like a new woman. The repetition of that promise is what I live in every two weeks. It fades and falls out just in time for me to report back to the Macalister shack just off the Staten Island pier. Sea time passes with no consequence. I stand at the bow as often as I can for the same reason I have to sit in the front row of a movie theater. I want nothing between me and that which my thoughts tumble into. The open ocean reflects no hard things back and is one of the best places to hear the book and the letter. Where the flat sky and the flat ocean somehow meet is where my eyes fall and Huck's story and my letter just roll on.

The thing you might want to know about the tugboats is that when we pull up next to a ship the size of Grand Central Station we laugh, feeling so small.

An hour or so before the sun comes up, I'll get an egg sandwich, a coffee, and head for some open and private place—the bridges, or the parks, or the Brooklyn promenade—and dangle my feet or pull up on some grass and tell myself the letter or the book out loud.

I have only one story of my own and sometimes just the right mixture of coffee and egg sandwich in the mouth gets the story started. Sometimes the sky needs to turn pink at the edges. Other times in order to begin I have to reach between my legs and see if I've got a pair.

It is my one story and God help me if I get it wrong. I digress often, because if I tell it all the way through, I'm afraid there will be nothing left. It is the story of how I came to own the letter that is kept safely in its Ziploc bag and pressed between the pages of *Huckleberry Finn*.

I don't know my own good story like I know *Huckleberry Finn* or my letter. Often the sun comes up on me before I ever really get started. I get sidetracked and worried that the parts which bring me to how I've come to own such a letter won't be told right. Won't do justice.

I bring my legs up and back over the railing which runs the length of the promenade. Tomorrow night I'll come back and try and tell myself about Panama. Go all the way through. Tell about the blue-blue butterfly that looked like it should have an extension cord, about the city of Colon, where you could get monkey meat on a stick, a girl for a box of c-rations, and where I got Paola, who wrote me my letter. Tell about scorpions and red ants gang fighting alongside the jungle paths, Paola's friend who belonged to a green and red bird that lived in her hair, about the good guys who would cry over whores, about a platoon sergeant who could read a jungle.

Paola is my good thing. I turn to the story of her the way foxhole Christians hit their knees in prayer. Religions have big books and in them are many long stories. But they contain only one good true thing. Mine begins in Ft. Bragg, North Carolina. I can tell this story.

1

Mr. Big–Tunisia–Hook–Why Not Me?–Afro Pick in the

Eyeball–Sergeant Major Tells a Story–

Peanut Butter–And in Which Richards and Limón Talk

I was a paratrooper in the 2nd 304 Scout Reconnaissance Platoon, 82nd Airborne Division. You don't know me without that. It's where I come from.

My guys, the scouts, we waited till we hit Ft. Bragg to get brought along right enough to be from someplace. In 1979, 1980, when a kid could still get himself out of a jam by getting into uniform. The service was only just getting ready to be picky. All of us had stories when we got to Bragg, but there's where we learned to tell them. Even good guys who weren't dopers could tell you a story, except you might could actually believe some of theirs.

Stories.

We had them told to us, too, and in that way believed ourselves connected back ten and twelve and fifteen years, to Vietnam. These Vietnam stories were even better if an actual combat vet were telling them.

Everybody gets kind of quiet if you or somebody else who wasn't there is telling one of these stories, usually for the benefit of some cherry in need of guidance. If the vet is telling the story, then all that are gathered round bow their heads and hope that the act of listening real hard doesn't make too much noise. The vets, our noncommissioned superiors, don't tell stories that much, probably because they're the ones who made the rule that if someone talks about it a lot, then they most likely weren't there. If you are lucky enough to catch one of these stories, know that it may have actually happened and that in the Vietnam, the moral always seems to double back and get you from behind. Sometimes happens in our stories, too. Like this one.

I tell about Mr. Big a lot. A good solid telling of Mr. Big sets everything up for Paola.

Before we left for Panama, Mr. Big got passed down to us. Sort of like a story.

We'd been down on Hay Street—Suzie Wong's Rock Palace—sitting with the frosted mugs offered out of the lay-down refrigerator at the center of the dance floor. Me, Limón, Ski, Togiola, and even Richards stopped by before heading southside to the blacks on Mercuson Road. Friday night, a week shy of payday. All of us except Richards—cause The R could hold on to a dollar, sent it home too—had a bandage and one wrap of sticky gauze taped to our left forearms, from the blood and plasma shops. The last one, the nice place on Yatkin Road. Ladies take it from you wearing all white.

The two old-timers, Corporals Quinton and Collins, popped up behind us, pointing fingers for barrels, thumbs for hammers, and the bird for a trigger, and shot me and Ski in the temple. A whispered muzzle flash blown gently into my ear as a reminder: "You stay alert. You stay alive."

They looked hard at the gauze, picked up our beers, and motioned for us to follow them to a back table. There they told about a way to make it to payday without ever having to sell plasma again. Even though we were still "Stupid fucking cherries" to them, they had decided to pass along their dirty deeds with a man they called Mr. Big. Really, they called him "That fat fuck Mr. Big." Quinton added that the dirty deeds don't come cheap, and he said this like it was official, not even a wink or a grin.

The two corporals were getting out soon and had been sporting short-timer attitudes for weeks, treating us like we were cherries all over again. You'd of thought they were super old-timers like Platoon Daddy, who was ready to retire after a full twenty.

They passed Mr. Big on to us, saying that we were to think of him as an uncle of an old member of our platoon and to know him as one who had been in the 82nd himself and liked to keep in touch with the young guys. What we were to do for Mr. Big was easy enough: put aside some of the loads of munitions—L.A.W. Rockets, Claymore Mines, M-203 rounds for the grenade launchers—that the scouts get issued and are half bored with cooking off anyhow. Put that way it didn't seem close to what it really was.

Almost a week later, early morning and just before first call, Collins and Quinton, who had started their separation paperwork the day before, came back to the barracks big-white-boy-scary-drunk and screaming, "Short!" up and down the hall. They banged on every metal door of the scouts save Limón and Richards, gave Ski a piece of paper with just a phone number on it, and when I opened my door I got the two of them holding on to each other and shoving two clipboards in my face, yelling "Paperwork, son! ETS! Estimated Time Of Separation—you stupid fucking cherry!" and "I'm so fucking short I could do a Parachute Landing Fall off a motherfucking dime!" They fell across the room and crawled into Frankie Meadows' bunk, harassing him and singing, *Be all that you can be. Civilian! Moth-Er-Fuck-Er!"*

We stood round the barracks phone the next day when Ski called the phone number they'd given him. Mr. Big's voice was loud and laughing, we could hear that clear when Ski held up the phone. Two words came out of the phone and Ski got serious and we moved in close.

Red Lobster.

He wanted to take us to the Red Lobster off Bragg Boulevard. Since none of us had ever been and the challenge of most bets around Ft. Bragg ended with, "Yeah, and you take me to Red Lobster," we were impressed.

We spent the next few days not saying anything to the other scouts, only had a hard time not being superior when we waved off the usual payday week trip to Morrison's Cafeteria.

The five of us drove out to the restaurant in Ski's Gremlin with the mag wheels and Limón and Richards argued the whole way about whether or not to burn one.

Limón really wanted to get high before eating that good chow, Richards liked to wait to smoke after his meal and didn't want anybody stoned without him. Me, I used to be afraid to get high around authority figures, but had kinda gotten over it when on a dare I had tripped down low on a half hit of the Malaysian's—which was more than enough to feel like the whole world was gently whacking you in the face—while humping the colonel's radio as he evaluated the 2/325 on a mission through the Smokey Mountains. But something wanted me to stay regular for this first meeting with Mr. Big.

As usual, Richards, ice brother from Detroit, won by getting himself quiet. Limón folded but rolls up five pin joints for later, just to be doing something close to aggressive while talking that Spanish all to himself.

At a red light there was a line of cars waiting to make the turn into the restaurant's parking lot. The cars looked like mostly officers' foreign jobs, with a few senior noncommissioned officers' American-made machines—Buicks and whatnot mixed in—cars belonging to people who probably came to this kind of place even when it wasn't payday week.

Ski turned the Gremlin with the mag wheels into the lot, saying, "The cuisine here is supposed to be excellent."

Each of us, in our own way, told him he should blow us as soon as possible.

Because Ski had worked as a roadie for Van Halen he thought himself to be a worldly man. We had heard the real roadie story one night a couple of months before, when on his birthday, Ski got piss-in-his-pants drunk and we wound up at the twenty-four-hour IHOP watching him cry as he told us how he lost the "best fucking job in the world, man." Turns out that he and a buddy got caught selling stolen tour T-shirts on the side. After making a small fortune they got busted in Dallas towards the end of the tour.

"David and Eddie fired us personal and everything. Made me feel bad, man, and then left us in fucking Dallas."

Every third word boysenberry syrup would bubble out of Ski's mouth and down his chin. But everybody liked Ski, and forgave him his cheapness, taste in music, and even those white Capezio shoes.

We walked into the Red Lobster and there was only one miserable fat fuck sitting by himself at a round table in a corner, sipping a red frozen drink out of two straws. It was Mr. Big, and he was fat, that fuck. Looked like an evil lumberjack retired into thick double knits. We surrounded his table, and he stood up and said real loud, "All right. Nice of you boys to take time and meet an old paratrooper. Always like to meet the new breed. Come on now, take a seat." As soon as we were at our places round the table, he looked across at Limón and hissed, "Stop staring at me, son. You're making me nervous." Limón clucked his tongue.

We got right into our menus, pointing and talking about "I'm gonna get that, and if you get this let me get some of that." Then a waiter appeared at Mr. Big's shoulder and Mr. Big said, "Surf and Turfs, Number Two, done well, all the way around, and a couple of pitchers of Heinekens. Good Airborne chow, right, fellas?"

He waved away the waiter and the scouts all folded up their menus and stared at Mr. Big, who was taking a long pull off his red drink.

"All right, goddammit. I give you the poop, we eat, and get the fuck out of Dodge. Just eat and smile. How you read me? Loud and clear, right?"

The scouts, answering more his shitty way of talking at us than the question, banded together in our answer.

"Loud and clear. Roger that. Airborne."

"Read you, Lima Charlie."

"Airborne. Coming in lickin' chicken'."

Mr. Big's right eye began to twitch, and he started to tap out a slow cadence with a fork as he spoke fast and soft.

"You don't fuck with me. Not even a little bit. Rule number one."

He sounded like a hillbilly gangster.

"Rule number two. You fuck up, you get dead. Don't even think about a buddy fuck rat job, because you fuck up you just gonna die, and then your mother's house will burn down."

We sucked it up, and looked back at him like who and what the fuck is that?

"And know this: You eat with me, you're in. I shit you not. If any of you want out, somebody better act like they had too much to drink and head for the door and the rest of you can follow, assholes and elbows, moving out."

The waiter was headed for us with the pitchers and mugs, and Mr. Big started talking about how he wished he could have jumped with that new Dash One Bravo parachute that he had read about in *The Paraglide.* The waiter circled and Ski almost knocked the pitcher over trying to take it out of the waiter's hand. Mr. Big laughed loud and said, "No, son. This here is a tablecloth restaurant. Let the man pour your beer."

The waiter poured, and Mr. Big ordered another "strawbarry dykury."

"I'm going to utilize the latrine. Y'all drink your beers and think on what kinda stories you want to hear. I think y'all want to hear that one my nephew was telling you about. But you let me know."

We watched him towards the facilities and then looked down at our beers. It was Friday night, we were thirsty, and nobody moved.

"Heavy drop rigging motherfucker. They'd have to put a cargo chute on this asshole," said Togiola while Mr. Big was in the men's room.

If Togiola hadn't been there, we'd all of been more nervous than we were. Having a Samoan for a buddy made a guy feel like a cocky little brother. There weren't but a couple hundred of them in the whole Army, but the NCO clubs were always run by the Samoans. They like to reach down for a guy's ankle and sweep up with one hand till he was hanging upside down, maybe ready to get pulled apart like an orange. That's one of the moves in their own kind of martial art called Kapu Kuialua, which means something about breaking bones. It's a four zone martial art, and Togiola's cousins are all fourth level and I think that's as far as it goes.

Everybody's scared of them, Grits, Mexicans, Ricans, and especially the Brothers. Say they don't want to mess with them. Called the Samoans them "Big Chinese Niggers."

Ours was a big sweet Samoan, with royal blood, and it hadn't gone by any of us that he'd taken to swearing very early this evening.

I looked at Togiola across that table in the Red Lobster like I looked for him just before exiting an aircraft. Togiola, as an Army brat, had played football against Tony Dorsett, been a kickboxing champion in Europe. And he wrote poetry like car radio love songs except with more trees.

Both Togiola and Ski were sons of Sergeant Majors, and they should have known better about this mess. Not that they'd put much attention when a Colonel or Sergeant Major, who had combat time with Dad, tried to pull their coat about hanging out with dopers. Still, they should of known better. It would have been different. The scouts rising up from that round table to leave the beers full as poured, and Mr. Big left shaking it in the latrine, returning to an empty table. Maybe different things would have come.

But that night, we drank his beers and smiled shitty.

Mr. Big returned from the latrine and seeing our mugs half empty said, "Yeah, buddy. That's what I'm talking about. Bunch of paratroopers getting all liquored up. Now where's that half a fag waiter with my beverage?"

He was playing us. Working us. No biggy, he got us thinking the way he presented it. Just some extra ammo, and shit. Like the old-timers said, it was stuff we were tired of cooking off and blowing up, anyway.

He got his drink and we ate his food: prime rib with a lobster tail gone from its shell. But not before Mr. Big got us even more uncomfortable by saying that the prime rib wasn't done well enough and making the waiter take all the plates back to the kitchen. Said he'd "seen cows hurt worse than this get better."

Richards stared at the lobster tail like it was a word problem on a math test, and said it looked like butt.

"You eat that, son. It looks like butt, and tastes like pussy. That's some good eatin'," said Mr. Big. "That's right. Y'all brothers don't eat pussy. Get it in some of that butter take the tang out of it. Me, I stay in the pussy. Wake up in the morning with a face like a glazed donut." He smiled at the rest of us with that eye going all crazy again.

Richards pushed the tail to the side of his plate with a knife, and Limón reached across and scooped it up, popping it into his mouth whole.

We ate, listened, and Mr. Big told us how it was going to go down—and he kept saying it like that, "go down"—in the form of an infantry operations order.

I wasn't used to his kind of table manners. He never talked with his mouth full. He'd cut up one small piece of food, then put the knife down before raising the fork to his mouth, chewing only when the knife and the fork were back resting on the sides of the plate. I thought he ate like a girl and it scared me.

He wanted all of the next phone calls made from a pay phone at the Pop-A-Top. This got us staring, not at each other, only together at a point just above the center of the table, cause Corporal Marty Jencks' girl, Yon Me, worked at the Pop-A-Top, a dink bar on Hay Street—her mom ran the place. It was like this guy knew us.

Mr. Big switched to being somebody's fake uncle whenever the waiter or some customers came close.

He didn't want us to call till we'd gotten a bunch of stuff. He told us that it was best to keep the stuff out of the barracks and better to bury it out in the woods. The whole deal would be done with maps of Ft. Bragg and grid coordinates. Mark up an acetate-covered map with grease pencil to show the location of the buried stuff, call him, and arrange a place to leave the map. He'll use an eight-digit grid coordinate to tell us where. Eight-digit grid's how the Special Forces types work. Later we call again, and he gives another eight-digit grid coordinate where the money's at. It would all take some figuring with map, compass, and scrap paper, by somebody. Not me.

"Y'all keep it coming in steady and we're talking maybe two hundred a month. Each. More if it's that stuff that blows up real good.

And I don't need to talk about keeping it quiet now do I?"

I shook my head and the other guys were looking at the empty pitchers and Ski was tapping on his empty mug. It was the quietest sit-down-at-a-table meal I'd ever eaten with these guys.

"That's it from me, and no dessert and coffee, either. Y'all make my phone go ringy-ring, and y'all get paid in folding money."

He called out for the check and paid it from a small and tight knot of cash wrapped with rubber bands, snapping the bands as he paid.

Mr. Big dropped an arm around Limón and spoke loud to us all as we walked out of the restaurant. "I hear that the 82nd gets to wear the maroon beret again. I'm glad they gave it back. I think all elite units should wear a beret. Wore a couple myself."

The maroon beret, the international symbol of paratroopers, had been given back to us, almost two years ago while I was still in basic training. A lot of stink made about it, too, all the way up to Washington, and mainly about whether or not we were a true elite force worthy of our own special headgear.

He was coming straight for us with that. Letting us know that he had been with a Ranger Battalion—black berets, and a Special Forces unit—green berets. We belonged to the 82nd Airborne Division, which was like the minor leagues for those truly elite units. We shared Ft. Bragg with the JFK Special Warfare Headquarters, and they never thought about us, while the rest of the whole Army either mistook us for something scary, or considered us a glorified infantry division with no purpose in a real world situation. They said the AA patch under our Airborne tab, which stood for All Americans, really meant All Alcoholic, or All Assholes. They called us Jumping Junkies, Wind Dummies, and we even called ourselves with pride, The Most Physically Fit Alcoholics In The World.

Mr. Big's comment had caused me to stutter step, and I saw Richards whisper to Togiola, "This motherfucker," as we filed across the carpet and Ski veered off to the latrine.

The truth about Mr. Big could've gone two ways. Maybe he had been some high speed, low drag, special op's guy, or maybe he'd learned the talk and about the star sapphire ring and Rolex that all Special Forces guys wear from sitting up nights with *Soldier of Fortune* magazine. Either way he had a bead on us, and was fucking with us no doubt.

We knew our place, didn't need to be reminded. Special Forces guys, Rangers, Marine Force Recon, SEALs, they were supposed to be humble and quiet about what they did, while we, the paratroopers of the 82nd Airborne Division were supposed to talk a lot of shit. Especially scouts, who woofed it big time. Except if any of the real guys were around. Shit, we trained with the SEALs in Little Creek, Virginia, and spent the two days like, "Man, don't even look at them."

We followed Mr. Big out into the parking lot. I was sure he had another block of instruction for us but instead told that he had his eye on a little gal cocktailing back in the lounge. Said he'd be waiting for the call, and be sure to wait till we had a bunch of that good shit, then he gave us the Airborne salute, which is like a regular salute except when the arm comes out the palm is cupped and then falls like a floating parachute.

"Now you know I come from self-experience."

Nobody thanked him for dinner, but we watched him back to the restaurant and felt sorry for the cocktail waitress. Looking at our feet as we walked to Ski's car, except Limón hopping and fishing the loose jays out of a flip pack of Newports held in his tube sock. Togiola spoke first. "Ain't no way this guy was SF."

"I don't know, man, but what about that fucked up eye he had? Going all crazy and shit. My grandmother got some kinda name for that shit. She'd be burning plenty chickens over that motherfucker," said Limón.

One of us had started singing the bass part to Rapper's Delight. Just the beginning part, the way they have it on the long version. We call it the *Bump-Bumps,* and it was, along with the dance called the Smurf, the scout signal that somebody needs the Hay Street real bad.

Smurfing out a little in place, just a few moves from the four of us, and Richards confirms.

"I heard that. I need the gook land like twenty motherfuckers."

Limón handed out our private individual joints, holding one back for Ski and himself, and lit a match which Richards blew out.

"Damn, Rican. In the middle of Bragg Boulevard, Red Lobster and everything. Like a addict. Can't you wait?"

"No I can't. It's that eye, man. I got to put it out of my head. Did you see the way it moved around looking at everybody at the same time, and . . ."

Then a regular sight: Ski running across a parking lot, those big white Capezios a-flapping, car keys tossing from hand to hand.

Forgot all about Ski and King Econo. It was a contest he'd made up: King Econo. Who could be the cheapest. Ski usually held the title, only knocked off the throne for short times here and there. It had taken us a while to figure out why we were really always waiting for Ski in parking lots. After that, Scouts had gone to the floor of the IHOP lots of times trying to hold Ski back from stealing the tip we'd left for the waitress.

Laughing as he came the last few steps over, he was yelling for us to hurry up even as we waited for him to unlock the car. We were all pulling hard on our skinny jays before the Gremlin was out of the lot.

"I can't believe you stole Mr. Big's tip," I said, glad to have smoke in and out of my lungs, happy that leaving the parking lot in a hurry sat me at shotgun, and happy again with the Red Lobster in the rearview. Looking forward to a Friday night on the 500 block, Hay Street—land of a hundred dink dancers.

"Yeah, and check this out: the guy's almost as cheap as me. He didn't leave that waiter half the tip what he's supposed to."

We took the back roads to Hay Street. Me and Ski fighting over the radio, twisting dials and punching buttons, and him not driving good at all.

In my dreams so nice, the whole thing slides away. Just left it back in the parking lot, and we take our chances on doing nothing.

'Course it did get brought up. Togiola spoke first in the smoke-filled car.

"So what about this guy? I say it's a no-go. Don't like him. Not even a little bit."

Sweet thought. Night drive to the Hay, search for the song, talk about something else, and leave it alone.

Limón leaning up to the front seat said, "It's that fucking eye. It's evils, man. I'm telling you he got the evils."

Richards exhaled smoke and said, "I know for know why for I say."

"Yo, black. That ain't right. For serious we got to figure this out," said Limón.

Richards apologized for fucking with Limón, and wondered out loud how the fat cracker could find his dick never mind wet it with a cocktail waitress.

The black, Puerto Rican, and Samoan didn't like the way Mr. Big had treated them. But neither did me or Ski, particularly, even though it was agreed that it was different for the darker scouts the way he seemed to call them "boy" without really saying it.

We all took a turn bad imitating him, saying, "Remember, you eat the chow, you're in."

We decided that he was full of shit about being SF and about killing us. It had worked out fine for the old-timers, and we could all use some easy cash and a little covert activity, real sneak and peek, snoop and poop stuff. Everybody wanted to take some of Mr. Big's money.

Limón was quiet like he gets when the good dope first hits him, and then he started to stomp his feet like sitting and running in place at the same time while screaming, "I want his eye. I want that little eye. I take it out with my K-bar and put it on a little string. I want heeez eyeeee!"

We all started chanting "Limón wants the eye! Limón wants the eye! Limón wants the eye!"

I take my comfort from *Huckleberry Finn*. The part that tells about people like Mr. Big and why me and my guys let him play us like he did.

> *It didn't take me long to make up my mind that these liars warn't no kings nor dukes at all, but just low-down humbugs and frauds. But I never said nothing, never let on; kept it to myself; it's the best way; then you don't have no quarrels, and don't get into trouble. If they wanted us to call them kings and dukes, I hadn't no objections, 'long as it would keep peace in the family; and it warn't no use to tell Jim, so I didn't tell him. If I never learnt nothing else out of pap, I learnt that the best way to get along with his kind of people is to let them have their own way.*

We had circled Hay Street twice and then a good song came in clear, no static: The Ohio Players' "Love Roller Coaster." I twisted the volume knob all the way right, and the speakers Ski had stolen and installed himself held solid.

The Gremlin swung across the railway tracks and into the parking lot behind the Bunny Club. We had a rule that all entries onto the Hay had to be accompanied by a good song. Sat and stayed singing along. Scouts and smoke—mostly cigarette cause they taste best after the good green dope—climbed out of the car. Except Ski, who gripped the steering wheel and screamed along with the end of the song.

Waited up for him and then out past the back entrance and onto Hay Street, walking tight, five across—Paratroopers—lit up by the signs, the unreal light, and taking the first bar of many from the front.

Airfuckingborne. It was a good night. But I felt Mr. Big's eyes on my back through all of it. Even when I was steady stroking the six foot tall, half black, half white stripper from Maine in her trailer an hour after last call, Limón doing right by her roommate in the next room, I felt that fat fuck's eyes going deep.

The next day I woke up on a pull-out bed next to the stripper named Tunisia. She was kicking on me, thrashing around and talking in her sleep. Could almost follow the story of her dream she was talking it so much. Was something about a guy, he had a motorcycle and he was leaving. Her long legs had kicked the top sheet off of us and her left foot had taken up a corner of the bottom sheet, showing the light blue and thin mattress underneath. Maybe the guy on the motorcycle didn't leave cause she stopped all the moving around and I watched up on one elbow as she smacked her lips and she settled into a piece of a dream where people stay put. I stared at her coffee-colored foot against the blue mattress and the white bottom sheet where the elastic corner was now hooked onto the tip of her big toe.

Left her sleeping and damn near floated on top of the thick white wall-to-wall, looking for the bathroom. I was smiling as I pissed all over the toilet seat and floor, both covered in white shag, and even a little over into the sink. Smiling cause I was still a few years away from the crippling hangovers and cause spraying piss in six different directions meant that maybe the last thing I did before I passed out was come. I was down on my knees getting up as much as I could with some balled-up toilet paper, when I heard noises coming out of the bedroom across the hall.

I opened the bathroom door nice and quiet; two steps and I'm pushing on the bedroom door to see if it would give just a hair. It didn't budge. I looked down the narrow hallway and could see Tunisia still sleeping on the sofa bed. Behind the door, I heard Limón talking fast and Tunisia's roommate, Rochelle, starting to moan. They were getting going good, loud, so I turned on the doorknob and cracked the door a few more inches than I meant to. I saw Limón's back, and that he was still wearing that green and yellow shiny shirt with the race cars on it, borrowed from Richards over two weeks

latrine or chow. Or Togiola, we called him Brah, just like all the other Samoans, Hawaiians, Guamanians, and Tongans called each other. It was island for Bro, and I would call him by it when the first glint of a buzz was coming down on Hay Street, or like when I came into his room in the barracks after his grandmother died, and he was upset. All I could say was, "Damn, Brah." And what he said back was, "Thanks, man."

Rochelle and Limón were really going at it when I looked back into the bedroom. Limón wasn't doing the hip-swinging dancing anymore. Now he was slapping her ass and bucking back and forth as her whole body worked like a sprinter rocking in the starting blocks.

"Hook. Hook. Oh, Hook. HOOOOOK!"

There in the hallway I stood with a thumb and trigger finger trying to hold down my grin and keep my own noises in. Without even knowing it, I picked up Limón and Rochelle's rhythm with my hips. Just a little.

Those first few weeks at Bragg went just trying not to piss anybody off, and getting the hang of stuff, like remembering where the mess hall was, and just how in the hell did Limón get that boss nickname.

One night the guys took me down to Hay Street, showed me how to be righteous on the 500 block. They told me, "Scouts don't buy no drinks for dinks."

The girls got some of every dollar they got off every GI dumb enough to buy them a Hawaiian Punch. Out of the dark corners and sometimes right up off the bar and above the tables you'd hear a voice from a young soldier, no stranger to wheat or slop or engines or mills, factories, basement apartments, back lots.

"What's in them drinks I'm buying you?"

"It's for ladies drinks, baby."

There was a sign up on the mirror of every dink bar on the Hay.

Ladies Drinks

$5.00

$10.00

$12.00

$15.00

$20.00—Special Drink

There were all these Korean girls working GIs at the tables and the bar, strippers and the barmaids, all of them called Limón "The Hook" a lot more than the guys ever did. Really, that's all the dinks ever called him.

"Hi, Hook."

"Look, it's The Hook, baby."

"Hooky buy me drinky? I love him no shit."

"Hooky, how is your hooky, baby?"

The guys fed me beer after beer and made me yell, "Scouts!" "Recon!" and "Airborne!" a lot. That night I also got a nickname that did not stick.

At the Yobo club there was a men's and a women's, right next to each other, and one had a sign which had the word STUDS wood-worked into it, the other BEAVERS. It was just a temporary thing, losing my drinking skills. Eighteen straight weeks of basic training, infantry AIT, and jump school, did that to lots of good guys. I stumbled into the Beavers like seven times to piss and then yell at the toilet, floor, and walls. I don't remember it. Got told about it, and about puking some more in a car. Woke up in the barracks the next day by Frankie "Country" Meadows, who got his nickname cause he just was, stone cold, Country.

"Hey, Beaver. Beaver, man. Hey, come on now, Beav. You got to wake up and go clean out Sergeant Kenan's car."

Beaver. Like I said, it did not stick. Only a couple of months.

So, I did have a hangover that day, being out of practice, and the next one, too. I hated being called Beaver. But was happy that I was almost for sure how Limón got to be called The Hook.

Then, one morning after the company run, I decided to try and get a shower in before chow and wait out the long line at the mess hall. I thought the latrine was empty at first, but as I hung up my towel I heard a shower being turned on and someone singing a Spanish song.

It was Limón.

I knew it was him as I walked past the sinks and into the shower area. I knew stuff about him cause the guys would try and pick at him. He was very private about things. He wouldn't let anybody use his shower shoes, which had PR and a little Puerto Rican flag drawn on them with black Magic Marker, wouldn't let anybody use the weight set he had in his room cause he didn't want " . . . anybody getting big off my stuff," would send his roommate, before it was Richards, out of his room because he had to talk private to the poster of Bruce Lee above his bed, and he would rather miss morning chow than have to take a shower with everybody else.

I stepped into the big open shower room and turned on the set of knobs closest to the entrance, all the time thinking, "Don't look, Don't look. Whatever you do don't look." But weeks of wondering about how he got that bad-ass nickname, and then being almost sure of its origination after my first night on Hay Street with the guys, put me in that shower with the chance to know for sure. Limón was at the back end of the shower and I was pretty sure that he was washing his hair and didn't know I was there. Here was my chance to know for sure and I couldn't do it. Could not risk the chance. I started soaping myself down still thinking, "Don't look. Don't look," but there I was with my neck craned. Looking. And there it was. But it wasn't like I was looking at it; more like it was looking at me. You know, like peeking around a corner.

I whipped my head back just as Limón turned off his water and said, "Hey, cherry. Come on, man, we're going to miss chow." I rinsed myself off and said softly and smiling, "The Hook."

Limón and Rochelle were getting real wild like it might be ending soon and Rochelle had a pillow in her mouth, shaking it back and forth like a puppy with an old tennis shoe, so I faded back into the hallway and shut the door. I walked over to Tunisia still sleeping on the sofa bed, thinking I might get a little something off her of my own before I asked her to give me and Limón a ride back to post. Got stopped by looking out the big living room window of the trailer. Out that window I now had clear observation of that small group of people I'd seen through the small window just past Rochelle's head. It was a cookout and Sergeant First Class Mumphred, the 2/304's mess hall sergeant, was at the center flipping burgers, and laughing, probably at those old Jerry Clower stories he likes to tell.

He was a big happy grit, a southerner, who loved feeding the boys. He had spent ten years in the infantry so he got all the respect most spoons didn't, was connected with supply sergeants all over Bragg, and didn't go cheap on any little thing. You could hit him up for ice and burgers for a company party anytime, and he put the whole deal on in the mess hall for the holidays.

I remembered that we had seen him when we rolled into the parking spot next to Tunisia and Rochelle's trailer the night before.

He had been sitting on the steps of his trailer drinking a glass of wine, and yelled over that we boys should have a good time and wouldn't we stop by for some cookout tomorrow. He raised and tipped his wineglass towards me and Limón looking like we were about to sink our teeth into a heap a chow he had prepared himself.

I turned away from the window thinking *never a day off for this guy* as Sergeant Mumphred wiped away sweat and fanned at the smoke behind three little grills up on cinder blocks.

Just about to slide in next to Tunisia—she was so fine, sleeping with her lips looking like they were about ready to meet a straw, and one hand cupping the smaller of her breasts—but I heard a whoop and holler come directly from the bedroom, followed by a crash and a pop of wood and metal.

Tunisia came up, out of sleep and sofa bed, saying "What the fuck," and we both heard Limón shouting, "Oh, shit goddamn. Oh, shit goddamn."

I turned to see what Tunisia was looking at through the large and long living room window and saw that the whole picnic were all staring at her trailer and now moving towards it as a group. Tunisia wrapped a sheet around herself and stomped towards the bedroom, asking over Limón's now even louder cries, "What's he doing to her?" I followed after her to the bedroom door as she turned the knob and kicked it open. Limón was still humping away and Rochelle still had the pillow in her mouth except that her head had pushed the screen out of the small window frame and was now being driven into and back out of the open air at a rate that was just getting faster. Tunisia pulled the sheet around herself tight and said kind of funny, "Rochelle?"

I found and pulled on my jeans and ran for the door, looking to join Sergeant Mumphred's picnic as the outdoor audience for all of this. As I peeled out around the corner of the trailer in my bare feet, I heard Sergeant Mumphred yelling, "Yeah, buddy. That there is The Hook."

From a distance of respect, about fifteen yards, surrounded by ten or twelve people, he was pointing at the little window. I saw what they saw: just Rochelle's little head—eyes shut tight, with a pillow hanging from her teeth—coming in and out of the window. The rest was just the white flat front of the side of a wide and a half trailer. Of course everybody got to laughing, especially when the head flipped up the pillow, dropped it, hung there a sec, and then disappeared back inside, the frame of the window filled with the swing down and drop of curtain. Soft.

What I wanted to know then, and right up to this day, is how did Sergeant Mumphred know it was Limón behind Rochelle, and not me?

Soon after this we all took to fretting after Mr. Big, full-time.

We had planned to get some stuff to him fast, and opportunities kept popping up, except we were without The R for a while. We wanted to wait for him.

Richards had gotten sent to the Retraining Brigade over at the Correctional Confinement Facility across post. It was because of this one night when the Grits from Charlie Company—they were just rednecks, but we liked to call them Grits—begged us for some of the Malaysian's. We tried to tell them about the Malaysian, who is this forty-year-old guy who works as a caddy at the golf course a half hour away in Southern Pines, and who has the purple double-barrel micro-dot mescaline that messes you up deep cause his shit's from Asia. But they didn't care and took a whole hit apiece, washing it down with shine that came from Asheville in big plastic milk jugs, cause they thought it would go good. We heard them on the floor below us in the barracks, singing that Elvira song over and over, and thought that would be the worst of it until we heard glass breaking. We ran down and saw one of the Grits with a hunk of glass the size of a pizza slice stuck in his bicep, the blood smearing as it pumped up. A Staff Sergeant who was Charlie Company charge of quarters that night and just regular drunk was trying to apply a tourniquet too tight made of a torn T-shirt and a wet toilet brush. Yeah, and between the wound and the wrist.

We tried to tell him, but he wasn't listening and after a few drops from the toilet brush fell into the wound we tried to pull him off. But he held tight and the guy screamed. So Richards, with his useless red, black, and green afro pick—which he still carried on account of good style and being from Detroit—stopped the staff sergeant by sticking it to his eyeball. Then a whole shit storm, a mescaline-moonshine riot, with the Charlie Company Grits beating on each other and the scouts sneaking back up the barracks stairs quiet as the paint. The

MPs and the medics came, and then a lot of Uniform Code Of Military Justice, with Richards getting a month at the Retraining Brigade for assaulting an NCO in the eyeball.

The day Richards got back to the company, the whole battalion was moving out to the field to support the National Guard guys. We sat on the wooden benches in the open air of the deuce-and-a-half trucks, bouncing out to the boonies. We sat, and Richards told us about getting run ragged at the Retraining Brigade, the good shape he got in, and did we know that half those Charlie Company Grits are from places like Ohio and Wisconsin and just played hard at being southern cause it goes good with being in the Army. We told him all the stuff he missed, and in front of everybody I said we had waited for him. I'd caused one of those moments of silence again, and Richards didn't know what to say and Ski and Limón bailed me out by saying some stuff about Hay Street and this dink girl that we all knew Richards liked, as if that's what I'd been talking about.

I hate getting looked at like that.

Later, he told us he'd almost forgotten about Mr. Big and we decided to let him catch up to us with the worrying on his own without saying too much.

We got our chance the first day of supporting the National Guard, which we had to do a couple of times a year. We'd run the firing ranges for them. Teaching some blocks of instruction and being the enemy out in the field. They were starting off with a live fire on one of the small ranges, and we were going to leave off from there to the woods, where our job for the next week would be to harass them on aggressor detail.

Their ammo was stacked up behind the far end of the firing range, close to the wood line and half concealed by a couple of deuce-and-a-halfs. Ski and Limón walked towards it very casual, the plan being that once the firing started, they'd toss some ammo cans into the wood line and come back for them later.

Our platoon sergeant stopped them before they even got close. He was sitting against a tree smoking a Pall Mall, drawing in the dirt with a stick and waiting for the word to move his men out, when he cocked his head to one side, and nodded at the two doper scouts on their way to the wood line. Ski and Limón now knew that they couldn't do anything behind those trucks except piss in the wood line, and when Ski and Limón returned they said, "He knows. He fucking knows."

He didn't know, couldn't know, was what we tried to tell them, but they said, "Fuck you, man. He wasn't looking at you." Then we all talked about how our platoon sergeant had been through so much shit that sometimes he just knew things he had no way of knowing. We'd talked about this plenty times before, only now it wasn't about how cool it was. Now it was about how fucked up it was, and worrying about what we'd gotten ourselves into.

Ten days later, we were worn out from being The Eyes and Ears of the Colonel. Every time Alpha, Bravo, or Charlie Companies made a move against the National Guard guys we'd have to get out in front of the battalion and pull a route recon and then probe the enemy lines. All those other companies in the battalion, especially the officers, got something they don't like about us scouts, so they get a good whoop about seeing us hop. Scout Reconnaissance is our job so there's no use in bitching about it too much. The problem with aggressing against the National Guard is that instead of being Swift, Silent, and Deadly, we had to make as much noise as possible or the goings-on would never get interesting.

On the last day of this mission my squad was ordered to be ambushed, so we move to the assigned grid coordinate and waited. No ambush. We moved back and forth over this ambush site, a small clearing set among the scrub oak and dry North Carolina brown-assed and yellowed brush, talking loud, kicking at the dirt, and generally acting the camouflaged fools. Then a transmission came over the Prick 77 radio saying that the National Guard guys were having a "navigational situation"—map problems—and the ambush was being moved to an intersection of firebreaks two kilometers north. We sang cadence—*Mother Russia you better behave/ Before we fill your skies with maroon berets*—as we did the Airborne Shuffle the two klicks through the woods to the new ambush site. But no one was laying for us there at that place where two dirt roads meet.

We just sat there all out in the open. This mission of playing with the weekend warriors during their summer camp had turned us into the anti-scouts. Cpl. Jencks called in the situation report to our platoon sergeant, and then, as the sun was setting, the word came back over that the other three squads would be heading towards our location with no regard for noise and light discipline in an attempt to bring the National Guard ambush to us.

First, second, and fourth squads, all joined us upon the crossed firebreaks, arriving from three different directions just after dark. Always in the Army, light and dark, the heat and the cold come on like they had been ordered.

The guys were concerned and wondering.

"Man, where is our ambush?"

Richards muttered something about not wanting to sleep in Area J again, our present Area of Operations.

Then Platoon Sergeant Timson, who we were allowed to call Platoon Daddy, said, "Oh, no we ain't even. I'm not sleeping in no Area J again. I'm sleeping in Area Jackie tonight."

His current girl was named Jackie, and he was moving with a purpose as he rose to address the platoon.

"Y'all lock and load some of that bangy-bang blank ammo, and get up off them artillery simulators you're thinking about saving till next Fourth of July and commence to firing. I'll get them peckerwoods over here."

We got on line, did as he said, and he talked to no one of us in particular over the sounds of twenty-eight soldiers cooking off round after round on full auto, "That's right, all of it. That's what I'm talking about. Ain't staying out here in this mess. Got me a date with Area Jackie."

In the middle of all the firing, he said, "Who gots the pound cake?"

He was looking at me. The muzzle flash from my M-60 was like a monster strobe stick and made Platoon Daddy jerk about like a big disco puppet. I ceased fire in the middle of a long belt of blank ammo I had snapped together and rotated the selector switch to SAFE. Then I reached down into my rucksack and handed him one artillery simulator, and my only damn fat can of c-rat Pound Cake I'd drawn during the whole week and a half. Taking care of Platoon Daddy was not considered eating cheese, that is, not an attempt to execute the act of kissing ass from the front side.

The huge firecracker-looking simulator was popped, tossed, and whistling, trailing a thin trail of sparks, and Platoon Daddy had a P-38 issue can opener halfway around the can of Pound Cake before the flash and boom lit up the beginning of this night. A few of the guys grumbled into their rucks and then they too pitched simulators into the woods, whistling and booming. Trees showed up good to their tops in the bright and brief moments of splashed light, all this above the rifles and machine guns steady ripping through the fake stuff, everybody now catching some strobe off the guns and still too casual and muffled to pretend a real world situation.

Better to make believe a woodland dance, stag, girls off and away so far might of been billeted on the moon. Except maybe later, in the quiet, when a good imagination might sit one down beside you for a minute.

The lieutenant's doofy voice came across Limón's radio, the PRC 77, "Whiskey Four-Niner, Whiskey Four-Niner, this is Delta Eight," just as the ammo ran out. Limón brought the radio over to Platoon Daddy, who took the handset, but didn't key the mike until he was done interrogating Limón as to the location of a certain can of c-rat Peaches In Juices that the Puerto Rican was known to hoard. Limón handed over the Peaches In Juices, and Platoon Daddy walked off with the radio, preparing his Peaches and Pound Cake while he talked into the handset, explaining that no, that noise they'd heard wasn't the ambush but only an attempt to bring it on.

Platoon Daddy walked back towards us, handed the radio back to Limón, ordered two cherries into the wood line to gather up some wood, and then commenced to ponder aloud the situation, the Army, and just everything.

"Building me a big ol' barn fire, whole motherfucking barn. Shit's fixing to give me a serious case of the ass. Y'all know what that's like? It ain't like when y'all gets you a little pissed off at something. I'm talking about some big time, lifer dog case of the butt. I hear y'all talking about being short-timers with your trifling-ass three, four years in service. I got more time than that in the chow line. Got more time in a parachute harness. Shit, I was in the Vietnese, I was in the platoom. . . ."

Somebody had let Platoon Daddy borrow a few of our vitamin pills, as he like to name them.

". . . that's right, I was in the goddamn Vietnese. Got me out here begging National Guard motherfuckers to attack me. Feels like I ain't had no pussy since pussy had me—Richards, get after those cherries make sure they bring up some fat wood, lighter knot, or whatever them redneck sons of bitches call that good burning shit— What y'all laughing at? Laughing at poor old Platoon Daddy. See if I don't rain some delayed stress on your ass. I was in the Indochina. Y'all seen my car? That's right, Deuce and a Quarter, Electra 225. I don't buy nothing them rice-eaten people make. Brothers in Detroit made my shit. Yeah, y'all be down Hay Street messing with them ping-pong people girls. No, buddy. I don't play with none of that crosscut pussy. I was in the Vietnese."

Richards and Limón grinned and muttered, "Damn."

Bonehead, bone-ass Hartel, taller even than Platoon Daddy, but not the brains or the pound weight God give a trout, come in the Army last year at thirty years old and struggling still, stands up official and says, "But, Sergeant. The girls we see down Hay Street are Korean."

Platoon Daddy's eyes gray big, narrowed, and then popped open wide enough to look like two white parachutes hung in the night.

"Ping-pong! Ping-pong! All them ping-pongs peoples. Cold cabbage in a jar, buried in the backyard eatin'. . . . They was the Vietnese before the Vietnese. . . ."

He started to turn in circles with his big palms reaching out to his men. "Why is this man talking to me, somebody why?"

Hartel sat down in the dirt next to me, and I whispered to him, "You're still trying too hard. Let the rest of the cherry wash up off you before you try and get next to him."

And then Hartel, old hard-to-tell, bending his voice like the strings of a pedal steel guitar, yelled, "I ain't no cherry!"

"Yes, you are," countered the rest of the scouts sitting in the intersection, Platoon Daddy, as well as Richards and the two for-serious cherries returning with the firewood.

Platoon Daddy wasn't satisfied with the size of the fire so he sent the cherries back out for wood three times, and then the whole platoon had to go. The guys with time in the platoon knew how to look for traces of a recent lightning fire to find the fat wood. It's like petrified wood, real dense stuff, caused by the heat of a fire passing over it fast, already dead and on the ground, without burning it up. A good-sized hunk can burn all night. But I must have been spending too much time minding Hartel, because as me and Corporals Quinton and Collins—the two old-timers who started that shit with Mr. Big—were piling each other up with a load of the stuff I said, "Yup, the seasoned scouts find the seasoned wood."

They looked at me like I'd just done a bit of fancy dancing for them right there in the woods. I was forever stepping on it, trodding on my richard like that in front of these two. Probably because they gave me the hardest way to go when I was a cherry.

The fire was burning wide and tall in the middle of the intersection of the two firebreaks. Platoon Daddy passed the word on to higher that we had lit up our location and that maybe someone should let the National Guard and Reserve guys know this so's they could come and ambush us right ricky-tick. The whole platoon was taking advantage of this rare fire authorized in the field by warming different c-rat mixtures balanced on flat pieces of wood at the fire's edge. Cans of Pork Slices Cooked In Juices, Ham And Egg Chopped, Beef And Potatoes (call them Beef And Motherfuckers if you want to sound weary), little cans of Processed Cheese, Cocoa, and Coffee from the accessory packs in canteen cups. Small, thin bottles of Texas Pete Hot sauce being tossed back and forth. All the non-issue foodstuffs—Pogey Bait—purchased at the Piggly Wiggly off-post, long gone.

A good-sized pile of little tins of Peanut Butter was taking shape away from the fire where Platoon Daddy was making time with another can of Pound Cake, no Peaches. Boxes of c-rats come with all different combinations, but chances are you'll draw Peanut Butter and a fucking Nut Loaf seven times before you get Cheese and a Pound Cake.

Something about Army guys and fire. It could be high noon in the middle of the Mojave in late July and if someone makes a command decision that it is a good time to sneak a fire, the soldiers will gather round.

The scouts never needed matches to start wuffing it, but this fire was taking all the chill off early October at night, and end of mission cycle excitement was loosening jaws. I'm a talker, but somehow being an ambush, and a deuce-and-a-half ride away from a hot shower, cold dollar beer on Hay Street, and maybe even a roll with a dink— though for sure a trip to the IHOP—made me want to listen. I pulled my beans and weenies off the fire, set them down to cool, and laid out with my head on my ruck and M-60 pulled in tight to my side. A sliver of moon still stood the boss of the stars and was licked up by the flames of the fire and from mouths full of food the talk began.

"How the fuck do you get a 440 engine in a Dodge Dart?"

"What, you don't believe me, needle dick the bug fucker?"

"You fucking ain't right, I asked a question."

"No. You said, 'How the fuck?'"

And around the big fire it goes.

"Wait, wait. She didn't have no teeth? How old was she?"

"Nah, nah, man. Not like that. Her teeth come out in a softball game. Catcher."

"Softball game? I thought you was down in her basement?"

"Forget it, man. Pass the hot sauce."

And goes.

"I been wanting to ask you. How can you be from Massachusetts?"

"What does that mean?"

"I mean fucking pilgrims from Massachusetts. What'd you do in that Massachusetts?"

"Same shit you do in Cabin John, Maryland."

"Oh no, buddy. I don't think so. I mean, just look at ya, son."

And then out of the east came a sweep and bounce of jeep lights on high. The cherries made for their weapons with no ammo.

Corporal Quinton sighed. "At ease, dickfucks. It's Sergeant Major."

Sergeant Major Macmillan, the rankingest noncommissioned officer in the battalion, looked like a combination of Frederick Douglass with a good airborne haircut, Napoleon, and General MacArthur if only because of the pipe. He swung his little body out of the jeep before his driver had brought it to a complete stop. Richards once described the man as a "deep brother."

The Sergeant Major, with no hands, switched his pipe from one corner of his mouth to the other. His eyes moved across the scouts, who were all standing, stopping briefly at each young NCO. I was hoping he would stare and really bore into Corporals Quinton and Collins, but instead I switched to thinking there might be hot-A's, mess hall chow, in the jeep's trailer. Then he spoke.

"You know I was just telling my dear wife how much I love this new army. Yes, I said, 'Dear, you know this new breed is so Strac, so field savvy that they do not even need to post perimeter guards anymore. Nope. Just done away with them. She said, 'Well, I know those recon baddies do not need any perimeter guards. . . .'"

Corporal Quinton motioned for Hartel and the cherries to get out on the perimeter.

Sergeant Major smiled and whispered to Quinton, "Good Airborne thinking, young corporal," before continuing.

". . . she says, 'I know your super scouts, they do not need any of that silly kind of security. They have eyes in the backs of their heads. They would never just let any old fool drive up on them. They could smell 'em coming two, three, maybe even four klicks out."

Hartel was muttering something about not being "some kina

dag durn cherry no more and why I gotta go be on perimeter" as he gathered up his gear and walked towards the wood line.

"Isn't that the young private that I caught sleeping on motor pool guard so that the Russians could come and relieve me of my modes of transportation?" asked the Sergeant Major.

Quinton affirmed and claimed Hartel's sorry ass as a member of his squad. Couldn't actually believe that Sergeant Major was serious about the perimeter guards, what with the fire spread across the middle of two crossed narrow roads cracking, shifting, flames roiling up three times the man's height. But Hartel was just plain stupid, in his Hartel kind of way, pissing and moaning in front of the Sergeant Major. It is just not done.

"Sergeant Major, how did Hartel get to be in Recon anyway? His ass should be in a line company, or driving for headquarters, something," said Quinton, speaking four times as many words to the Sergeant Major as I had ever seen a man below the rank of E-7. Sergeant Major walked towards the fire, looking like he really might begin a conversation with Quinton.

"You don't think he was put with y'all for a reason? Recon's had it too easy lately, taking the best before the line companies, the most promising newbies. That soldier there is a walking talking mission for y'all. Do you Hollywood scouts some good to bring that troop along properly. You scouts are hardcore, right? Recon dogs? Gung ho?"

The temptation here was to get too casual, roll our eyes and respond in the spirit that Sergeant Major asked the questions, with that creepy smile he gets, just begging you to step on your dick.

Instead we sought safety and answered him with a round of all-purpose dog barks.

"Do any of you scholars know the origin of the word 'gung ho'?"

"Nooo, Sergeant Major," we replied, pushing it a bit.

"It is from the Chinese, and it means . . ."

He took the pipe from his mouth, tapped it out on the sole of his jump boots, and finished the lesson.

"Men, it means teamwork."

Just then, Platoon Daddy's voice: "Y'all get away from that Sergeant Major!" He was quick-stepping towards us from out the wood line.

"What are you doing, crowded up on the man like that," he said. "Sorry about this, Sergeant Major. This bear can't even shit in the woods without all hell breaking loose."

Sergeant Major nodded his head towards Platoon Daddy and marked his arrival with a simple "Tim."

The two men both had patches from the 173rd Airborne Brigade on their right shoulders—a winged sword coming down from the sky under an Airborne tab. Combat side and rare. The 173rd, the rumor went, was disbanded after Vietnam because there wasn't hardly anyone left.

"Brought you some hot A's," said the Sergeant Major, pointing the stem of his pipe towards the jeep. "Figure we all will be heading back in sooner than later."

"Thanks, Mac. If I can ever get attacked out here. Recon! Go and get you some of that good chow the Sergeant Major brung you."

Heard it. So did the others. Platoon Daddy slipped up and called Sergeant Major Macmillan "Mac" in front of God and everybody. The scouts looked at each other, searched for the faces of their best buddies to make sure we'd all heard it. That we all understood that our Platoon Daddy got to call Sergeant Major a nickname. Then I guess we remembered that Platoon Daddy was about to retire pretty soon and would be leaving us, so we moved out towards the chow not wanting to think about it for serious until we had to.

The green thermite cans held warm chili, macaroni, rice, green beans and okra. Ate first helpings still standing around the jeep—all of us—cause two weeks of C's make you more than just a little like a dog. The cans lasted enough for seconds which we sat back down to the fire with.

Sluguski ran some of the plates over to Hartel and the cherries, though not as heaping. He did it only for the fine promise of future loans from the cherries fresh out of jump school and flush.

The weight of a paper plate, its center heavy with the wet and warm mess-hall food, felt like cheating out in the woods. Grimy and rank, I knew something that is true if you display it in a certain style: My stories would have white paper plates in them.

Sergeant Major and Platoon Daddy, after a few private words, moved over to the fire where they stood over us. Platoon Daddy eating from a plate of okra, which was about eye level with the Sergeant Major, who was packing his pipe. It was the most time we'd ever spent around the Sergeant Major other than when he talked to the whole battalion in formation.

Sluguski returned, shaking his head. "Man, that Hartel is so ungrateful."

The pipe was lit and its stem rattled between upper and lower teeth, and Sergeant Major said, "I'll tell you scouts a secret. That soldier. Hartel. He was a little going-away present for your platoon sergeant here. Yes, my old-time buddy Tim." He stuck out one of his short legs and bent at the waist, cackled, and kept on.

"I saw that man coming through Battalion and I just knew you had to have him because he reminded me of that guy you liked so much when we were over in the place. What was that boy's name? Tim? Come on now. What was his name?"

"Renfield . . ." said Platoon Sergeant Timson fast between bites, ". . . and I don't want to talk about that peckerwood."

"Yes. Yes. That's him. Renfield. And when I came up on that Hartel sleeping on guard duty I just knew it again and didn't he look just like Tim's buddy from back in the place. Then I leaned on the horn of that deuce-and-a-half he was sleeping in and boy if he didn't act like Renfield. . . ."

"Come on, now, Mac. Leave that lay."

Sergeant Major sure was enjoying himself, stomping his little jump boots in the dirt and blowing pieces of lit tobacco out the top of his pipe.

"Now, Tim. When was the last time we saw him over in the place? Was it, Binh Dinh? Nah, way before that. Dak To. Was it Dak To?"

Platoon Daddy nodded solemnly and said softly, "Yes, Sergeant Major. Roger that. Dak To."

Sergeant Major stared at Platoon Daddy, dead into his eyes, as if there was something in them he hadn't seen in a long time but was once common. He then looked out and into the eyes of the scouts in the firelight, one by one. When he got to mine I felt safe, seeing that I hadn't popped a vitamin pill since noon, but even still, when I locked eyes with the man I felt read for all the good and bad I had ever done and would ever do.

Everybody should have a Sergeant Major.

Before the eyeballing, we thought we'd been about to get the once-in-a-lifetime chance of hearing our Sergeant Major tell one firsthand and in person. Still sitting, the scouts gathered up the greasy paper plates and plastic spoons and forks and tossed them into the high flames. Boots kicked at the fire's edge.

Sergeant Major refilled his pipe and lit it. He then began to puff and slowly rock back and forth on his heels, a small, thin cloud of smoke gently blown up on each motion.

Platoon Daddy spoke. "That was a bad day, Sergeant Major."

"Could have been worse."

We stopped moving.

Platoon Daddy looked at the Sergeant Major like a proud day laborer looking to get picked by the hiring man, and then he said, "Yeah, Mac. It coulda been lots worse."

"You remember it was that Renfield, right?"

"Yeah. Yes. I remember."

They were both laughing now. Just little laughs, made them look different.

Still standing. And would stay that way.

Looking into the fire, this time Sergeant Major spoke first. "Yup, so there we were."

"Yeah, Mac. Dak To."

"You scouts should listen to this. Might tell you something about your man, Hartel. You never do know how a troop's going to act in a real world situation. Now, Renfield was a redneck of the first order. Yes, and the boy was from L.A. And where is that, Tim?"

"That would be Lower Alabama, Sergeant Major."

"Yes. Yes. And boy, did Renfield and your platoon sergeant get into it. Do you all have any idea what your platoon sergeant was like? Yes. Well, I guess you do. Him and Renfield would have knock-down-drag-'em-outs over any little thing. Why did you? . . . Tim, help me out here. You broke his nose for something? . . . Singing wasn't it. Yes. That song he was forever singing. What was it?"

"Something about, *Hello, I'm Johnny Cash* and then he'd make guitar sounds and sing some shit about his momma and prison. . . ."

"You know and it doesn't sound so bad when you do it. Tim? Yes. Yes. Anyway, Renfield had people home in the Klan, and his own daddy wrote him letters kidding him about having to fight a war with niggers. Mean, nasty people. Renfield would read them out loud so the whole platoon could hear. And he would not soldier for anything. Biggest ghosting goldbricker you have ever seen. Make your man Hartel look like the division trooper of the year."

Platoon Daddy quick cocked an eyebrow and said, "I don't know about all that."

"Hush, Tim. And let me talk to these troops. One day we're out doing our little bit in the bush, no big thing. Some small contact here and there. Well, all long-range recon units have met at the rally-ing point, and we're ready to move out to the clearing where the choppers were going to pick us up about a half a klick away. Then all of a sudden the ground starts turning up, and then small-arms fire from all directions . . ."

"A whole shit storm," adds Platoon Daddy.

". . . I heard that. Victor Charlie had our ORP all plotted out, and was just waiting for us to come back from looking for him. Two of our guys got zapped right off the bat and I don't remember any return fire. You, Tim?"

"Not me. I was gone. Booked. Jetted. There wasn't nothing but assholes and elbows moving out for those birds."

"It was the longest half a klick I ever traveled. My little legs pumping like crazy. I turned around and caught sight of black pajamas not more than two football fields of loose jungle away, turned back towards the front and saw the choppers landing in the open and didn't know. Did not know. But I kept moving. Me and everybody else dumping butt packs, ammo, web gear, everything except the weapons. Moving. Now we have been on patrol, probing enemy lines, and it was hot. We're worn out. Still, nothing like ordnance flying past your ear to get you hopping. But my little legs didn't want to carry me. They felt all swelled up, and lots of our guys were a good ways in front of me.

"Then I start to hear Chuck behind me. I got moving right for a bit, but then the legs started to feeling all thick again. I kid you not, I started to cry. Running, trying to hold on to my weapon, and wipe the tears from my eyes. Young fool that I was, guess I didn't want anybody to see me crying.

"The choppers had landed a long football pass away, and most of the guys were on board. They were yelling and hollering, waving their arms for us to move! Move out! Make it! There were about five of us still running and, man, Chuck was so close I could smell him at my backside, but what I did not see at the time was that most of the small arms fire was being directed at the choppers. The morter fire was coming right up behind everybody. Whumping. And I could feel it in my chest, the sound."

"That's right," said Platoon Daddy. "I was in one of the birds and the shit was pinging all over. Punk-ass door gunner was hiding somewhere, and his sister the pilot talking about they gotta go, gotta go. Pilot started to lift us off the ground. We turned our weapons on the pilot in my bird and I guess the guys in the other birds did the same. We had us a fast Mexican standoff. We were yelling at the pilots, 'Don't go! Don't go!' Then yelling at our guys on the ground almost up on us, 'Come on, motherfuckers! Make it.'"

"Well," said Sergeant Major, "I saw the choppers lift off the ground right in front of me, and come back down a bit, and it was like my whole life came and went."

Platoon Daddy, almost interrupting, "Our pilot screaming like crying now, 'Shoot me, but I gotta go!' And wasn't nobody gonna shoot him, and we were screaming too, and hitting our own selves in the helmets with our hands just to have something to do. The bird was jerking all around and we fell on our asses while he spun and then leveled it back out."

Then Sergeant Major again: "I actually calmed down for a second there on the ground. I was about to stop running and turn and fire a few rounds when I saw one of the birds spin a few times. I thought it was hit, then figured, no *I* must be hit. But I wasn't hit, just waiting to be and not wanting to turn and face the enemy and not wanting to watch the choppers take off either. And then I see Tim's bird get ahold of itself, flatten out, and start to go up straight, real fast. Leaving. But, oh, what a sweet sight I saw next. An American soldier, a paratrooper, with an M-60 machine gun just drop out of that chopper, hit the ground, execute a combat roll, and commence to laying down fierce suppressive grazing fire. The zips didn't know what hit them. The pilots must have seen them scatter, because the birds all came back down and my boys came flying out. John Wayning it like all get out.

"I made the few meters between me and them like a cakewalk. Shoot, Smitty on my right flank, shot up as he was, hippity-hopped on over. Yes, except for the two that got it right away, we all made it. Made it. Now who do you suppose was the super duper paratrooper who jumped out of that helicopter? . . . I'll tell you. It was Renfield. Who was more like your man Hartel than any other soldier I've seen in this man's army. It goes to show you, men. Under fire we never know who is going to come through for us. Remember this."

I wanted to get up and take a walk, but before I could even look at the faces on the scouts, Platoon Daddy spoke again.

"Damn, Mac. I mean, damn—I been listening to you tell that story to young troops for almost fifteen years and I can't have it no more. Yeah, remember I said, the bird started to spin and we got dumped on our butts? You remember that, right? Well, right as that bird leveled out and just before it tipped on up I saw that Renfield's sorry ass was sitting right in front of me and I couldn't help it. My leg just kinda straightened out real fast and it was me that kicked that raggedy-assed peckerwood right through the door. He fell out on the ground it was all he could do to save his own racist, redneck, dog-fucking, music-singing, punk-ass self, but to lay down a base of fire."

It's hard on guys when you know you've been told a bunch of things that could help you in your life, but you're not sure what they are exactly. If we were allowed, we'd of all said "Wait a minute. Wait a minute," but there is no question-and-answer period that comes with the Vietnam stories. So we had to help each other out later when we had the chance, till we all agreed we'd got it right.

But it was so difficult not knowing how to behave around that fire, with Platoon Daddy and the Sergeant Major looking like we should give them money. They definitely were not looking at each other, except once, and then Sergeant Major sucked hard on his pipe like maybe trying hard not to laugh.

We were saved from the uncomfortableness by one of the cherries coming in out of the dark to stand by the fire and say, "Excuse me, but Private Hartel sent me to ask if there is any more chili mac left."

Corporal Quinton with one fist balled, whispered, "Directly, I'm fixing to knock the Redman down his throat and out his backside."

He never got the chance, for then we all picked up movement from the wood line to the north.

"That's what I'm talkin' bout. That's my ambush come to take me home," said Platoon Daddy.

He was flustered about how to react to an ambush such as this. First he told us to get on line facing the direction of the movement. Then he told us to pull back behind the fire, and then he just said to pretend like we were asleep. He shrugged at the Sergeant Major who laughed and took off in the jeep, grinding gears with his driver bucking in the passenger seat.

Hartel low crawled over towards us and whispered, "I got big-time movement at three o'clock."

Quinton kicked him in the ass and told him to go and fetch the cherries. We all laid down around the fire and pretended to be asleep. From fifty meters away we heard the weekend warriors advancing. It sounded like a tavern was trying to sneak up and attack you. I, honest and God, heard one of them whisper, "Are we there, yet?"

They almost got quiet as they got closer and I found myself rooting for them. I peeked over towards their position and I saw big butts in the air low crawling even worse than Hartel. They got it together and were almost stealthy in their last push towards us when an electronic chime broke their brief silence—*Do do do-do do do-do do do-do do-do.* It was the opening chords to "Dixie" followed by a voice from the wood line, "Damn it all, Phil! I told you to leave that watch at home!"

So they attacked us and we let them. Just DIP'd, Died In Place.

Corporal Collins had placed the tins of Peanut Butter in and around the fire just before they attacked. After they shot up all their blanks at us and they had started a little victory celebration, we snuck off and left them dancing by the firelight. We moved out into the woods in two Ranger files, towards the hard top road where the rest of the company were waiting with the cattle cars to take us back to post. Collins was on point a few men in front of me. He gave the hand and arm signal for halt, which got passed down the files. He looked at his watch and said, "Just about . . . Now."

He was off by a good thirty seconds, but then came the sound of three dozen cans of Peanut Butter napalm starting to daisy chain off in the distance. That and more than a few "yeoowws!" "ahh shits!" and one "Incoming!" The Peanut Butter napalm was the perfect peacetime weapon, flung burning on faces and hands, sizzling and sputtering all over uniforms.

We moved through the dark woods, barracks bound. Swift, Silent, and Giggling. Except one old combat paratrooper who belly-laughed us all the way.

It was weeks and weeks later and the doper scouts had had a few opportunities to get some stuff for Mr. Big, but now every time we were around live ammo, it seemed too risky, and we got scared. Did get a break from all the worrying when word came down about Panama. Heard it from guys in Headquarters who saw the paper-work for transportation and everything. The battalion was supposed to have been going for forever, but politics and Jimmy Carter kept messing up our time for jungle training. It seemed I'd never get to put the jungle school patch on, only have my guys giving me a hard way to go for the rest of my life cause they caught me in line at the PX buying the patches three months before we were really going official.

Even with the word coming from Headquarters, we tried not to talk about Panama, which would definitely be a jinx. So all these things we weren't saying or thinking about Panama took our mind off Mr. Big. Once we got on the aircrafts, we'd be looking at a whole month of training in a foreign country without having to fret about the fat man.

The night before we were leaving for Panama, Frankie Meadows wanted to sneak this girl he's met at Nashville Station into the barracks for an overnight in our room. So, I slept in Limón and Richard's room on an air mattress on the floor. We had stayed in and fixed up our photo albums, getting them ready for the new pictures we'd be returning with.

It was late when Frankie Meadows got back and told about the girl he had in the parking lot. He was going to sneak her in wearing a uniform and web gear and helmet like she was coming off moter pool guard and could he use Limón's shit cause of the size. He had it all figured out that she could pee in a mop bucket if she had to, and don't nobody act like anything is going on.

It was later when none of us were asleep in Limón and Richard's room—only lying down pretending cause of the excitement that we were really going to Panama tomorrow—when they started like I wasn't even there.

"Hey, Richards . . ."

"Hey, Richards . . . You asleep?" Limón from the top bunk stirred the sleeping Richards below.

"Damn, Limón. What you need?"

"Hey, Richards—"

"Limón. What?"

"Hey, Richards. Who you think is badder? Exorcist or Aliens?"

Richards rolls over, pushes down the green wool blanket from his chest and pulls close a chair next to his bunk. He props himself up by one elbow, reaches out for his pack of Kool shorties from the chair, taps one out, and lights it using a one-hand strike and cup.

"Limón, you wake me up for some stupid shit."

"No, for serious R. Who you think is badder?"

Richards takes a long pull from the Kool and blows the smoke up the side of the bunk bed, squints his eyes and says definitively, "Exorcist."

From the top bunk, which is lit through the window by the tall lights that line the company street, Limón whispers, "Damn. Damn, R, just like that?"

"Yeah, man. You ain't even got to consider some stupid shit like that."

"But Aliens got them teeth. Like a skillions of them, shoot out its mouth and chaaa cha cha."

"Limón—"

"And that's just the front and he gots that tail—Wham!—and all them little Aliens kids and—"

"Limón—"

"And that shit that drips out its mouth and don't even let that motherfucker bleed on you with that battery acid—"

"Limón!"

"Come on, man, and what if Aliens got some of its hot breath on you? You know that mess has got to be stinking like twenty—"

"Dag! Shut up, Limón. For a second, man. Wake me up to explain this simple shit."

"But."

"Limón, Exorcist could be Aliens if it wanted to."

"What?"

"Exorcist can be anything it wants."

"Come on now, R. Oh, oh, and Aliens could gets inside you, remember? Sucks all onto your face and shit and comes out your stomach. Hungry too. Chaaa, cha, cha cha."

"Limón, Exorcist gets inside you. Exorcist probably made Aliens. Exorcist gets inside your mind and your body makes you anything it wants."

"Hunh?"

Richards exhales smoke and sighs, "Exorcist fucks motherfuckers up along the lines of the holy trinity. Mind, body, and spirit."

Silence.

"Damn, Limón. When was the last time you saw Exorcist? You forget the story or what? Which is probably why you asking me this shit in the first place. You don't think shit out."

"I just asked you who think is badder—"

"Exorcist is the devil, Limón, the devil! It gets inside your mind and does whatever it wants to your body. Exorcist controls your mind! Runs your spirit, and does whatever it wants with your body."

"Okay. Okay, R. So let me break it down. If you take it all the way down, Aliens, like you said, was probably made by the devil. So Exorcist got like trumps over everybody, all the monsters, because Exorcist had something to do with all of them, right?"

"See, Limón? You could've had that all by yourself. Waking me up for this mess, but you are my brother."

"You wasn't sleeping."

Richards drops his cigarette into an empty can of Mountain Dew by the side of the bunk, rattles the can, and then turns back facedown into bed.

"Good night, Limón."

"Good night, R."

"And really go to sleep. We're going to Panama tomorrow."

Silence.

"Limón . . ."

"Limón . . ."

"Limón, I know what you're doing up there so don't even think about it."

Silence.

"Limón?"

"What, man?"

"I know what you're doing."

"I ain't doing nothing."

"Yes you are. You're up there looking at that poster of Bruce Lee and don't even try it."

"No, I'm not."

"Yes, you are."

"So what?"

"So don't even try and put no Bruce Lee in with Exorcist and Aliens."

"Come on, R?"

"No, cause that's just wrong."

"Check it out, Richards. What if that ugly little Exorcist girl just, like, looked away for a second. Bruce could be in there all fast and Whaaaaaaaeeeeeooooww, and, and. . . ."

"And what?"

"And I don't know. Fuck her shit up."

Silence.

Giggles.

Silence.

2
_____

New York

I know the length of the stories by the subway stops, or by the numbered streets I walk, and if I'm just sitting, then by just sitting.

Light out in any point of the compass, and I will find a rhythm, by tracks or sidewalk, to accompany me while I tell.

If it be while quiet and still, park or bridge, then before that boat passes or another one docks, this . . .—*will happen.* As this plane's nose disappears behind a building both old and tall, that . . .—*must have already begun.*

I have to tell on lots of things. Still, tonight, I will go all the way through.

All the way.

Panama will be told tonight and . . .

Subway stations missed. Walking in circles. Stare out and notice nothing.

C-O-Ws, Indian-Anna, Hay Street, Ordnance and that mess, Corvette, *This one time there was . . . ,*

I've only thought about her as often as I notice the time.

I hate Tom Sawyer.

That has nothing to do with anything much except I just like to say it out loud to myself sometimes.

There were other letters from Paola that came saying, *Please . . .* and the last one saying just that in big letters, *PLEASE.*

But after we got back from Panama, back at Bragg, between the shit I was taking from the guys, the weekly staredown lectures from Platoon Daddy and Sergeant Major making sure I wasn't going back to Panama either over the fence or by reenlistment, and being in that mess with Mr. Big, I didn't write her.

When we got back from Panama, after Kansas, we went to Ft. Campbell, KY, for three weeks of air assault school, away from Sergeant Major, Mr. Big, and Platoon Daddy, and the guys eased up on me.

That school, we just got run around, dropped for push-ups—Which arm? How many?—and taught stuff we already knew about rappelling out of helicopters. Whole days began and ended about Paola without her around.

Outside Ft. Campbell, on a half-assed strip of GI bars, I got jerked off under a table by a dink. That's what you get over there for tipping a dollar on a dollar beer, ten times, and being polite about it, too.

The dancer had flecks of asphalt under her thighs. I let her work me and I let it fly so's the guys wouldn't know what I was really thinking about.

I had listened to other people about things that did not concern them.

When we returned from air assault school somebody had broken into our rooms. They stole photographs, awards, diplomas—our televisions and stereos were already at the pawnshops. The scouts were fanatics about their photo albums and scrapbooks, especially the dopers, who would call it a night in, get lit, and spread out on the floor with scissors, rulers, tape, and paste, being very exact about the order and lining up.

The doorknob to my room spun in my hand and when I found my fat album gone out of the drawers below my bunk I threw up for the only time from emotions. It was the only time from emotions. That whiny-voiced rebel little shit from the Four-Deuce Mortar Platoon down the other end of the hall had done it. He'd gone AWOL, after steady-stepping his dick into the dirt since he'd gotten to Bragg, and the four-deuce guys came down the hall with some bended up photos they'd found in his room. They apologized for their dirt bag and said there was some more of our stuff out in the dumpster if we wanted to look. And did we want to see the hell he'd left in his room, who knew he'd been into that devil shit, especially cause he'd scared his cherry roomie so bad that the cherry was crying and telling it all to the first half of his chain of command down in the First Sergeant's office.

I was hours in that dumpster. I didn't care about the smells or what all I found, only what I didn't. What I didn't find was my pictures, the one in particular. The guys would come out and bang on the dumpster, telling me to quit, but I'd just fling over the things of theirs I found. Nothing of mine. Not my diploma from Recondo school—second honor grad, not a picture with those kids in Egypt, not even a Polaroid from basic. Panama, gone.

Days later, Limón showed me a postcard he'd gotten, all in Spanish. It was from Paola, and when I asked him what she says, he said, "What she says is why are you such a fucking asshole, shit."

He'd gotten a letter from his girl in Colon, too. All the guys got a letter from their girl, and none of them planned on writing back. Somewhere between Panama and Ft. Bragg they had decided to listen to all the stories about guys who had been burned by bar girls from Korea to Germany. Limón too, he had been on me with that word, saying it whenever I got quiet and looked like I might be thinking of doing something crazy. Citizenship. The word was just thrown at me.

So I didn't understand Limón getting serious now, calling me "so fucking stupid" before he walked off. Maybe it was because Paola had written him for help in finding out what was wrong with me, why I hadn't written. Maybe Limón realized then that me and Paola had always been a real thing and that I had given in too quickly to the forces that always try and ruin real things.

They caught that four deuce mortar man that stole our stuff. A retired officer had reported seeing him on a plane out of Fayetteville in dress greens wearing ribbons last awarded when he was in grade school. He'd put up a good little chase back in middle Arkansas. When they brought him back he was in dirty civvies, wild-eyed and broken. They gave the captain first crack at him, hands cinched at his back with plastic handcuffs like garbage ties.

The captain had the whole company in formation at the rest position waiting for the MPs to walk him by, and the bastard stuck his tongue out at me as he passed.

Her picture. I'd given a whole album page to the wallet-sized photograph.

Paola had hesitated before she went ahead and gave it to me. It took her a while before I understood that in Colombia girls only have their picture taken, all set up like that, twice.

Twice. And she made motions with her hands swirling in the air and then down and up and away, and I took it to mean she was now out of little wallet-sized photos.

The photo was thick with fancy edges and on the back she had written her real name.

After the photos were stolen I fired off letters addressed to

Paola Rocha
C/O Bar Le Fleur
Calle Maciel
Colon, Colon
Panama, RP

They all come back with lots of marks from rubber stamps that Limón told me said, "no address like this exists." But it was the address that all the guys had, and the one on the back of Paola's letters.

Three times I got rolls of quarters and Limón called Colon, Panama, information. Nothing listed under Bar Le Fleur. Limón wouldn't do it anymore so I asked a Filipino guy in Charlie Company and he tried but his kind of Spanish didn't work over the phone at all.

I can't remember her real name.

She had said, *Please.* I do believe that you only get to let a person down once like that, once.

I know not to be asked again. Not asked like that, anyway.

Please.

Grateful just to not have been blinded by it, and my burden is a blind and dumb heart.

3

The Scouts Jump Into Panama–White Wooden Barracks–

Gov'mint Cheese–Our Spot–Platoon Daddy Pours–Soda

Truck–Stream Drinker–Colon

The standing up and sitting down had started in our C-130 just after the aircraft had dropped to jump altitude. The forty guys in my bird were all standing up, hooked up, and holding their static lines, which connected their chutes to the jump cable running overhead. All of my squad, and half the rest of the scouts, were peaking on two hits each of the Malaysian's purple double-barrel mescaline. We scouts had the first fifteen jump positions on each door being that the little mission we were going to pull before joining the jungle operations training center was to take us on a route reconnaissance north of the drop zone. We had all synchronized our watches and popped the mesc two hours and fifteen minutes out of Ft. Bragg.

The jump doors of the C-130 were opened over the whitecaps of the Atlantic just as the aircraft began its descent with a low-pitched whine of hydraulics. I felt the mesc coming on strong from the base of my neck, slowly inching up the back of my head. I watched the mesc travel the same route up and over the heads of my OD green and loam-faced buddies. Their cammied up, tiger stripe faces breaking out into big, cool green smiles as we rode out over an ocean boiling up low. My cammie job was as close to a happy Emmet Kelly as I could get away with. The camouflage stick I had run back and forth, thick, over my teeth, was now dancing in my mouth, and a smell came and joined us in the C-130 just as a swatch of deep green appeared in the jump doors replacing the blue-white ocean like a thought.

I wanted to retie my jungle boots so bad.

Other than that, my hundred pounds of weapon and equipment hung off me solid and comforting. The jump masters ran through the jump commands fast and I wanted to ask questions, but the jungle below rushed by like an assembly line out of control. We got the order to stand up and my old-style, rip stop, slant pocket cammies had a hard-on straining under them and the crossed parachute straps. No underwear was one of the rules of the jungle and the green and the smell and the mesc and my uniform made me want to rub one out at 2000 ft.

I couldn't stop looking out the open jump doors at the top layer of a triple canopy jungle below. At the jump command of "One Minute!" I sat back down on the iron and cotton webbed bench and so did Richards, and Ski, and Country, and Limón, and Togiola, and Shattuck, and all the high scouts lined up by the jump doors. We looked across at each other, smiled, and wrinkled up our foreheads, nobody was going to freeze in the door—no, fuck that, never happen. But the smell and the ocean, and then the green and a jump, and that smell and the sky a blue almost like the ocean before the green, and I was sure they all had hard-ons and a guy just had to sit for a sec. Then we were standing and then sitting, all the while holding the static lines and trying to stand up for good but then sitting back down.

The jump masters were not laughing as the men at the forward ends of their jump sticks continued to pop up and down with their jump command—"Thirty Seconds!"—being repeated down the lines. Richards was told to "Stand In The Door!" on the left and I was told the same on the right. Me and Richards both, out of habit, put one funny foot forward, the toes of our boots just hanging out the edge of the door and in the breeze, while at the same time slapping our palms to the outside skin of the aircraft, cool and wet like a beaded-up can of pop.

All the high scouts were still trying to sit down, our knees bending every other second, even as the paratroopers in the aft end of the bird began to push. Wanting out. We wanted to sit and then stand and then jump, but what we did was moan and giggle until the light by each jump master turned from red to green and my stomach got happy and I exited the aircraft elbows in, knees together and up, a tight high ball of green camouflage with an old green chute that deployed with a sweet squeeze at my shoulders before I thought to ask.

It was like falling through a painting that you see real and in person. It's too good, too much like everything should be.

The blue ocean with white tips meeting the blue sky with white roads of clouds at the far end of what the eye could see.

Green floor at my feet rising to meet me until I passed over it, cutting across a square of yellow which rose too fast, too fast, my body rattling through stiff grass and I attempted no standard parachute landing fall, instead began to move my hands and feet like a dog in water until the ground, and I crawled across the earth until an old green chute fell over me with a blanket of silky nylon and a thin shadow, as if a god had put me to bed.

Lying on broken grass so thick it almost held me aloft, I stayed under the chute and listened to the scouts fall and rattle through the grass, forming their own private clearing. I listened to the sound of men who have fallen through a day's beauty too high not to feel a part of it. They talked to themselves, laughed to themselves, drank water, gargled and spat and giggled. I heard them begin to move into the tall grass. Others moved out towards the center of the drop zone to the parachute turn-in point. The scouts began to stand up and sit down.

I heard them before I peeked out from under my parachute. My wrecked pals stood up and then disappeared back into the big grass, making the sturdy blades klack and whoosh. Shattuck—a moon-faced Hawaiian, Chinese, Irishman, from California and "San Pedro Tough," the way he called it—moved towards me clutching his parachute at his neck with both hands. I stood and gathered up my chute the same way and we strode out to greet each other like kings without horses.

"Man, it's like a warm pot of jasmine rice," he said, nose up. He reached out and shook my hand, our chutes falling to the ground. Nobody shakes hands in the Army.

"Look at the boys," I said, as we turned in circles, watching as dotted streams of other paratroopers beat back the grass working their ways towards the parachute turn-in. "Fucked up." He laughed as we sat down and he began to pull four Newports out of a fresh pack. He gave me three and lit one for himself. I lit my cigarette twice and we stretched our legs out straight and watched the good guys stand up and sit down, each time coming up with a different expression and stance. Me and Shattuck smoked and joined this gopher dance. We found the sea and pointed back to it, and we found the edge of the grass over at where the jungle began on all sides and pointed at it. We pointed at the pretty birds in formation nosediving into the jungle; we pointed at everything and after we pointed everything out we broke down our equipment, rolled up our chutes, and then moved out to collect the gophers.

We found Limón sitting Indian-style and petting the M-60 in his lap like it was a long cat.

"M-60 my baby," he said to us. We agreed and kept moving.

"Goddamnit the motherfucker shee. This is like my fucking country. Do you understand me? Like my fucking country!" says Limón, the Puerto Rican from Queens, New York, as he falls in behind Shattuck and me.

At the turn-in point we dumped our chutes and there a couple of permanent party soldiers on drop zone detail told us that the mission was canceled, all we have to do is get to the assembly point and wait on transportation. We snake along the drop zone, as the rest of the tripping scouts fall into one Ranger file—one in front of the other, six arm's lengths between men—like dots of mercury. It still takes a long time for us to get to our assembly point, what with all the standing up and sitting down still going on and the lieutenant had a serious case of the ass when we showed up all laughing about a cloud.

"If this just doesn't frost my balls. Men, we are scouts and scouts are supposed to be in front of the battalion, remember? And what is so goddamned funny and where the Christ have you been?" went the lieutenant, spitting the words out a mouth with no lips.

I said, "Tree landings, sir," and the men behind me made sounds like they were trying to move their bowels. More excuses were offered up.

"Too much sun."

"Heavy air."

"Mean Panamanians."

"Got lost."

And, "I don't feel good."

The lieutenant spat "fuckers" as he unbuckled the chin strap of his steel pot helmet fast like he was going to do something.

Standing next to him was Platoon Daddy and "Hot like twenty motherfuckers out here to-day," was all he said.

Platoon Daddy, who had done his three tours in Southeast Asian jungle—three tours because he liked it—and because of the muscle was the only man in the Army authorized to leave the top button of his fatigue shirt unbuttoned.

The rumor was that he got all the muscle from chopping his way out of the Georgia woods to get to the recruiting station.

He had only those two months until his twenty years in service was up. Stood all of himself off the ground and out of habit we formed up into squads and a traveling wedge formation.

"Hot like twenty motherfuckers" was all Platoon Daddy said till he passed Togiola on point at the threshold of a wall of jungle. Squads closed back to files, and he slipped into the foliage like an— I mean no disrespect—old whore into bed. He'd begun humming a song that was an old one and just a little sad.

Limón popped out of the file, threw down his rucksack, and nodded his head at me, fast, with eyes big. He then put his back to me and let me check. Yeah, it had happened again, I told him so. He turned back around, still nodding fast, but with eyes now narrowed with satisfaction.

We all hadn't become less impressed by the miracle, just irritated with Limón for being so sure he was special. There was always the talk of calling up the *Army Times* or *The Paraglide*, never did though, wish we had. But I'd swear to it to this day on a stack of Hucks that whenever the scouts got up to half speed on foot, Limón's back would sweat up into the sign of the cross. Clear, dark, with angles like that looked like they'd been outlined with marker and the large space filled in with hot wet wax.

The scouts followed Platoon Daddy into the jungle. And though he had slipped in easily, we, all thirty of us, lined up to get snagged on vines, trip on roots, and curse. No more than twenty meters in, the first ten scouts lost the big man until he shouted at us from the east, where we heard the sound of running water. It turns out the sound was Platoon Daddy taking a long piss, not a stream or small river to be skirted or crossed. He yelled for us to get the hell out of his jungle, pee somewhere else, and what did we think we were doing anyway, loud sneaking up on a man like that? It was just like the scouts—and not just the high ones—to follow Platoon Daddy into the jungle even when he was just ducking in to take a leak.

All the scouts were "imagiced"—a Limón word—hypnotized even, by the way Platoon Daddy looked with the jungle all around him. Even if this wasn't Indo-China, it was still triple-canopy jungle, and Platoon Daddy looked, against it, just like he was supposed to.

There are few things in the world that are better than when a thing looks just like it's supposed to, except sometimes when it doesn't.

Before he moved towards the jungle he was just standing there, holding an M-16 like a stick, sweating through his cammies, and the colors in the sky, blue and white, were separate, crunched behind his head, like deep finger paints. We just wanted to go where Platoon Daddy went. We'd waited so long to see him like this that we'd forgotten our last order, which was to head to the rallying point and wait on the deuce-and-a-halfs.

I wish someone would ask me, cause I'd tell them all about coming out of a plane with good friends, some just the right kind of high, all wearing cool clothes, looking to land someplace you've only heard about for two years, landing soft, finding everything and everybody where it's supposed to be, with a good guy who knows everything which you like especially. You let your high fade cause stuff just looks new and like you'd hoped it would, which is kind of like what getting high is about anyways. You let the high go because the man who knows so much suggested that you do, and to tell your pals, too.

Trying to put the high away was easy, even though it would come up like a laugh you weren't supposed to have. We didn't talk with the permanent party soldiers—the guys stationed in Panama full-time—when they drove the long line of deuce-and-a-halfs onto the drop zone, stopping alongside our equipment. Instead, as best I could see, each driver gave us one look from their cabs, and the look said, "It's different here, and you're gonna like it." We climbed onto the wide beds of the trucks, which were open, and the entire battalion got licked by trees more like big plants, as the convoy left the drop zone's edge on a hard top road leading into a green tunnel.

The speed of the warm air cooled and dried us. We passed under shade and sun like little whole days. Rocks and rough ocean on the left until you thought you had it down and then beach sand and still water on the right, so's that those who had never been nodded their heads and thought of the coast of California. The entrance to a military base came up fast—a long road, new blacktop, with no gate or checkpoint. All eyes followed it towards the rows of white buildings kept in line by trees, then snapped back quick to six or seven brown girls in shorts and tube tops who stood by the entrance and waved and said stuff in Spanish. The deuce-and-a-halfs slowed by five

miles per and we all thought, "This is the place." But they didn't
turn, only crept the trucks past the girls, and the soldiers in the first
trucks stood and waved back saying Hey! and Buenos Dias Senorit-
ers! We did the same and turned and watched all the 2/304 in convoy behind us come up like dominoes in reverse and yell, politely,
cause we were guests.

One loud voice from the girls returned above the rest asking a
long "Where are you goooing?"

We wondered because that place seemed fine. The drivers got
back up to speed and we liked them for the slow pass of the ladies
and thought them the good guys. Rides in trucks usually meant
sleep, but our eyes alternated between the wide and the squinted,
with seats being swapped across the bed of the truck for fear of
missing something good on either side. Quick neighborhoods we
passed, whitewashed half houses, half built along the bends in the
road, looking like they would fall just after a tenant family's midnight move. The wind bent the palms on both sides of the road so
deep that they looked like they could be working yo-yos and I
believed that this ride would have been the same without the mesc,
cause all the scouts—the whole battalion, from what I could see—
were acting like, "Hey, I get to do this. Be here." All the dopers know
that what with all the electricity pumped through the brain on a
jump, a lot of the chemical is burned off. Plus we'd been doing as
we'd been told, trying to push what was left of the high out and
away. I was very busy just sitting there.

The trucks swung through S curves, and our driver yelled praise
out his window as he and his fellow transportation experts found
gears high and low at the same points in and out of the turns. That
these drivers were good was not lost on the scouts, who came to
notice the line of twenty trucks moving as one, noting the details
that made the drivers experts so they could be remembered, discussed. Then we'd all laugh, cause who'd of ever thought that we'd
come to Panama to admire the work of no-grunt, non-jumping, leg,
gear jockeys?

The ride got supreme as the drivers wound out the final high
gear, adding speed to the shared precision and before us, the last
tunnel of palms liking to suck us through a particular spot on earth
more dark than light. Country began singing, *"Traa-in Traa-in . . ."*
and the drivers all coaxed on their engines for just a little more
speed: *C'mon just like before/ make it just like before/ make it just like*

the last run the last time/ and make it fast like the last run the last time/ and make it fast like my boys at the wheels/ in front and quick behind.

Round the last bend, deuce-and-a-halfs found extra turning room off blacktop, tires crunching thin gravel dirt. The trees, the lead trucks, and everything that lay before us lost all patterns of shade and instead caught and held the now steady light. Drivers backed down clean through the gears. Ft. Gulic welcomed us with just those words spelled out by painted rocks set on crushed clamshells, and our flag waving from a pole so high it made you wonder if somebody in charge and way back when hadn't gotten carried away.

There had been this one time on a bus, years and years before, a cross-country bus, and that's what Ft. Gulic had me thinking after. Cause this one time, between me at the window and the grown man on the aisle of that bus, was a seat with not a thing on it except, one on top of the other, three *Model Railroader* magazines. The cover of the first one was a close-up picture of a silver Lionel train running across a valley towards a bitsy village where no real thing lived, though it looked like a place where people—especially me—should live more than any other. I wanted to live there in that picture bad enough that I knew it was very wrong. Being a kid on a cross country bus all on his own, I figured it was okay to look at the man's magazines while he slept, and picked one up to look closer, but he woke up and took it right out of my hands and fussed over a couple of page corners I might of bent. I stuck my head right at that window and looked out at the highway thinking, "Jeezum," about a man all grown with magazines about special toys, knowing that if I was to wind up like him, then I hadn't done half bad for myself, all things taken and considered.

If a train had run out across our field of vision when we arrived at Ft. Gulic it would have been good. But if it had been a silver Lionel train like on the cover of the man's *Model Railroader* magazine it would have meant we had really done some traveling, and that would have been best.

Soldiers in flat green fatigues and green ball caps worked lawn mowers out in all directions. In a narrow inlet that just sliced halfway towards the center of the base sat river patrol boats and bigger LSTs. Ft. Gulic's headquarters was a village of many short old buildings you'd want to call bungalows, connected by sidewalks

lined with trimmed tough-looking plants. Everything not growing
was a painted white that could hold a polish, and I joined Richards
and Limón talking about, "Dang, bro. You know they got multiple
motherfuckers pulling all the extra duty on this clean bitch."

Lines of palms picked up after we passed the little buildings, a
parade field. We took a right turn along more palms—which were
the only things keeping the whole base from being in the open—and
full in front of us, across another perfect field, was a fat row of six,
seven, maybe eight tall white barracks, run out in front of the ocean
and still more palms, and this time close enough to the wind coming
off the ocean that they seemed to bow down together, almost marking time. I looked down from the truck at the blacktop, catching
myself wondering why we were stopped, why were we still here
instead of across the field forming up into companies. Even the
blacktop was worth a look and told some of the story. This place was
old and used, but everything about it was kept so good, cleaned and
reconditioned, that it looked like new history.

When the trucks finally made their way around the road, stopping in a line to match the length of barracks, I went to grab my
gear and found a K-Bar knife in my hand. I brought it close to my
eyes and stared at it, as across the bed of the truck my pals leaned
into one another and stared at me. Not knowing which way this was
going to go, I stayed with my eyes on both the knife and the men.
The three-way staring contest was broken up when the guys began
to shift their eyes over to my right, and I saw that I had dug my ini-
tials and the year into the end of the wooden bench. That the letters
and numbers were set permanently in the wood clean won out over
both the laughter of my pals and the rise of worry which comes with
the completion of a task you hadn't even realized you'd started.

In formation, standing with bag and baggage along the tropical
company street, the 2/304—the whole battalion, five companies—
faced the old white barracks with backs to a sea barely glimpsed but
still felt as if the water behind them held sway over the water in
their bodies like a worn ancient magnet over slim pieces of metal.

The sun went on over the men held in formation at the rest position like it could burn you two inches in. And still like no bad news
or trouble would come your way under a sun like that—it was all
just good light across every little thing. Yet southwestern, western,
and southern boys would come to burn under that sun for the first
time, and the burn would come up a pink just short of red that bub-

bled and turned hot white when fool enough to press on. This burn changed the tolerance of the skin they lived in ever after, following and haunting them as a primer for fresh burns under the long sunny skies of home.

And if someone would ask me about happiness I'd tell on that too, because it might be that I've got a kind of answer. At least as I feel the stuff visited around me in the days when I was a soldier. And young enough for hopes to repeat, and that these hopes were hoped hard, and made beautiful when the repetition of them was answered almost always.

By the time we stood in formation outside the white barracks and the fanning fingers of the green palms of Panama, I'd come to anticipate the call and response of wants answered. So's that just by hoping, we'd soon be able to see the ocean's breeze alternately wrapping our blousey, old-style camouflaged fatigues tight to our bodies, only to drop and hang just a little heavier with collected mist and condensation. Just by hoping to see the water, and knowing it was fast what we all wanted just for then.

Sergeant Major—a religious man—stood before us and commanded the 2/304 to attention. Down the ranks, the order echoed, each time in a higher register. My lips were set to smile, and then I did, as the Sergeant Major ordered an about-face, tens of voices repeated again and hundreds placed one toe of one boot behind and swung about catching a face full of river ocean and a few thoughts uncontrollably private. Then the Sergeant Major walked again out across his men, dead reckoning the center of them.

It must be we are issued an allotment of desires that will be met, and I, and most of my kind, burn through them before we know enough to wish for the practical. It must be that.

Sergeant Major yelled to the battalion in formation, his men; and I heard nothing save his tone, and the word Colon, which came every sixth word. He was high-hatting us, that much I knew, in a brief and futile attempt to keep his men from that myth across the water. It was a city so vile, he said, that God's hand would soon come and raise the waters and wash it all away. His address ended and as it did I heard his challenge: for us men to prove his suspicions correct. To prove that we men of the 2/304 were too smart, too Strac, and too wise to fall prey to the city which held nothing for us that we didn't already have back home on Hay Street. With this, his pipe switched corners in his mouth, a smirk ran up the other side, and he shifted his weight from one of his little jungle boots to the other. He was cueing us. Sergeant Major was undermining his own speech. It made no kind of sense military or otherwise and when the first dog bark, more like a happy canine moan, came from Charlie Company, hundreds of others followed like hounds finished running something up a tree.

We were letting him know that we weren't smart or bright that way, at least not most of us, otherwise we wouldn't be with him in the first place. Just like he really wanted us to be was how we were, same guys he'd been humping next to for damn near his full thirty years and who would definitely be going to that city. We were headed for the jungle and then to Colon and a trail of peacetime casualties, Article 15s, court-martials, bad conduct discharges, less than honorables, separation for the good of the service. All that and more we would leave in our wake if only to make Sergeant Major know we were that same bunch of guys.

The scouts were assigned a large section of the third and top floor of a barracks. We passed rows of cots in the empty open bays, our boots sounding with a sharp report on the wooden floors as we found our place, smiling at and passing under the ancient and gently wobbling ceiling fans. Smiling again because ours was behind a half high partition which gave the scouts semi-private lodgings, with long and wide hand crank windows looking over the tops of palm trees towards the water.

We each dropped our gear by a cot—very natural, nobody upset with another's choice—and went down to check weapons into the arm's room and pull linens. In line for the sheets, Limón whispered to the dopers that there were stairs that went up the outside of the barracks. We could take those outside stairs three flights up the ocean side of the barracks and right into our quarters. Officers and noncoms were everywhere and not a one said boo to us when we tried it. We made some noise about it too, and decided that the more they saw us on those stairs—between the leaves and trunk of one big palm—the better, rather than saving it just for the times we'd need it for sneaking.

The windows were cranked open wide, screens checked for holes, cots were made up and lain down upon scout-style with the lightweight poncho liner at the feet. We had been cut loose until evening chow. A few hours to rack out. Sleep came nice in the scented breeze, and the scouts fell to it. And as if shifts had been drawn, and a guard roster posted, one by one, men came to stand alone, at the windows smoking, or spitting chew or snuff quiet into a soda can.

Sleep, motherfuckers. I got your back. This ain't going nowhere. It'll be waiting on you when you rise.

One by one.

I waked up to Togiola standing over me saying, "Past that time."

Giving myself a minute while the men started down the outside stairs towards chow, I stared at the fans clustered in threes across the ceiling and asked myself to not think about those who came before. Think about the ones who came *long* before you, long enough that they wore different uniforms. Bring those old-timey guys up close to your own and then go on about your business. Find a way to make that work.

From the company street my name was called twice, and at the threats that followed, I moved.

The mess hall was big. Two serving lines at each end, and you could have gotten lost in this mess hall. The whole battalion seated and you had room to spread out with your good chow, not all up on each other like at home.

I had been saying just that to the guys outside after the meal and got a strange look for it, too. Like I had gone round the bend for lifer, calling the mess hall back at Bragg "home."

At the center of every table, big pebbly, frosted plastic bowls held Panama fruit. The fruits were different shapes and none a color you could name, but all were the size of softballs and a flat kind of sweet loused up with seeds. The same kind of machines for bug juice you find in any mess hall except here it was real juice, regular sweet, and over ice good enough that the spoons had lots to do refilling them. Each table also had a Panamanian soldier at it. We smiled at ours, a corporal, when we sat, but he returned it like he was an old friend of Sergeant Major's. He was skinny, didn't talk, and best I could see, none of the Panamanians at the other tables talked either. All he did was peel at the fruit and then eat in a way that looked more like licking, spitting out a stream of seeds into a glass only after each piece of fruit was vanished. We just sat looking at his dark green fatigues, which were tight and starched, the darkness making them look cheap, his brightly colored glory patches, and his sew-on jump wings which were U.S. like ours, except that the cloth was white.

When we set to eating our lobsters, he got up from the table without taking his tray and went for the door, the other Panamanians either beating him to it or close behind. I was going to ask him for some help with my lobster, cause I'd never seen one like it. In one of the places I was raised you'd see lots of pictures of lobsters, and in tanks in a corner of the Star Market they'd be climbing all over each other. I'd even had one bought for me in a restaurant except what they served was twins.

Me and the doper scouts had been to the Red Lobster on Bragg with Mr. Big, but that time, the whole deal was done up for you, no shell.

Never saw a yellow lobster before, a little on the small side. There was nothing to crack the shells with. Like a lot of the other guys, I stared at it for a while, then went up and got two burgers. I came back to the table and the little yellow fucker was still there sitting on a plate. They had all kinds of other food up there, fish, and a steak that looked a little gray. After we'd had our fill the lobsters were still sitting there.

Limón said, "Man," like he was from around here and stabbed his lobster with a knife. The shell folded in a good bit, popped back out, and the knife slid down and hit the plate with a loud clank that told us we'd been too quiet. All eyes upon our table now. Some at tables far away stood to look. Frankie Meadows came out of his pocket with a folding Randall, opening it with a solid klick, one hand, as it came. He flipped the lobster and gutted it with the sharp and always oiled blade. Soon the mess hall was filled with the sounds of Bucks, Gerbers, and more Randalls being flipped open and I thought, "crickets."

Outside the mess hall, we were still talking about the lobster, how watery it was, the funny color, and that soupy meat which was not what I remembered at all. But everything else about this mess hall raised it high above any we'd ever seen, so's that comparisons would have to be made with restaurants. The dopers—plus Corporal Jencks, who by coming along made it an occasion—walked along a wide piece of grass with the white buildings on our right and to the left only the ocean. Within steps, the complaining started. This mess hall wasn't nowheres near as good as a Morrison's, but why, shit, couldn't our mess hall back at Bragg be anything like this one. . . .

Limón and Jencks, who were big fans of our mess hall back at Bragg—especially since it had started having snack mess where from 8:00 to 9:30 in the evening a soldier could get hot dogs, hamburgers, and his fourth hot meal of the day—protested. Jencks said that *any* mess hall sure beat the hell out of day-old kitchen bread over and under a fat piece of gov'mint cheese.

Came up on the enlisted men's club directly. It was ground level of a white building just off the row of barracks. No door, just a wide-open front and a bamboo bar where a seat could give you a view of the ocean and lights beyond it, except that the place was already full up with our Alpha, Bravo, and Charlie Company line dogs at the Stroh's. They nodded at us friendly enough, but we knew if we stayed it would be as guests.

We got handfuls of American change from the bartender and walked it back out to the beer machine. A can of Balboa in each hand and likewise in the cargo pockets of our cammie pants, the doper scouts walked the grass along the rocks and water away from the barracks and got back to it.

"Gov'mint cheese."

The pronunciation came from Richards, but the gov'mint cheese was a thing shared across early versions of many of our lives. A common disgust and humiliation, but with the relief and comedy that came from putting ourselves in the service of the government which made the damn cheese, and that took us off far from the three-foot-high blocks of the stuff which in memory stood taller than any tall buildings in our hometowns.

"Big block of thick-ass gov'mint cheese."

"Yeah, moms like to just set it down in the middle of the table standing thick, tall and nasty . . ."

"Yellow."

"Yellow. Yellow like some banana cheese."

"Yeah, Mom. Just stand it in the middle of the table and let the kids come and gnaw on it when they get hungry."

"Gov'mint cheese."

"Imagine if you got hit in the head with the gov'mint cheese?"

"Shit would say, 'Dunk.'"

"Yeah, and Limón go to school the next day with little x's for eyes all the kids talking about, 'Oh, shit, Limón got hit in the head with the gov'mint cheese.'"

"Cause they'd know."

"Of course they'd know. Get hit in the head with the gov'mint cheese, everybody'd know."

"Be plain to see."

"Need to drop some of that mess on Iran. Kill a bunch of mother-fuckers on the head and the rest would be all fat and depressed from eating the gov'mint cheese and leave everybody else the fuck alone."

Me, Limón, Shattuck, Meadows, Richards, Togiola, and Corporal Jencks found a walkway made of big rocks that went a good sixty meters out into the ocean. At the edge, we sat and hung our feet, and we noticed—marked, finally—how the light faded and darkness fell by degrees in Panama.

Everybody got their own skinny joint so's there'd be no orange tips to be spotted being passed round, and even still not all of us lit up at once. We'd never been more out in the open. Practicing Platoon Daddy's number one rule for the peacetime soldier—*If you don't want to get caught don't look like you're doing nothing wrong*—had become an easy habit. Meadows scooted down a bit around the edge of the walkway to be able to keep an eye out, and said, "Shee-it." Turning we saw it, too: those trees and the barracks, the little bar, beer machine glowing, officers—by their walk—saluting and stopping to talk, soldiers in groups, all this misty and a little washed out in yellow from the streetlights tacked into telephone poles, circles of old metal, like pie tins, covering the bulbs.

Turning back, cans of Balboa popped, the water an ocean of bat wings easy aloft, Limón smiles at the lights that must be a flat water mile across the river shining from the side he doesn't yet know is Colon. Hugging himself tight against a wind that ain't even cold, he say's, "This shit's nice."

We got four days of training before they began to throw us in the jungle. After jungle training in Panama, we'd be authorized to wear a patch that said Jungle Expert over a pirate ship with a cross on its full sails. Soldiers from the 2/305 had come back talking about how the patch should read "Jungle Barely Familiarized" because they weren't experts at nothing but the city of Colon. Turns out that the story we'd been told about the cadre eating bugs was true. The first block of instruction we got was survival-type stuff and a guy did eat a bug. Another half swallowed a centipede and then opened his mouth wide so we could see it from the rickety short bleachers crawl back up and out along his tongue.

The cadre run us through their little zoo, which looked like it belonged back home off an interstate south of Ft. Bragg: a little beat-up bunch of cages with some supposedly bad ass animals look-ing tired and bored. I did see my first sleeping monkey, and the black guys got freaked about the snakes and scorpions, cause that's what the cadre was trying to do. There was a caiman in something that was just a metal tub. It didn't do much of anything till poked at with long sticks, then its tail came to life and the tub scooted across the cement floor like a Knoc Hockey puck.

We got blocks of instruction on booby traps, too: that was just cadre showing off. And they said that the jungle was no more dan-gerous than Ft. Bragg—safer than Hay Street. Which was supposed to be real funny. They had it down. That annoying military way of saying whatever they'd seen was harder and scarier than anything you have. Platoon Daddy walked behind the bleachers as the instructors went on about how, ". . . the weaknesses of guerrilla forces include their sense of numerical and technological inferiority to counter-guerrilla forces."

At this, Platoon Daddy hissed, "Don't you listen to this shit. Bitch must be mad."

He lay down behind the bleachers when the instructors brought out training aids—big pictures—of jungle fighting position, grenade sumps and all that. At the words "fortified jungle fighting positions" he smacked his lips, said, "Digging in the jungle, and for Recon that shit's insignificant. Don't you listen to nary a none of it." And he fell asleep.

The sleeves of his cammie shirt were slit for extra room and brigade rolled high. From my seat in the bleachers I couldn't really make out the tattoo on his left bicep, the ink in his skin faded and spread out over time, but I knew what was there: Bugs Bunny in a floppy boonie hat, wearing tiger stripe cammies, holding a smoking M-60 at the hip, and a big ol' bunny foot on the neck of a dead pajama-wearing Viet Cong whose tongue was hanging out. Above this were the words "Rice Paddy Daddy" in script.

Most of the brothers didn't get tattoos, and the ones that did were divided between those who Richards said were half white boy anyway and those who were country to the bone. Get up close to these country boys and the jump wings, skulls and berets—colors barely seen, black lines a shade or two darker than skin—make them look dangerous in a I don't give a fuck kinda way.

White guys get tattoos because they want to be cartoons—better than people—but wind up looking worse.

Two hours of instruction on radio antenna rigs for the jungle and our whole company was giving in to the heat and sleep, scouts leading the way. By the second day of classes all but the big time cheese eaters had given up attempting to stay awake.

Most nights after the good chow, we'd head back to the barracks for a while. Limón hadn't brought his radio, so all we had for music was Corporal Collins' 8-track, and all he had was two tapes of Neil Young. One was *Decade* and the other *Harvest,* so there was some doubles. It fit nice, especially the slow ones, and not one black complained. I'd read the Huck book on my bunk, and some guys played cards, but everybody looked out the window a lot. Maybe Shattuck could say that the wind coming in smelled like jasmine rice three more times before somebody'd have to do something.

It wasn't long—maybe an hour, hour and a half—that we'd all get to looking out the window more than reading or cards, so we'd put up all our stuff, and down the stairs along the palm tree we'd go. The whole platoon would go to the little enlisted men's bar and have a Balboa as a unit. Then the dopers would wait outside a few minutes to see if Collins and Quinton were coming. They weren't and that was a shame because they had got all of us high—wanting to find out about us—when we first come to Bragg, and it would have been nice to take them out in a foreign country on our dope. They were short-timers, though, and wanted to leave the service honorably and at their current rank, which made them careful. Besides they'd been here already. It should have been real obvious how careful they were going to be, seeing that they gave us Mr. Big a month before we left Bragg.

We'd find little groups of line doggies at the dope as we walked out along the water. We'd join them, sharing a jay of ours to be friendly, not staying too long cause their spots were uncool, but we'd invite them to ours and sometimes they came.

Low on dope and money. Paychecks would be sent over to be cashed by the paymaster at long tables before our first weekend loose, and that was fine. Rationing kept us mellow in the evenings and word was you couldn't get drunk on Balboa anyway. It was a different kind of quiet sitting out at our spot. Not like those other good scout quiets, most like it was for us in Egypt, but it wasn't really like that either. The ships here had something to do with it. We were at them always. Catch one coming a ways off by its running lights and then lose it, especially the long and low narrow ones. In front of us, edges and surfaces bleeding into the dark water, ghosty ships known only by little sets of lights at both ends. Sometimes one voice carried and we heard it, not from our alphabet, and sometimes a song, which made all it passed very quiet.

Classes ended the morning of our third day and after lunchtime chow we practiced jungle insertions—rappelling down from helicopters—and after that we smoked the rest of the battalion through the longest obstacle course in the US Army. Over paths cut in the jungle and loaded up with wall, log, low crawl, rope, tower and nut buster obstacles, even down a cliff and a run along a beach, the scouts finished and triumphed as a platoon, and if we hadn't had to carry Hartel the last 150 yards, we'd of set a course record. Even so, our time was good enough that the cadre said we could use the post craft center to make a plaque to put up at the finish line.

On our last day before the jungle, my platoon whupped up on the rest of the battalion again, tearing up the morning on the land navigation course. Cheating dogs is what we were, though. Quinton and Collins had acetate-covered maps still marked up from their first cycle through this jungle school three years back. All the rest of us had to do was put our heads down and hump. The land nav course was well traveled and almost jungle. Still the hills hadn't been worn down, and between that and the black palm, there was plenty cussing. Black palm. The tree was common as scrub oak in North Carolina, and the thick needles that covered it were barbed so's when you ripped it out quick cause it burned, you pulled up skin and made a wound. All those hundreds of steep little hills messed up with wait-a-minute vines, and whole systems of fat tree roots living more above ground than below, had us tripping and sliding back. We each made the mistake of breaking the fall with a hand against a tree maybe once.

Have a paratrooper wearing issue black leather gloves in hot-assed Panama. First time I'd heard of it I was still cherry-cherry, the motor pool sergeant was talking loud with his kind gathered round.

"Black Pride Week. Shit, seen them posters in the mess hall? When we gonna get us some White Week? Black Pride? Shit, down Panama they got some black palm that'll fuck everybody up with equal opportunity."

Waiting for us at the finish, Platoon Daddy was happier about the cheating than that we'd won and upheld the 2/304 Scout Reconnaissance platoon's reputation. He didn't even have to say, we knew it by his big man's little laugh that he did believe he'd taught us something.

That afternoon, the whole battalion was formed up and waiting along the inlet where the boats were going to pick us up and take us for a ride. We were all laughing a little and trying not to.

We'd heard the boats were the same ones used to carry troops from ships to beachheads during invasions in World War Two. But seeing a dozen of them coming for us manned by small crews wearing green ball caps puzzled and annoyed the battalion of hundreds of paratroopers in maroon berets. Till now we'd tried to be polite to the permanent party legs—it was their base—but the sight of Army guys driving little boats was too much. As the boats got closer the snickering began, and junior grade officers tried to go diaphragm deep with the command, "At Ease!" which never sounded right from them. It might have gone like that, the boat soldiers pulling up and us loading on smiling at them, if it were not that one voice from the back of Alpha Company which rose up like a southern ballpark peanut vendor working the bleachers, "Hey, Nice Hat!" That minted our next few miserable hours, cause after that came, "Squid!" and then "Hey, Fucking Popeye!" and the Popeye song, and then a couple of years old disco song about the Navy with the little dance that went with it, all this from hundreds used to yelling and singing and marching together. The boatmen ignored this as best they could, pilots backing down the engines making the budda-budda deep and slow, the crews manning the landing side and the 2/304 boarded talking shit, our captain not being around and the lieutenants buried under the momentum.

Charlie Company line doggies were mixed in with the scouts in our boat and they continued to ride the pilot and crew halfway out to the canal, which we were going to see for the first time. At our passing of a cargo ship that Shattuck said was from Turkey by its flag—its name, *Halcyon*, barely readable from all the rust—we were surprised and near giddy about seeing the women holding drinks on the top deck, but we waved and acted respectful. After they saw how respectful we were they waved back, and so did their men in sports jackets.

Some of the guys said the ship was the biggest thing any of them had ever seen, and with the locks coming up with even bigger ships at the wait, the whole world was out of scale. Paratroopers got to pointing and saying "Wow" and then we ran into some waves from the big ship just passed. Old war movies came back to me as the slanted front of the boat both rode and slammed the wave with a thud and whip of sea water across us all. The boats quit their staggered formation and rode in a file, which kept the waves small but steady. 180 degrees away from the locks, the boats in front of us turned hard and ours followed.

The boats cut across the current and into the trail of rough water left by big ships. Just like in an aircraft, once one soldier let lunch go over the side, the rest followed. The boat men kept us out there a long time, not saying much except that if we looked at the water it would help. It made it a lot worse and the sickness was a constant. They could spin these things in one spot and as they did, they sang Airborne cadence under the retching that was now almost dry.

C-130 rolling down the strip /64 troopers on a one-way trip . . .
And
Momma told Sally not to go downtown/Just a bunch of paratroopers a hanging around . . .
And
. . . backed off, jacked off, fucked the other two.

There would have been a violent response to this kind of treatment or at least threats, but nobody could come off the side for very long. Those few paratroopers not afflicted were awestruck by the amount of sickness that their pals had heaved into the ocean and the boatmen were stone-faced and tending their craft. They kept us out there a long time.

The boatmen dropped us off where they picked us up without a word and we went and lay out, a whole Airborne Infantry Battalion, facedown, on the cots and under the ceiling fans until the sickness passed. When evening chow came we were famished.

The word around the chow hall was that none of the officers had gotten sick.

Togiola had gone out with girls back home who went to junior colleges and community ones and so I tried to get a good conversation going on about the connection between college and not throwing up on boats, but nobody was having it.

And nobody wanted to go back out to our spot that night, either.

Ski bought a bottle of rum which had a treasure map for a label from a civilian working at the mess hall. We stayed with it in the barracks with the breeze, listening to the two tapes on the 8-track, until Platoon Daddy came by to kid us about the boat ride. Instead told us about what dumb asses we were cause he smelled hard liquor in the barracks over all the Kools and Winstons before he was halfway across the Charlie Company side. Like your good dirty grandpa, he stood among us sitting on cots, and he stayed put and silent till he'd gotten his fill of attention. Then he began to talk fast about all kinds of things and then narrowing to one in particular. The bottle and why were we taking it off the neck like porch dwellers on assistance?

Corporal Collins sent the cherries after change and the soda machine, and the rest of us waited and hoped.

Platoon Daddy stayed and not just the dopers but six or seven others—even if they didn't drink brown liquor—were strewn tight down our outside steps with enough room between the feet to set your drink and a pack of them down.

When the cherries came back, he first took the top off the Mountain Dews with a P-38, then poured some soda out and added just enough rum in to make what he called after a stir with his finger, "a nice drink." Each one was prepared slowly, his elbows out and high, and after the stirring and tasting and before the passing down the stairs, soldier to soldier, he did in some way pronounce each and every drink, nice.

"There, that's a nice drink."

"Give that to a paratrooper, cause that's nice."

"I like a nice drink."

"Drink is nice."

"Nice drink."

"Nice."

Again, he asked us fast where we were from, and what it was like. Cutting us off with his own versions of what a soldier's hometown was like, and fixing more drinks, until he cuffed me off the side of my a head a little hard, saying, "This motherfucker here from everywhere," and not like it was a bad thing at all.

We were out there long enough that sleep was a nap. No officer or cheese eater said shit or nothing about Platoon Daddy up drinking Mountain Dews outside with his scouts till all hours.

First call came an hour early and the morning came on gentle and dusty, already familiar. After chow, we sat chuted up in the parade field waiting on the birds. The vitamin pills from home were divvied up, pink hearts and fat black beauties tapped into the corners of Ziplocs and tucked away. We swallowed one each, for this might be the day the hangovers began, and lord knows lifer and a wife might be next. The Hueys came in low and staggered at the far end of the field setting down, still in formation; within minutes the entire battalion was on board and flying the Chagres River NAP of the earth. There seemed to be no waiting in Panama.

No doors to the Huey—Indian–style, my knees had nothing underneath them except a river in Panama. Alpha Company close on our wing and pilots followed water just above the top of the jungle. Crazy water, no kind of good sense river, banked turns so hard you felt it under your butt and at the same time watching Alpha Company taking the same turn, fast enough that a helicopter should spin out, and this was flying. No slow-down before getting drawn up skyward out of formation and over fat green, climbing while we made one pass and then a circle route once over a drop zone that didn't look big enough for a softball game. Jump commands came and went and pushing off the edge was like scooting off a table. A full canopy set me up as insignificant against all that sky and with a full chute taken for granted, all I wanted to know this time was how they figured out that my drift, mostly over jungle, would land me in the clearing.

Almost got fallen on once, twice, and that had never happened before. I looked up and ran over my chute on the ground with a little wind puffing under it, only to run back cause down comes another paratrooper; it must of been the vitamin pills that had me running back and forth like Charlie Chaplin, cause that's what they said.

Left the parachutes where they lay for the detail to police up. Moved out across the little clearing in a platoon-sized traveling overwatch formation, which we held as Platoon Daddy moved us into the jungle. It was like running into a green wall that gave a bit when you whacked at it enough. After an hour that was like all day, the traveling overwatch dissolved into a platoon on line. Horrible too, speedy in the head, body wants to follow only it's mostly stuck still except for the whacking. We hadn't covered a hundred meters and loggers at their work couldn't of made more noise. Platoon Daddy called for the squad leaders, and the platoon took a knee where they'd stood, breathing hard, sweat still pumping and without one splash of sunlight to hold accountable.

Jencks came back to us folding his map into a small square, and

squatting before us said, "First, he wants to know if anyone has bothered to look around at all this shit and second if we heard anything."

We looked around and listened.

"He was over there saying that right after we moved into this
shit we dropped into a draw that has a crick running through it
come rainy season. Y'all know'd that? Whole country like low country to me. So then he says that all he wants us to know is that the
noise we're hearing is birds and animals and that they sound this
way when we're over here and different when we're over there. I
dunno, something like that. Here, I got to show this part on the
map. Battalion wants us out here in thick shit like this here, but Platoon Daddy says we're going ridge running. There, I told it all."

When we were back at Bragg, the scouts would take to the low
ground for ghosting, making cherries take turns running up and
down a nearby hill with the radio sending transmissions to the captain to make it seem like we were traveling.

Platoon Daddy now had the whole platoon moving along the
ridges with decent concealment and a poor view of the route we
were to recon, but still it was a lot better than being down in the
thick mess making all that noise and not getting anywhere. Besides
we were learning how to ridge run keeping the enemies on the other
side and we'd know that by the noises of the animals, which you had
to wonder about especially if the enemies were from around here
and might could know the animal noises a whole lot better than us.
All I really understood was that in less than two hours the jungle
had me smoked and I was knowing everything I wanted to know
about getting whipped on my face with vines and branches and
rough, sharp pointed leaves with flat surfaces like 40 grit sandpaper.
I did trust my Platoon Daddy and knew that like always and forever,
he was teaching how to stay alive by avoiding work.

By squads we separate and Platoon Daddy gave us sectors to run
loose in with no mission—just see what we could see. He'd take care of
the captain. Jencks and Country on compass, Richards and Limón
working pace count, with me safe from the navigating, but doing my
bit for the squad humping Limón's M-60, and we're lost on a wide dirt
road kicking at rocks, and calling names for fun within an hour and a
half. The road narrowed and opened, as it twisted and turned, so regular that when I paced the distance between they did prove to rhyme.

The jungle complete all around the road, but above, just then,
clear enough for the thick shadows to turn to shade and it was nice

to be out from under the jungle where everything was a thin and pale night. Jencks stopped and knelt back over his muttering about how everything looked like either a dang mountain or depression. He said, why don't somebodies go shake on a big tree to see if anything moved on the map.

Frankie Meadows fish hooked some old Copenhagen out his lip and packed some fresh dip back in tight.

"Damn, Country. Even in this fucking heat?" said R.

Meadows replied with a rich brown blast at the jumbo ants running between us in the road, tossing some up in the air, end over end, and sprayed others into the road, where, away from their fat black column, they lit out for twenty directions a second. We took our seats from where we'd stood, peering down at the cluster fuck of ants, Limón coming out with the pack first, cursing himself while handing out the Newports to me and Richards, cursing me again in Spanish as he gave me a light cause I still had my issue black leather gloves on like the black palm was going to jump out and stick me in the middle of the road.

"Motherfucking Chinese ant fire drill," said Richards as he tried to redirect ants back towards the ant highway with a stick, and we other three pointed at ones he was missing.

"You fucked up their whole society," said Limón, and I guess I deserved it when he punched me in the chest for blowing smoke on the ants and I got told, Great now they got cancer and it was a menthol, too, and why didn't I grow up. I knew it was a big wrong by the way the smoke hit them, making them stop and go again faster than ever, and I got a little sick to my stomach only for a flash.

We were going to break for afternoon chow off the side of the road, but at the sound of gears grinding, we were on our feet and following that sound as it repeated and listening to it brought back all the other sounds of the jungle which we'd forgot cause they're constant. The engine didn't belong to the US Army, though it did sound broken, and it passed behind the jungle coming on strong. A strange rattle—sometimes dull, sometimes sharp—came too, promising to loop around the green and head straight for us down the road. Bottles, the sound was bottles, knew it before I saw it, that bottle truck with empty bottles, row after row, out in the open and up the side of the old bottle truck. It was red with faded carnival paint colors advertising American sodas though we recognized none of the bottles, except for a half row of Fanta, by their long necks.

The truck passed us, Jencks' arm across my front as we moved to let it go, but the three men on the outside of the truck were scrambling as they passed till one was hanging upside down into the driver's window, and the truck stopped with bottles all clanked forward. The men sprang from high on the truck's side, jumping higher than necessary, white and yellow shirts buttoned once, twice, blown up as they came down, bare feet slapping the road hard.

Shorter than Limón, all three with home-cut hair, and it would be good if they were brothers the way they moved almost in a circle, in between one another, arms always in contact, speaking Spanish, and waiting for us to do something. Limón approached, speaking a faster Spanish than theirs, which surprised them, their faces like children invited to a dirt bomb fight by pelting. The three men, who were definitely brothers, spoke back to Limón, trying to speed their words up, till two pushed one forward and he extended a hand holding a beat-up pack of Panamanian cigarettes.

Limón took the pack and we motioned him back to us. Inside the pack were thick and bumpy joints rolled in mustard yellow construction paper.

"A-O-A-O-A! This is it. This is it. It's—" and Limón wiggled his nose back into the pack for another snort and coming back to us serious like angry.

"Give me all the money you gots. Just the singles. Come on, come on."

Nobody really takes money on patrol, and Limón was doing small calisthenics, mad and original, in place. But Corporal Jencks pulled from deep inside his ruck a Ziploc bag, and inside was his wallet. Corporal Jencks didn't really smoke dope although he had taken a few hits at our place on the water and was now acting crazy like he thinks we act when we're high but we ignored that as it was above and beyond, him paying for our dope and him being a squad leader just waiting for the paperwork to clear division for his sergeant E-5, hard stripe. Making a fan with the bills, Limón walked them back to the men who immediately began making eating signs, like out of a can, and waving off the money, which one of them did then take, but not until they pointed at our rucks, and continued with the eating signs.

"C-rations, these fucking guys want C's," said Limón as he skipped back to us—there is no skipping in the 82nd Airborne Division—and we dumped our rucks and this time it was the three men who came to us.

We started to stack the cans in one row, but the men were at them fast, grabbing them up, and smiling at the various size and weight of each can. They started to put some cans back on the ground in front of us, and that got them to arguing and picking up and putting down their favorite cans like they were trump, till Richards said, "Shoot, take all them shits." He sounded a little Frankie "Country" Meadows when he said it, proving that we were all starting to talk like each other—mostly southern and western just cause of the numbers.

Limón translated and these Panamanian guys suddenly got very casual like they knew all along that they were going to get all the C's. They even acted a little conceited if you ask me, but later when we all had a chance to talk about it, nobody else thought the conceited part and we all did agree about the driver.

The driver had jumped out of the truck and he too did jump very high and showing off like there was nothing that could hurt his bare feet. These guys had already waved off our offer to get them high and the only other thing they wanted was a P-38 for opening the C's. They were ready to go but the driver ran right past all of us and then stopped to part the jungle at the side of the road, and bending down at a small stream took a drink. Pulling us over to join the driver, they were making a big deal about it, and I was thinking, "Big deal, so you know where the water's at and you're supposed to, you know, because you're fucking from around here anyway."

That wasn't it, though. The driver was making the water come up out of the stream and into his mouth in such a tight thick jet that it looked like faucet water was coming up backwards and into his mouth. He did it with wicked fast moves with one cuffed hand and even though he showed us how, we couldn't get it. Even after they pulled away down the road, the brothers way up on the sides like perched birds, Jencks running after them yelling, "Hey, a sody!" and coming back amazed that in this country you can get reefer and stream drinking lessons off some guys in a soda truck, but no damn sody, and even after we burned one of those joints, the smoke heavy and kinda sweet, the vitamin pills rising again, we still—and we tried and tried—couldn't get that stream water to do anything but splash. Everybody wanted to know why I was so mad and I said, "Cause those guys think they're bad," and truth was, it bothered me to see people liking c-rations that much.

We walked down the road, both ways and each for too long, till we found our right way. The whole time being followed by dogs.

Wild dogs had shadowed us all over Ft. Bragg, not on the short day missions or one-nighters, only on every single mission that went over two days. In the mess hall we asked men of our own battalion if they hadn't seen the dogs, heard them, and on Hay Street had asked others. Not one had. They paid careful attention and were serious and asking polite the questions they had about the dogs.

Some said, then they must be ours.

On that jungle road nobody said, "Wonder if it's the same dogs from Bragg?" though Limón did wade into the jungle going after them the same way he does back there. He scared them away the same here, except it sounded like a few more of them, circling, barking, taking off.

Once my squad decided to not be lost for serious, we joined back up with the rest of the platoon and we told them all about the dogs.

"Dogs are here."

That's what we told them.

"Aww, Son-Of-A-Bitch" and "Ain't no fucking way" was what the platoon said, but they gathered round us fast and fell in and got caught up with us about the dogs and then they too believed it much as we did and the whole platoon didn't quit off talking about the dogs till we got back to the barracks.

The guys are moving around the barracks with shaving cream on their faces, letting it soak in, done cleaning weapons, turning them in and moving fast cause there aren't many buses to Colon and they're leaving soon. Shaving cream is the only thing that takes the cammie stick off of your face, unless you rub it on over insect repellent, but that's for dirtbags cause then it shines, which ruins the whole point.

In the open bays men are getting ready to go out, borrowing cologne, and anybody not a cherry is wrapped in a Myrtle Beach towel and standing on a wet OD green one except for the brothers in proper shower shoes and Limón on top of flip-flops with P.R. written on them in black Magic Marker.

Civvies: jeans, pocket T's, button shirts or collar shirts, by where you're from, plain or snap ones with flower designs at the shoulders are all pressed with travel irons on the barracks floor. Brothers ironing knits with a kerchief between iron and material, and shiny shirts with pool hall scenes and cars, action across the fronts and backs. Stacey Adams dress shoes with the knits, except Limón, who will be working his black knits off green New York Style Pro-Keds—stripes on the side. Some of the boys shining Western boots, which is what you have to call them cause Western boots got bullshit on the outside of them not like cowboy boots that got it on the inside. Ski, in white flat shoes which if you mess with him about he goes off on nobody knowing anything about being a rocker.

We're ready to let them all know we ain't from around here.

My boys got space standing on the first deuce-and-a-half out so we didn't have to get into any of that panic we watched starting to get physical as we left. I felt it enough to mention that it must be a kind of old feeling, that: trying to leave someplace when there isn't enough room. And mentioning that got me looked at hard and silent, again.

They had put on a special early chow for us—didn't want to send us off on empty stomachs—figuring there'd be problems enough, and didn't try and warn us away from Colon, since they hadn't even given us enough time but to get to Panama City and turn right back around.

The deuce-and-a-half moved back into the green tunnel at dusk when you just begin to notice it and it became a second or double dusk under the curved green above, thick with trees, shot with web sprays of vines. You'd think it had been thought up by a man and executed with a trellis, but you'd be wrong, and traveling now the air different with speed and time of day. The same girls outside Ft. Sherman and if they weren't the same girls then they all know each other and this time we all just waved, them too.

A loping left turn after the girls, out of the tunnel, and we saw new things. Suburbs is what it looked like, but the names on the mailboxes were Colonel This or Lieutenant Colonel That, and lowest down was Major Somebody, which were things we couldn't be without college. Something we couldn't be. The flat long houses shrank as we sped past and the ranks stopped dead at Captain Anybody. We could imagine the noncommissioned officers—Sergeant First Class and above—with families, their homes a good walk away with one toy or bike lying on a lawn.

The driver slowed to a crawl as we passed a big house, taller, older, and set back, darkened by the half dozen palms scratching its sides. Okay, so it's a nice house but we were confused by the slow pass, why this house, but why so much when it wasn't something. . . . Then the mailbox with fat black letters spelled it out: Command

Sergeant Major Putnam—a CSM, something we could be—and the men standing in the back of the deuce-and-a-half rushed to one side and barked like big dogs at the house, as if the thing itself had shown off moves the paratroopers liked very much, instead of just being the home of an enlisted man they didn't know who had done the long thirty, and that math told he began not with the last war but the one before.

Under and in the shade again and slums like in the magazines, not even whitewashed like the ones before, but most like the long narrow homes forty miles outside any military base in Georgia and Alabama. Their length slanted, sliding towards the ground, and still lived in full, and we passed them fast like all country slums never our destination. Even the homes that sold shine weren't like these, and even if a guy did come from a place like this, he was from a different place now so it's always just the scenery.

Riding in trucks and wearing civvies. So much fun that a fake fight broke out between two guys from A company all cause one guy said another had been born by a mid lady, not in a hospital at all, and maybe even in a crop field. It wasn't a real fight even though it got good like a real one, the two paratroopers being best buddies since basic.

And now we were beyond where we'd been before at a bridge guarded by the La Guardia, who we'd heard of but now saw with their tan police hats pulled low, the bills touching their noses. We said, "Hey, man," and "What's up?" but they wanted no part of us, not yet anyway, and just swung the striped gate and we passed over the bridge.

As we crossed we looked up and down at the canal, each side with yellow trucks and tractors abandoned for the day, turned-up dirt, and you'd of thought they'd just finished the waterway. As we left the bridge, soldiers talked about what they know good, reminding themselves of what was familiar before going to experience something new. It was that work kind of talking that they had heard their whole lives, with words like Gang Box, Skitter, Combines, Back Hoe, OT, The Plant, 3rd Shift, Tool and Die, and After At The Icehouse. They talked about a brother hired into Caterpillar but now locked out, and then pointed towards the equipment on the banks of the canal cause "that's the company made that there," "used to run one of them," and "twenty dollar an hour job that was." Always these certain guys. Since basic, I'd been hearing about their twenty dollar an hour jobs back home, looked like they were born with girlfriends and a car, looked right living under an airborne haircut, and why'd they come in the Army in the first place was what I didn't know.

Hightower and Richards had a buddy from basic who was permanent party waiting for them where the deuce-and-a-half dropped us. They introduced us, and their buddy looked just as their stories drew him. He was a big, joyful country brother, who was sent to the Army by his college football coach—National Guard—to keep him in basic and AIT for the summer and out of trouble. But he'd liked the Army better than anything he'd seen, so he went regular Army, got Panama, and stayed happy. This happy soldier had some of his buddies with him, and with Hightower and Richards, they walked back to their little cars made from the parts of many other little cars—but very clean all of them—wearing knit dress shirts untucked, hanging neat, and swinging the one leg stiff, a walk Hightower called the Church Usher.

It was okay that the scouts broke up to have a time. Richards and Hightower would go off with the permanent party soldiers for a place like the ones on Mercuson Road outside of Bragg, probably need a collar shirt, shoes, membership, or know somebody, with mixed drinks and all. Frankie Meadows was back waiting on the next deuce-and-a-half for his roper boys from Alpha and Charlie Company for a look see, traveling with too many of them for much to happen. Shattuck wasn't with us. He had made the announcement before leaving for Panama that he was going to reenlist for a Ranger Battalion, and was so bold about it that nobody gave him any shit. We all knew that he'd given it careful consideration, talked it over with his folks and all—improve your life for the future and we all expected him to be careful in certain situations. But didn't really figure him to start spending most of his off time with two goofy Hawaiian guys from headquarters company right in the middle of jungle school. Some guys are given a hard way to go when it looks like they might be re-upping, and some aren't. Some you know the first time you see them, you just think 'Lifer' to yourself and go on about your business. It's supposed to be your buddies or good guys you say "Hey" to all the time that you give the hard way to go, but sometimes cause you know stuff about their life before, you just let it and them go.

Not this trip into Colon, maybe the next, or the one after that, but before we left Panama, all the scouts, we'd meet up for a time together and we'd show each other the good places we'd found. The spots, and they'd be almost familiar from all the telling at the barracks.

Couldn't walk it from where the truck dropped us, and there was a chiba-chiba bus stopping every few minutes, right in front of us, painted with dancing scenes and village life. Every inch of these buses was covered, a little story except where the colors got wild, real psychedelic, and the music from the bus was loud even to us outside and Limón started to dance—"AOAOA"—and the drivers laughed like his dance didn't go right.

We never got on a bus, even though Limón could have got us on the right one, just kept goofing around and the drivers kept taking off before we could get on. Across the street was a man waving to us and pointing to his little blue car. We'd all taken taxis before when on pass in basic and jump school, so it wasn't any big thing.

Limón, me and Ski in the back, Togiola up front, and Limón spoke to the taxi driver in Spanish. But the man answered in English, saying that no, Panama City was the place for us to go. We told him about the curfew, and that we had to only go to Colon tonight, and this time he spoke to Limón like we were being unreasonable, and Limón told us that he wants to take us to the racetrack in Panama City, and then bring us right back to the base. The whole time the man was nodding his head like he was ordering us. All of us now told him that no, we had to go only to Colon and he threw his hands up like Okay, Okay, and then he muttered names which sounded like streets and names of places, bars, softly as the little car dropped down a hill and out of a turn, too fast, and as we got used to his driving, he said, louder now, "Colon, where I have to go."

Before he dropped us, the man said to call him Mike, and by then stopped acting like he was mad at us for not wanting to bet on horses. Limón said, "Miquel" at him and the man said, "No, Mike."

He stopped at the foot of another small hill that only partially hid the miniature city. He turned around and said that tomorrow, he knows this, we are off duty all day and he would take us to Panama City, all day, and ask around tonight what the price should be for that and tomorrow we will see that he is our friend. "Okay, Mike," we told him and crawled out of his cab. "I find you tomorrow" was what he tossed out his window as the tiny wheels peeled out.

Before we had got much up the hill, Mike was back behind us.

"Tomorrow, I wait for you. The good boys. Yes? One night Colon okay for you. Tomorrow the Panama City. Yes, okay?"

"Okay, Mike," we said. "Okay." Fucking guy.

That first night in Colon it was Hay Street rules: one beer in each bar and no ladies drinks, treat them just like the dinks on the Hay. One of the first bars we found was one we'd heard about and they had the room in the back for smoking and we burnt one of the long yellow, bent and bumpy joints, and the La Guardia must of come because the owner locked the door just like he said he would if La Guardia came, but only for ten minutes before someone came back and clicked it again from the other side.

The main streets were tight with buildings like our own old wild wild west—second-story balconies even on the ones with stores below them—and the streets had many Pharmacias, but none sold rolling papers cause Limón asked and we really needed to break these joints up, even white boys knew that.

The alleys, wide and long, jammed up with bars, looked like they were for us, and we stayed mostly to them. Bars with awkward entrances, strange angles leading into them, but walk in sideways, and there's lots of room inside. Only one bar that night had the disco ball and the red pulsing lights that make everything look like dull velvet and Depresso, which was a scout word for things like that.

Street lights fuzzy, but so were we, and it was an ocean haze coaxed to shore through the canal, everything starred and splintered at the edges like in a rain.

Back out in the alleys and for a while it was only the La Guardia that made noise. Their boots—or shoes for the officers—when they walked in step, together, a sharp scuff of the pavement, and they passed in twos and threes with their headgear down low, ignoring us until we warranted their full attention.

Something had happened while Colon had been off-limits. Soldiers who'd been before had told us about Colon, and it was different from what they told. A cherry would know it. Know it by the sound of the boots and shoes and the headgear worn low. Know it good that the canal zone, Colon, was now Panamanian. Even though not yet written out that way, it was no longer international or U.S., and the La Guardia now off and away down some other alley or proper street did not need to walk by us again so boldly. The whole little city, if a city can tell such things, dared the happy scouts to get comfortable and call it ours. The way Hay Street was ours, the way some hated us on Hay Street for the way we walked it. That the other soldiers and the few bikers in their two bars were only needed for atmosphere. It was for us.

The same way everything on that river is for Huck and Jim, good and bad. Huck and Jim is all that exists and everything else but them two is what they make a creation. All for them.

"Jim, this is nice," I says. "I wouldn't want to be nowhere else but here."

And then, just a little later.

We got an old tin lantern, and a butcher-knife without any handle, and a bran-new Barlow knife worth two bits in any store, and a lot of tallow candles, and a tin candlestick, and a gourd, and a tin cup, and a ratty old bedquilt off the bed, and reticule with needles and pins and beeswax and buttons and thread and all such truck in it, and a hatchet and some nails, and a fish-line as thick as my little finger with some monstrous hooks on it, and a roll of buckskin, and a leather dog-collar, and a horseshoe, and some vials of medicine that didn't have no label on them; and just as we was leaving I found a tolerable good curry comb, and Jim he found a ratty old fiddle-bow, and a wooden leg.

That's Huck and Jim taking all they need out of a two-story house come floating down the river—*tilted over considerable*—and it's all the real things they'll need cause the rest they can take care of themselves and the rest they themselves will conjure up along the banks of that river.

The streets and alleys would turn from crowded, like a fairground's first night midway, to nobody but us, and when it was the first way, the walking was slow, lots of bumping and no shoving, just a slow move to the next place and guys yelled to each other in languages you couldn't even imitate, and many of them were squids in black navy uniforms which made them sort of cool. I wasn't worried cause their kinds of talking came mostly from countries I do believe ours had kicked the shit out of some time, at least once and, they'd have to respect that. No matter where we were or how clear the way, the men selling monkey meat on a stick did not sing like the men selling stuffed animals on a stick; they sang lower, not trying so hard and not pretty at all. Their songs could be heard everywhere in Colon.

That first night taught all of us that a place lets you know right away just how it feels about you being in it.

That first night Colon liked us very much. No matter how bad we had messed up before, no matter how many times we'd given the wrong answers, in some way we'd been right all along cause there we were on those streets and walking, waiting for what was next and another chance to be right.

The Bar Le Fleur was the spot. Knew it when we passed the wooden cage like an old bank teller's tucked in just four steps left of the entrance. Even though the man behind the thin iron bars didn't pay us any attention as we walked by and waded right into the middle of the tables crowded up with foreigners, sailors with beards; not military by their long hair, and rootless attitudes. Girls got up from the tables and tried to bring us to an empty one like we were the cherries and this hadn't already been tried on us many times. A man at the bar moved over two stools and that gave us an objective as we slid sideways from the tables, excusing ourselves from the girls, polite, though they didn't seem to take it that way, waving us off with flicks of their wrists. They pouted out their lips to each other as if they were saying *we'd rather be with each other* and that was not true at all cause these were special girls, knew it.

At the end of the bar towards the door were three guys of a type that were everywhere in Colon. They haunted the city. Panama City—they were there too, we were told—moving about and making people uncomfortable. Former GI's, still young, maybe only three, four years, in service—six tops—finished up enlistments and stayed on, or came back. They looked guilty. Like someone can be kind of short or really tall, these guys were guilty. I never seen such guilty motherfuckers, not even in the places built to hold them. All had AWOL haircuts like backwoods country mechanics from twenty years ago, and that didn't help the guilty-looking part.

They got up to leave as we sat at the bar. The guy who had moved over the two chairs nodded. He had on clothes that at some other time and in some other place were probably nice. At the tables, a laugh came up, more than a few voices mixed in it, male and female, a fake and forced laugh, and it was at our expense, though it stopped a few feet short of our backs, just shy of provoking. We took our time ordering the Balboas, making the lady bartender ask each one of us what we wanted and pretending to think about it before answering in the Spanish way that Limón had taught us, even though the question she asked came in English.

There was a woman dancing on a small stage, and after a while the men at the tables changed, still different kinds of guys but they came in regular like in shifts and we stayed for more than one beer in the same bar.

The man sitting next to us moved over one more seat when it became available, making sure we were not offended, waving his hands to say we could all use some more room. The man seemed okay enough, but after you stopped noticing him, out of the corner of your eye you'd see him start making little head moves and noises like he was agreeing with his own thoughts. The girls kept coming over to check on the man, running their hands up his forehead and massaging his shoulders and then pestering the hell out of us.

While the girls were on him, he crossed his arms and dipped his hands into the inside pockets of his dress jacket and came out with two large flat chocolate bars which were brown paper over shiny-shiny brown foil. The girls stopped talking and pulled back from him just inches. I hated the way he opened the candy, sliding, and unfolding the foil at the corners, carefully, at each end, the pen knife he opened and then moved over the lines in the chocolate before breaking the bar a row at a time and then the pieces, placing one piece at a time into one girl's open palm, just one piece, and that seemed all the girls could handle, the taste so good making their eyes flutter under closed lids. Then he handed the other bar to the bartender lady and turned to me across the empty seat between us, asking, "Would you like a square of chocolate?"

Where the hell is this guy from, was my thinking, and I pointed to my Balboa silently like *the two don't go so good.* He said, "Ahh," short, like a short stiff jab, and came out with a small Tupperware tub from an outside pocket of his jacket, peeling the top off and pushing it down the bar towards me, saying that the black disks inside the Tupperware were good with the beer. I took one and checked to see if the symbol stamped into it wasn't the same as the ancient tattoo on the valley between his thumb and trigger finger.

I started to pass the tub down to the guys, and then thought to ask him permission first, thinking that his politeness was rubbing off on me just sitting there. He said, "Yes," but not like it was a strange or unnecessary question at all. We all liked the salty licorice and he said that certain other liquors went better with it and that licorice—real licorice—came in different grades of salt, these being of a medium sort. I didn't like that this man with the heavy accent had more words for things in English than me and that he could really put them together, which added in to all the other reasons he got the special treatment at the bar. The girls left to tend to another shift shaping up at the tables after giving us a look that set us apart from the man, who then took back his old seat. He begged our pardons and asked if it was all right, not too forward, if he asked a question of us? We liked that we had a choice and listened.

"You are not familiar here, that is obvious—you are here for the training only. And yet you do not buy drinks for the women, which even the oldest sailors never learn not to do. This confuses me, but will serve you well."

I was still wondering where the question part was while the other guys were smiling like the recently commendated. Ski asked the man where he was from, the man offered cigarettes which, just like you'd think, were foreign and from a pack that did not hold twenty. He insisted that we take one, even just to save for later, and maybe we were supposed to have been offering him ours, which were on the bar—green packs and red packs—and smoked from since we sat.

He was from Norway and Finland, and not Europe at all like we had thought, and I knew if the woman hadn't come to the man's side Ski would have been asking him what he knew about the Polish Cavalry in World War I, his one big cheese-eating question.

He had been waiting for her, and I had seen her enter the room, her hands under her chin, fingers spread, and eyes up towards the bird by her right ear. He spun slowly in his seat and she came to rest, stand between his legs. This woman, who belonged to the green and red bird that lived in her hair, said to Limón, "Jefe" when he pointed to the bird, and that was a word I knew, meaning that the bird was the boss of her. We all fussed after the bird after it dropped from her hair to hop on the bar and inspect us one by one and we came to attention, saluting the bird. All this was fine with the lady cause she wanted the man to herself. After he finished his drink she led him by the hand and they walked away as if this was a much better kind of place, one where you walked slowly, appreciating each step.

Togiola and Limón both told me to look towards the girl dancing on the small stage which looked like it had been built for her. It was Paola, and I didn't even know it yet. She wasn't looking at me. Not when I turned to see. She was dancing casual, not like a stripper, or even a go-go girl. She danced looking down at her white sandals that had a little shoe heel. And they must have been new. It was a Spanish song about the heart which had played more than a few times since we sat, and she moved her lips to the song and you could tell she really liked her sandals and the way her feet moved in them. The song was too fast to be very sad.

Her dress was bright green. Her legs like great ones only shorter. When her head came up she was still looking away, and her hair was also short and close to her head, fancy.

She had a favorite part of the song. With it her eyes became even larger, happy, but then the men at the tables tried to speak to her and she seemed disappointed that she couldn't even be left alone to just dance to her favorite part of this one song. The girls kept coming back over to us, sometimes one each in front of Togiola, Ski, Limón, and me, tracing the inseam of our pants, with one finger, sometimes soft, sometimes harder, with one finger only to hear—politely—that no, we didn't want to buy them a drink. They went away mad, and other times walked past us wondering aloud in Spanish if we were fags. We could be alone together anywhere, why here in their bar? Limón translated, but you could have got it anyway.

The man with the woman who belonged to the green and red bird that lived in her hair returned the same way they had left, slowly walking hand in hand. This time the man sat down next to Limón and talked behind his back to Ski and Togiola. He had lost—really, misplaced—his ability to put together the fine sentences in English, and now with words from his countries mixed in, he spoke about a ship he was buying that needed a new name. "Halcyon" was the ship's name, and at this he laughed till the bartender lady brought him another drink.

"What do you think of this name? Really, because it must be changed."

And he said he was considering a name that in his country was the name all northern children give to imaginary friends. He asked Ski and Togiola what they thought about that name for a ship. I told the man that the Army boat guys had taken us right by the *Halcyon* during our throwing-up voyage, not even mentioning the rust, only saying you could hardly read the name of the ship anyway.

He took to laughing again, which turned into a hack, and facing me now asked what I thought of another name. This one he explained, meant all Christmas tree ornaments saved for decorating the lower branches. I said, I liked the first one better about the kid's friends, only to have something to say.

The girls came for us again, leaning on the bar or pulling up chairs, sighing because there were few men sitting at the tables who had not already taken the trip by the man in the banker's cage upstairs.

Or maybe they sighed cause they saw us for what we were, which was experienced about these places. International.

The song came on again and I had found the tape player above the bottles of rum, many different colors of rum with labels all crowded with Spanish words and girls and pirates and old-timey ships. It was a reel-to-reel, a German kind, and I remembered you could get something for that kind of unit. The music was from a radio station that someone had recorded and in between the songs, an announcer said the word *Caliente* and that was the bartender's cue to turn the volume down during the commercials. I tried not to look at Paola on the stage, but did anyway and this time she was waiting for me.

She narrowed her eyes at me, dropped her hands from her hips and she danced away cool. I spun back around to my beer, promising myself not to look ever again and then everything would be okay, but she yelled fast Spanish words to the girls, whose hands went to their mouths.

Limón said to me, "Man, she says, 'You have such a baby face she can't stand it.'"

I snuck a look and she was really dancing now, showing moves for the girls, who were making a half try of it with some new sailors with hats like Scotty dogs. Paola was very happy dancing around the little stage all by herself.

One by one, the girls came over to Limón to talk Spanish about me and Paola, they even got the man to join in and he bought us each another beer like we were celebrating. I think I was even slapped on the back and everybody seemed so satisfied with themselves about me and Paola.

The man said it was a good time to leave, and we told him thanks for the beer and that we all liked the first word best for the ship. The woman who belonged to the green and red bird that lived in her hair nodded like she understood, though I thought she just wanted to be in on it even though she hadn't been asked.

The girls came from our flanks and right up the middle and they must have been thinking that Ski, Togiola, and Limón were surely going to buy them ladies drinks now. Confident and sweet-talking, goofy English and sexy-talking Spanish, they leaned in against my guys. There were four or five besides the woman and Paola on the stage, but it was difficult to tell one from the other with all their moving around, talking that yang, and tag-teaming my pals. They came by me and pointed to the stage and said things that I'm sure meant I should now be ashamed if I wasn't buying. Limón laughed. Paola—and I did not know her name then but it seems silly to pretend I don't now—flicked a wrist without looking our way. If I had been by myself, Hay Street commando or no, I'd of gone for my wallet directly. Instead, I did something in some ways worse, which was to notice that her skin must have had beauty stuff on it because it just couldn't come regular like that. The woman who belonged to the red and green bird saw me looking and smiled.

I tell you now there was nothing on that skin.

Togiola said it. "About that time," and we gathered up our green packs and red packs off the bar. After a few steps, and at the end of the bar, Limón stopped our short column, and I tripped, bumped into Ski. Everybody was looking at me. Though it took me a few seconds I got it and I turned and waved towards the stage, not really looking at her. Still I could tell she'd been waiting and the other faces told me that I'd done good, proper respect, and they all seemed satisfied, even if it was mostly with themselves.

If we didn't know for sure we'd be back, they did.

They said Bye-Bye many times as we left the Bar Le Fleur, following us out into the alley-street. We walked the middle and spun, marking the location, landmarks, and the position of the few steeple tops in the distance. I counted the steps up to the main street and once there panicked because I'd lost my pals and my count. Dozens of bars, the entrances and signs lit with lights mostly red and blue, and I had to walk quickly to avoid getting bumped into by more guys with strange uniforms, and above us all were sticks with meat and balloons and stuffed animals, all of this shiny and blurred from the mist and too many lights.

There were men outside the bars singing in broken-up bits of many languages and promising satisfaction for all who entered. One of them was looking at me and pointing, and above all the noise he was yelling words so familiar, personal to me and I told myself that I was imagining things and that this night had held enough adventure and it was time to go. But even as I tried to rush past this man looking straight ahead and falling in behind some drunken merchant sailors I heard the words again, "Too Easy. Hey, Too Easy. Over Here. Too Easy."

And from the doorway of the bar, behind the man, it was my pals calling my nickname, perfect for times like this.

I joined them and the man turned to us and said, "We are all together now?" Limón spoke to him in Spanish and they argued until Limón said that to see the show with the donkeys cost a lot more than we'd thought. I didn't have a say in it, only listened to the guys going back and forth over whether or not we were getting taken by this man, and we did pay him and follow him in and out of many doors and down an alley to see the show that cost so much.

We'd cashed our monthly checks at the long tables set up by the paymasters when the sun was still up and the cammie stick still covering our faces.

4

New York

Regular people were still out when I began into this night.

I got an early start to be able to finish, to go all the way through in one night's walking. I've gotten to the Colon part of the story, the first night in Colon.

It is too early in this night for the girls on Eleventh Avenue. Eleventh Avenue is empty of my friends, all my girlfriends. Eleventh Avenue, between Twenty-fourth and Thirtieth Streets, is where I stop telling the story, let the girls take care of me, and let the walking dream begin, but it's too early and dark for the walking dream.

It begins with the avenue forcing me to pay homage to it.

After being taken care of, then wiping down with the Wet-Nap and stepping off into the early-morning gray—only the absence of other colors, not really a color itself—I imagine twenty-dollar bills flying like little magic carpets, hundreds of them. They dive, veer, turn corners, double back, and then they laugh at me. Just before they snap their lengths and strive for the stars they laugh little thin green lipped laughs. At me.

And then I go back to the letter from Paola, which reads like a book of its own.

There are things hinted at to make you keep going, pull you along. Suspense: the Russian sailors, will the owner on his rounds catch Paola and Marta in his attic office at the typewriter?

Her question of will I be making the switch to Special Forces and come to Panama forever? And I love her for not saying anything about how hard the training is, about the high attrition rate. She just asks like all I would have to do is make the decision and there we would be, me and Paola living together off-post, and I would have fights with the men who she had serviced and had mouths, all those who did ill to her name. But what would her name be? If I reenlisted, learned to read a map and made it through Special Forces Phase Training and got orders cut for Panama, would she go by her real name? What name would she use when I went to the jungle for three weeks out of four?

It is in this walking dream that I am able to let the story of Paola go for one more night.

Them Guys Again–Panama City–Euclid–Tall Warm

Horse–Taken–Paola Up the Stairs

What they don't tell you about the donkey shows is the eyes. Sure, you can get up close and all, but they don't tell you about the eyes. That the girl's will be closed most of the time, but that she will open them once or twice and you will be able to see them. The donkey's eyes the opposite. Big, round, and open, closing a few times and then like it was only to re-grease the wet brown eyeballs, large. Small globes. Both pair away from you and still calling you witness, customer to this.

The drawbridge was down over the canal, and the taxi driver said we would make our curfew no trouble, so we discussed the show which was two bars shy of ending our night.

"Maybe all the guys told us about them shows saw different ones."

"I think we was just too close."

"Maybe she was new."

At that we all were quick to agree and then just that quick to silence.

Over the canal and past the La Guardia, the ride back to post was becoming familiar, twists and turns, people sitting at their steps. The little white houses. Now after midnight and the driver keeps it steady in the tree tunnel straightaways. With the sights almost regular now, we noticed the changes in air, coming in all the windows, however small, received by faces tilted up to catch the shifting warm, cooler currents, the patches of chill and heat. The air played on us and brought back to mind what we would do all day and night tomorrow. Dropped off at the entrance, the talk got back up to good. We made a stop at the beer machine and joined other scouts at the barracks, taking a seat on the open-air stairs where the CQ counted us for bed check. And many whole stories were begun and finished about first nights in Colon, Panama. Looking straight to the water from the stairs it was now reckoned that across that river, where the ships were lit by their running lights, was the spray of many more lights that was the city. We'd been staring at Colon for a week without knowing it. At the cots, solitary thoughts of the donkey show were kept away by all that had come since. It kept returning just not for very long. That night sleep came with Colon pressing gently and full against our sides.

Most of the scouts made it to Saturday morning chow, the tables loud with last night talk. Guys from other platoons and even other companies kept coming by and saying we should really come with them tonight cause they were going back to this one place they'd found. All these different groups of guys had found themselves a special place and liked to say its name, fitting it into as many sentences as they could, and some even just repeating the name over and over.

The mess hall emptied fast once the first group of soldiers, Bravo Company dogs, left quietly for the trucks. We got seconds on eggs, Saturday SOP here, drank the sweet real juice, and even sat with a third cup of coffee not caring about looking lifer or missing the deuce-and-a-halfs cause we gotten the poop from permanent party legs that there were three sets of trucks leaving one every half hour. Turning our chairs towards the water we kicked back and through the screens that wrapped the whole mess hall we watched our battalion in civvies on the company street heading for the deuce-and-a-halfs, hundreds talking shit, and the air was blowing a little hot even at breakfast. The Mess Sergeant came and asked for the trays, said we could smoke 'em if we had 'em right in the mess hall, there was just all kinds of special shit happening in Panama. Double checked with him about the deuce-and-a-halfs. Then we all got a little wild, a little crazy, doper scout style, deciding right there to visit that bar we liked in Colon, the Bar Le Fleur, before going to Panama City.

Richards, Hightower, Jencks, and Frankie Meadows sat with us and asked how in fuck hell them girls we met was going to be around before lunch, and wouldn't the bar be closed, anyway, shit. We had already told them about the man from the northern countries who needed help naming ships and that he liked the woman who belonged to the green and red bird and the upstairs and all. But we hadn't told them last night on the steps that the man had said the girls live at the bar and the only time the Bar Le Fleur is closed is on Good Friday and even then it's only the front door that is locked for show, you can still get in through the back.

The other doper scouts sitting with us were very curious and acted concerned and upset.

"Not this guy again . . ." and that was Frankie Meadows.

"Motherfucker from the northern countries . . ." laughed Hightower.

"Yeah. Y'all listen to the man who talks to his own self cause sensible people won't, and can't even name his own shit," said Marty Jencks.

And Richards just stared at us.

Them guys tried to get serious with us, saying that maybe they should split us up and each one of them take one or two of us, except Jencks, who was hanging out with sergeants and whatnot, cause it was plain to see we were fixing to get all unnecessary in a foreign country.

We told them that we were Airborne Scouts, Recon, Paras, and didn't know about them anymore, but that we were also adventurers, and that they should just go on about their business of having a regular time in a foreign country.

If there was real jealousy and real hurt feelings around that table they got taken care of by slap boxing and throwing all the balled up napkins and empty boxes of individual cereals at each other. Richards' and Hightower's friend from basic came to get them in a Privately Owned Vehicle, and Jencks left with other noncommissioned officers from the company in a POV belonging to one of the jungle school cadre.

The deuce-and-a-half dropped us right in Colon, the regular part. There were restaurants with tables out on the sidewalk and families eating, dressed nice. The looks we got said it was kind of early for us in their city.

We walked too far in the wrong direction, round a corner and came out of the sun onto the edge of the city at the water, stepping along on the tar that was worn in places that showed wood underneath. Shaded by the tall shacks built more for business than living in, we looked for somebody who didn't seem like they'd mind telling us how to get to the place we'd been last night. How to get back to the part of Colon that was for us.

Along this waterfront walkway, there they were. Again. Americans, young, and not long separated from the military. You could tell by their still growing out haircuts.

It can't be just memory making trouble the way those guys still get me.

In the shade of the shacks that ran along the waterfront there were groups and groups of these guys sitting with Panamanians, clusters of them all sitting on barrels or leaning on each other, grinning and not talking.

We'd of liked to have turned around, but they'd seen us. Seen us stop walking too.

They looked like a grown man's way of pretending a pirate, wearing the straw hats that we'd seen sold in the city. Been seeing them stacked the last night and this day, on the tables, the sidewalk, more than a few wore them or fanned with them, and the hats had been customized, cut and shaped to be cowboy, or just close to beanie, and cut shredded in a hanging-down style that seemed most appropriate for the region.

Walking again, and kinda fast, we couldn't get past all of them. It seemed that way. Another bunch and another bunch. No damn shoes either, flare jeans, and plain green fatigue pants, them too cut up at the bottoms in strips, some off at the knees. Machine grease smeared across T-shirts, green and white, putting these guys with the boats floating ugly close up to city shore. Guiltiest men I've ever seen. I'm easy admitting this kind of stuff; any group of them could've taken us. Silently they sent that information and out of one bunch came, "Y'in lose something?" and I waited for laughs that didn't come until the last of them called after us, "What? Y'in got what? What?"

Later I did ask around about the "Y'in" and Frankie Meadows said that was straight up Arkansas, though Corporal Marty Jencks said boys he went to jump school with from Missouri had it that way, and Hightower, excited, swore that was anywheres, deep back road country ocean water motherfuckers, and it became a thing to talk about in order to wind Hightower up because soon he'd be going off about how didn't none us know nothing about no Maryland the way they did it around his way. Y'in.

The first left turn, after the last of those guys, brought us to a wide empty street leading away from the water. From back in the sunshine, Ski spotted some steeple tops clustered up northwest and we doglegged from the regular part of the city over for a second visit to our part.

Up and down streets more like alleys, and the doors to all the bars were open wide and out of them came the same music, loud. As we passed, mop buckets swung by just a pair of hands out the frames of doors, each sending a small body of water into the air until it slapped at the pavement. Togiola and Ski were taking turns pretending that they were Limón trying to talk to a Panama person in Spanish, and I got in trouble from Limón just for laughing at them. It was true: none of these regular Panama people would talk to Limón, not even in the daytime.

At the end of a street that was close to our part of the city were four soldiers. We knew they were, not just by their uniforms, but by their walk. We'd know it in a man naked. They were coming right at us—they'd seen us first, what with our fooling, and set their faces. All the classroom work since basic, all that OPFOR, opposing forces, training since basic training chambered into our brain housing groups. Russians, and fucking paratroopers by their blue and white striped undershirts. Both groups of soldiers, us and them, must of veered just a little cause no shoulders were clipped at the passing, and it wasn't obvious that room had been given even though at first sighting it seemed like somebody was going to have to move over. They passed close enough to smell, and it was like wet tents. One of them muttered something in that yang, and Ski told them just louder, "Hey, where's your headgear?"

On another street, and a good ways gone from those Russians, I hoped we wouldn't see them again, especially cause they got to wear their uniforms in town, but with no cover.

It bothered all of us that they probably thought we were Legs or maybe even squids.

"Probably ain't got no other fucking clothes when they're all Russian and shit," said Limón.

Togiola kept it going, "Dang, Brah. Wish they would see me with my cammies all hooked up," and he strutted his self more than usual.

Togiola, like all the rest of the scouts, had every authorized glory badge sewed on his duty and field uniforms.

"And where's your goddamn headgear?" yelled Ski, like a jump school black hat, over his shoulder at where they might have gone.

I didn't want to see any more Russians.

The Bar Le Fleur didn't look sad at all in the daytime. A young guy who didn't talk let us in, and we sat at the bar facing the bottles, not looking around. Another man, older, with lots of keys off his belt, came behind the bar, welcoming us in Spanish and English. We ordered Balboas and didn't feel like losers drinking in a bar when it was late Saturday morning, instead like soldiers off for a whole two days in a foreign country. Adventurers, not like the men we grew up knowing real good who drank in bars on Saturday morning, and who had put that only second of worry on us sitting there thinking that maybe this is how they got started. But we shook it off quick cause this was Panama. The man took his time, pulling the beers from the bottom and saying that these being the firsts, they were going to be extra good cause they were extra *frio*—that's the way he called it—and they were icy cold going down before the heat outside had really kicked up.

Still, the man turned on all the fans overhead, behind the bar and over by the little stage, where even empty I was shy to look. We tried to protest that he was fussing after us too much, and we did this like men we'd known over to another's home, relation to relation, old friends to old friends, guys from the same mill, shift, plant, neighborhood. "Jesus Christ, now John, Bill, Frank, Sammy, you do too much, now" is how'd they say it, and we tried to imitate them with the man, but it didn't come out right and he just laughed.

Men from our hometowns and past seemed to be hanging out with us this morning.

The older guy left us with our beers and we were at Limón good now, saying maybe this guy would talk to him if he used his Rican Spanish, and why didn't he give it a try so we could see if the girls were around without looking like we really cared. Rican.

Limón tried to play it off. Pretended like he was up in his rack talking to the poster of Bruce Lee. "Bruce, they don't understand me, Bruce. Is why I have to be all the time fucking motherfuckers up, shit."

Still, you could tell Limón was pissed cause it was like we were really almost messing with him about his people for serious, but not in a way he could prove, and by trying he'd look ridiculous. So he talked to Bruce and swore to get even on all of us, which was a Frankie Meadows, Marty Jencks kind of thing to swear.

Limón did get the man to talk to him, bending his Spanish to fit that yang of the man who set up more beers without being asked and it might of been that we were getting nervous about settling in here; too comfortable in a bar, too early in the day.

The quick skiffle of slippers and the knick knock of the balls and heels of small bare feet on the floor and the girls, a bunch of them in their sleep clothes, at the chase were threatening one another with plastic dish soap bottles, yellow and white and filled with water. The bottles now squeezed hard, eyes shut, arms out, and advancing on each other, the girls screamed high to start and ending in Spanish, swearing, and shaking the water from the last of the bottles.

I was helped up off my stool from behind by wet hands used to that sort of thing, and was led past the entrance and the few steps up to and then beyond the booth with the window like an old-fashioned bank teller's to the right of the stairs.

I stay only in my room up of stairs and make no money and boss mad.

She was standing at the top of the stairs leaning against the banister rail with a big towel wrapped and tucked all the way around her little self. Behind and beside her were her wet friends and behind them were the rooms and a couple of doors were opened but not wide enough to see in. Paola was smiling down right at me while talking to her friends.

My pals had gathered behind me and Togiola whispered, "Dang, Brah."

The girls were giggling, and one of them was saying Spanish things to Paola that made the others scream, and me and my guys tried to look as cool as possible standing there with our necks craned.

Paola said, "Hello" to me like she was talking to a baby bird.

I said, "Hi."

Paratroopers and working girls alike got to wooo-woooing in any language and Paola was given a plastic bottle still dripping from the filling and she shrieked loud above everybody else, both hands and bottle in front of her face, taking them down only to then nail me directly full blast in the face from a pretty good distance. Nothing made me, I just did: tilted my face up to meet the hard stream of water, hands by my side, swallowing some still soapy water. Paola now, almost on her knees as the bottle emptied, backed into a room and the door slammed and there was damn near applause to go with all the hilariousness

The man handed me a stiff, clean bar rag, and so much was

understood without saying, like we were now leaving to go to Panama City and that we would be back that night to see the girls. Maybe everything new was bringing out the better parts of people, cause it was Ski who remembered about the beers and went back in to pay the man but came out smiling that the man had told him to pay tonight.

Down the street we went and I was pushed from one to another, my nickname used in a good way.

"Too Easy."

"Too-motherfucking-Easy."

"You see, Brah. It's cause you wasn't trying too hard, Easy."

Togiola sounded proud of me, and it was nice to hear my nickname used in a good way. I got it in the first place cause I sure could fascinate the guys by turning a really easy task into a new kind of difficult.

We were on our way to Panama City, and back here tonight, you might could say, I had a date.

We got a cab on a main street and thought the driver was cool cause he went so fast, squealing tires around corners and passing all the chiba-chiba buses on any side at all, but he wasn't. Limón, happy with himself and being very Spanish now that the man in the bar had talked to him, pulled out one of the long, bumpy, yellow joints, and asked the guy in Spanish if we could smoke 'em por favor, and all that shit. The driver pulled right over and said, "Vamanos." And when he opened the passenger side door and said it again, you didn't have to be from around here to know that he was not at all cool. Ski pulled some dollars out of his pocket and tried to pay the driver, like now he couldn't help himself, and Limón told him no, and then a few more words that the driver understood. Limón and the driver got it going pretty good, and outside the cab on the street they were still going and the driver bucked the cab and came back half in reverse and Limón ran towards him, but we got a hold of him and told him we could see the fucking train station from here. The driver took off, and Limón told us in English what he could do to the driver, and we didn't doubt him cause the driver was old enough to be an uncle and probably just the right kind of slow.

They give you these train tickets in Panama that are the size of folded maps, and we moved all the way to the back of the train and it was almost empty, just a few regular Panama people. The windows all open and soon out them you could touch the trees and the smells inside the old train, which moved a little faster than you'd thought, and were like the jungle only lighter from the speed and passing through.

We sat for a while. Then stood at the back of the train that was open to the air and you could see where you'd been. We smoked cigarettes pulled out of green packs and red packs, hung a leg over the thin iron railing and were travelers.

In the seats we argued about a new hiding place for the big joints Limón had been keeping, which stuck out the top of the same beat-up pack of Panamanian cigarettes. Ski was worried that the La Guardia might get us on the train. Togiola thought it was an okay thing to be worried about, but Limón was getting pissed off about us acting like worried old ladies and went to walk the length of the train looking for La Guardia. When he returned, he looked hard at me and raised his hands fast like tossing a ball over his head, and I sat like, What? I hadn't even said anything and if I had it wouldn't have been about the La Guardia, it would have been about wondering how bad Limón was sweating on the shit held tight under a tube sock on his right calf?

When the cards came out, I was real happy to be going somewhere new on an old train with pals that were always thinking. A man like you saw all over Panama—little, not young, and wearing a brown suit jacket gone gray—gave us his blue suitcase to play on. It looked new, but it was nicked and smelled strong of cleaner. We played Hearts and a couple of games of Tonk, getting like we do— slam-slapping cards down, talking mess. The man didn't mind cause he liked that we were having fun, Limón said so. After a while I quit the cards. Looking out the window, clack a clack, seeing water, jungle, green up high, and a town, even saw them all together from a bridge, which made you say "whoa" but out the window on another bridge and the whole scene repeated and that made you sleepy, except when the horn blew, even on a bridge, everything all at once, and train horns were different here, the sound deeper for longer.

The tapping on the window woke us up. We were at a dead stop in Panama City. It was that cab driver from yesterday, Mike, the one who picked us up and brought us into Colon on our first trip. He was smiling, tapping and pointing at Ski and Togiola, who were still sleeping, and then motioning fast with his hands and starting to laugh, cause maybe the train was moving again. The blue suitcase was gone and so was the man who had lent it to us. The cards were tight back in the pack, under Ski's palm on the armrest.

Speeding along in his little blue car, Mike talked to us in English like he had spent the time since we had seen him practicing with a book, and what I remember about Panama City was many rotary drives around statues, and long streets, and parks, to be passed on the way to everywhere we went and back again. Mike said that he knew inside his own head when we would be coming to Panama City, and after dropping a very important businessman off at the train station he decided to wait for us, "The good boys."

He asked about Colon, and then let us talk. When we were finished he said, "Colon, where I have go." He didn't think much of the place, that was for sure, but was very careful that we understood about the girls . . . that we knew that the women who work at Bar Le Fleur, all the bars, are not so shameful, that they support whole families by their work. They were from Colombia, mostly, some from Costa Rica, but most from Colombia. To do this work, they had cards that were kept in plastic wallets like a passport and were checked regularly by the government. Mike made sure we understood about the card being in an official thing, and kept making the moves that go with pulling the card out of such a thing and handing it over official, until Limón helped him finish up about it cause his driving was suffering for all the explaining.

Not so shameful. He probably said, "Not so shame," but I can help the guy out.

I'd never heard anyone say this work wasn't a damn shame or worse. Usually worse. Starts when you're a kid. Cracking and snapping on each other. Saying that's what your sister and mother do. Kids say this stuff even before they know what it is they're saying. There was a time when I was real young, in between relatives and placements, that I kept winding up back at this home where we got teased for not being able to afford to be greasers in this comic strip, Top Cat city. It was just a town in New England where there were sagging wooden fences everywhere, and bars that most people lived right above. In this place that called skipping school "Bunking" and named firecrackers "Salutes" there was a street called Euclid and everybody thought that was a kind of tree that got diseased a hundred years before so they weren't around anymore, and you learned about that Euclid Street early.

"Saw your mother standing on Euclid singing, 'Pussy for sale.'"

The cab driver talking about shame made me think about the whores at that end of Hay Street, too. So scrappy that if you looked too long and weren't paying they wouldn't hesitate to step right over, threatening to jack your jaw. I thought about the Booger Queens by the train tracks, forever tall and stumbling, telling any man walking slow that they'd "Create a disturbance in your mind" and riding their dusty ankles in those high shoes.

But it was Euclid. Real early in life, kids talking about other kids' mothers out on Euclid, especially during Scatter Dodge Ball when the taunts came with, and still faster than, the red pebbly ball. I was already trying too hard and new there when I caught a wicked beating for laughing, trying to be all in it, under the arch of the school's Boys' entrance, everything gray cement. They stopped the game and asked me why I was laughing and so I told them it was just me imagining all their mothers out singing on that Euclid Avenue.

It was funny. I didn't know what they were singing about. Knew it wasn't cats but a whole bunch of kids' mothers outside on the street singing was funny to me.

Get that kid.

I was back there a couple of years later when there was this lady supervising on the weekends that would get all the kids up and piled into the house van early Sunday mornings to go look at the people out on Euclid Avenue. We all laughed extra hard at the fistfights between women.

And then the last time I was on Euclid, a teenager now, I walked up the steps of a slanted and rotting porch and gave fifteen dollars to a big Cape Verdean guy that I recognized from sixth grade. He was much older than the rest of us and he hated to be called Cape Verdean. He wouldn't speak that brand of Portuguese even to his cousins, pretended he couldn't play soccer. He'd wanted to be regular black so much that it became his nickname. Then Black disappeared. But not really. Sent up is how they call it around there.

From information passed during homerooms we kept track of him as he went to the Diagnostic Center to Sockanosset, right to the Adult Correctional Facility, where he must have served out because here he was taking my fifteen dollars. He shook his head, saying "Ain't no John Holland Middle School discount. Any room on the second floor." He stood blocking the door and laughing at me for a few seconds about how I wasn't even drunk, but I just waited for him to move and wondered if everybody lost their accents in jail.

Off from the porch, and up inside that big falling-down house. His lady left me at the bed, quick after, to cross for the sink, where she spat out like a dog. Sneezing hard, with her whole head.

I hate a bare mattress, that and I was sure I would never pay for it again. Better to wait for it to happen natural.

After we'd been around I don't know how many rotaries with an old statue of an officer on a horse, a religious lady, or Jesus, I figured out that the cab driver was trying to treat us like tourists. Like he was helping us. He told us about how it was before the Spanish from Spain, and about the Panama Railroad which came before the Canal, and showed us a historical place to go with everything he told.

"If I had wanted to go to school I'd of stayed in school instead of joining this man's army," said Ski, and the man looked at him in the rearview mirror. Limón was up front talking to the man in Spanish, but you could tell he was fucking with him, asking him questions that were nasty in some kind of way.

I thought that Togiola could have been interested in all the stuff we were seeing if he had been traveling with a different bunch of guys.

The cab-driving man was now ignoring Limón no matter which language Limón used.

This cab driver had a lot of "try." That's what Marty Jencks would have said if he were here.

It was true about his patience and I didn't know it then, but it was that of the reformed. This man who was so clumsy and anxious with his kindness had flat knuckles with scars like a flaming star and his arms, when he turned the wheel hard either way, rode up a shirtsleeve and showed more traces of what had once lived there bold: naked mermaids on a rock, ships, pirates and lady pirates. It had all been made to fade with lemon juice and a needle—I know cause I've seen it before—and it looked like someone had jiggled the drawings on an Etch-A-Sketch. I think it must have been hard for him not to stop the cab and give us all a beating one by one while imagining he was giving thrashings to younger versions of himself before it was too late. He could of, and wouldn't, that much we knew. Like sometimes when you are in the country and you know that this old farmer, being polite and selling good corn and vegetables cheap, could beat the shit out of you and everybody you know. But wouldn't almost ever cause he's a farmer who sells corn and vegetables.

"Okay, we go to see my friends."

He let all his frustration out with those words, and after seemed happy with his decision as a way to keep us in his cab on a tour for the day rate and abandon the historical stuff which had us acting so rude.

It was important for us to know that he was taking us to places where his friends had good jobs. After a short ride, he walked us from the sun into a casino, which was deserted except for a few men working and who smiled and waved. We passed the slot machines, across the carpet which had designs of casino games in it, and his arm swept the air in front of him and he said, "Very respect."

Into a room that had lots of round tables and chairs, all red, the stage at the front empty too like the rest, and the man called out for a friend and one appeared from the side of the stage holding a fist full of thick wires with fat plugs of many colors in each hand like bouquets of flowers. The friend didn't seem to understand why he was being introduced to us. There was some silence and we left.

The next place wasn't far, but it was a night racetrack where the cab driver's friend worked cleaning the horses and was a famous place for people from Europe. Being at a night racetrack during the day was almost as good as jumping the fence to an amusement park that is closed down for the season. When it is quiet and empty in a place where there's always noise and too many people, you get to make it all up. You just fill it in the way you want.

Ski and Limón stayed with the driver while they talked and pointed out at things with a man whose clothes were stained with sweat, it being now that time of day. Me and Togiola walked over to a field away from the white-railed, perfect dirt track and leaned on a white fence to watch the horses led by men so much smaller than them.

The horses, many hands tall, like it's said, and their double long legs were taped tight where they were thin and dangerous. They walked in that field, each holding in them what it is was that you remembered about a tall pretty girl. Walked like her, too.

The men let the horses go where they wanted, eating grass, and the horse nearest to us came closer until her man made her stop, which seemed to surprise her, not just me and Togi. We motioned for the man to bring her close if only to see just how big she really was, but the man smiled and came only a little closer, then waved and shrugged like it wasn't his fault.

He did let the horse stay where it was, for a few minutes, and we three all watched as the horse stood still for the watching, then moved a front leg high to flip a hoof up at the air like it was playing with something flying. The man smiled again, and the horse began to turn away in its eating. After a while, they both seemed to forget about us. The man talked to the horse and reached up to pat it hard.

Turned from us and farther away now, the man talked some more and patted up higher, where the sun made the horse's brown turn golden, and after a time he put his cheek down against a place near where it was golden and still surely warm.

"I have many friend," Mike told us as we walked to the taxi. The racetrack was great, everybody said so, and the taxi driver was happy, but we'd had enough, and on the way to see more friends we were about to say something when he spoke first. He'd been hearing my name tossed around the car and he turned to talk to me, still careful to the road, and he talked to me in Spanish assuming I would understand at least part of what he said, this long string of words in Spanish ending in a question which he repeated and repeated.

"Ahhh, Roberto Duran" was my wise-ass answer, the only Panamanian thing I could think of. Right away I wanted to take it back, at least for the horses, and him trying. But the guys laughed too loud and the man stopped. Not the cab. Just stopped. Then he laughed. He stopped again and looked in the rearview mirror, coldly, and at me. Before we left the cab, he was going to keep showing this look in the mirror and hold it for me to see.

It was because he had finally decided about us. Not just about me alone and not speaking Spanish, but about all of us, our not being grateful for his kindness and special tour, our rudeness. Now that he knew it for sure, on the quiet way to the next friend who had boats, he let us know. "You are not the good boys," he said.

And soon after that, "You should go again to Colon."

He spoke the names of streets, bars, and he had mentioned them before, the day before when he told us to call him Mike, but now we'd been on some of the streets and we listened for the names of more bars, and if he mentioned the Bar Le Fleur. He spoke Spanish to the windshield and out the open window. Ski in the front seat turned all the way around to listen as Limón translated softly in the back, "Colon. Where I have go. Where there is no God. No God, and where they burn candles in windows for the saints."

Limón shrugged.

He left us at the train station. Ski went to pay him and the man took some off the price cause it wasn't all day. We should have felt worse, but everything in the day was new and there was momentum from that.

There was a train for Colon leaving in an hour and so we bought tickets and sat in the shade under the peaked roof by the side of the tracks. Limón went searching and came back with fat sandwiches wrapped in wax paper, mostly bread with the meat and the cheese tasting the same, and orange sodas, sharp and extra fizzy even though they were a little warm.

Limón called himself stupid for getting sodas instead of beer, "so fucking stupid," so he went back for beers, bringing Ski and their sandwiches with him.

Me and Togiola kept eating and looked at each other. It was like on a good night when we were in a doper's room in the barracks where the wind was blowing out, fresh duct tape sealing the cracks in the door, the company CQ was cool, and something like *The Dirty Dozen* on a TV in the room from the Rent-A-Center, or somebody's own with pawn stickers all up and down the sides, and the beers are still cold, more in the machine downstairs, and later order pizza delivered right to the barracks. Everybody's there, and a pact has been made and sworn to: there will be no going out tonight. No Hay Street. Limón and Ski look at each other, cause it's not far past pay-day, and they get up and pull on the door that makes a sucking sound cause of the tape and they go and get their gloves. They used to make up silly and lame reasons for excusing themselves, breaking the pact, until they just starting going without saying a word.

They'd walk around post till they found a cherry, and they're easy to spot: Airborne T-shirt with jeans tucked into Daniel Boone suede fucking moccasin boots that rawhide lace all the way up to the goddamn knees, and either a floppy suede hat to go with it or a big-time beezer haircut from jump school. Put a pathetic, lonely and eager face on it all and you got your cherry.

"Hey, man. Wanna get high?" And there's a good chance cause of the whole situation that the guy's going to want to, I mean, cause he's in the Army. So he goes with Limón and Ski off into the woods, and the cherry's talking a mile a minute so when they get far enough in Limón or Ski or both are irritated at the cherry so they hit him a little too hard with the leaded leather sap gloves and they come back to the room with extra money, sure, but the good night's a little lost. Plus, cause Limón and Ski are going to say a bunch of times that they hope the cherry's okay cause they "Heard some shit say, 'Snap'!" And no matter how many times they'd have to say it and tell the story on top of the movie or whatever, we let them have their laughs too loud. Never even told them about the rumor that went around behind their backs that they had first found out about that trick the hard way.

Kind of the same sitting there with Togiola. Those two came back only to give us a beer apiece, and it wasn't Balboa and damn near homemade. Gave us most of the money they were carrying to hold, and then took off again after a little argument about how much money they were supposed to bring back with them.

By the time me and Togi figured that the cab driver must of graduated ugly from Colon and couldn't stand it anymore with all his friends being respectable and everything, Limón and Ski came back sweaty at the quick step down the train tracks.

Knew it before they climbed off the tracks that they had a story to tell. They'd gotten taken off by Panamanian versions of themdamn-selves who promised real cocaine, but instead delivered, in a little back-yard, two Walther PPKs, one each, pressed against my pals' heads. It wasn't that me and Togiola didn't believe them that got us quiet and riding in whole different sections of the train back to Colon. It wasn't that they had gone and experienced new stuff in a foreign country without us. It was that those two now thought and acted like they were immediately extra rugged cause they'd had guns to their heads.

The train chased dusk back to Colon and the train was winning. The air through the windows got damp and my lungs were creaky like they get after a day at the beach. Those two found us before long and sat right across, making the story real gaudy just to be difficult, and about how'd they'd have all the stories to tell their grand-kid's about when they were para's and traveled the world.

After a time when we were done throwing things at them, me and Togi said, remember, we still had the rest of their money and maybe it just wasn't their day. And like that it went on. Panama flying at the open windows.

6

I don't know but I think I might/Jump from an aircraft

while in flight–C-O-W-S–The Last Time It Was Good–

We'd been back at Bragg for four days, after our month in Panama. Still tan, and not just GI back and arms, but all over from the relaxing. At the routine again but still sun warmed to the bone.

Guys from other battalions, around post and on the Hay, greeted us, "So, how was it?" And we'd tell them perfectly, and carefully, everybody helping with all the parts. When we had them to the point where the most they could manage was a soft, barely heard, "That sounds all right, now," we'd tell them that they'd be going soon for sure. Heard something coming out of Headquarters Company about their battalion, from a buddy, for sure. We wanted it to be true. Especially when we'd be seeing them around and if they never did get to go, and we had to see that sad look on their faces cause we built it up so much, that would be too awful.

There was a cherry waiting for us when we got back. If he didn't feel bad enough about being a cherry, it was worse when he had to listen about all he'd missed. Cause he was our cherry, it got told like he'd have to re-up twice to be sure to get to Panama and by then the stuff with the United Nations giving back the canal zone and all, they probably wouldn't let him go anyway.

This cherry coming into the platoon pushed the cherries before him out of cherry status and Hartel stayed locked in as he was. Like me, this cherry came from the repo-depot all by himself so he got lots of attention. Didn't get to watch Corporals Quinton and Collins go to work on him, though, cause soon as they got back from Panama, they decided to use their accumulated leave days to get out early rather than turn them in for cash. No ETS party for them, no send-off. They came by the barracks once in civilian clothes, invited guys down to Hay Street for a few quick ones. I couldn't go cause of motor pool guard, but others did, no biggy was what they said, and then the corporals were gone.

And there was a night when Corporal Marty Jencks became King Econo.

It had been a payday and a night before a mission which took us off-post and out of state, either one reason enough for the scouts to hang together on Hay Street; 3:00 A.M. found us back on the steps of the big brick barracks sipping on Stroh's in a bottle.

We'd been watching the carloads of lit paratroopers drive slowly up and down, trying to find their barracks. Years before any of us got to Bragg they'd painted the barracks all kinds of light pastel colors, each one different, cause somebody did a study that said prisoners and soldiers would be happier that way. Then, three months ago they'd changed them all back to red, and guys still had trouble making it back, especially around payday. After finding ours, we liked to watch.

Corporal Marty Jencks' re-up money baby blue Honda Civic that he'd just bought off a widow came down the company street and turned into the parking lot.

"Marty Jencks," said Frankie Meadows, pointing, and letting his north Texas accent slide westward for a go at the corporal's border-speak. Frankie Meadows, even with a nickname like "Country," was forever giving Jencks a hard way to go about his accent, tricking him into saying words like napkin, which Jencks pronounced "Nakin."

We had a clear view of the parking lot across the street from the barracks as Corporal Marty Jencks parked the Honda under one of the powerful streetlights that makes Ft. Bragg look like a vast and shimmering minor league night game.

Since his accident (tree landing, stick in the balls), watching Jencks do just about anything had been a quiet pastime for the members of the 2/304 Scout Reconnaissance Platoon. In Panama the injury had gotten infected all over again, so we got comfortable on the steps and waited for some movement from the Honda.

Several minutes passed and then Limón whispered, "Come on, Marty. You could do it."

"Shhhhh," said the scouts and a few guys from Charlie Company who had joined us on the steps, bringing our number to almost a dozen.

Then, in the parking lot, a door popped open, bouncing on its hinges, and a long leg shot out. The boldness of this first move was noted and other possible tactics quickly discussed.

And then the leg retreated, the door shut tight, and we were quiet.

More beers were opened. It was a few long slugs off those last beers until the passenger side unlocked and two big ol' gunboat feet tapped the door open. It seemed that Jencks was lying across the front seat, moving his spotlit feet back and forth, in and out, over the same six inches of air.

Sluguski raised a trigger finger and announced, "Stick shift," as the source of the young corporal's trouble in his second attempt to jettison, unass, his privately owned vehicle. The soldiers mumbled low and moved together as if the command to nod had just been given.

The feet were sucked back into the Honda. The door left open. A sigh in the key of high lonesome caught some June wind just heavy enough to run it across the company street.

We could see Jencks' silhouette pop up like a target. Then he reached over to shut the passenger's side door. The Honda jumped with a turn of the key and pedal punched in neutral, taillights flashed red and faded as the engine died in place, and clicked to quiet.

The cherry—the FNG, the Fucking New Guy—just like a cherry thought that this was a good time to talk. He stood up, knocking over his beer, and pointed towards the parking lot talking about how ". . . the '79 Civic's much bigger than the '78, I know because my cousin has the '79 and it was his wife who made him wait to get it and if Corporal Marty Jencks, sorry, Corporal Jencks has an injury, you'd think . . ."

Ski reached up and pulled the cherry back down with one good yank, whispering in his ear, "You're not allowed to talk."

When the cherry knocked over his beer, a drop had landed on Richards. The R hadn't yet taken his eyes off his shoulder where the drop had spread to the size of a dime on his dark blue Qiana shirt with the street life corner scene printed on the back. When we were sure the cherry was about to say something like, "Sorry, Mr. R," the hatchback to the Civic opened and all eyes witnessed Corporal Marty Jencks slide headfirst onto the parking lot pavement in a perfect tuck and roll.

We lifted what was left of our beers to him and he executed a bow from the hips that was so slight as to make it royal. We cried, "Airborne! Airborne! Airfuckingborne!" Limón said, "It's just like I said. He's got no problem with the front and back kind of moving, it's just the side to side that messes him up."

Corporal Jencks silenced us with his outstretched arms. He reached into the back of the Honda Civic and then came back out with something that looked to be a doll about three feet high. He set it on the ground.

Man Hightower, who had been keeping himself between Richards and the cherry cause Richards was back to staring at his shirt again, says, "Sweet Petey the Jeez the Booty Doctor! A midget love doll."

We get to call Hightower, "Man" cause that's how his sisters ask for him on the barracks' phone when they call from his hometown of Cabin John, Maryland. Turns out that ever since he was a little Hightower all his brothers and uncles and father been in jail, so he'd always been the only man around.

One of the guys from Charlie Company says, "Nah, love dolls can't stand up on their own."

Togiola agreed, "Yeah, that thing looks hard."

Another guy from Charlie Company, keeping a bead on Jencks' exaggerated, bow-legged, quick stomp kind of a walk asked, "Wasn't he supposed to have an operation or something?"

Togiola laid the Island Boy accent on thick—when I try this it comes out Mexican—and begins to explain, "Yeah, Brah. But it would lay him up for three weeks . . ."

The rest of the scouts finished the sentence with the Samoan, ". . . and he don't want to miss nothing."

Then, as Jencks walked across the street and up the walk, I guess we all got to wondering why Corporal Marty Jencks would need any kind of a love doll when he's got Yon Me. She was his steady girl who we called Ping Pong, but not so much anymore because the relationship has gotten serious with plans and everything.

"It's a damn poodle doll," said Hightower, as Jencks came up to us and set it down, front and center, at the foot of the steps.

It was a three-foot-high pink poodle, filled with yellow shampoo.

"And this here is a receipt from the Piggly Wiggly for two dollars and seventy-nine cents," said Jencks, handing the receipt to Sluguski, who, until this night, had been King Econo. He'd earned the title for life except when he was kicked off the throne for a night and a day cause of the one time he was observed buying a dink a Ladies Drink. He ended up at sick call with alcohol poisoning and got busted down one pay grade and had lots of money taken out of a few months' pay. The reason for the punishment, according to the Uniform Code of Military Justice, was Destruction of Government Property. They do you like that. Like they done to Hernandez for getting *Bertha* in cursive up his neck, and like those guys in second platoon Bravo Company, who all shaved their heads before Panama and got sun stroked on the obstacle course and burned bad enough to not show up for duty but at the sick call. They all got busted just like Sluguski. We had to give Ski back his throne quick. He looked so horrible when he got back to the barracks all through the night telling us how the Army had it in for him and what the medics do for alcohol poisoning at the aid station even if we did keep on drinking cold ones from the machine and all the time offering him sips.

The scouts are devoted to cheapness. We are Econo Men. That's the thing about the Korean girls on Hay Street. We don't buy them drinks on account of having principles or because we're not stupid enough to get taken, but cheapness. We like them and want to go with them, but only when they're off duty.

Econo Men. Two weeks after payday, and we'll be pawning everything in sight. Even nonessential equipment that was issued to us. This is an excepted practice and even if there is a surprise inspection with the whole company out in front of the barracks with all their Ta-50 laid out per SOP on green wool blankets all you have to do is place the ticket where the piece of pawned equipment should go. Pawn your equipment. Paratrooper tradition. A week after the pawnshops and we're selling blood and plasma, weak-kneed and pale, at three different locations. Red, White, and Blue beer is a $1.48 a six-pack at your local PX. We have pulled drunken raids on motels and hotels all over the South when we relieve them of their works of art. We do this to finance our covert operations to keep the world safe from somebody. Floor plans are drawn up on bar napkins, and then operations orders given with some Dirty Dozen, Alexander Monday type shit, and then attack—Swift, Silent, and Deadly—combat rolling out of elevators, shooting guests and security with silenced fingers, throwing empty beer can concussion grenades and disappearing into the night aboard Ski's Gremlin loaded with the art collection.

In my room alone hang five oil paintings of covered bridges.

Except for Jencks and Man Hightower, who is squatting in front of the poodle and staring in its eyes, we are all walking around the poodle. Silent, respectful, envious.

"Damn, Corporal Marty Jencks. You stay a paratrooper with a good Airborne haircut this here 'il last you your full twenty," said Frankie Meadows as he picked up the poodle, palming it by the head and testing out the full weight of it.

We all jumped a bit when he touched it.

Jencks took the poodle out from under Meadows' hand and said, "Damn, Country. Me and Yon Me were just talking about that over dinner tonight. We figure we'll be washing our gran' kids with the poodle.

"Oh Yeeezz. Corporal Marty Jencks and Old Ping Pong gonna get married. Oh Yeeezz," sang Man Hightower. He did a little dance, scout style, that was half parts The Freak and half The Poppa Smurf.

"About that time ain't it, Recon?" asked Marty Jencks, trying not to laugh, not taking any offense cause none was meant. It went right with the moment. Wouldn't of at others and pals know the difference.

The 2/304 Scout Reconnaissance Platoon, plus poodle, danced its way up into the brick barracks towards sleep and a wake-up call two and a half hours away.

6:30 A.M.—O-Dark-Thirty—and we're back out on the company street, lined up in formation and ready to run Ft. Bragg. The Colonel's got a hard-on for his scout platoon so we've got to run in boots, and always in the front of the formation. Which is a good thing, too, because after a payday, even when it falls on a Thursday, the guys in the back don't really run, but more like swim through the warm, toxic fumes coming off a hundred bodies.

Lieutenant Goody from the mortar platoon has fallen out to the side of the formation to call cadence this morning and he can rock a little. Since he got to the company about six months ago he's been steady on being a prick and on exposing us to the old-timey music of his home state of Louisiana.

We start out at the quick time march, and he calls, *"Oh, yessss. Ernie K. Doe, A Certain Girl."*

He's priming us for the call and answer that will soon have both a river of payday and a whole company running.

"There's a certain girl I been in after a long, long, time."

"WHAT'S HER NAME!"

"I can't tell ya."

"AWWWW."

It goes on, the company starting to up rock, and then Lieutenant Goody switches fast and calls for Huey "Piano" Smith, telling us, you know how we do it, and to sound off like we got two of them swinging this Airborne morning.

"Hey, pretty baby/Can we go strolling?"

"DON'T YOU JUST KNOW IT!"

"You got me rocking when I oughta be rolling/Ahh ha ha ha."

"AHH HA HA HA!"

"Hey-ay-O."

"HEY-AY-O!"

"Dooba/Dooba/Dooba/Doo-ba."

"DOOBA!/DOOBA!/DOOBA/DOO-BA!"

"Ahh ha ha ha."

"AHH HA HA HA!"

"Ahh ha ha ha."

"AHH HA HA HA!"

Before that part was finished and before the part about *"Baby, baby. You my blue heaven,"* Lieutenant Goody snarls "Doub-le Ti-me. Who-Arch!" and the company's off into the step-stomp that is the Airborne Shuffle.

We push out through the darkness, passing other singing paratroopers from other brigades, battalions, companies, singing about Jesse James and what he wanted to ride: *A bicycle, tricycle, automobile/A bow-legged woman/And a Ferris wheel.*

Groups of paratroopers, hundreds and hundreds of them in formation, running and stomping the left foot down, trying to drown each other out singing about the same girls and what we've been told: *Eskimo pussy is mighty cold.*

And about bugs: *A green grasshopper got a red asshole.*

But mostly we sing about jumping.

C-130 rolling down the strip/Airborne Daddy on a one way trip/Mission unspoken/Destination unknown/He don't even know if he'll ever come home. Everybody's hurting, and the singing helps. Sort of like how the way talking about yourself helps.

We tear up two miles of hard top, turn into Area J and then run the fire breaks for another two, singing to the trees.

If my main don't open wide/I got another one by my side/If that one don't open neither/I got a date with old Saint Peter.

Out of the forest we appear with a full up, red Carolina sun at our backs. After we return to the company street, double time to quick time, quick time to halt, a facing movement, parade rest, and then at ease, we get released from formation.

Smoke cigarettes, and head for the chow hall. Even the pukers.

Inside the chow hall, Limón is up in some Mess Corporal's face. Something about no Frosted Flakes: "Goddamnit the motherfucker shee. Where's my fucking Tony. I can't be jumping without my Tony."

We jump today and superstitions are being tended to. Frankie Meadows won't talk until he's on the aircraft. Hightower won't stop talking. Jencks will be on the pay phone to Yon Me a half dozen times before pre-jump. Sluguski will start drawing souped-up pictures of his Gremlin in a little notebook, but will soon switch to page after page of the same river until Togiola helps him by taking over and making them all nice. Me, I don't have any jump day habits except being scared and wanting to retie my boots before I go out the door.

Because of the jump, the scouts are off the day's duty roster. There are a few hours before the deuce-and-a-halfs carry us across to Pope Air Force Base, which means there is ghost time for the taking. We draw up an operations order over breakfast and follow it, leaving the mess hall in three-man teams that fan out in all four directions. After successfully escaping and evading all officer ranks the scouts ghost up the back steps of the barracks and move for their rooms. Swift, Silent, and Napping.

Our Platoon Daddy, a month shy of his twenty and retirement, is already ghosting out on my bunk.

When I walked into my room he woke up just long enough to squint at me and say, "Y'all look after your Platoon Daddy, now."

Hendricks, who I shared the room with, had unofficial off-post housing with this reformed biker girl, but he kept his bunk in the room squared away. Not wanting to mess it up, I grabbed a field jacket out of my wall locker and using it for a pillow, pulled up a piece of floor and tried to imitate the biggest ghost of them all sleeping in my bunk.

For the year and a half he's been our platoon sergeant, Sergeant First Class Timson has taught us the good stuff. He's passed on the poop that's kept him out of trouble enough to stay alive and in for the full twenty. Of course, the three tours of duty he did with a Long Range Reconnaissance Platoon of the 173rd Airborne in Vietnam lays nice smoke for his ghosting ways.

He wouldn't have liked our movement from the mess hall to the barracks. He'd of critiqued us using the good thief rule: "A good thief don't never look like he's doing something wrong."

But right now there's the bigger lesson from Platoon Daddy—and there is always a bigger lesson with Platoon Daddy, it's just that he never tells you what it is. You're supposed to get it on your own and it's okay if that happens much later. The hint is that he always leads by example.

I looked up at him in my bunk and learned that I should be a senior NCO who drives a Buick Electra 225 and a BMW, and because the BMW with the fat tires and smoked-out windows that I had shipped over from my last tour in Germany is only for nice ladies, I should drive the Buick in from my quarters off post, stopping for an Egg McMuffin, and arriving on the company street just in time to miss the morning run. As far as taking my bunk went, it came down to the big peacetime rule of "Be there first. Play fuck around later."

Once in a while Platoon Daddy would go deep on you. Like when he'd give long blocks of instruction on how to read the woods, swamps, or jungle. About how listening to the ways the noises of the animals changed could tell all about where everybody was at. Some of the country boys were starting to get it, and they said it didn't come from trying to figure it out just by listening.

There was one time Platoon Daddy was waiting with us for transportation on top of a small mountain in the Mojave. We had already pulled off our mission and he let us wander off to burn a thin one. While we smoked, it was decided that the time was right and I would be the one to ask. We walked back over the big rocks and came upon Platoon Daddy from the rear. He was sitting still, looking out over the whole desert, and somebody said, "Oh, shit— Check out Black Moses." Or else I just thought it loud enough to remember that he did look—with that shiny black head that had most of the cammie stick sweated off it—like the tough kid's Isaac Hayes album of the very same name.

He asked us "What the hell y'all looking at?" and then told about how the birds will be coming in about One Five, and that we should get our little bit of stuff together. I checked my gear, sat down with my M-203 across my lap, and just up and asked him about it.

"Sergeant Timson, we heard that the 173rd Airborne was disbanded after Vietnam cause there wasn't hardly anyone left. And we want to know, like in a real world situation, how do you come back?"

I looked up and he was petting the Airborne tab above the 173rd patch under the right shoulder, the combat side, of his cammie shirt. You wear nothing on that side till you've been to combat. He just smiled and kept petting it with his heavy fingers, which were ashed up from the nights of cold desert air. It meant something like luck or magic. Sometimes we would pet the Airborne tab above the 82nd patch on our left shoulders, saying it would keep us warm in the field or safe before a jump, but as always with peacetime soldiers it did little. The point of it was to show you could imitate the real thing, because you knew one or two.

He kept on petting the tab like it only got better and my team began to whine like kids begging for dessert. We were saying "Come on, Platoon Daddy. Ain't no one around. Give us a something."

Platoon Daddy stopped smiling and petting and said, "All right. Y'all think you're on the mount and want the sermon. I'll tell this. You look good and you look twice at anybody that makes it out of the shit. It's what the books leave out. Vietnam. Uganda. Holocaust. Motherfucking Stalin's. You look good at those folks who come back. I ain't talking about no judgment, just look hard. You might fuck up and learn something universally. Now get out there and make your Platoon Daddy some nice 360 security and at least look like you're securing an LZ."

When we got back to Ft. Bragg, the platoon met up at the IHOP just off post and my team filled the guys in on what Platoon Daddy had said.

Limón, while floating his eggs and pancakes in boysenberry syrup said, "Now why he does he gotta do that? When he's giving out the good poop he gets all 'Listen to my forest.' I don't get it."

Frankie Meadows, after calling for more boysenberry syrup, says, "I know it. I didn't come in this man's Army for that college stuff. I mean I'll get plenty of that at the CC when I get out. I mean. Damn. Stalin. He said, 'Stalin.' Right?"

———

Still on the floor, with the big bear in my rack, I burned off the rest of my ghost time dwelling on how much time we'd spend thinking about Platoon Daddy after he was gone. The man came in the Army in 1961; here it is twenty years later and he's tired. It was understood that, after Panama, as his twenty came up, we would look after him a bit. The scouts would play it a little safe and keep everything mellow so that Platoon Daddy could go out nice and easy. What we didn't expect was for Platoon Daddy to come right out and say, "Y'all better look out for me cause I'm tired."

We'd be cutting back on the drugs, in the field—making jumps, live fire exercises, and patrols—and back in garrison. We wouldn't gas anybody on aggressor detail. We'd even talk our way out of any messes with visiting Marines down on the 500 block. It was as if we were trying to be careful the way we believed combat guys are careful when someone's about to go home.

The biggest thing we did for Platoon Daddy was win the division-wide scout platoon competition that year. It's called the Military Stakes and our battalion had a long tradition of its scouts being wild and Hollywood, but effective, too. The colonel had eight trophies in his office. He didn't get one the year before because we had lost a good number of old-timers. A few had re-upped for Ranger Battalions, others for Special Forces groups and the rest just plain went civilian. Except for Quinton, Collins, and Jencks, we were a platoon full of half cherries and even still Platoon Daddy brung us in a distant second.

This year we sneaked and peeked and snooped and pooped like home-grown ninjas. Platoon Daddy had us working in two-man teams like the hunter-killer teams of old. Each team had a radio and we held tight and undetected, not only on the other scout platoons but on anything that moved west of Preacher's Road. We were swift and silent topography, calling in situation reports fast like old ladies' good gossip. Our sit reps had effectively compromised all the other scouts by midnight of the second day so that the competition was called with no need for the third day and that was a first.

As our two-man teams moved through the dark woods we fell in behind each other like little brooks into a silent river, until the platoon was whole. Then we fanned out into the most perfect traveling wedge formation. We could have hooped and hollered our victorious selves all the way back in, but instead we just went quieter. Nobody wanted this precision to end. If each man's thoughts could have been amplified that night, the woods of Ft. Bragg would have been laced with the whispered pleadings of thirty men: *Give me something to finnnndd.*

That night, I believe we could have moved over and across Ft. Bragg and set out to pull reconnaissance on the whole world.

We'd had times close to this. Times when I thought: these guys are too good, and we need a real enemy. But those were during war games, at the end of Reconnaissance Commando School, live fires, or in Egypt after Sadat's assassination. Maybe it was because this night was for bragging rights, but I wanted to go with these guys and call in everything everywhere. Not for artillery or F-16s, more like pointing stuff out: *One hundred and twenty-two passengers heading north on the Red Line two miles out of Boston proper, sixteen in line to cash checks in Mexico City, two babies asleep on their mother's back in Peking, one anteater moving slowly and without purpose in a zoo in Istanbul—How do you read me?—Over.* We needed a military-sanctioned scavenger hunt. Find everything.

What we got was congratulations over the radio from the Colonel and much slack for the Platoon Daddy. After the call from the Colonel, our shared stealth vanished and we *walked* it back in. Twigs snapped, weapons' slings creaked, and breathing became an individual task.

Just as my eyes began to flutter, Platoon Daddy walked over me and standing by the door he said, "Young soldier, let's go."

I love it when he calls me that.

We pulled our weapons out of the arms room and went through the pre-jump drill in front of the barracks. The scouts in a big circle, practicing immediate action drills for partially and fully collapsed parachute canopies, what to do when another jumper swings into your risers—the lines of thin and woven nylon that connect the harness to the canopy—and the weirdo malfunction that we think someone made up called The Towed Jumper. In the 82nd Airborne Division, which was built and held together by tradition, myth and bullshit, nobody I ever heard of had laid claim to seeing one towed jumper. You wouldn't want to have to mess with a chute that streamers, or one that opened between you and the stars looking like a twelve-year-old girl's training bra, but being a towed jumper might be kind of cool. Except if you were tripping.

We talked about how being a towed jumper on mesc would probably fry your brain. Out there in the night, twenty yards of static line pulled taut between you and the aircraft, your chute still on your back and rolled inside the patray as tight as it left the rigger's shack. Maybe you were at the beginning of the stick so your buddies who lined up behind you on the ground are now blooming in your wake like popcorn. You are too high to give the signal to the jump master, who is leaning out the door of the aircraft. All you have to do is place your hand on top of your helmet to show that you're not unconscious or anything, and then the jump master will make a cutting motion, first just with his hand so you get ready, then with a knife across your static line and you will fall free until you pull the reserve at your chest. But because you and your pals went to see the Malaysian your brain is now thinking about sunflower seeds, the way dirt smells, only to then start sending out messages of the kind only received by babies who die during birth. Cause of that you hang in the breeze like a stick figure without arms. It's impossible to get the towed jumper back into the plane so the jump master and the Air Force crew chief will haul you up as far as they can. They're supposed to be able to get you up close enough to the wing of the C-141 Bravo where you will be secured by special straps designed just for the towed jumper. The runway will have been foamed and you will touch down as a new piece of the plane lashed to a wing. The brain would have abandoned the baby terror and will begin searching for a way to receive and protect itself from the mesc, the ride, but will fail and give in to the landing. The brain will open up clean, and as the tires hit and screech across the runway, foam flying like ash, it will open again and again, each time trying to take in too much. Like C-Ration Pork Slices, your brain would be Cooked In Juices.

I know this cause one earthbound night me and Limón figured it out on a hit of the Malaysian's Orange Sunshine.

The Malaysian goes in and out of a southern accent, especially when he's trying to tell us about golf. He says things over and over about his drugs, like "Fucking crazy guy, you. This make your brain suck your dick"—which is how the whole brain thing got started—and he pronounces dick like "Dit." The night that me and Limón figured out about the towed jumper on mescaline, we also decided that the only thing worse would be to have to hang out with the Malaysian while peaking on his mescaline.

After pre-jump training, the scouts got carried across to Pope

Air Force Base in one cattle car. Stopping on the grass just short of the tarmac, we filed out and towards the two riggers standing on the bed of a truck piled high with parachutes and reserves where one each was thrown down.

The Colonel owed this jump for winning the Military Stakes. Instead of a couple of trash barrels filled with ice and beers or a long weekend, we get a day jump into Kansas with a light mission and no officer.

The scouts were punishment for this lieutenant, who had fucked up so badly as a CIA field officer that he was sent to Officer Candidate School and then to us. A guy we know in Headquarters Company told us this, and that the lieutenant had lost all this very important equipment while on the job in the Middle East, and that the big time spooks wanted him far away from spook land, but where they could keep an eye on his sorry, inefficient, scarecrow-looking, lanky ass.

Like most of the officers we had already burnt out, he just got in Platoon Daddy's way during mission cycle. He tried to make up for it by mentioning, half in code, little things he'd done here and there with the "company," and even dropped hints that he'd been sent to us because he'd seen too much and needed some down time. When he'd get happy with himself, we'd wait some minutes, and then have a platoon singing of Secret Agent Man while doing this very cool jerky dance.

Higher was doing a good job of keeping him away from us, though. The Colonel had sent him for another try at jump master school two days before the competition, and lucky for the scouts he hadn't no-go'ed his way back yet.

So, the Colonel's giving us a Hollywood jump and a couple of days to run wild. The dopers held a big meeting on Hay Street after word come down about the jump. It was the perfect time to visit the Malaysian: a rare daytime drop at 3000 feet instead of nighttime at 800, no hundred-pound rucksacks, no lieutenant, and a big ol' field with no trees at the edges for a drop zone. It took three rounds at the Pop-A-Top for us to decide that in honor of the Platoon Daddy and his super short status, we couldn't risk what might have been the most beautiful jump in all of paratrooper history.

We argued about the possibility of it being the most beautiful a lot longer than we argued about whether or not it would happen. The cherry—who we had claimed as one of ours—mentioned that civilian parachutists do crazy stuff all the time when they jump, and that got everybody to jawing. But we all agreed that the adventure shit civilians do is just people trying too hard, and their deal ain't getting it cause they have a choice and have to pay for their jollys. It's not authentic.

And like the saying and the bumper sticker goes, "If you don't jump with a weapon and a rucksack you ain't shit."

What the cherry didn't know was that he was the reason it only took a few beers for the doper scouts to settle on jumping clean. Not that Platoon Daddy would be all that responsible if somebody did step on it, but this was the first cherry doper we'd ever really had, seeing that most of us came in at around the same time, and that meant we'd be in charge of giving the cherry a boss Cherry Blast: his first jump out of jump school and with the platoon.

We all had to try hard not to overdo it too soon, so we all held back until after we were chuted up and were waiting to be inspected by the jump masters who were two staff sergeants from Bravo Company. Frankie Meadows started it off real nice by just staring at the cherry's chute. He stayed on it long enough that the cherry lost his nervous smile and asked, "What, man?"

"Oh, seen it before. It ain't no thing," said Meadows, sounding like Hightower and Richards, which made the brothers watching, sly at a distance, giggle at their roper pal.

The cherry nodded, trying to be casual, and then he was grabbed and twirled as the jump master did his thing. The jump masters check everything on you from top to bottom, using a system practiced hundreds of times in jump master school. Working you over, they give you the good to go or send you back to re-rig. The jump master finished with the cherry and his rig was right, but Meadows asked polite if the jump master would give the cherry another look, "Seeing he's a cherry and this is his blast and all."

The jump master was hurrying because our bird had just swung down the long tarmac, past rows and rows of fighters and transports, and jerked to a stop in front of us. He moved back over to the cherry and looked hard and pulled roughly on his gear, only to state flat out, "He's good."

The cherry said, "Thanks, man," and Frankie smiled back and shrugged. "Thought I'd seen something like that before."

The back end of the C-141 opened and the scouts barked. Paratroopers bark when they like something. Not only had the Colonel gone and got us a C-141 when we were expecting an old prop-driven

C-130, but he got us a tailgate, too. That means we get to walk off the back of the aircraft instead of popping out the troop doors on either side.

This was going to be my forty-third jump and I'd only tailgated two other times, both times at night. Hell, I only had six day jumps total.

With our chutes on our backs, reserves on chests, rucksacks hanging high and light between our legs, and weapons cases strapped to a leg, we did the elephant walk across the tarmac, and up the ramp of the aircraft, waving at the imaginary crowds. The cherry was in front of me and I asked how he was doing, but he didn't seem to hear me.

We got from the barracks to sitting inside the aircraft in under an hour. If this were a regular mission with the battalion, the whole mess would have hurried up and waited a good ten hours.

Ten thousand feet in the air. The C-141 was meant to hold one hundred and thirty jumpers, now held twenty-five scouts plus medic. It feels like an empty show. Sitting in the aft end, the men crowd together out of habit, and Corporal Marty Jencks is fixing to wind up Man Hightower.

"Ho, Hightower. Tell us about the Big Water Head Boy."

"Ummm. The Big Water Head Boy—I miss him. Rode in the back of the bus with him all through junior high and high school. Shoot, the Big Water Head Boy from Cabin John, Maryland just like me. We'd play Hearts and he'd tell me about his chickens and his cat until the little yellow school bus would drop him at the special school. I miss the Big Water Head Boy. Hey, Corporal Jencks. Did you go to school in a big yellow school bus or a little one?"

"Man Hightower, I went to school in a big yellow school bus."

"Yeah, I knew it. I can always tell whether a man he went to school in a big yellow bus or a short one. I mean, you know, not good or bad. Can just tell."

The body of the C-141 Bravo is divided into four rows of thick nylon webbed benches, and the jump masters had divided us up along them according to their manifest. I was across from Man Hightower pretending to sleep as he tried to draw Richards all in it.

"Hey, Richards? . . ."

"Hightower, we didn't ride no buses in Detroit."

"Dag, R. No buses? How'd you get . . ."

"The shit was right across from the projects."

"Hey, Richards. What do you think happened to the Big Water Head Boy?"

"Damn, Hightower. Now how the fuck should I . . . All right now."

One of the only ways to mess with The R is to ask him stupid questions and then watch him go off.

I peek across at John "Man" Hightower, who, like the rest of us, is cammied and chuted up and half loaded down. His brown and sweet round face, crowned by a steel pot helmet worn low, shows through the dark green and loam cammie stick. The green cotton elasticized band on the camouflaged cover to his steel pot says in blue ink pen: "Cabin John, Md." and "Sweet Petey The Jeez The Booty Doctor." This is both a favorite thing to say and an imaginary friend for the Man.

Hightower is one cock-strong country boy who plays football for the post team and gets to report to the coach for three months out of every year. He gets sweeter than usual before a jump, and only gets mad when he pulls a box of c-rations with a can of Nut Loaf for a dessert. When this happens, he stomps the horrible can. In two years I have seen Nut Loafs stomped deep into the jungle floor of Panama, the mud of the Everglades, the red clay of Georgia, the deserts of the Mojave and Egypt, and across Ft. Bragg. Like a complicated map of land mines. Hundreds of years from now, smart people in earth science will uncover this trail of Nut Loafs under exactly the same amount of ground and will figure them correctly to be part of some kind of ceremony.

Richards makes you wish that Spade wasn't an old fashioned insult cause that's what he's like—all black and bold. Before a drop he chain smokes Kool shorties that he can only buy across the bar of private clubs on Mercuson Road. Rarely has his own pack on the ground, but be in an aircraft with him and watch The R come out with a full deck. Can't bum one off him, either, and it's not out of cheapness. That's just him, The R.

Frankie "Country" Meadows is going to be singing the same damn song over and over, which is the reason why he's not allowed to sit next to Richards.

"Damn, Country. *Put another log on the fire.* Fuck kinda song is that?"

"It's a good goddamn song, R. Help me sing a little."

"Song's about a fireplace."

Funky Town. Oh, and that's a good song. *Take me down to funky town.*"

"Don't talk to me about that record. That record's played."

"You played it enough. *Funky Town.*"

"Country. You will at ease that singing."

When Frankie Meadows gets out he's going to get married to the finest girl any of us have ever seen. I'd say she looked like something in *Playboy,* but she's classier than that: *Penthouse,* maybe. When he first come to the platoon, Meadows showed me a picture of her and said, "Now, ain't she prettier than a speckled pup in a red wagon lapping cream?"

I couldn't say anything but "Yeah, man." Then after taking the picture from his hands to get a closer look, I said she looked like the ladies on the show *Dallas,* and Frankie told me how she gets all her clothes at Belks. After he does his three, he's going to work for her dad in Houston, and we just can't figure it out so he got another nickname: Sweet Meat. That's what's written on his steel pot helmet band.

I have a little bit of the right kind of blood to sometimes get with The Island Boys. They come together on Sundays from all over Ft. Bragg—Samoans, Tongans, Guamanians, Hawaiians, and some of your Filipinos—to play combat volleyball, pig in the pit, the whole deal. It's a nice safe place to be.

The scouts look so cool right now, I think, looking down the rows. On our cammie shirts we wear our sew-on glory badges. I've got an Expert Infantrymen's patch, Parachute wings, Recon Commando, Egyptian parachute wings. The Jungle Expert has just been sewed on by the dinks shop on-post, and the Air Assault wings are coming on next. We've all got our little collections going, except the cherry, and Platoon Daddy, who is at the end of my stick, asleep and drooling until drop time. He sits with shrapnel embedded in his shoulders and nothing on his work cammies but name tag, rank, the two division patches, and US Army. Combat don't wear any glory badges.

Up inside the bird, my time is always spent pretending to sleep, but I'm just about to get busted, and know it sure as there is jet fuel in my nose and the turbines rumbling in my ear.

"Ho, wake up motherfucking Spickanese, Flipapino, White Boy. You ain't sleeping."

"Yeah. You can't be sleeping with all them nationalities running around inside you."

"And put that book up. Been carrying *Huckleberry Finn* for fuck-all years. Shit's been around the world. Hey Too Easy, buy a new book. Better, borrow one, and don't return it, cheap motherfucker."

I yawn, stretch, smile, and send back, "About that time, ain't it, you little cherry bitches?"

I get the whole shit storm in return, but it's cut off by the jump masters standing in front of each stick at the aft end of the bird. They're straining to be heard above the turbines adjusting to jump altitude.

"Twenty Minutes!"

All jump commands are to be repeated. "Twenty Minutes" is supposed to be yelled back, then we're supposed to elbow one another, each side, back and forth, to make sure everyone's awake. We just bark.

The Air Force is now flying NAP of the earth. That means the flight path follows the earth's contour, and because we are jumping into Kansas means we are flying low. And the world's second largest aircraft rides bumpy down low.

The bench disappears from my butt for a while and then slams back up.

"Ten Minutes!"

The fuck it is. Somebody's stepping on their dick. "Twenty Minutes" was given three minutes ago. I hate jumping. I like *having* jumped.

Richards lights another Kool, and ignores Meadows singing about the fireplace, cause it really is about that time. Hightower and Jencks finish their hand of Tonk. I get right into the book where the Duke and Dauphin are claiming their titles riverside, and hurry up to spend time in the part that goes *"Drot your pore broken heart," says the baldhead; "what are you heaving your pore broken heart at us f'r? We ain't done nothing."* And cause it always gets me goofy in times that are good for that.

Everybody's doing something.

Sometimes I do try to read other books, the made up and true books about war and paratroopers that get passed around the barracks, and even some of Shattuck's Casca: The Eternal Mercenary series. But I come back to Huck cause I always feel like I'm missing something there, like the story's going on without me.

Not wanting to miss something is why I only pretend to be asleep before a jump. That and because I'm too fucking scared to sleep. The back end of the aircraft is being opened and lowered. It's not time to look, yet. The hydraulics and the rush of air mask the sound of the jet engines, and the ears adapt to the new sounds. There goes my seat again, and back again it comes.

"Six Minutes!" come the jump masters.

The tailgate is down on the big iron bird and it's still not time to look. Tailgating. Means we walk off the back of the aircraft, right off the back where they load the tanks and stuff. The inside of the aircraft gets real interesting about this time. How it's lined in gray plastic. The alternating red and white grids of the nylon webbed benches. The Air Force issue sunglasses of the crew chief which make him look from the 1960s. Limón's big fucking nose three guys down.

"In Board Personnel!—Stand Up!"

The two jump masters are facing the rows of jumpers and raising their hands, arms outstretched, palms up from the waist and over their heads. Behind them is a whole lot of big blue sky and patches of Kansas earth rolling along like it was on a conveyer belt. Cigarettes, books, letters, and playing cards have been put up, disappeared, as half the scouts stand and sway.

"Out Board Personnel!—Stand Up!"

Hard to hear the jump commands, but we know the drill: try to stand up with all this shit on. Even though it's lighter than usual by half, some will fall back once and twice, and then lift and secure the benches to their upright position.

Forty-three jumps in almost two years. Weird to be freaked about a day jump. I'm jumper eight on my stick. Up front the guys are already on the cherry. Fresh out of jump school so this is his Cherry Blast. Can't really hear them that good but I know how this goes.

"Cheeeery! You're gonna fucking die, Cherry!"

"Die, Cherry! You stupid fucking Cherry!"

The jump masters are holding their hands high and making hooks with their trigger fingers, moving them up and down.

"Hook!—Up!"

We are wearing two chutes: the main chute is on our backs, and the reserve is worn at chest level. We unhook the main chute's static line from the top of the reserve chute and attach the gated long metal end to the jump cable that runs overhead. When we exit the aircraft the static line will pull taught, exposing the nylon chute and leaving a bunch of patrays—canvas chute covers—flopping in the breeze.

As we hook up, closing the gate around the jump cable, the sound of thick metal clicks are heard up and down the lines of jumpers with the rhythm of a lit damp pack of firecrackers. A cotter pin is pushed through a hole in the metal end of the static line, then bent down, and hookup is complete.

The aircraft has settled down as our knees absorb the ride with a slight sway sideways every three seconds. We steady ourselves with a good grip on the static lines. An occasional dog bark up and down the lines, until fear finds its voices.

"You get hot Recon!"

"Ree-con!"

"Motherfucker! Motherfucker!"

"Airborne," manages the cherry.

Poor guy. Sluguski is up on the cherry's back and screaming.

"Dead Cherry! You're fucking dead! You die on this one, Cherry. Die, Cherry!"

One time when I first got to Bragg, I was big time lost hitchhiking back from Hay Street. I had gotten dropped off at the wrong end of Ft. Bragg and two MPs in a jeep picked me up. They said they'd take me up close to my barracks. It was a long ride, me sitting in the back of the open jeep. Every once in a while the driver would say something to me and the MP in the passenger seat. The two of us kept answering his questions at the same time, although I wasn't doing so good cause how was I supposed to know what they were doing when they got off and other stuff like that? Finally, the driver started laughing and motioned for me to come close so I could hear better.

The driver said, "Look, Man. I wasn't talking to you. I'm not calling you Cherry. His name is Jerry. Okay, Man?"

They both said something about "Jesus Christ. These fucking grunts, man," and spent the rest of the ride using the radio to tell all their MP friends the story over the radio. Maybe they felt a little bad cause they passed me back a pack of Winstons with three left; told me to keep them, which was great cause I was out.

———

The jump masters nod at each other and yell, "Check Static Lines!"

We all check the static line of the man in front of us, tracing our fingers along it to check for rips or frays, and following it into the patray. Then you tell the guy in front of you "Looks good" or something official like that.

Sluguski says, "Fuck you, Cherry."

"Check Equipment!"

One of the jump masters falls backwards as they give that command. On the deck he must have looked up and saw the earth and sky from 3000 feet all upside down, and got freaked because he looks like a flipped-over beetle trying to get up.

We run our hands over our gear, unable to remember what we'd been taught to check for long. Togiola, who is behind Sluguski, starts up in thick Island Boy.

"Hey, Brah. The cherry's shit looks all fucked up."

The cherry had been doing "Check Equipment" like they tell you in jump school, starting with his hands searching the rim of his helmet. He heard Togiola and now both his hands are holding on to the static line and he's trying to look over his shoulder. Togiola is one of the nice guys in the platoon, and has been decent to the cherry so far.

Sluguski says, "Nah, He's fine. The Cherry's good to go."

"I'm not fucking around, Brah. Look at the broken bands. I can see the canopy."

"Ahh, that's nothing. I've seen worse."

"Sound Off For Equipment Check!" go the jump masters, and the last man in each stick slaps the rear end of the man in front of him yelling, "Okay!"

Slaps and Okay's move quickly up the sticks, until the first jumper on each side steps forward and points to the jump master with one hand's fingers extended and joined, and sounds off mightily, "All Okay!"

Corporal Marty Jencks, from the other stick, looks through the webbing separating the two sticks and waves his hands, one over the other, mouthing "No Go" at the cherry's chute. Everybody knows that Jencks has just graduated from Jump Master School. Even the cherry.

"I'll just shove it back," says Sluguski, pushing around on the cherry's chute.

Jencks is now pointing at Sluguski like he is giving him a direct order for serious. The cherry keeps trying to look behind himself like a dog tied up by a two-foot length of rope. The word gets passed up the sticks that the cherry's chute is bad, but it just doesn't manage to make it to the jump masters, who've just shouted, "Two Minutes!" It sounds like a demand that is only answered by the scouts chorusing as a pack of hell hounds, focused and intent. The men are yanking down hard on their static lines making the jump cable bounce wildly.

Ski's hands are moving all over the cherry's chute. Yanking it this way and that.

"Fuck Cherry. It's really fucked up. This ain't no Cherry Blast bullshit. Jump Master! I need a jump master! No Go! No Go . . . Shit, sorry Cherry. Shit. No Go!"

The dog barks and the metal rattling along the two jump cables drown him out. And then.

"One Minute!"

The scouts at the back end of each stick begin to push. We've got a forty-second drop zone, and it's a large meadow, but the guys are worried about winding up in the trees if there are any. Which is what happened to Corporal Marty Jencks. He made a tree landing and got a stick in his dick. His balls blew up and he refuses to go back to the doctor. That's why we call him Sack Man or just Sack. Really though, we stopped calling him that same time we stopped calling his girl Ping-Pong.

As the C-141 makes a pass over the drop zone, one of the jump masters is on his stomach and leaning out over the edge of the tailgate checking for ground obstacles, fires, hostile farmers.

Hightower is always saying that his girl tells him he feels like warm hard mocha ice cream when they do it.

The patches of earth out past the tailgate are so clear. Clear like when you've got your face in the eye doctor's machine and he clicks it too clear.

I like this kinda overweight girl I met at Nashville Station, but she only goes out with Special Forces guys.

One Minute's taking too long. Ski had let the cherry alone for a bit. The cherry's this college dropout from a rough and famous place in Boston called Charlestown who never liked it there and now he's up here with us wiping at his eyes. He keeps trying to get the jump master's attention, but can only manage to paw the air with one hand.

"Thirty Seconds! Stand-In-The-Door!"

The first jumper in each stick steps forward towards the ramp. The pushing from behind has those in front losing ground like in a tug-of-war. Every few seconds they give in a step towards the ramp and the open air. Dog barks. On tailgates, you free fall for six seconds instead of four. Don't pull the reserve until after six seconds.

Maybe I won't jump this time. Freeze on the ramp. Not be forgiven.

I want to retie my boots.

The guys in the other stick are leaning and jawing into the webbing, their faces distorted, the skin poking out through loosely woven nylon straps.

"You're gonna die, Cherry!"

"You're gonna burn in, Cherry! Fucking Cherry!"

"Die, Cherry."

Sluguski's steel pot helmet is bouncing off the cherry's steel pot helmet and he looks like he's trying to bite pieces out of the cherry's face.

Many voices. Now a chant: "Die, Cherry! Die, Cherry! Cherry Gonna Die, Cherry! Die, Cherry!"

And it don't stop. . . .

"Die, Cherrrrryyyy!"

I whisper it once, and then scream it so loud I come off my feet.

The cherry's knees have gone and he is sobbing into the man's chute in front of him, pushed there and held up by the force of the jumpers at the back of the stick who are frantic, leaning. Wanting out.

All eyes are fixed on the two lights by the side of the tailgate. The red one on top shuts off and a thin tight surge drops from my stomach to my balls. I want to live in that time between red and green. There isn't even a second between the two, but the time that's there is big enough to move into. Live there.

The green light pops, and wedged together, we shuffle stomp towards the tailgate and into the sky beyond. The seven men in front of me are dropping off one at a time. I hear the jump masters: "Go! Go! Go!" And smile as I go. My buddies look like little kids taking a walk off the end of a diving board. Goofy. Hey, look at me! Drop. Silly.

I take the air proud of being aware. Never saw the whole thing through before, cause mostly blacked out like in a fight.

Live where you can.

One thousand, two thousand, Three Thousand, FOUR THOU-SAND, mmmmmmmm, umph! AHHHH. I always count a little too fast and then moan. I know how long my moan should be before I feel that sweet tug at my shoulders.

Nobody lives in that four to six seconds before your shit opens. Not in one enlistment. Not in this man's Army.

My risers are twisted up—falling too fast—gotta bicycle the legs—open it up—spin a little—and I'm good.

It's so fucking big up here. The different colored patches of earth and the clouds and all this blue, they aren't running anywhere now. Below, in front, behind, everywhere that isn't up, they are there. Rectangular, square, and notched up like pieces of a puzzle. They are orange, yellow yellow. Hee wackety green. Green. There's no wind, and I get to sit in the blue. In it.

"Yeah, buddy! That's what I'm talking about."

Aw, Country. Shut up. Frankie Meadows' open canopy just moved under me, close, but still clearing easy by twenty meters.

Up here is the only time I get to be alone. I pull down on my left risers which only changes the view a little. Steerable parachute my ass.

I think that's the cherry over there.

Back in the bird he was crying. My old-timers made me pee my pants on my Cherry Blast. Not a lot, just one big spurt. Everyone gets it. Except Richards. When they tried to start with him, he just gave them that From Detroit Look and they backed right the fuck down. At least that's what I heard. Richards looks at a man like a panther finished eating a small animal that was just enough to piss him off.

Might be him above me, moving off and away. All around me my pals are hanging under full canopies and you can pretend you're not falling it's so slow and steady this jump. But look to see everything because you *are* falling and the green patch below comes rushing up and barely enough time to pull the straps for the lowering line and kick at the weapons case and rucksack until they drop. Stare at the horizon, don't look down, knees together, bent, loose. Don't reach for the ground, let it come to you. Fall into it. Feet-ass-head. Chutes collapsed. Look up at the big blue sky and get to say *I was there*.

Richards had caught whatever wind was up there and was run-ning with it as we all watched him, the last jumper in the air. He did come down out of sight into a small valley, from which we heard a lot of yelling. We fast-stacked the weapons, left the cherry to guard them. We ran over and I was worried that we'd find The R's hipbone sticking through his skin and cammies, or his feet turned all the way around like the guy from headquarters I found after a bad jump into the Smoky Mountains. Some of us fell and rolled down the hill to where Richards was standing and yelling trying to get some cows from stepping on his chute. He must have come down in the middle of them, cause part of his chute was draped over a few of them and they were moving around and sniffing him, this black guy who fell from the sky. Richards didn't like them coming up on him and smacked one and set himself up like he was going to knock another one out. The cows answered with what I guess was a Mooo, and Richards panicked and yelled to us about them being so big.

"Get these nasty pink lipped motherfuckers away from me!"

Some of the country boys went over and drove the cows off, acting like cowboys, and asked if Richards hadn't ever seen a cow before.

A few of us tackled Richards as he picked up his M-16. He did manage one swing but missed by three feet, and as we held him down he swore out all the things he would do to us I felt him trembling.

Everybody got calmed down and the country boys saying they hadn't meant anything by it just a question, till somebody said, "Oh, shit, Charlie Oscar Whiskeys," and Richards went off again and we jumped him and the cows stopped their slow walk across the grass to turn and watch.

We left Richards to police up his chute and gear and headed up out of the little valley. Even terrified The R was still cool, his eyes moist like crying except no wet trail of tears coming down.

Just back up the hill and here comes the National Guard guys in four gun jeeps, dress right dress, gunners behind the mounted M-60s. In one of the command seats sits our Platoon Daddy. He's jiggling his head and faking like Old Combat's got to do everything around here and he can't leave us alone for a minute.

The National Guard guys dismounted and we all said, "Hey." Their lieutenant said it looked like it was a good jump and when nobody said anything he got into his map, showing stuff to Platoon Daddy with the thin end of a pulled up piece of grass. Okay, so this National Guard–butter bar–LT knew not to point to anything on a map with his finger, and he had jump wings on his flat green fatigues, but it bothered us that our Platoon Daddy—Combat—this close to retirement, was obligated to call this half a civilian, who looked like his favorite thing in the world was softball, "Sir." All because this five jump chump from Kansas had college.

And his troops looked like they were wanting college real bad, too. Except now they were staring at our uniforms, glory badges, and maroon berets folded down and sticking out of the right cargo pockets of our cammie pants. Remembering how the Navy SEALs were during joint training in Little Creek, Virginia, we tried to look casual.

Richards, dragging his gear, comes up the hill. He sees the National Guard guys, turns his back to us and tends to his eyes with the sleeve of his cammie shirt, his head coming up once or twice to shoot a look back over to the cows. The lieutenant has been watching and walks towards Richards, who must have sensed his approach. Richards walks fast to the junior officer, eyes locked down on him, daring him to ask if he is okay. He stops inches from the lieutenant's face and stands there waiting for the question that would not come. The R had just dropped cows from the number one position of most hateful things and put white boy lieutenants back where they belonged.

The National Guard guys froze. We smiled, and The R picked the lieutenant's person clean of all classroom blocks of instruction on the execution of a command military bearing. Richards stayed on him and we watched the lieutenant wonder what his report should look like: *Specialist Fourth Class Richards approached me in an aggressive manner and engaged hostile eye contact with me for an extended period of time. My purpose, as ranking officer of the drop zone support detail, was only to insure that Specialist Richards was fit for duty following a tactical parachute jump . . .* But Richards had turned up the volume on that small voice in the lieutenant's head which overrode everything defined in the Uniform Code of Military Justice. Platoon Daddy knew that something must have happened to Richards on the jump—something we all knew about—and that Richards needed something to put himself back as The R, so he let it go on a little longer. After the young soldier's face—smooth black, green and loam now with drying trails of salt—goes through all its changes, it rests at the point where it is martial, more weapon than face.

"All right now," whispered Platoon Daddy, coming between the two, "let's get back to those chutes."

We climbed aboard the scout jeeps, but not before a short line formed to slap Limón on his head to try and put an end to his Spanish giggling.

Wedged in the jeeps tight, we watched the National Guardsmen, and critiqued the very lame performance of their drivers and gunners.

We'd been steady humping since Egypt. Not one mission with the rat patrol jeeps since we rolled three of them on the rocky dunes, and these guys were stiff legged behind the gun, jerky at the wheel, and pitiful.

The rest of their drop zone detail had already collected up all the chutes except for Richards', and were sitting around listening to our cherry, who was way too happy for a cherry. His back was twelve arm's lengths from the stack of weapons, which wasn't much like guarding them. We left the disciplining to Platoon Daddy who dropped him before the jeep came to a halt.

"Just get on down, Sweet Pea. Start knocking 'em out. One Two Three Four One Two Three Four. Get up get down Get up get down Get up. Now beat ya boots. Get on down and elevate your feet, Stud. Get 'em up on that jeep. Airborne pushups, Son. All the way down. You just keep knocking 'em out till I get tired. Have arms like Popeye. You gonna push Kansas into Missouri. . . ."

The first time the cherry's arms failed him, his feet stayed up on the metal bumper of the deuce-and-a-half, and face in the grass managed to say, "Wow, Sarge."

And if there had been clouds overhead they would have parted for the fury the cherry had summoned with one word, his world now a storm of shit and smoke, could be traced to ancient soldier gods who rained Death From Above long before it was a tattoo.

"Sarge? Sarge? A Sarge is some fat, lazy, inefficient, Main Post, puke non-jumping, leg, sissified strutter, who sits behind a desk and likes to suck dick. My first name is Sergeant, my last name is Timson and I'll be addressed as such. How you read me, Junior?"

The cherry said, very softly now, "Wow."

We lit cigarettes, and understood the cherry completely. The National Guard guys—who stood in the field like trees planted funny by Job Core delinquents—looked surprised that you could smoke during something like this.

Platoon Daddy walked over, sank to his haunches and began to whisper in the cherry's ear. The young soldier got wise and pushed back up, locking his arms with his feet back up into the position on the jeep. We'd all had these little times with Platoon Daddy. Your arms on fire, the old soldier telling you what life ought to be like, what it would be like, and how you could find your way somewhere between the two. You'd become grateful for the man's attention, private and focused, and push ground until muscle and tendons fried, collapsing, nose in the dirt. Platoon Daddy'd get you back into the up position—The Front Leaning Rest—and tell you short stories you could do something with, and then with a change of voice, no adjustment of tone, he'd let you know it would be a good thing if you got to pushing again, because he liked to do his talking while a man was working. Your body and mouth could be screaming from the pain, sweat dropping off the tip of your nose, the pushups all totaled way past 300, and there would be a quiet part of your brain that listened where Platoon Daddy's words landed. Even as your body rattled up top and repeated the fall into the dirt time and time again, what you heard seemed like all you ever had missed, and the beauty part of it was that it stayed.

The cherry went down hard one last time, both feet sliding off the jeep. Falling then, prone, face full in the grass, and Platoon Daddy left him with his cry.

"Good training," said the National Guard lieutenant, and I hoped all these Kansas guys knew that none of this was for their benefit.

Ignoring the lieutenant, and referring to the cherry's time with Platoon Daddy, Corporal Marty Jencks said, "Twelve minutes. Not bad." We argued about the time, and about who had lasted longest.

Someday soon the cherry would learn how to mess up a little bit on purpose in order to bring on that good attention from Platoon Daddy. We'd all done it on the way to be called by the names on our uniforms, and when we were lucky, maybe a few others.

The National Guard ran us out to their firing range in their gun jeeps. Just a long stretch of dirt for a firing line, no range shack and I was expecting them to set up tin cans, but there were pop-up targets in the grass and from a small electronic box their lieutenant brought them up at 50, 100, and 150 meters. The National Guard guys carried their weapons like hunters, like they had a choice. They were wanting to see us fire, you could tell, especially the 60s.

They had the ammo waiting for us. National Guard ammo. The colonel had gone through trouble to get us this live fire, the whole deal here in Kansas. His present to us, and it was all just kind of dumb, but still a present, and Platoon Daddy looked after us knowing that all we'd been through the last few months put a live fire in Kansas as no kind of thing at all. He knew any scouts of his would be happy cleaning weapons and watching, so he got their lieutenant up on one of the gun jeeps firing the mounted 60. Platoon Daddy could sometimes just know everything, and he knew these guys hadn't ever fired live from the gun jeeps. Soon all the gun jeeps had streams of spent brass casings clinking on the metal floors. The 60s high cyclic rate of fire sent rounds downrange that were absorbed by grass and earth until saturation turned clods up to the air and then vanished while white targets rose and fell and rose wobbly like mummies shimmering up out of caskets.

We coached them at their sides, shooing the rest to break down and fire up the boxes of M-16 ammo that we had dumped out of cans marked KANSAS NATIONAL GUARD. We kept the same gunners on the 60s and the barrels began to glow, seen red hot right in the day. Their guys on the 16s bumped selector switches over to Auto, and the doper scouts shoved half belts and handfuls into cammie pants cargo pockets.

Platoon Daddy, with his fingers in his ears, helped the lieutenant until he got bored, then raised his arms to conduct the whole firing line like it was instruments with music.

It seemed fine with him, that one of his last days had him standing in Kansas and playing with the sounds of automatic weapons fire. So many rumors about Platoon Daddy. Mostly about being a good guy and fucking people up. Long Binh jail. Some college. Played football, but got in trouble cause he just liked hitting dudes, even his own, and didn't never notice where the ball was. This one seemed like a stretcher even to me, but the old-timers swore that Jack Tatum—a few years retired from the Raiders—came by the barracks, and he treated Platoon Daddy like a dangerous older brother. The former pro looked tiny as they walked out to the parking lot to talk about their Buicks.

The Platoon Daddy had conducted the firing line till all the ammo was spent by the National Guard guys save the loose rounds and half belts snaked by the doper scouts. They had laid on some hot chow for us, and we ate, told lies, and Ski traded some loose jays for four canteens full of shine. We left them and humped off the afternoon chow. There was no mission, so we just walked the many fields pointing at what we found in Kansas. Just the farms, how that one was different from the last, animals, and the country scouts told about crops, "them's wheat, them's soy," and which ones were a pain either planting in or harvesting out. High ground isn't saying much in Kansas, even still we got ourselves up on a ridge, damn near a bluff, and I had no idea where in Kansas we were at, and hadn't seen water, not even a crick or a creek. Still I got to wondering if Huck's river hadn't torn wild through here thousands of years before the book and left us a little elevated piece to set down on.

The PRC 77s squawked out the National Guard's offer to run us out some hot A's for evening chow. Platoon Daddy—his scouts having picked over for favorites two cases of C's from the back of the Guardsmen's deuce-and-a-half—declined and then gave the order to switch all the radios over to the alternate frequency. Up on the ridge, firewood was gathered as the sky turned the orange and red of a thousand screaming hot rods flung out across the horizon. Quiet was spreading, begrudgingly security went out on perimeter, and the scouts rested easy. P-38s had already worked their way round the green cans—no swapping tonight—Texas Pete hot sauce tossed round and round, no sound but that of the big fire, until the radios began to jump alive with no transmission. Corporal Marty Jencks, just as his Beef Slices were hot and ready for the thin tin of soft cheese to be spooned out on top with a military ID card and lacking only the red dot sprinkling of Texas Pete, got up and walked towards one of the radios by a tree and, because we'd switched to the alternate freak, spoke his mind freely.

"Now, look here you little cherry bitches. Y'all quit it keying the mikes. Quit off laying on the handsets. Men are trying to eat."

Once, twice more the radios broke silence but were ignored; the scouts feeling too full and fine to even come up with punishment or future brutal blocks of instruction. Canteen cups of water were placed in one flat wood at the fire's edge, c-rat Hot Chocolate and Coffee, at the ready.

Ranger cookies are made by adding a packet of Sugar to a packet of Instant Creamer, folding it up tight and watching it closely in the fire by those that had the patience.

Then the radios again. The guys round the fire muttered "can't a guy even eat," but the radios once again and now with transmissions not from the cherries. Urgent. Formal.

"Ahhh, Delta Eight. This is Delta Six . . . Ahhh."

And in the background was heard Hightower's "Hooo. Hoooo."

"Delta Eight Delta Eight Delta Eight . . ."

Jencks has dragged one of the radios over by the fire, and having identified the voice on the other end to be that of his fellow Texan, spoke accordingly.

"Goddamn Country. What are you and Man doing out there with them cherries."

"Hooo. Hooo . . ."

"Hightower, get off that mess, and put Meadows back on."

"Delta Eight Delta Eight. This is Delta Six. We got big-time movement outside the perimeter. Over. Aww Jeez. Delta Eight? . . ."

And Corporal Marty Jencks, way more confused than concerned, curls himself in towards the handset.

"All right, Country. Godamnit. You got a sit-rep for me? Over."

"Ahh. Delta Eight . . ."

"LAND SAKES, COUNTRY, WHAT?"

"You didn't say 'over.' Over."

"COUNTRY!"

"Delta Eight, this is Delta Six. Sit-rep as follows, I say again, sit-rep as follows: Size—four, five, goddamn . . . might be half dozen, it's dark out here Delta Eight . . ."

"Hooooo-hoooo."

". . . Activity—probing our lines . . . Might need night vision devices. Can't see . . . I dunno . . . Oh, shit. Location—two zero mikes and closing. It's dark out here, Delta Eight . . ."

"Hooooooo."

"Delta Six, you're coming in broken and distorted. And keep Hightower the hell away from that handset . . . Over."

"Delta Eight! Delta Eight! They're in the perimeter! They're . . ."

"Sweet Petey the Jeez! Hoooo! Hoooo!"

"Delta Eight Delta Eight. We got Charlie Oscar Whiskeys, I say again, Charlie Oscar Whiskeys in the perimeter. They're coming over us! Tell my girl I done my best! Over . . . Ahhhh. Ouuuuut."

"Hoooo. C-O-Ws. Run! Run! Hoooo!"

You had to be there, but Richards himself got to tittering and when he did, all the scouts, even the ones he wasn't tight with, fell out round the fire. Platoon Daddy got raucous, his whole body shaking, and with all his years we knew this was the good stuff. He told us we were right.

It was the night where everyone indulged. Even Jencks. The dopers taking guys out in twos and threes, away from the fire, out of respect, to burn the good thin ones. Country boys from down way sat together with the canteens full of shine, till after tipping big sips up to the stars, sloshing back and forth through clenched teeth, and spat out, the shine was declared to have been run through clean pipes and safe. From out of his ruck, Limón pulled the AM-FM with PR and little flags written in faded Marks-A-Lot all over it, and hot-wired it to the wet cell battery off one of the 77s. No arguments about music cause Limón's radio could only pull in the one station wherever it went, and it was always just fine. We watched the country boys sip shine, no longer suspicious of Kansas stills, and when the canteens came our way, backed off their pulls by half. The good smoke was thick, the shine thin and strong, and the ridge gave away just enough dark distance, cross fields, between it and the horizon so's the mind could fold out and a long Pall Mall straight, bummed off Platoon Daddy, tasted best.

Limón's radio, hung in a tree, brought in a college station where the DJ talked too much and then way too serious, introduced song after song. Fast jazz music by a guy named Louis Jordan. The talk round the fire was nice. Everybody's poke at that fire, the four-foot dead pine dragged over and draped across the flames, was like their addition to the talk, all perfectly timed, and well placed. Appreciated. Some of the guys were off sitting and talking at the edge of the ridge, lured by the dark open.

If it got quiet that night, somebody'd go "Mooooo" and Richards would act mad and make it right, then the talk—and I swear the flames, too—would flare up again and you'd learn something. The shine, trips away from the fire, you couldn't go wrong and another DJ, who played dance blues, got Platoon Daddy—who was only messing with the shine—up and doing little steps with his whole big body, face scrunched up with a Pall Mall in the center. Every new song, he'd stop to tell us "I got this record" and if not "I like this record."

The radio in the tree held the signal all night, and after midnight a girl DJ came on and said, like she was embarrassed, that this was the station's one night of disco and it was going to be a long one. The scouts heard the word "Disco" and everybody yelled "Limón!" It was a year-old routine that had begun one Saturday night in the barracks' wide hallway. Everyone was waiting for someone else to get ready to go out, and Shattuck asked Limón what time it was. Limón, like the other rabbit that was late, looked at his watch, and announced, "Nine-thirty! My lady! The Disco! A O A O A! Nine-thirty!" And down the hall and stairs he flew, while the rest of us barely made it out that night for all the reenactments.

The music the girl in the tree played meant high school to any scout from private to sergeant E-5, and even if they only went for a day that meant old home and old home was where they ain't, so even the Disco Sucks ropers got up and moved. Limón got Jencks to up his squad leader strobe light meant to signal helicopters in the dark, and that too hung in the tree spanking out hard light—A O A O A. Prom music played and former football stars never recruited, three lunch takers, class skippers, bunkers, dropouts, kicked outs, geeks and goons, all worked on out, and Platoon Daddy like he was at the Mercuson Road clubs for real.

Richards said, "Why do white people all the time be thinking that if they move more it makes the dancing better, cause it doesn't, you know?" and this just made the time better for everyone with everything now all out in the open.

The strobe's flashes sent light deep into the woods like lightning, the back edges of the pulses hanging out and then falling past the ridge, repeating.

The scouts danced alone together, until the girl DJ announced a song she called seminal, and Curtis—second squad's quiet, half blood Florida Seminole Indian—looked confused and then proud. The song was the long version of the scout's call to the Hay Street: Rapper's Delight. The men closed ranks and Freaked, Smurfed, Poppa Smurfed, and modified Bus Stopped, as a unit, till the rapping part came in, then all arms went out from the shoulders— . . . *And guess what, America? We love you.*

The song, like all good ones, never wanted to end and when it did, the girl, she played it again.

Up rocking, the shine and dope held out, and when the girl said good night at the end of her long shift, Limón cut off the radio and strobe, and back round the fire the rest was all talked away and then the scouts, one by one, slept where they lay and slept long.

New wood was burning low when I woke to the sound of birds and P-38s turning around Cs. The good night before hung over the camp and the morning fire popped out sparks that fell by my head and then lay burning bright. The sun stayed behind the one cloud like it was waiting on y'all, and the scouts woke quiet till coffee, still early in payday week with nothing between them and The Hay except an easy jump back into Ft. Bragg, hot showers, big drooly naps, and maybe some had to hide ammo for a fat man.

I walked over to the cherry to kick him awake but stopped just short of boot to the backside and long enough to pick up the notebook he'd been scribbling in forever since he got to us, thinking it was full of stuff he needed to remind himself of in order not to be a cherry any longer than necessary. I carried it over to my chow warming by the fire, and sat with it. No do's and don'ts were what I found in those pages, instead the cherry had written things the scouts had said to one another since he landed in the platoon. The guys wanted to know what I'd found so interesting for reading that wasn't my book, and I said, "Just some cherry bullshit" and felt bad for reading it because besides all the things we'd said—and he'd gotten a lot of the good shit—the cherry had written his feelings and stuff.

The last lines written, which must have been his last thoughts from last night, ended with " . . . and never again would it be so easy to try so hard."

I read that and stayed with it a while. Then I got up and kicked the cherry into this fine day. Hard. I thought the words had come from some college book. Now, I believe them to have been his own.

7

New York–How I Got the Book

A good thing to do is to ride the 1/9 train going uptown. At all hours there will be foreigners in small groups or maybe alone with back-packs and maps and guidebooks, trying to look casual but remembering everything to tell back home. They're looking for the youth hostel and don't know whether to get off at the 96th Street stop or the 103rd. Sometimes I'll walk them right over to it, almost getting to tell them that I, too, have been in foreign countries.

On Riverside Drive I keep an eye on a tugboat; sometimes through the trees of the park and sometimes with a clear shot across to the Hudson. Pace the boats, you can do it if you just pay attention to your stride, just past a saunter. If you walk that way anytime at all you should know it means *the walk of the saints* and this I was told by the captain of the tug I work myself.

I would like to know that there are people who pace the boat I work.

When later morning comes I'll be back to Riverside along the Hudson River to watch the man who throws punches in the playground.

Huckleberry Finn. All that exists in the world is him and Jim and what they choose to allow. Their adventure: The Duke and a Dauphin *that smell a nation*, Camp Meetings, Grangerfords, Shepardsons, what comes off the river and what goes on beside it is up to them, all the time knowing plain and good that *You can't pray a lie* and a lie is all there is towards the end when that Tom Sawyer shows up. If we're not supposed to stop reading there, then everybody should see it for what it is mostly and that's a lie and no fun at all.

I have the tug I work tattooed on my left bicep. You have to work on a tug for a respectable amount of time before you get one. Back when I got mine I wanted it to have a cartoon smile on the bow and a big red clown nose, but the guys threatened violence cause they all should be uniform.

It is good to have a reason to get one.

I got all mine back when a tattoo on a guy could tell you something, and I got my first in the '70s. You would know something about a man with them, like if you were stuck on a bus for a few states next to him, you'd have stuff to talk about. Not anymore. It's like how those guys in the Army used to be talking about how they were country before country was cool, and I know I'm that way about tattoos but it was really a thing when I got my first: Pink Panther starting low on my wrist and coming up tall wearing a top hat and holding a cane and my special addition to the design was that the Pink Panther was looking down like he lost something. All everybody else got was just how it was straight off the wall. Pointing to it and calling the number out to the guy.

All the way back then, anybody learned early how to do it. When people from out of your neighborhood places start staring at you, you just smile and stare back almost singing the thoughts to yourself that—*Yeah, I know it's stupid looking. So what? I mean really, so what? It's a cool kind of stupid though, right?*—and you do it bold like you meant it to be just what it is, and when you can't do that anymore you get it covered with something new.

I'm what you call a cover-up kind of guy.

The longest place growing up, I had an Uncle Lou: small half-slanted eyes, and his skin slowly getting whiter as he aged, time losing the dark yellow, and he had a Jesus on his arm looking up with thorns poking him in the head, the black dots of blood dropping. All the work on his body had been done in foreign countries and now the lines were thickening, spreading. The India ink fading, and I don't think any Jesus would mind that. More than anything else, he's a guy on my uncle's arm from where I used to swing.

I ran Paola over with roses. It was going to be crossed swords over her, but through her is what I would have meant. Years after I got the tattoo it messed with me bad that Paola wasn't her real name. I wished it was okay. It's the name I knew her by. She had told me her real name—wrote it down on the back of a photograph—but

I let it get stolen before I could remember it always. The thing I hate about myself the most is that I cannot remember that name.

So I had her whore name on me. There must have been a reason why she had told me her real name, and that would be the same reason why I shouldn't have Paola on my back.

It was below parachute wings with a skull wearing a maroon beret at the center of the wings, and 82nd Airborne Division written above it all.

The nurse at the school I tried at for a while was taking my blood pressure while the doctor tapped on my back, and after she saw it she said to herself, loud enough for everybody to hear, "Yeah, that looks real intelligent." The doctor gave her a look and maybe she felt bad for insulting me cause she asked where I worked, trying to make conversation, and I know she meant on the grounds crew or at the physical plant. I told her I was a student and she stepped back as if she might challenge my statement, but instead quietly went back to her work. Even still I wanted to tell her about Paola under the roses.

The captain of my tug makes you try out for school. Stay with him long enough and he makes you. It started with studying for the GED, says he wants everybody on the tug to have one, and anybody that's spent some time with him and his boat has got one, even the salty briny one. He looked like you couldn't go wrong listening to him, and he had a way that you wanted to follow. He'd been a professor of stories in old languages and before that even played in a weird band that some guys said was very influential but he never would talk about that.

After the GED, he'd be after you to try out for college, even though guys were all the time telling him that they liked working on the tugs, loving it some would testify, and then faking annoyance: "Damn, leave me alone, Captain."

He would say softly, looking right at you, that he just wants to make sure you knew about your options, that's all. He knows all kinds of people, and how if you went off the books for a year, you could qualify for a scholarship. Then through a friend get you a job working security at the same college even if you had a record. Around every five years he gets a guy to try, and like me they all came back to the tug after a year or two, and every single one of us grateful for the chance, that we saw what he meant about options for our life, and now we're sure. It's a university, too, not just a college.

I let the tug I'm pacing loose and it breaks away upriver unescorted. Don't even know whose it is when the trees block a good look at the smokestack, but I need to walk regular when I tell about how it was when I got the book.

A guy I hadn't known too good in basic training gave me my copy of *Huckleberry Finn*. I don't remember his name cause he left before basic really got going, but he was from the Ozarks, slight and friendly, who said that one time his whole hollow had joined up for the reserves right off the stage from high school, even the girls and all. He could run just fine, and had a real good attitude, just couldn't get up for the minimum amount of pull-ups, or swing arm to arm down one set of monkey bars. None of the guys gave him a hard way like they did the other no-gos who were trying just as hard. Maybe it was because he had guys from other training companies who were from his hollow sneaking over across post to check on him. They'd come in packs of seven or eight and go off under a tree to talk and sit wih each other. Where he was maybe even shy of slight, these guys were long and wirey and looked like they could fix anything, especially if it went fast. They looked like they were from a place where it was always autumn. One Sunday they came for him and I walked them over to the PX, where his squad had just gotten its first privileges. On the way they asked after him and I told them about the pull-ups and the monkey bars, but also about his running and good motivation. They said—almost like they were mad, though not at me—that he was the best player around their way and that he could sing it out loud like nobody's business. As I walked with them, I wished I could say I was from a hollow.

We spotted him on the steps of the PX, where he was sipping on the first Coke soda of basic—that's how people from his way call it, Coke soda—and picking at some loose white paint. He saw them coming and got up just like someone whose good home place was coming for him. Before they run off for someplace private, I asked one of his guys what it was that he played. I got looked at with "dummy" loud and implied, and was told "Dulcimer." I knew what it was.

Before he got sent home, he gave me his book of *Huckleberry Finn*. He said it didn't work for him no more, and he wished me luck going out for Airborne, being a paratrooper, and everything. I was sorry for him, lots of ways sorry for him, but mostly because his book didn't work for him anymore, even though I never knew one could work for you at all.

After he got put out, his bunk mate told that it was his third time trying basic training and supposed that he'd find a way to keep coming until he got it. There was some talk about him maybe having had a little kid's disease, and then some shoving and words, but we'd all agreed about him having a lot of heart and that he would keep coming back and finish someday.

I read that book, and then just kept on reading it, and some time after jump school began to understand what he meant when he gave it to me.

I know a part of it word for word. Have for some time. It's good for when you're going somewhere. A real place, or even just a spot picked out, a corner up ahead to walk to, and it's sort of an all-purpose section that works day or night, even though it's written for the daytime and lets Huck do the talking when things aren't going right and you're sick of your own self anyway, but if you're feeling okay it works too, cause this part of the book is so familiar, and you really don't believe him about the serious mournful parts and there is something comforting about a kid sounding weary.

8

After Panama City, Colon

From the train station, in the night there that never falls but just beyond bottle green, we found the sure way, in one try, to our part of Colon.

In a pharmacia we bought soap. It was the first one we found that was still open and it had black and white tiles on the floor that swirled in the center. Everything to buy was behind glass so you had to break the silence of the place to ask the man or woman dressed all in white. The only noise was the sound of the long fixtures overhead that hummed and pumped out light harsh and unnecessary, just the same as us ourselves. On this our third entry into the city of Colon, we had not gone deep enough into the part set aside just for us.

Maybe the rumors we'd heard about being able to buy the good strong drugs in pharmacias was true in other pharmacias but not this one, and we were alone there with the man and woman in white, and we all said, "Soap." Limón stepped forward to translate but the man put up his hand at Limón's "Por favor," and the woman had a bar dropped down into a narrow white bag which was quickly folded and sealed with an inch of scotch tape. Leaving, I knew we offended them. That they knew what kinds of girls we were washing up for.

It wasn't long that we found a hotel that was for us. The lady who rented us the room asked Limón what we boys wanted with a room for one hour and what was in the white bag from the pharmacia?

As soon as Limón was done translating she started with that laugh.

"Hanhh Ahha Hanhh Ahha Hanhh Ahha" and then she'd make clicking sounds with her tongue just waiting for you to laugh too, which we figured out we were supposed to do, and she showed us to a room on the second floor, up stairs patched with the metal of coffee cans.

We'd all stayed in hotels or motels before, all of us, stayed the one weekend on pass in between basic training and AIT, and at least two of the weekends during jump school, so this wasn't any big thing at all, a hotel. There wasn't any thermometer on the wall to mess with the way the guys like to do. The temperature. No place to get ice for free and for everybody, but Togi went for sodas while turns were taken in the shower and damn near everything in this hotel was wooden, not like the Motel Six's outside Fort Benning.

We smoked on some of the stuff from the Soda Truck Guys, and handed the joint to Limón in the shower and that was cool and had us like we were really paras and on the town in a foreign country. Forgot about towels and went to see the lady who burned us for two of them, bad. Limón, wearing one, was smoothing out his knits on the bed, and doing a good job of reviving the creases in each leg. Out the window there was a whole world lived in up above with its own noises, family and dinner, candles in the windows. Togi was back with cold Cokes in thick glass bottles, and when Ski came out of the shower he went to the window and started yelling his fake make-fun-of-Limón Spanish.

Everything above us got quiet like we were in nature, and then Togiola at the other window yelled up a long string of words in Samoan, and Limón now too, singing a Spanish song, but in a way that sounded more like we did when we imitated him. Soon the free air in the alleys between our windows and the rest of the buildings was filled with all kinds of crazy singing and shouting as people stuck their heads out and joined us until, above it all, a young woman shrieked about her children and there was nothing but distant laughter and then quiet.

In the shower there was more graffiti, English, Spanish, all different kinds of languages, strange markings belonging to the enemies, I was sure, but couldn't read most of them good for more of the coffee can patches. Still, under the weak spray of water I washed myself and found some words and whole phrases in English.

Back down the stairs of the hotel and the woman was waiting for the return of her towels. She made gestures that asked, "All finished? Everybody get done?" Her fat, no thick, no fat, moist tongue whipped around the whole outside of her mouth wetting the old uncracked brown skin up to just shy of her nose. She scooted behind us as we went down the hall towards the door with dirty lace hanging in its window, us guys thinking she's coming wild like she is for slaps on our asses. But it was both her hands squeezing nuts, two guys at a time, with a sharp twist to the right and at the door now we're bunched up and hopping, her hands about us like a snapping blur of angry turtles—"Hannh Ahha Hanhh Ahha Hanhh Ahha."

Back in the street and safe, we walked, not wanting to be too early for the girls, and ate the monkey meat on a stick. Stopped at a little outside cafe where we sat at a table and had beers brought to us on a tray. After ordering a second round we waited for the waiter to leave and in low voices we argued about what kinds of drugs the men at the tables all around us packaged and shipped. Even without hearing us they didn't like us, but we finished all of our beers, and then left for more meat on a stick.

Three times we ate what was handed to us from different vendors holding high the many sticks of charred monkey. Soldiers, sailors, and merchant seamen wandering Colon like lost movie actors, uniforms, and no one alone. Some we knew from our battalion, only nodding and us too, across streets, respectful of everybody's wish for it not to be too familiar here, and me, Limón, Sluguski, and Togiola, stayed by the doorway off a main street and watched it all go by, and Togi said the word "Lurking," and not one more was spoken as we stayed watching until the streets were as crowded as they'd been our first time, which had been the night before.

The sign for the Bar Le Fleur was wooden and plain. Seeing it stick out from the building after we rounded the corner laid in solid a clear and clean sense of glee and expectation and there are many things people know better as they age, but feelings like these in particular are not one of them. The joy of expectations answered. Promptly. Look for the bar. Go down more streets. Some like alleys. Look. Argue a little with your pals. Look for the bar with the girls who like you. Smile cause you're really looking now, and this is right. This street. This one, and round the corner there is the sign. Smile again cause you're right, and always have been, you and your pals. Right. Must have been. Must be cause there's the sign. Just the words Bar Le Fleur in wood that maybe should have a picture of a girl below them. And then words remembered. In English and readable in the wooden shower of the old woman's hotel.

*IF IT SMELLS LIKE FISH YOU GOT A DISH IF IT SMELLS
LIKE COLOGNE LEAVE IT ALONE.*

We went in the first door and angled through the next. The man
who is boss of everyone greeted us and left off talking to the man in
the bank cage. Walking us to the bar, he and Limón are talking fast
in Spanish except when the man asks Limón to repeat and then
turns to the rest of us and says in English that our friend has funny
ways of putting the Spanish words. Ski thrusts dollars at him for the
beers we'd had that morning.

The Bar Le Fleur is not empty. The girls are all there. A few men
wearing blue work shirts stained with the grease of big engines sit
familiar and like they will be leaving soon.

With our return we have surrendered, lost the best kind of bar
fight, and the girls enjoy this with casual greetings from all but
Paola in her tight bright green dress, sitting at the edge of her tiny
stage, head down, tilting up the toes of her white sandals with the
little heel, staring at them as they bounce from side to side and she's
talking to the woman who belongs to the green and red bird that
lives in her hair.

Alone at the bar is the man from the northern countries, and we
sit on each side of him. He has not noticed us or pretends not to as
he repeats in a whisper the same words.

"Silence, exile, cunning."

His hands both wrapped around a drink melted and white yellow. He chants like a religious child in a corner serving out their
punishment.

"Silence, exile, cunning."

This thin man, repeating.

"Silence, exile, cunning."

We leave him to his task and Togiola signals for four and the
bartender woman sets up the Balboas with short glasses. He points
to the northern countries' man's drink and goes to hand some
money for another across the bar. The man shakes his head no, and
repeats the shaking in time with his repeated phrase, and Togiola
lays two bills in front of the man's drink, who stops and looks up
close at Togi and says, "Must you cheapen everything with money?"

The Samoan, no stranger to weird customs, recoils and waits.

"I was here first," says the man slowly, "and I am much older
than you, though you are more than me in number, but in numbers

with much different meanings. Do you all understand me very much?"

Togiola looks like he's adding up the ways Samoan that he should jack this guy's jaw, but the man comes back with the explanation that would he dare to visit the home of Togi's grandparents without several cans of corned beef hash?

"Yes. Yes. Yes. I know some things. Yes. Yes." And the man has coaxed a smile from our large pal, and all is well and returns to the regular kind of strange when the man crosses his hands along his chest and dips them both into his inside suit pockets and comes out with two big candy bars.

"Would you like a square of chocolate?"

This time we knew just to accept.

"Yes."

"Okay."

"Yeah."

"Please."

"Yes, please."

He runs a fingernail under the sealed edges of the chocolate bar, removes the cardboard, folds out the layer of tin foil, takes out his knife, and polishes the bone handle on a pant leg before flipping open the small blade which will run across the chocolate the better to make perfect our portions. This ritual doesn't bother me like it did before.

"Or maybe you prefer the licorice? For your beverages?"

No. No. We assure him that chocolate will be great, and it is really hard not to start acting like this guy even after only a few minutes.

The woman behind the bar has her own chocolate bar in her fist and the reel to reel has a big switch she has flipped and all of us seated at the bar watch as the reels bump from side to side, inches in each direction, left and right, before music, sweet, and just the smallest bit too fast to be sad, jumped from speakers of all sizes mounted everywhere on the walls of the Bar Le Fleur.

We asked the man from the northern countries how it was going, putting a new name to his boat, and he said that it's called a ship and that he supposes we know this and that we should not tease him like we do men from our navy and that his family has made its way with ships for many years do we understand him? Do we understand him very well? About the difference between boats and ships? About very old families?

"Okay."

"I am for different things this night. Not names, except for yours. I have not yet had the pleasure."

We introduced ourselves by rank followed by first and last names as we should of done the night before.

"It is my imagination that you have your own name for me."

He was getting quiet again and the woman who belonged to the green and red bird came to him, and Togi gave her his seat. We all shifted over to stay on one side of this man. The bird ran back and forth from one of the woman's ears to the other, along a trail across the hair which fell down the woman's neck and bare back. From ear to ear the bird ran and hopped and the woman still would not let it visit the man from the northern countries.

The music got louder and the Bar Le Fleur filled up. Many Greek merchant sailors sitting in a corner breaking white plates. The boss of Bar Le Fleur kept the plates just for them, since the Bar Le Fleur served no food. The Greeks talked to one another constantly. Even on their way across the floor to the man behind the banker's cage, their hands all over one and sometimes two girls, they spoke Greek to the men left at the table. Yelling still, as they disappeared up of stairs.

When more plates were brought to their table and smashed to the floor, the bar woman would stop what she was doing and go round to the Greeks' corner with dust pan and broom, muttering bad words in Spanish. The Greeks laughed and matched her words in Greek. The Americans had also come in the bar. Two the same as ones we'd passed at the waterfront in the afternoon. Grown-out military hair, with none wearing their straw hats, but still with the scissor-fringed blue jeans or the same style flat green fatigues.

They stayed at the end of the bar close to the door, and girls and the boss came to speak to them, but serious, and these guys looked at us, and the ways we thought we knew them faded from their eyes. The skin around their faces darkened until they were just eyes that looked at us unblinking, saying something that came across as We see you We see you We see you. Things had a way of repeating in the Bar Le Fleur.

Like those slow to dress according to the change in seasons, it took longer than it should have for us to understand that the bar was not ours alone, as it had been that morning

Men came in and walked around the room from table to table,

selling handfuls of Violet Chiclets in the tiny boxes that have two pieces to a box, and the sailors and soldiers bought these up by the fistfuls emptying them into the laps of the girls by their sides while pocketing for themselves only one or two.

We each bought some and had mounds of them piled next to our cigarette packs on the bar, green packs and red packs, and we had money, and beers with a glass before us on a bar like men we'd known our whole lives and the difference between the men we swore we'd never become and those we knew we would, not yet much of a difference at all.

Men came in with stuffed animals on a stick and walked the same path as the ones before with gum. Everyone moved their chairs, or stepped forward or back to let them by, and no one bought an animal, and no one seemed inconvenienced by all the moving.

The girls were holding the hands of uniformed sailors from New Zealand and they were bending their middle fingers back across their palms, and marking the spot where the tip of that middle finger reached and then unfolding that middle finger and doing a measurement with their girl fingers. They would squeal in delight no matter what it was they found out. We wondered how they would do with Limón.

Men came into Bar Le Fleur with blow-up wading pools. The men who came in one after another to sell in the Bar Le Fleur were all Indians, the bones in their faces making ridges under their skin halfway the color of Georgia red clay. The wading pools guys each had one blown up, bright colors, and the rest deflated and folded neatly across a forearm and they walked the room, bumping people with the pools, careful for the cigarettes and no one bought, but the Indians were smiling all the same because it was early and they knew that later there would be plenty buying.

Three cherries from Alpha Company, all in leather floppy hats, cheap blue jeans bloused into their Daniel fucking Boone boots, Airborne T-shirts, and two with Government Issue black glasses are at a table and drinking with Russians.

Paola has not left the edge of the tiny stage and is never alone but always tended to by one or more girls who come to sit with her in shifts. We stiffen in our seats when men from the tables shout out to her and wave their arms for her to join them, but the other women take care of this by double teaming them and paying extra attention and quickly blocking their view of Paola. The man from the northern countries has passed us the licorice from the Tupperware that fits inside his jacket and asks that we take two, so now one black disk joins the green packs and the red packs, bills and change, bottles and glass, and piles of Violet Chiclets before us on the bar.

More and more Balboas, and the money on the bar holds. So little is gone that only a trip upstairs would require reaching back into pockets. A while ago the music was turned up and men began to walk into the Bar Le Fleur only to turn back out, for there was no room left, and as these men departed they ask each other to remember this place and to come earlier next time you could tell.

Limón is called over by the woman who belongs to the green and red bird, to join her and Paola at the edge of the stage and Ski got to ask the man from the northern countries about what he knew about the Polish Cavalry in World War I, which it turns out is a lot, and me and Togi sit facing the tables and watch everything as if in a moving picture, wrapped and held by the silk banners of soccer teams from all over the world hung on the wall next to the dozens of dusty military headgear, and posters of ports of call, these tokens left behind by men who meant to say "Remember me" and Christmas lights blinking and steady, unchanging on walls of plaster, stucco, wood paneling, next to speakers of all shapes and sizes, some working, some not ,and always the music too fast to be very sad.

Men outside the window deciding where to next and me and my guys we stayed.

But didn't go with a girl to the man in the banker's cage and up of stairs following the banister rail. Not that night.

We did pair up that night. And buy drinks. Not hiding while doing it, not out in the open about it either. The man from the northern countries and the woman who belonged to the green and red bird would not tell us their names, but they nodded at each of us when we bought their fruit drinks. That it was okay to buy girls in bars drinks, they had admired our worldliness and restraint, but now was the time.

Limón came to me before I had bought. I had been sitting alone, happy and still only sneaking looks at Paola.

"You need to put more attention. Do you know what she says now?"

"No."

" She says that you now have such a baby face she wants to die."

"So."

"Come on fucking guy Too Easy, you just have to put more attention to her."

"Okay."

Boldly I looked over to the stage not caring anymore and Limón
walked me over and Paola kept her head down. One of her legs was
wrapped aound one of the woman's who belonged to the green and
red bird and the two were bouncing together as one.

Limón had bought the drink for the woman who belonged to the
green and red bird and she left when we sat, and she thanked him
for it before leaving to tend to the man from the northern countries
who was singing terrible with the bartender.

I was awkward and a little ashamed buying Paola her drink.
That it should have been more natural, no biggie, a guy buying a
drink for a girl, and really that nobody was watching would have
been nice, too. I had the money out and in my hand before Limón
introduced us. She said, "Que Pasa" and some more words, and only
then did she lift her head, but only to look at Limón to let him know
he could now translate.

"No, shut up, man. She means—how she say it?—like way
down, in your deep places, where you keep yourself, how are you?
That kind of Que Pasa. Some shit."

Till then I don't know if I had ever thought about it before, and I
think that since then I've never stopped.

And maybe that's because the person who first told me about
those places moved in and I had only the one. Place.

Limón took the money from my hand and gave it to Paola, who
went to the bar. I wasn't given a chance to answer her question. The
Que Pasa.

"She said other shit, you know? This deep place, ghosts, no,
secrets—shit, something about ghosts and secrets—but she stopped
and said to make it more simple. I don't know, bro, she got words
like from the country, Indian or something, but she's very sensitive.
'Sensitivo,' all the girls say."

She returned to us at the edge of the stage and gave Limón
change back which he gave to me and I tried to give it back to her
and I said, "I don't want it," and I think she said the same as she
pushed away my hand and I pushed it and back and forth we went
until Limón said "Quit it" and in Spanish and we all laughed till he
got up to buy himself a beer with my change money. The drink she

had gotten was very small holding it with both her hands sitting next to me and we were alone on her little stage.

I pointed to her drink, and still looking at her new white sandals, she handed it to me, one eye peeking out from just behind her fancy lady hair which fell across her sweet round face. It wasn't Hawaiian punch, like the Ladies Drinks on the Hay, though the color was close, and the smell was of flat and unsweetned root beer. I pulled away from her drink, making a face and handing it back, and she looked up, receiving it like she had played a joke and seeing her even before she hooked her hair behind an ear and took a sip from the straw, and even before I realized that I was looking for the first time, on purpose, I knew then that I had a place like she had been talking about.

Right from there I sat just as I had been doing before. Happy at it then too, except now with a girl next to me with a drink I had bought and she was watching with me. She would not dance that night, only sit with me at the edge of her small stage and only a few times did I look out at the men at the tables like I would twist the neck of a broken Balboa in the face of any man who bothered her. Knowing this for sure relieves you of having to be brave and also replaces all the fear of being among men with a woman. It is also very rare, and is best with a woman who would never incite any trouble ever, only stay happy knowing you would go at it if you had to but that it would always be terrible. Some men appreciate it by instinct and leave you alone for your precious golden time and maybe cause they remember their own. All this very rare. Especially in a foreign country.

The girls came to sit with us on the stage, Ski and Togi each being tended to by different ones and showing polite that there was the one in particular they'd like to be with, which was working out fine because the two they liked best were the good friends of Paola. Limón was getting highly irritated for all his translating back and forth and you could tell he would have liked to spend time with the woman who belonged to the green and red bird you could tell.

The girls would call Limón over by saying what sounded like "Limonay" and they said it real quick and then Limón would come and translate the words.

"Limón, man. Come here, man. What the fuck is she fucking saying to me, man?" is how Togi and Ski would go, and Limón started messing with them, saying things like, "She says you are such a big American soldier it is very much too bad a thing that your penis is so fucking small, shit.

"And that you are very much the needle dick the bug fucker and that you should be buying drinks for the little cucharacarchas, and their little friends that crawl along the fucking ground because maybe you could keep the bugs in your bed instead of like the girls back home around your fort who go find civilian men to be with whenever you go to the field because your fucking dick is so fucking small that only the bugs like you and the birds that fly in the air make fun of your fucking needle dick the bug fucking motherfucker, shit."

The girls knew the bad words and had their fingers in their ears and Limón apologized and complained in Spanish to them like they had always been his sisters.

To get a girl sitting with us on the edge of the stage to go up of stairs with them, other men in the Bar Le Fleur had to ask the owner. They would go but only after being told twice and the owner man told Limón to tell us that it could not be helped. Paola was not asked.

The woman who belonged to the green and red bird left Limón's side and went back and took the man from the northern countries away when he looked like he was drawing little circles on the bar with the tip of his nose. They walked arm and arm again across the floor to up of stairs and the slow and grand way they went was not as easy as it had been the night before.

The girls had rolled up Ski's sleeves and were looking at his tattoos on each arm. Now, for most guys, one Airborne tattoo is enough but, Ski, when he was Ski the Cherry, went and did just what you're told not to do right from day one on Ft. Bragg: Don't go to the tattoo parlor off Yatkin Road that's called Poison John's after 9:00 at night. It's cause John up in his trailer, where he works and sleeps, is deep into his second jug by then and don't draw the tat's so good. Imagine the shape a guy would have to be in to forget that kind of advice and knock on Poison's door at 1:00 in the morning talking about some shit like "Hey! Hey! Old Man! Fucking Airborne, okay? I'm a fucking paratrooper, right? Fucking tattoo. Fucking two tattoo's. Two fucking tattoos, all right? Airborne. Right?"

He got the classic. Two of them. The word AIRBORNE over a set of jump wings. One on each bicep, and guys all over battalion acted out different versions of what they figured Ski and Old John talked about that night, both of them so grateful for each other's company.

Thing was the word "Airborne" got laid in without the second "R." Both times.

AIRBONE.

Yeah, and it got to be a kind of a nickname.

Except that it was just too awful what happened to Ski's face when he got called by it, and it reminded us of the way bad things landed before we wore uniforms, his face when called like that, and it was an old hometown feeling like we all had before we were responsible for our own messes, and still had others the boss of us.

We used Ski's nickname mostly when he wasn't around and we were looking for him: "Hey, you seen Airbone?"

And that way still got to use a good one and keep our buddy right.

That's what we were doing on the edge of the stage, and without Limón's help. Trying to explain to the girls who had seen their share of paratrooper tattoos that Ski was special for the spelling, "Especial" and very "Serioso"—an honor kind of thing, really.

Maybe they didn't believe us, but they left it alone and sold us some speed. Ski treated, and the odd-sized baggies full of black pills took the girls two hands to palm over to Limón. Paola pointed at me and said, "You. No. Okay." I said okay, and would have said anything to have her look right at me again.

From the tables, usually after the music stopped and before the big tape player was reset by the bartender woman, first one hand would shoot up holding a Balboa or a liquor drink and more hands and then foreign phrases repeated, imitated, and anyone would know that what was being shouted was full of pride for a country and maybe a whole way of life. We didn't know what we'd do if the Russians drinking with the cherries from our battalion spoke up, but they didn't and neither did we, and in that way incidents international were avoided and then one of the cherries raised his fist and shouted out the name of a Lynyrd Skynyrd song which resulted in no incident at all, cause these foreign guys knew the song and shouted out some others by the same band and soon the whole Bar Le Fleur was making guitar noises till the Spanish music came back on and the man from the northern countries returned across the floor led by the woman, who dropped the man back off at his stool at the bar like he was a child to be cared for by others. She sat next to Limón with all of us, guys with girls, everybody with drinks, on Paola's stage that must have been built just for her.

The owner man went to the tables as the night wore on and it came to look almost dark outside the one window of Bar Le Fleur. The clock moved above the bar woman's head like those hands only do in bars in foreign countries when your life is around men, uniforms, ships, except for now and these hours when you are treating women good and you can't get drunk, or if you are can't notice it and you haven't yet reached the age where you've caused enough trouble in other people's lives to have to begin to pay it all back.

Because you are here, you and your friends, you have always been right, and each glance at the clock tells this by the way it moves and at the change of each o'clock or this, then that, one hundred hours military, you have sat, remaining as you look, already gone from small boy to old man and back again many times since the little hand moved last, wisdom and ignorance traded freely and at each glance at the clock you know some more and some less, but always that you are right.

The owner man came to the tables and told groups of men when it was they had to go. He knew the curfew of each ship. He came to us at the stage. Said it was the end of our first week at the Jungle Operations Training Center so our time was coming too. It did nothing to lower our spirits cause he says they would see us many more times in the Bar Le Fleur before our training was finished and we had each bought a drink for a girl who asked for not one more, and still they stayed and they didn't ask us to go up of stairs, and had not measured us with their fingers. Through the window of the Bar Le Fleur, men still passed in groups, but we had done good here. Inside this bar for many turns of the clock we'd been very good and leaving soon was the way this night was supposed to go.

One more Balboa apiece and we stayed watching on the stage with Paola and her friends till the owner man came and told us that the military buses back to post would be leaving, but it was up to us, and the cherries at the table with the Russians left with promises to their new friends that they would meet here again next weekend to finish their good talks.

Paola hooked my leg with hers. A light brown foot in a small white sandal hugged my ankle and she bounced our legs together just slower than the music. She pointed as if to make sure I noticed, or to see if I agreed that this was nice, or even maybe that I liked her new shoes as much as she did. Her drink was finished and I made motions that she could have another, but she wasn't looking at me when I did.

We didn't know what Paola's friends and my pals were talking about. They were right next to us at the end of Paola's stage and we looked together to make sure everything was okay with them before going back to just sitting together, maybe closer, but definitely her foot now very tight on my ankle, and now double legs making small circles cause some kind of movement was necsessary.

The owner man came now to tell us that we had stayed so long that our destinies would be decided by the position of the bridge.

The woman who belonged to the green and red bird went to the bar to wake the man from the northern countries and then asked him what our chances were. She returned saying that her friend believed that at this o'clock, on this day, the bridge should be down if we left now in a cab, unless some lonely asshole with a ship and political friends would be rude enough to demand the manipulation of millions of gallons of water for its miserable passage through the locks and under the bridge on a perfectly wonderful Saturday night when everyone is having such a good time, in which case we were screwed. He had told her this in his language, her language and ours, which is how he went when drunk, and she had told Limón in English and in Spanish and Limón, who was getting very fancy with his words, told us it was time to go. Paola unhooked my leg and said her Bye-Bye only once before leaving for up of stairs by herself, taking with her the smell of smashed melons just shy of ripe.

Everyone in Bar Le Fleur said Good night, Buenues Noches, Bye-Bye, to us and the bridge was down, our curfew would be made, and I had looked right at Paola three times that night.

On the road back to Ft. Gulic where long stretches begged for a spray of streetlight this cab driver we did not know was speedy and mindful of the time without being asked and he slowed only as we approached the entrance to Ft. Sherman and the shiny short short and tube top girls were still out not asking Where are you gooooooing? but only pointing at their wrists and urging us on. We stuck our heads out the window after passing them and they were out in the street now pointing to watches that maybe they didn't even have and waving us on, and I laughed before and after yelling to them not to worry.

We took bed check in our drawers and shower shoes on the steps outside of our barracks looking back over towards the city of Colon, all scouts present and accounted for drinking rummed-up

Mountain Dews. The beverages provided by platoon members who'd sat there all night, and Platoon Daddy, who'd accompanied the duty officer during the accounting, called us "Some Happy Motherfuckers" before going back to his room with a door.

We woke up in the cots with the sun full on us through the screens to pain-driven moans and high-pitched vowel sounds from soldiers in the latrine at the first morning piss. Maybe three different voices almost together and belonging to some who had gone up of stairs somewheres, probably on that first night in town, and then the same voices asking "What the fuck is that shit?" and all that I saw lined up at the urinals that morning were concerned soldiers each one braced and looking down whether they'd gone or not. The infected standing stock-still, squeezing Richard, eyes teary, short breaths, and waiting for someone to tell them what to do. All I heard was the laughter of the healthy and "Hope it was good" and more stuff just like it that wondered "Wasn't they told enough?" and "Damn, Airborne. You ain't supposed to put your dick skin in it, son."

We spent the day at the beach on post. At one end were the permanent party soldiers who had weird-looking American cars, some of them were Opals, but most a thrown-together rig of mixed quarter panels and bumpers, none any one color and running god knows what kind of engine. They were with dark girls, but not at all Indian-looking ones and probably real Panamanians, not Colombian and working girls. These guys had coolers full of Balboas so they got to sit and swim all day instead of fighting over who was going to run back and fill a rucksack from the beer machine. Smoked the rest of what we had brought with us and some of our guys swam in the ocean for the first time, and many others the first time high, which in the warm water blue at a distance and clear to the bottom up close, was giving unstoppable boners that had to be dealt with by swimming away and following the shore around out of sight and getting it over with before the lifeguard blew on his whistle and called you back. Some tried to wait it out but the shit stayed harder than Chinese Arithmetic in that warm water and you couldn't leave the water cause of the girls at the other end who would be able to see.

The whole platoon hung out that day and we told about the Bar Le Fleur. Everybody was definitely going with us next weekend, though we said we weren't sure cause the place was kind of private, but we'd see what we could do.

There was a lot of talk about how there was this one girl at Bar

Le Fleur who was stone in love with Too Easy and how that had a lot to do with our special treatment. Though they did make sure everyone knew that they'd all found someone at the place, it was emphasized that with me it was different and guys said, "Shithouse mouse!" and I even rated one "Sweet Petey the Jeez the Booty Doctor" from Hightower and not cause they were so surprised or anything, just that I was big time for the day and some even said they always knew I had my ways.

9

Jungle

Spent the whole Sunday on the beach and the whole night on the long steps high of the white barracks. No more Mountain Dew in the machine, so it was spiked Cokes and jokes up and down those stairs; we knew how to pretend it wasn't a Sunday. Had some weather out there, too. The wind pushing the palms around enough that they looked like they were fighting to stay planted, and the fat leaves over the stairs bouncing down to pat you damp on the head. The boats out between us and Colon moved slow, their running lights bobbing in place. White water could be seen here and there with no particular pattern.

One by one, men declared that it was about that time and left the stairs for the cots, Corporal Collins leaving his 8-track on the steps. The two tapes of Neil Young played so constant that even Richards and Limón asked the corporal, "Where the songs at?" if they weren't already on. Brothers and the Rican made fun, saying "Yo, man. Punch on my Pocahontas jam," but listened afterwards with no complaints. Everything tropical and the old white wooden barracks and the salt air smell of this place, which was what Shattuck still swore was jasmine rice. It eased the tension on what for soldiers is a very dangerous thing, and that is some very different ideas about the tunes. I probably don't need to tell about it but there have been hospitalizations.

Twice and separately I caught Limón and Richards humming and singing "Heart of Gold," but mixing up some of the words. Both of them, when I busted them, said "Fuck you, bitch" and threw stuff at me.

It was the doper scouts who stayed up late. We were so bleary at first call the next morning that we didn't even join the rest of the

160

guys around the latrine to mimic the howling of the afflicted soldiers. A hurt dick dog symphony.

On the walk over to morning chow we were deciding to definitely try our girls' speed. We'd share a bit with the rest of the scouts, who would take it too because it's not really considered a drug in the 2/304 Scout Reconnaissance Platoon.

After morning chow, the staggered line of helicopters were seen in the air before they were heard. Then came the calls to get it on from small clusters of soldiers laying out in the big parade field on the other side of the barracks. Weapons secured, web gear fastened, rucksacks swung on backs, and Ranger patrol caps pulled down low, and we stood ready as the old Hueys set down without a hover.

The line companies were already on their aircraft, but Platoon Daddy was having an extended conversation, yelling into a crew chief's ear. The chief had been just about to wave us on board, till Platoon Daddy pulled on the right shoulder of the crew chief's flight suit where there was a 101st Airborne patch. Platoon Daddy kept tugging on the man's shoulder and kept on in the man's ear till they both smiled and then Platoon Daddy showed his 173rd patch, right side, combat side, like he was saying 'Wish you had this one, dontcha?' Even though this must have looked strange as hell to the officers of the 2/304 with the whole battalion on board except the scouts still standing on the grass in front of three empty Hueys, you'd be right out of your military mind if you think any of them other than the colonel would break this up. And because the colonel himself had been in what was called "The Place" himself, he would let it go a while longer.

In the air with us at the rear of the flying formation, Platoon Daddy stayed with the crew chief, both of them now with headsets, as the chief tried to do his job talking to the pilot and copilot. It was clear that Platoon Daddy had found his best kind of audience: one that really knew what he was talking about, and who also wanted Platoon Daddy to like him. Platoon Daddy held out his big hand, palm flat and fingers tight together, telling a flying story and the hand started to wobble and dive down. Platoon Daddy bent his knees and exploded his cheeks as his hand simulated a crash. There was some friendly pushing on each other by the two men and then they gave each other the thumbs-up.

I was the only one still watching this, thinking how much a helicopter's flying really was like Platoon Daddy's hand in flight, tight and nimble. Me and everybody were sitting Indian-style along the sides of the helicopter, knees sticking out over the edge, and the girls' speed from after breakfast was already a kind too strong and the scouts were jumpy coming up on irritable.

Like this one day when one of our lieutenants tried to get us to quit it with the speed in the field. He gave us vitamin B$_{12}$ pills, saying it was healthier, legal and also kept mosquitoes away. Something about that stuff just pissed everybody off, plus giving half the guys blotchy rashes in the shape of continents. Soon we were a scout platoon full of old hens on a route recon, bickering about who always let the wait-a-minute vines slap back in their buddies face and who never washed out the sink after shaving. Even over the radio, from squad to squad, guys were wanting their extra poncho liners back, and gas money was brought up, and trips to Wrightsville Beach were canceled on account of "This guy fucking ain't right the way he don't never share his pogey bait." It got worse that day, rifles clacking together when bodies clashed cause they just had it with one another, rolling in the forest. The others who broke it all up got into it too after catching stray blows, except nobody got hurt when that vitamin B$_{12}$ had guys so irritable and pissed off they forgot they knew how to fight. At the end of that mission the whole platoon met up and this lieutenant allowed a fire, but couldn't understand why nobody was talking, just eating c-rats cold and wrapping themselves in poncho liners all humphy far away from each other. Maybe he got it when the next day he asked for the vitamins back and we looked at him hard cause we had taken all the vitamins he issued when he gave them. He had not made it at all clear that they were supposed to last us the week.

The staggered formation of helicopters veered hard right, tipping the guys on my side into the safety strap. For a moment we were looking straight down onto the top layer of the triple-canopy jungle, and all the birds dropped low across a green so thick you couldn't see any of what it grew out of until they banked and dropped again one by one and we followed the river low and it was like race car helicopters, fast along that water.

At the center of the bird, Platoon Daddy and the crew chief had both taken a knee and were looking at a map and you could tell by the pointing that they were discussing two different spots, the crew chief shaking his head and Platoon Daddy just smiling back and not having it. Every few minutes the lead helicopter would rise up out of the formation and soon all that were left were the three birds full of scouts. The crew chief was still shaking his head, but smiling too. He spoke to the pilot, who then talked on his radio to the other pilots who were lined up and bouncing slightly on either side of us, and thumbs up went all around and off we went again. Because our lieutenant had been called back to Bragg that morning to fill an open slot in Jump Master School, his third attempt, we knew Platoon Daddy could be up to something and it probably had to do with being set down in a place that had nothing to do with the battalion's mission.

The river snaked and turned so wide that sometimes you'd worry about the pilot's steering, cause they do it with their feet on floor pedals. But they kept the river under us. The real birds were getting scared out of trees so much I got to saying "Go on. Get. Go on. Get," quiet and steady.

Fast above water in thin air and me and my guys too speedy ourselves in helicopters with no doors. The girl's pills had blown right past irritable and were coming on stronger and stronger in waves. The only worry was that it might go right up to tripping out, which we hadn't planned. But it didn't. It stopped at the point where you almost speed yourself straight, only to have it come back speedier and matching the turns of the helicopter's props and the bends in the river everything matching as we rose up high atop this river.

I miss so much. I miss the flying with drugs.

We set down one Huey at a time, the landing zone was so small. Corporals Quinton and Collins came right over to Platoon Daddy, asking him where they were cause this wasn't like they remembered from the last time at all. Platoon Daddy asked back about where the vitamin pills at, and how dare anybody hold out on the Great Jungle Navigator Timson?

Platoon Daddy put Quinton and Collins on map, but each with different ones. Quinton got the one we were supposed to be using to provide reconnaissance for the battalion, and Collins got the one given by the crew chief that showed where we were really at.

There was a trail, leading into the darkened covered jungle. It was narrower and less well traveled than the ones we'd seen at the training center. We followed it off the open LZ, really understanding how much the terrain changed once under the triple canopy covering, still hot but without the direct heat of equator sun. The eyes didn't adjust to the lack of sunlight for a while. It wasn't drastic, but still a change, like the ones ignored by children at the edge of forests.

There was nothing rotten about this jungle. Not like you hear about jungles near rivers. The only smell was of the living. It was the terrain demanding attention. Not like Bragg or the deserts—Egypt or California—or any southern state we humped. There most of the time, even pulling recon, you could just hump, think, and look at new things with a mission you had to accomplish and a paycheck every month.

Here you had to put attention where you walked. That's what Limón told me when I fell back on him going up a small hill. The black palm everywhere was making the hills worse cause you can't grab ahold of anything going up hills or brace against going down. The roots of all these trees more above ground than in it or so it seemed and if you were another kind of fucked up and more, maybe they'd appear the tails of mile-long serpents diving, burrowing and winding, up and down, stitching through the earth.

Once in a while you got some flat ground where you could look around and see where the last bit of sun hit the woven clusters of leaves way up high, and up ahead where the sun did fall all the way through there were armies of fat ants, thick and climbing over each other and moving alongside you, always on a flank. You can't stop to stand in the middle of the ants. No matter how your buddies tolerate from you.

My Army stories that surround my Paola story are mostly just about walking around places in the world with a weapon, all fucked up and thinking about girls. Or about fires and guys something like you, and being able to jump out of planes and keep in shape, having good motivation, cool headgear, bloused boots with the dress uniform, and all that. But really about walking and thinking.

And about the wild dogs that followed us everywhere, barking unseen and pacing us through the jungle. Their calls at us regular enough to become jungle sounds like the rest. The word went down the long Ranger File as we worked our way through the jungle.

"Dogs are here."

"Mo-ther Fuck-er."

"Dogs are here."

"Son-Of-A-Bitch."

"Dogs are here."

"Aww, Jesus shit."

Even in Egypt they found us, and there it wasn't even when we were on patrol. Right there in big tent city they came sniffing around our area, trying to steal our stuff with dog teeth under the sides of our tent.

"Dogs are here."

I think that half the pictures of armies and war that I've seen have dogs in them. Dogs. A tradition, and an excuse for the scouts to feign weariness: proof that we'd been around.

At a place where the jungle thinned, Platoon Daddy crossed a deep stream, and we followed.

There is a sound water makes as it becomes still after the sloshing.

Through the stream and pushing on, we stayed as a platoon, with Platoon Daddy on the crew chief's map. Corporals Collins and Quinton had the other map, on which they plotted out false movements with grease pencils and called in fake situation reports. Platoon Daddy probably wanted the last few patrols of his twenty years of service to have some zip to them, and who knows if we were really in an unauthorized area, but it did put some pride in our stride and pep in our step and made the imagining a little less of a stretch.

My imagining went to the French Foreign Legion, which was where I was going if they hadn't taken me out of the Mortar Platoon. I had threatened boldly for a cherry.

The Four-Deuce mortar platoon was shorthanded when I got to the battalion. Even though I had signed up for Infantry and it said so right on my orders—11-B-1P meaning Airborne Infantryman—they thought I'd jump at the chance to ride in jeeps with the heavy mortar "High Angle Hell" guys.

No way, I told them.

I want to hump.

That's what I said. Told them if I had to go in the Army with no good choice about it, at least I had made sure that I'd be walking and not riding in no armored personal carrier or jeep. That's what got me to the 82nd in the first place; they still walked after the jumping. I'd checked. I was so scared of the thought of having to ride in a jeep for a whole three years that it was all I talked about, and the Four-Deuce guys who were some good ones were insulted. They didn't understand cause shifting that base plate for the mortar was plenty physical and could be counted as suffering. I bitched so much that they gave up trying to treat me like a cherry.

Not two weeks in the company I walked right into the First Sergeant's office and asked politely for my rights. He locked my heels and tore me a new one right ricky-tick and pushed me out of his office, still telling me what it was like and how it would be halfway into the company street. I got Motor Pool guard that day and many after. Later, the scout guys told me that the First Sergeant was smiling about it all day long, but I didn't know that. A few days later I told the Mortar Platoon Lieutenant what I was going to do and when I was going to do it if I didn't get my rights soon. I'd walked right into his office, too, asking him what kind of Army is this if a man can't walk after signing up for it, sir?

You couldn't talk to me about anything else and some of the Four-Deuce guys pulled my coat to the fact that there was talk going round about maybe I was a Section 8 and might be getting evaluated by a doctor soon if I didn't shut up or give over, one of the two.

Then I'd done just like I said, and left. I took a cab to the Fayetteville Airport with nothing but the civvies on my back and a pair of drawers stuffed into a black AWOL bag with the rest of my personal effects. I'd done just like I told the mortar platoon lieutenant, waiting until the next payday and putting near the whole thing down on a one-way ticket to Marseilles, France. Before I went to the airport, I put the receipt part of the ticket into the book *March or Die: A New History of the French Foreign Legion,* and left it lying on my bunk.

The Four-Deuce Lieutenant was waiting for me when the cab pulled up at the airport. He grabbed me kind of rough and told me to At Ease cause he was out on a limb and I was walking a thin line. He took me to a Shoney's—his treat—where we sat and he said everyone in the company was saying I was hardcore more than crazy, but that things take some time and besides they were having fun watching me go through these changes. Anyway, Absent Without Leave was not the answer, and would mess up things for my whole life.

I asked about my rights, and he laughed saying I'd get them and did I even know how to speak any French?

I said that they teach you when you get there. It says so in the book.

He shook his head trying not to smile and then took me back over to the airport for my refund, telling me that he really didn't think I'd go through with it. But I looked out the window of his car at the civilian planes coming and going and knew I would have done it. Gotten on that plane. Now, I wasn't going to cause I didn't have to.

Back at the barracks there was all kinds of guys gathered around my bunk like it was in a museum or something, looking at the book with the ticket receipt sticking out of it, centered on a bed made regulation and tight.

They said that it, and me, we were fucking beautiful.

A week later I was transferred to the battalion's Scout Reconnaissance Platoon, which was part of CSC Company just like the Mortar Platoon and right down the hall.

The First Sergeant told me that he didn't want to hear another word out of me or about me for the rest of his days. Even if I made general next year and was the officer in charge of this man's whole Army, I better hope he didn't have to hear about it and that me and the scouts, we deserved each other.

The scouts that were around back then—lots of them gone now— had been calling me Hardcore like it was a joke, but really didn't think it was funny. They all had a buddy from basic or jump school who was plain old ground pounding in a line company and trying to get into the scout platoon for all the good training. So whatever cherry time I had missed in the Mortar Platoon, I got back double in the scouts. They even made a rule that even when it wasn't a serious nickname, nobody was allowed to call me Hardcore—only cherry.

Platoon Daddy got us back along the river, and I stayed an arm's length behind Meadows in front of me. But I had also gone off to the French Foreign Legion, where it was a tradition for the enlisted men to have affairs with rich ladies in Monaco when the Legion trained there every year. These affairs were brief and impossible to continue, everybody knew that. But in a French way, that was what made it great. There were songs in French going back years and years about the rich ladies on the beach and the enlisted men of the French Foreign Legion. Being in a foreign country now with palm trees and good speed helped me with the imagining, and then we got ambushed.

From up high in the trees came oranges the size of golf balls.

Some came hard and stung off the side of the head and one on the bridge of my nose hurt wicked. Then another hard one got me on the shoulder and when we hit the ground it got worse and I had to stop myself from yelling I was hit.

Looking up and sweeping the trees for the snipers got me hit in the face again, and I got dizzy trying to separate out all the layers of foliage and the noise of the oranges falling through leaves. The cursing from the guys who were hit was awful.

The mad minute ended, and then there was silence, until we heard the attackers laughing and climbing down closer and screeching. One of them got out in the open on a low limb and fired little rotten oranges that exploded on the ground and got a few guys and Platoon Daddy sprayed with nasty pulp.

"Little ugly motherfuckers," said Platoon Daddy, and he searched for a rock and then whipped it. It missed the bold sniper, and then the whole platoon was looking for anything to return fire. Some threw cans of c-rats and the cutamonga monkeys mocked us as they scatter-dodged, moving from tree to tree, vine to vine, in a circle above us.

When they did leave off, it was easy pretending that I'd survived to return from the jungle again to see my beautiful French lady on the beach even though our love was impossible.

We left the monkeys behind and were back following Platoon Daddy through the jungle and skirting the river we could barely see for the thickness. I'm feeling so stupid for imagining the French ladies but then remembering something real and better, which was Paola waiting in the Bar Le Fleur and I was a para in a foreign country. I'd get to say *This Fucking girl, man* and she could be the heavy load I would carry and my buddies would ask me if I was okay and be worried about me cause of this girl, and not in French either.

The trail brought us alongside the river for much of the afternoon and the good speed held with no disgusting feeling when it faded. Platoon Daddy signaled with a raised fist for us to halt and then to take a knee. Then we too heard the putt-putt coming upriver and the voices in English. We stayed down and saw two Americans pass slow, in a long green tin boat, wearing eastern bloc cammies. They had long hair, and beat-up, short AR-15s across their laps. They were Special Forces or Delta and didn't see us, a whole platoon-sized element at the halt. Soon after, proud scouts set down for the night along the river.

We slung our jungle hammocks in a circle, low, just off the ground; every two hammocks shared one mosquito net. Built a small fire and waited down the beginning of darkness before the cans were warmed. We'd been told that you really couldn't see your hand two inches waving in front of your face with the sun down, and we waited with a hand ready to see if it were true. The old-timers had first shifts on perimeter guard and took the dopers with them to burn thin one's, refire the speed, and watch how the smoke hung heavy in the jungle.

Limón sat at the fire, telling all about how the monkeys were playing in his head and that when they leave they don't put their toys away.

Platoon Daddy napped and we watched as a scorpion—small and clear almost to see-through, not like the desert ones—crawled up the tree where the back end of his hammock was tied. Nobody moved till it was almost up to the nylon rope, Quinton and Collins quiet at the tree passing a K-Bar back and forth—You do it. No. You do it. No—finally Collins turned away, knife in hand, and struck at the scorpion with the heavy blade. The stinger fell and the head drove on. We jumped up, searching the ground for the headless stinger striking blind and furious.

Night came slow and it was true: not your own hand two inches from your own face. The speed was not an irritation in the dark like it had been in the day, and sleep would come our first night in the jungle. But not before the dogs, and off in the distance we heard them. From inside our dark perimeter came a voice, and it could have been any of ours being now so much alike.

"Motherfucking dog terrorists."

Sleep would wait again, even after we knew to adjust to the sounds of the dogs. They weren't leaving, and inside the perimeter the men were quiet. Many of the men went for sleep wearing their Ranger patrol caps and when they rolled in the hammocks all that could be seen in the night was the two strips of luminous tape sewed into the cap's back.

You knew the river was there, but it was quieter then than we were. I was almost asleep when I heard the little, heavy, wet steps of fast feet on fallen, waxy, leaves approaching from many sides. Luminous tape popped up from the prone, and the noises were from down low, as they neared, and I swear I heard one coming fast then slide right up under my hammock inches from me.

Inside the circle now the water rats came at each of us, and you could barely hear them stepping across the rucksacks. The yelling and lashing out from the hammocks pushed them in waves back and forth. Guys saying to Stay Away, one asking Please. Some guys who were under attack attacked back with rifle butts. A cry went up: "I got one" and we heard its gurgled hissing anger as it limped off. But many more stayed in the circle till M-60 machine gun blank fire lit up Hightower's face wild in strobe behind the big gun, his body twisted up in the hammock under a mosquito net. We all locked and loaded, firing in the perimeter. When the river rat meant for me reared up on its hind legs just beyond my weapon's muzzle flash and showed me his teeth and the whole inside of his gummy white mouth, I knew then I'd have problems in a real world situation. I know cause I left out of my hammock and ran—more like hopped until the jungle was a black wall.

I wasn't alone. We checked with each other to see who was moving around us, and the calls and responses were not challenges or preludes to Advance To Be Recognized—nothing military—only short questions asking who else was out there. Here and there the dot of voices, more like those who had abandoned ship on a moonless night in oil black seas, bobbing, drifting, calling out.

Not twenty jungle meters from us, tactical flashlights clicked on inside the circle. Men moving around in it, tending to rucksacks, empty hammocks, everything glowing in the warm red light shifting from hand to hand. When the rats came back to probe, briefly, and at half strength, the firing resumed and those of us who had retreated waded back in, bitching and kicking, and becoming all the same again. Perimeter guards, who had bolted towards the circle of hammocks when the firing began, were not re-posted, and the guard roster was ignored all together. Platoon Daddy muttered about how he knew better about such things and had us throwing all the empty c-rations over by the river, and the getting to the river, even with the red glow of the flashlights, was not easy.

The rats stayed by their river. We could just barely hear them with the cans and wrappers, and when sleep did come I slept the dreams of a thief. I awoke to Limón in the hammock next to me, under the same mosquito net, whispering in Spanish and coaxing a scorpion into an empty pack of Newports with a white plastic spoon. It was almost cool in the circle, some sky visible through the layers of green tangle above, and the scorpion fighting that white spoon, its stinger tail tipping down repeatedly attacking the hard plastic with a clicking sound on.

"Limón, man. Please," I said rolling back towards him and wishing the scorpion had some color to it, anything, white even, or that Limón would hurry up and capture it already. He kept at it, ignoring me and making little spitting sounds and calling the scorpion little this and little that, till he closed the flip top of the Newport pack and said, "Shut the fuck up cause this is my project. Okay, shit?" He rolled out of the hammock and out from under the mosquito netting, dumping himself on the ground, where he began punching small holes in the cigarette pack with a pin so the scorpion could breathe. He whispered to me, "If you at-the-fuck-ease, I'll let you in on this and we could make some money. But you got to keep your mouth shut or you are completely out, shit."

The scouts didn't talk much about the rats, and there was no sign of them over by the river, but there were plenty all over our gear, little muddy rat footprints like Japanese writing saying the same thing over and over. Corporal Marty Jencks and Frankie Meadows played at being cowboy trackers, sniffing the air and then the rucksacks, saying the tracks smelled like shit. It was true: we all tried it out and when we smelled it started rubbing clean wet dirt on our rucks and rinsing them with quick splashes from the canteens. Everybody agreed that it must be pretty bad to have to be a river-living rat, but to have shit-smelling feet all day every day would just piss you off enough to be a real nuisance.

We ate the c-rats, which had held at the good temperature inside the rucks, and Platoon Daddy went off quiet with three accessory packs, but we saw him and yelled to watch out for Jake The Snake. He showed the machete up to the air and we wished some snake would just try and bite our Combat, squatting over the morning one.

Quinton and Collins talked loud enough for everyone to hear how they didn't have none of this the last time and that Platoon Daddy must be bringing us out far as Nicaragua, or some shit, where we were sure to run into rebels and Sandinistas.

The true part was that before, they hadn't come to the jungle with a Platoon Daddy who was maybe a little mixed up about coming up on his twenty cause a jungle's where he started from and where he got all the stories different than ours.

Platoon Daddy gave the day's operations order, which had nothing to do with the battalion's mission. He said "Fuck battalion," and that we stay as a unit going for a long walk in the jungle, sending bullshit transmissions reporting our location on up to higher. When the op order was finished, maps were folded away and all the soldiers moved for their web gear and rucks. Frankie Meadows stood in the center of the trail playing doofy, urging us to hurry up so that we can go and see what we can see, wearing a Margaret sweater.

Margaret sweaters belonged to Ski and were sent to him by this girl in Duluth, Minnesota—Margaret—who had seen Ski in her dad's copy of the *Army Times*. She had picked Ski out of a group picture of soldiers who were the guests at a convention of Polish American veterans. There were like fifty guys in the picture, which was not big, but it did list their names and units. Ski started getting letters. He answered them and then the sweaters started coming in. I'd never even seen him wear a sweater except the one red V neck one sometimes. She usually sent thin ones cause of Ski being in North Carolina and they were always brown because she thought, from the picture, that brown would go good on him. They came from the store in thick clear plastic and always, always, had a zipper in the front with a big ol' round pull ring. They were awful.

Ski tried to defend her and the sweaters for a while and once during her school vacation, Margaret, who we had only seen from the picture she had sent, comes to Ft. Bragg. Her mother and her stayed in a motel off post, where the mother says it's okay for Ski to be alone with Margaret in the room while she goes for a walk. Ski tells her that nobody walks on Bragg Boulevard except crazy people and hitchhiking GIs, and the mother winks and says just don't do everything at once.

Margaret's so happy that Ski's wearing one of the sweaters which he always threw out, but that we always got back out of the dumpster for the collection of them we kept in Hightower's room locked in a squad box. She's wanting for him to keep it on while they do stuff in the room. Ski told us that she definitely knew all about everything at once, and it was still daytime and he couldn't, but Margaret understood and took care of him in another way.

That weekend was hard on Ski. He brought Margaret and the mother by the company. We'd had a doper scout meeting about how he was going to have to wear a sweater and we owed it to him to mind ourselves in front of Margaret and her mother. We took Polaroids of them together and gave them a couple, keeping one for ourselves. Ski brought them over to look at the Airborne Museum, but Ft. Bragg's not really fixed up for guests and seeing it that way, through their eyes, was depressing everyone when we watched Ski drive off to show them the Peachtree Mall. We had wanted the Polaroid to torture Ski with, but it wasn't going to work. It was too sad: Ski in between and tall over these two ladies, their arms around his waist, and the picture showing three people trying hard to look like they knew each other and that this visit was a normal thing, really.

The scouts sat on the steps of the barracks and Marty Jencks tore up the picture. I'm sure we didn't know what was wrong with us on a Saturday and why we were going to head out to Hay Street early. That night we stayed in one bar pounding, almost the whole night. Ski joined us late saying he left them and wasn't going back.

It was okay to come from a mess of a place like Margaret and her mother. A mother that lets a GI have a throw with her daughter who looks in an Army magazine for a guy to love far away. We were all some ways familiar with whatever it was that drove these two women to come all that way and then say about how they couldn't really afford it, and not just to Ski himself, but to us his pals just as a something to talk about after the introductions.

It was okay to be from that kind of place, but to see it land in your own fort and not even be blood was not. It did get talked about late in the night. We agreed that it sort of felt like it did when a buddy had said fuck it, and surprise reenlisted at the last minute, and took whatever they gave him.

We didn't mention by name any of the guys who had done that, and there had been a few. We just stayed talking about the frightening understanding that some guys reenlisted—gave up another three or four more years—just to keep away from their own versions of what had come to visit Ski. That we might become those some guys, someday, was left alone.

We'd all done it once already. Raised our right hands and swore to what the man in the uniform told you to, just to get away from some mess. Those messes happen with your people while you are still tied to them, and make you grow up bent, faster, and in ways you'd never plan. You raised a hand to get away, and maybe keep raising it every few years to stay away. If they came and found you anyway, at least you'd have some Army stories.

We had left Ski alone about Margaret sweaters after that, let them stay down in the dumpster when he took the collection out of

Hightower's room and threw them away. But here was Frankie Meadows wearing one in the middle of a jungle path, telling us all to hurry up, pointing to the early morning sounds coming from the birds as if they were getting the jump on us. Maybe what he was trying to tell us was that this morning, in this place so crazy and different, no depressing mess would get us even when wearing a Margaret sweater.

What stunned us at first was that Frankie Meadows had thought far enough in advance to now be standing in the jungle by a river in a foreign country wearing a Margaret sweater. The hilariousness of Margaret sweaters themselves was brought on by Platoon Daddy, who said, "Damn, if Ol' Sugar Britches ain't vectored in and found Ski in the jungle."

That day of the Margaret sweater in the jungle the guys learned to like the speed. The way it came on fast and a little too hard, playing out nicely for the rest of the day.

Following Platoon Daddy, we snaked along the path that ran by the river, sometimes breaking inland towards deep jungle where the path faded; then it'd be map and compass, slow stepping, vines whipping back, hills and black palm everywhere, keeping a soldier's mind on the next step. The heat coming on that guys who always used Kool-Aid powder in their canteens were bumming sips of plain water, their mix had gone past warm and difficult to keep down. Later, at a halt, K-bar knives were drawn and pants dropped. The blades sliced through skivvies and sent flying, where they landed on the ground and up in trees, as trail markers green and white. T-shirts, too, were modified. Sleeves gone and then cropped up to the chest, some wearing just these under their rucks and web gear, stowing the cammie shirts till the bare arm skin was whipped on too badly.

The jungle thinned before a clearing, and spikes of light came down all around. Platoon Daddy signaled us into a traveling overwatch, and my platoon passed through and into hard sun and stood on yellowed elephant grass. From there we could see two birds drop from separate perches to fly at each other with no squawk, not a sound, then only a mess of black feathers beating wildly at the crashing. With one hand covering the sun, the scouts watched as one bird tipped up against the blue sky and across a white cloud before it was lost to the sun, the other turning in lazy circles, waiting. Another crash, then the two lost altitude, their wings beating out a loud report like the flapping of wet sails.

When they separated the scouts cursed like we'd been balancing them ourselves, and the birds kept at it, one climbing, the other staying low, circling, and more crashing, falling and flying together.

"Them birds just like me! Don't know whether to fuck or fight!" That was Hartel clear across from the left flank at the trailing edge of the traveling overwatch.

Platoon Daddy would have let us watch the birds for a long time, but there was Hartel scaring them off. We didn't need to say anything about it, the uselessness of trying to tell Hartel anything keeping us quiet even as his voice continued over across the clearing, comparing himself to birds.

That night, again, we slept by the river. Hightower took all the guard shifts, refusing to be relieved after he swore individually on his mother and all his sisters that he'd seen a crab come up and rip a c-ration can in half right in front of him. He saw it as a personal warning from the crab, since he was a Pisces and had the jewelry to go with it.

Several times that night, while we hung low in the hammocks, a dull red light popped on across the circle. Each time it stayed on only a few seconds. It was Garcia from New Mexico, I was sure, looking at his homemade tattoo laid in by his cousin many years before, the ink fading and the letters wide and misshapen on his forearm, but still reading clear: *Mi Vida Loco*. He hadn't ever tired of it, and when things were happening, like this crazy kind of shit out there in the jungle, Garcia would be found looking down at it and shaking his head. It had become a kind of show that Garcia put on for us, and he seemed obsessed with finding confirmation for what was written on his arm, his eyes wide with expectation.

When the light came on again, I whispered, "Garcia?"

The light went out.

"Yeah, man?"

I laughed a little, and so did some other guys. Then the light came on again, this time just for our benefit, and when it went out I said it.

"Good night."

Cause we mostly never said and it would be nice sometimes.

"Good night."

———

Late the next day, the permanent party soldiers came at us down the trail and fanned out on the flanks without warning. Maybe the birds and animals hadn't sounded that alarm cause they assumed we all knew each other. Or maybe cause they'd been talking to themselves about both sets of soldiers on the trail all day and were sick of us, bored, and just letting us pass.

The soldiers were all wearing flat green jungle fatigues, the pants lashed tight to their legs—making them appear skinnier than they were—and they *were* skinny. Could've nicknamed them all "Tent Peg." Their faces were drawn and heavily cammied, not just with the green and loam, but with wide stripes and shapes of black cammie. The black isn't issued, you have to buy it yourself, and lots about these guys made me think they made this kind of cammie themselves, cooked it up from leaves and roots that were boiled and then dried. When we all come up on each other, a young staff sergeant of theirs came forward, the rest of them at the halt and then to one knee. Half of them tended to their cammie jobs with small mirrors cupped easily by one palm, while the others looked out with both hands on M-16s that had no red blank adapters screwed into the barrels. There were no green drive-on rags flowing from their heads, just one canteen hanging off their web gear, two ammo pouches, one compass—none of the mess we carried. All that shit: extra knives, ammo pouches from WW II, mini-aid bags, more knives, butt packs full of pogey bait, drive-on rags you're only supposed to get from a medic if you've been injured, but that we bought at Ranger Joe's off post and wore under patrol caps, around the neck. Ski tied them around each wrist like a rocker. Platoon Daddy would laugh at us sometimes, and say if we were willing to hump it and it didn't make a noise, then we could keep it. Always adding that in a real world situation, we'd be jettisoning that shit and leaving a trail of it for the enemies to follow and kill us in our sleep. We were trying for a look that was like the covers of the mercenary paperbacks we read, or the real stories by Vietnam guys who had all been fucked over and lived to suffer about it, and we wished the same for ourselves so bad.

These guys looked like soldiers. They were silent and hard to find again if you looked away. There didn't seem to be any fuck around about these guys. They wore no unit patches, no glory badges. They weren't SF, weren't nothing special ops about them. If they were plain legs soldiering hard without the glory, we'd be ashamed. We wanted them to be paratroopers from the one permanent party airborne battalion the Army had here. But they weren't, they were high speed, low drag and even gotten the extra weight off their own bodies to be that way.

Their staff sergeant came towards our Platoon Daddy with his eyes fixed on the 173rd Airborne patch and it was the patch that he spoke to, saying that he knew we weren't lost, but what were we doing out here? He was careful to smile at the patch after he asked. Platoon Daddy flopped an arm across the staff sergeant's shoulder, calling him young soldier, and they went down the trail a bit. Platoon Daddy coaxed a laugh out of him twice as they bent over a map. We swept the area with our eyes in five meter increments looking for the soldiers, and found them prone all around us, 360 security. Me and some of our guys began picking out the torn leaves from under our gear. If you wanted to go through the trouble, it was good soldiering to look like a bush back at Bragg, but here it worked real good to be a stick.

They rose straight up to standing, as a unit, and walked off without even looking at us. Our guys shifted their feet, propped weapons over to the other hip, and talked in twos and threes about guess we ain't supposed to be around here.

"Hasta la bye-bye," said Limón, as the staff sergeant brushed by him. The man stopped for just a second, and then walked off behind his men without looking back.

That whole week we stayed as a platoon and when we rested or lay down for the night, Hartel got put on permanent radio duty and had to run up and down high ground, with the radio giving fake grid coordinates. So when we walked into that village, it was the whole platoon. In Egypt, or in the swamps and mountains in states south of Ft. Bragg, and even once north in the Smokies past Asheville, smaller groups of us had done this same thing: walked right into a place where people were living, and they looked at you like you're the problem. Looked at you like you should be in *National Geographic*.

This time, I guess they looked a lot like you'd think people would look living in the jungle, this day and age, with huts made out of trees and leaves helped a whole lot by cardboard with the names of

Spanish companies printed on them. The generator—there's always a generator, no matter where in the world you found these people—ran a television and some work lights. Which messed you up cause you're ready to treat these people living in the middle of the jungle like they're different, but there they are watching reruns of *Mannix*.

They had television and T-shirts, all the same T-shirts that said:

THE REHOBOTH BEACH DAYCARE CENTER'S
1975 ANNUAL PICNIC AND FAIR
REHOBOTH BEACH, DELAWARE

And there were clowns holding balloons on the T-shirt, too.

Hightower said, he just didn't understand anything anymore, and ran out of the little village back along the path. He sat down in the middle of it, and it turns out he'd been there—not the actual annual picnic and fair, but Rehoboth Beach in Delaware. He yelled to us that he wasn't coming back over and I wished I had a good reason to go sit by him till it was time to go. This feeling came on especially when I saw the two men kneeling and holding a huge white bird down to the ground and a third man hacking at it with a machete. The giant bird's long legs—longer than an M-16 and skinny like long white birch branches—still quivering along with all the hacking. I moved behind the men as they hacked so's their backs blocked the rest of the kill, not wanting to see its head, or its face if it had one. The guys talked about it later. Said maybe it was a pelican.

We also talked about how come nobody in this country wanted to talk to Limón in Spanish. Limón said that Garcia tried, and they wouldn't talk to him either. Garcia said he didn't care, but that the people in the village did have pictures of the Virgin in their little homes and that was good for them. We wondered when the dogs would show up again.

Someone said about how these locals didn't seem to care about our weapons. Somebody else asked: would you, with big red blank adapters screwed into the barrels?

Whenever we'd run into people living where we didn't expect it, they never cared about our weapons, blank adapters or no. They would always recognize Platoon Daddy as the leader, and would ignore him with more respect. Once, the Egyptian dune people had offered Platoon Daddy a seat on a bed. Twice, he replied with the same response to the men who gestured for him to sit.

"No. No. Oh, no. No, thank you. Y'all be fucking each other on that."

If they understood, you knew they were thinking worse about us, and probably called it even.

We'd hadn't ever been lost when this happened. Just following a path or a compass to someplace else, and wound up where people live.

The smell in these places always the same. Under all the different smells, there was one like spoiled orange juice, only it's urine from their piss spot: burnt by the sun and maybe generations old, and too close to their living quarters. This is always found when people are living where you don't expect.

Later that day, when Platoon Daddy let us break for chow, Limón told me his scorpion had died from overfeeding. That he found another so fast bothered us, especially cause Platoon Daddy hadn't allowed us to use the hammocks the night before, and wouldn't for the rest of the mission. We'd have to hump right until dark and then lay the poncho down and drape the mosquito netting over us to sleep in the dark, with one arm hooked through the rucksack straps and the other holding your weapon. You had to surrender to the fact that every little itch on the back of your legs or high up on your back was probably something alive.

The last days of that week in the jungle we stayed with the girls' speed but left the red dope alone, barely smoked cigarettes. The air itself under all that green almost thick like a drag. We were liking our fast movement through the jungle, Platoon Daddy picking up the pace every day, and still trying to teach us how to listen. We only got resupplied twice that whole week, once by Huey, the one we'd come in on with the crew chief Platoon Daddy'd talked to. That resupply got dropped at the edge of the tiniest piece of open ground before we were there to see it fall, so's it took a long time to find. The second time, Corporal's Quinton and Collins took a full squad to scoot down the river right after first light to meet the resupply boat, over where we were supposed to be operating. They didn't catch up to us till after we bedded down so we went a whole day with no food.

Otherwise for those five days, we were pretty slick out there, far away from the battalion. The villagers let us fill canteens half full from the big pot they had boiling, and the permanent party staff sergeant gave Platoon Daddy two sets of grid coordinates where canvas lister bags hung full and condensating. Platoon Daddy called higher and told them that us scouts didn't need no more resupply, we were moving fast, too fast for anything they had for us. He said we'd already reconed whole sectors three times over waiting on them, but we had to move, godamnit over and out. We never came close to having to drop the little blue purification tablets in a canteen of river water and wait two hours before we drank it. One box of C's was lasting a whole day and then some. Even though we moved as a platoon, and that's noisy, Platoon Daddy was getting us used to the jungle by keeping us all together, but also sharp and alert cause we were totally disobeying orders. He was teaching by fucking off, teaching us slow, maybe the way he wished it had all come to him.

On the last day, when we separated into teams to arrive at the rallying point, I was put on compass for my team. I remember standing on no path with my guys sitting and smoking all around me, and I'm staring hard at the compass, holding a map, directions and grids flying around inside my head, nothing sticking, and wishing all I had to do was walk under all those leaves and vines and trust another's calculations. Because to stop and take a knee, laying the map out, with a protractor and doing the math, was to try and will myself into being someone else. Someone who wasn't always fighting off the panic that came with any task, worried that if I failed, it would set me aside.

The guys, smoking now, left me alone to work it out. The taunts of "It's too eaaassy" would come later, much later, after completion. I am grateful that most every time around men when I've needed to perform a thinking task, when many things were at stake, something has come to make me like another, and with a little grace I come through, just needing extra time and exhausted. Taken care of like an addled, well-meaning little brother.

That far into the jungle, the smell of living and rotting plants compete, and any little piece of jungle lying fallen on the ground holds my attention better than the map and compass, and then over from the radio—left behind a tree by my resting, patient and still smoking pals—comes a transmission. Not the tree speaking, but I do sympathize with those that get it that bad, just a corporal's voice on the alternate frequency, directed to me.

"Yo, Talented. What's your major malfunction? Over."

10

New York and Indian Anna

I keep my body nice for the expensive ones. My super's got a little gym rigged up in the basement, and when I'm on ship, it's push-ups, pull-ups, sit-ups, dips. Me and the guys who work the tugs and like to stay fit, we do circuits of these exercises, running around encouraging each other, and it's quite a sight especially at night: the boat slow down a river or channel, us under the stars or city lights if we're that close, running the deck, yelling, grown men on the water at follow the leader.

The expensive ones have to see all of me, touch, spend time. Four times a year I'll go, more if the tug is pulling long trips. I don't have many bills. Dress up for these nice places, and they can always tell just by looking that I don't need to take a shower before we go to the room. I make the call from home, and take a cab to the place. If they know me or it's a real good place, I don't have to call again from the corner, but these places have to move around, so sometimes I do have to make that second call, even though I'd rather not. It's a precaution, they tell me.

Most of them are over on the east side by all the embassies. I sit on the couch, the whole place decorated like the furniture ads at the back of the television section and the women introduce themselves and I choose. On the nights right before and after I go, I'll scare myself with nightmares where I know all the women on the couch: the daughter of the man who owns the deli, wives of guys on the tug, my super's sister, women from the past, the champion lady pool player from over on Eighth.

I like when the girls comment that I'm in good shape, and that I'm nice. Not like some of the others. They tell me about them, and I listen cause that's what tells me how to be a good customer. Don't do what the other guys do and I get to be the good customer. I don't kid myself about going out with them, even if I see the same one several times in a row and they give me a number that's different from the place, saying they won't be here much longer, but would like to continue seeing me—they mean seeing me just like they're doing now.

2:00 A.M. and it's time for the girls out on the avenue, the streets west from 24th to 29th. I'll walk down to there through the Pasture, the low 40s and 30s on 10th Ave., where they get sent when they're too ragged for the twenties, too dope-scarred, lips too burnt up by the pipe, too gaunt from the sickness so it can't be hidden. I recognize some of them and they me. I travel through the Pasture. Never around.

There's always the same one under the bus shelter. White girl, foreign, trying hard to look like a late-night office worker, gray raincoat with a belt, pocketbook held with both hands, scarf over her head. But eyes so heavy with paint that a blink takes too long, like maybe she'll just keep them shut now.

Wherever she came from, she brought a lot of it over with her. Buses don't run much at this time, but still they come. More than her customers. She looks at the bus coming up the avenue, and rummages in her shiny black pocketbook to look for nothing before closing it. The clasp catches with a hard solid click, which I can hear perfectly it's so quiet now. She steps from beneath the shelter for a few paces up the street, watching her shoes, and turns on one—a spin really—back towards the stop after the bus passes.

The pros can always tell when somebody has sold it before. They say that. Even when they're working a street and an expensive green car gets stuck at a light and there's fancy people in it—they say they can tell that the woman in the passenger seat sitting up straight and looking dead ahead has sold it before. It's a certain look. They say it marks you for always, even if you've only sold it once. They say they can tell.

Out of the Pasture and I'm looking for a red minivan with Mississippi plates. The women ride now, some of them, and I like it in the parking lot after giving the attendant a five. When we're parked, facing out, their hair falls in my lap. Tonight, I've circled the streets from 20th to 30th on 9th and 10th avenues many times, and the red minivan still hasn't shown.

"Hey, Walking Boy."

A lot of them know me, and the newer ones take time to tell me that you really need a car unless you can get one of them pretty girls riding in cars and vans to pick you up. I listen politely, and look for the few who will throw anywhere, walking till one says, "Come on, walking boy."

Behind a dumpster—in an alley, or under the backboard of the basketball court—but there's always a dumpster with a lid to put up for extra privacy. She's on her haunches before me and then she's standing, her hand pumping and the cheap dry rubber will thwap up and down cause I like to finish, hands on their breasts—costs extra—with them talking, working me towards finished.

"Let it go, baby. I know. Yee-ahh. Yee-ahh. Fill up that tip, baby. I got you. You know I do. That's it. Oh, yee-ah. I know."

I say thank you and she turns on her heels and clicks away. Months before there was one named Cat, whose hand would go to my cheek before she walked. I take the rubber off slow, wipe myself with the Wet-Nap, and I walk.

I had a girlfriend for a while. She was an upstate Mohawk Indian and I met her at 4:30 in the morning on the N train. She was reading *Huckleberry Finn*. She had a tattoo on her back that said STEVIE'S GIRL over blue and red flowers. The tattoo had a circle of scars around it like someone tried to lift it up with a paring knife. I don't ask about things. Anna cleaned office buildings and was trying for her GED. She had left her people and never said why. I assumed it had something to do with Stevie.

I woke up one morning to her sitting at the end of her bed staring at me. She said her brother wanted to meet me and have a talk. By myself, I had to take a train to Elton, NY. From the station I took a thirty-three-dollar train ride to a place where the rural route stopped and a long stretch of road began. The cabby reached back, unlocked my door, held out his hand and said, "This is as far as I go." I headed down this dirt road which had weeping willows hanging over each side, thinking how much Anna looked like a Gilmore. I did some juvy time with a couple of Gilmores at Sockanosset, the Rhode Island State Reform School.

The Gilmore family was from Chapachet, the town outside Arctic. They were Blackfoot Indian, Black, and French Canadian. The two I knew were scarier than all get out, and there were more of them, and the place they came from, though I never saw it, became, and still is, to me, the scariest place in the world.

At Sockanosset, we were housed in cottages lined with cots. The Gilmores would trade stories about home after lights-out, making some of the younger criminals cry. The Gilmores kept a roster of Duck-Duck opponents. Duck-Duck was grasping a bowie knife in your right hand and having it wrapped around your fist with duct tape. With your left hand you did the Soul Brother shake with the Gilmore while the other Gilmore bound those hands with the rest of the roll of duct tape. And then you went at it. No stabbing. Only slashing. If you refused, they came for you at night with a small can of Ronson lighter fluid and a gag. First they would burn off your pubic hair and then would burn small amounts of lighter fluid from between your legs, snickering madly as your groin became engulfed in a light blue flame.

I remembered the Gilmores as night fell, and kicked at the dirt road, making my way slowly under the hanging willows. I had been sent back to the St. Jerome School for Boys outside St. Louis before my name ever found its way to the top of the Gilmores' list.

Twenty years later, I felt like the Gilmores knew this dirt road.

The dirt road began to twist and turn, then dropped. I was meant to turn left off the road at the top of a hill, where the willows follow a path leading into the forest. At the crest of the hill I saw that the path was lined with burning trash cans. The moon was bright enough that the road seemed lit by streetlights, and the trash cans threw off sparks like the vats of a steel mill. As I moved closer I could count six burning trash cans, and each has a group of people around them. The path seemed to go into the woods for a long time.

At the top of the hill, my right foot pivoted in the dirt road and I executed a very military left face onto the gravel path. The groups around the fires were all men and they marked my arrival. They were speaking the talk I used to hear from the Gilmores and their relatives on visiting days—Indian, French, African—I don't know, like too many M sounds. As I pass the third trash can, I stop and ask for Anna's brother, Pasco Taylor. A firelit face with gold teeth and red curls stops the M talk and tells me he's by the house, keep going. He pulls on his sweatshirt hood and laughs go round the fire—something about Anna—as I continue up the hill.

All the faces I see look beaten, like someone was trying to beat the black or Indian out of them. And it looks like it was done with a pipe—not a baseball bat, a pipe. In these faces lit by the fires, I remember every beating I ever took like it was one long one, how a pipe feels against bone cheek, how I become softer with every blow, soft on top, with hard angles to hit underneath. After I pass the fires I can make out the house, which is A-framed with cutout trim like a Swiss chalet.

Pasco steps off the narrow porch and I know it's him because he looks like Anna and Anna looks like a Gilmore, and the Gilmores look like the dune people in Egypt, and it goes on. He's smiling and holding a plastic milk jug filled with a clear liquid. He is tall with the bulk of a man who can move as he wants. I say, "Hello, Pasco," and he tips up a long drink, his arm taking its good time returning the jug to his side. Looking through me he says, "Come on this way. Let's talk the talk."

We walk down the path and I notice a Marine Force Recon tattoo on the back of his shoulder. He isn't wearing a shirt. I think about showing him the Airborne tattoo under my sleeve, and telling him about how I was originally going to get mine put on where he put his. But I know when I've been trumped in the old soldier way—Pasco having been special ops and me a jumping grunt—so I just walk. He takes another pull off the jug, hands it to me, and then sits Indian-style. After sticking my nose close to the opening I hand him back the jug without drinking from it. I expected shine, but this smells sweeter, thicker. Pasco shrugs and mutters, "Won't drink with me" towards the ground. We are in a grove of moonlit trees: a circle of trees, and a swing set is at the edge of the circle. Pasco speaks, but the sound comes from and hovers above the tops of the trees, "When you fuck her does she fuck you back?"

I look down and towards the clearing. Lying on the ground are two pig sticker knives and a length of rope with a knot the size of a fist at each end.

He notices me staring hard, and asks, "You know how to play?"

"It looks familiar," I respond, immediately regretting the way it almost sounded cocky.

"Yes, Anna said you knew some people. From before. Some Narragansets, Blackfoots, some kind of fucking state of Rhode Island cooperators."

His words that followed were soft and instructive. Pasco did not bother with a history lesson, instead he brought me up-to-date with the operations of his organization, who were an offshoot of the American Indian Movement.

"We have found the need for an In-ci-dent," he said, washing down the word with a sloshing drink from the jug.

His tribe was divided three ways over the idea that a casino might be built on their land: there were those who believed that their blood, from one one-quarter to full, was like a guaranteed lottery ticket, those who opposed a casino on tribal land—Pasco spat, ". . . like all these drunks, fat women, and dogs are preserving our heritage"—and Pasco's bunch, "the righteous consenters," who would gladly turn over a few square miles for their cause.

"Lawyers, guns, and money, Bro," he said, with another swallow for punctuation. "You're lucky, aren't you? I mean most all the time, yes? I know this: you are lucky now. Lucky that I like to drink more than I like to fight, but that is an old story for me. . . . Man, I almost said, *And for my people.*"

At this he laughed a little. The laugh of the truly sad, born sad, that resonates in the chest and lets you know it's okay to believe them.

"You like to watch me drink?"

I felt the need to speak, to head off the return of anger which was held calmly in his voice, to keep him talking about Indians, not me, not Anna.

"Shut up. Sit down," he whispered before I spoke. "Did I have to break a state seal to drink from this jug? No, my uncle sold it to me."

Pasco's head began to shoot up from his left shoulder and towards the moon, and a song of words with too many M's warbled from a mouth wet with liquor.

He stopped only to say, "John Truesdale song."

I wanted to drink with him, tell him I had heard all about the A.I.M. guys from Ogalala when I had all the time with my book and letter. That I had once been tight with a set called the Island Boys, and that my own blood had bought me no favors. This kind of talk from me to Pasco, on this night, could only come from drink. Later I would be thankful for my silence and clear head, imagining Pasco just watching me try to get next to him, giving me just enough room to piss him off.

Pasco's song settled into almost a ballad, a pop song, and the rhythm now made it nice to follow. This is not saying much, but it was the happiest Indian song I had ever heard.

I watched him sing towards the moon and the stars, sitting in his blue jeans styled with red thread on the pockets. The tattoo on the back of his shoulder looks riddled with scars like the ones around Anna's "Stevie's Girl" tattoo. Her other tattoo, it also had the scars around it. The one of a kitten playing with a ball of string. It was on her hip, and during our first overnight together we stared at each other as I stroked the tattoo, my fingers falling in and out of the scars. Finally, she told me about how, during the beginning of Pasco's involvement in the movements, he had convinced all those around him to begin the process of digging out the tattoos, the white boy marks. "It's okay," he had told her, "it can happen over time."

Pasco finished his song, and said, "I hope you like it. I sang it for you. It's a good song about all the people who try too fucking hard."

Like the Island Boys went, like some of my relatives did too, he was now, unlike ten minutes ago, very drunk. A wrinkled pouch of Red Man chewing tobacco was in his hand, and as he pushed the long leaf into his mouth, he gave me a smile and said, "What, you never seen an ironic Indian before?"

He reached over for a pig sticker knife, then another, and stuck one in front of me and one in front of him, like gravestones.

Wavering on his knees, he smoothed out an area of dirt for me while speaking his words with care. "Won't drink with me. Won't fight me. Mister, you will sleep by me."

"But I'm not tired," I said, looking for him to confirm my quick assumption that he meant beddy-bye time.

"Oh, so now you want to talk?"

I watched him as he lay down, his face turned away.

"Anna told me about you. That you are a good man. So I know that you understand how it can be. Good night."

With that he spit out a long stream of tobacco, and fell to sleep.

It might have been an hour or a few minutes that passed until I followed him, but before my eyes shut I felt his arm flop across my back. Soon after that, I heard men approach and depart.

I too left, for sleep full of safe dreams where the dirt was familiar and where the earliest memories of an imagined older sibling were revisited.

I awoke fast, like I had something good to do. Sitting up, I wiped the dirt from my mouth and listened to how the birds had turned Pasco's song of last night into a flying-around-in-the-morning number.

Waking up in the morning to a place you have only seen at night is a neat trick to play on yourself, as long as you haven't been drinking. The grove of trees was in tight focus, and the seats of the swing hung on chains like thin girders. I liked being there very much.

The ground where Pasco had slept was smoothed out, and the knife which had served as his headboard was gone without a trace. Above where my head had lain there was a row of objects which struck me as the booty of a short and strange scavenger hunt: a blue and white flecked tin cup of black coffee with a test tube of milk leaning against it, a high-protein bar, and the other pig sticker knife laid out on the ground. Under the knife, written in the dirt, was the word YOURS.

Food tastes better in the country, so I took my time with the protein bar and the coffee, which was the same temperature as the morning breeze which blew by me. I tipped the milk down in one shot, its cold traveling fast towards my feet. I drank the coffee black. Platoon Daddy used to have it that way and called it Barefoot.

The knife slipped into my boot, and I walked the tin cup and test tube back up towards the A-frame house, where I placed them on the bottom step of the porch. A sandwich bag scooted down the steps and past me on some new little wind. I snagged it only to drop it fast and back on its way. What got on my hands and what gave it weight was still sticky. Glue.

There was no one around, just a few more bags stuck low in a bush, and a small pile blown up against the foundation of the house, and I followed the willows and the path back down to the road. It took me all day to walk to the train station, which I reached at sundown. What I recall from that walk was how it made willows my favorite tree, and that for the miles I passed them that day, I never saw or heard the moving water they need to crowd a landscape.

After my trip upstate I spoke to Anna one last time.

All your stories, and you couldn't even drink one sip with him? Just once, for me? You didn't fight him, not one pass. Your big stories. Now I've heard stories. No. No. Not from Pasco. He just said you were harmless. Harmless. I didn't prepare you? Where did you think you were going? Oh, oh, and now I've been on the phone telling stories. That's not how it works.

Her mother and cousins had told her I was not the man for her.

Since then, I have decided that whatever it was I failed at had more to do with Anna having a very strange family than it did with any kind of Indian tradition.

She was only reading the book for some GED class anyway.

The cars are backed up from 29th to 30th. Up 10th Avenue, down 11th.

I pass the men in their cars, only the older ones' eyes meet mine. The young ones keep their heads down, until the traffic lurches ahead and their heads bounce side to side, searching the swirl of girls out working tonight for the one just dropped off, the one just now stepped out of an alley, the one they've never seen before. The embarrassment, the fear of being seen, vanished in their search for her.

I'm long finished for tonight.

"Walking Boy's finished."

Taken care of.

A daredevil works a guy right in his car under a streetlight on 27th. He's leaning back, like in a recliner after a meal, and her head is bobbing fast, fist jacking in time, and she is having to work too hard, too long, making it a good guess that it's past four in the morning, the bars have closed, and this guy one of the recently departed, too old for the after-hours, and too drunk to come nice for the pro.

On 30th, just off 11th, a woman has left a car. She is standing with her back to the passenger side, the door still open, and she's waiting for her breasts to settle down and smoothing on her white stretchy skirt. Now ready, she wheels about on her heels and begins to shout.

"Don't be pushing on my head, Motherfucker! Told you about that shit. Chicken-bone dick motherfucker, I told you about pushing on my head—Don't be pushing on my motherfucking head!"

The man has started his car, quick. She slams the door and leaning on the hood with her left hand keeps up with the car as the man rolls towards the light trying to play its change from red to green. Her right arm winds up high in the air—something cupped in the palm—arching down—a softball pitch—and the hand slams into the door. Even over by me I can hear a splat buried into the bang of metal. The spent condom plastered to the side door.

"Take that back to Riverdale, Motherfucker!"

The light pops and the man's gone for the bridge. She's lost and found her balance, composure, and walks towards me. I clap.

"You like that, Walking Boy?"

"Yes, ma'am."

"Shit. Chicken-bone motherfucker. Hey, ain't you been done?"

"Long time. I'm walking."

"Heard that. You better get. Squad's out like crazy."

"Good night."

"Good night, Walking Boy."

Just in from the corner of 30th and 10th, a man is up on a loading dock platform, his back braced against the door. Two girls on him—yanking, fondling—one standing, one squatting. Whispers. "Yeah, baby. Don't die on me," and lower, quieter, "No. Nothing but keys and mints."

Walk closer, right up on them. The man's eyes are shut tight and he is ignoring the view from the platform. Past the hair and earrings of the one standing, and over the curved back of the one crouching, are the tops of low buildings, 11th. Ave, the river, and above him the whitened gray night sky. He's feeding his lower lip into and back out through his teeth, in and out. The girls have seen me and continue, until something else spooks them and they leave the man leaning into the large door of that loading dock. His hanging shirt covering him to mid thigh, pants and drawers collapsed to his ankles. His back arches, his eyes stay shut, short breaths now, and he remains there alone. Two other girls join me at the crossing and the one to the other:

"Damn, they stripped him."

That man, like me, probably a veteran of these nights, with all except his girl money in his shoe.

Walk east to be away from this whole town within the city at night, and through the first residential area the security lights pop on over the stoops at my steps for their appointed seconds, leaving a string of strong fluorescents burning in my wake. The bright trail leading away from all my girlfriends.

The wives of the guys on the tug used to try and fix me up—no disasters, no hard feelings. Just didn't work out. They stopped asking, but I still get invited to things, their times, and I'll go just often enough not to being taken for rude.

Back west on 11th. Close to my home. Coffee and egg sandwich at once in the mouth can, if at the bridges or under the open of the parks, rush a story on. The temptation to buy an egg sandwich at the corner, where Hamid, behind the counter will cook for me with no problem about the hour. Waiting, I imagine Hamid asking me about the promise to walk until I've told myself the story all the way through.

The promise being made only to myself, I could walk across the street, put the keys in the locks and wait down morning by the window. Go back on my word and wake up knowing the story is still there, quiet and untouched. Not spoken. Unheard.

Wouldn't think of it.

The nights and early mornings at sea, I can play with my story. Don't worry about telling it all the way through cause with the views off the tug, I can pretend that there is still more to come. Another Anna held in days ahead, or some southern port in the middle of a long haul and I walk after some good-byes and thank yous, duffel on my shoulder, into a new city.

Moving onto 11th Avenue, my promise to tell being stronger than the pull towards home. This neighborhood remains salty. Old-timers retired in the booths at the Munson or Market diners, where the waiters still wear the white jackets, calling anything east of 11th, maybe 10th, "Inland." Small groups of these boatmen live in three buildings in a line, each separated by a taxi garage. Men who took the steady work with the tugs rather than scramble up and down the coast looking for a merchant ship before the expiration date on a National Shipping Card turns over. No, these men stayed with the boats, which are different than ships, ships being a vessel of some gross tons that need towing or that Navy aircraft carrier permanently docked down the street and visited as a museum.

They worked the boats and now stay way west in this city, knowing the Tranies seated across late night at the Market Diner, asking after their well-being. They offer condolences to the same girls walking into the Munson late morning with horrendous hangovers. Keeping up, knowing their names till they disappear forever.

There is open space here on 11th Avenue. Sky, and the water is just across the highway. New car lots, Mexican music stores, places where people call far away to home from rows of phones separated by dry-wall partitions, and a huge all-night ping-pong hall with wide webs of netting over and along the sides of each table, which blurs the action for the watcher at the window. Third-shift workers and light sleepers, at fifteen tables, and it's dense layers of sound, ticka-tocka, ticka-tocka, ticka-tocka, a yell, and paddles thrown down hard. Caring about a game, which is perhaps a better way to spend the night.

A street off the avenue, between two tenements, and below a wide piece of fence, run the railroad tracks. Quiet, and littered over.

I walked there once. On a night filled with snow and lightning, I bought cigarettes, and along those tracks I traveled out of the city far enough to stand in the middle of a spot where the signals still flashed. Red, steady yellow, and green, many sets of tracks, and one circular, not one train in sight.

Inland.

11

Back–Platoon Daddy Is Gone–Mr. Big

Haunting–Cherry–Fireflies–Corvette

After Panama, after Kansas, and Air Assault School, the scouts set-tled back into Bragg for a long stay put. Platoon Daddy was gone, retired now, and Mr. Big was everywhere.

We'd brought him back some M-60 ammo from Kansas, called the number, talked to a woman who said she'd tell him we called, and waited for him to contact us just like he'd said. A happy-sounding kid called the barracks like he was an old friend asking to speak to any of the scouts. A cherry from the Anti-Tank platoon took the call, and when Ski spoke to this kid, he was practically yelling he was so happy, and said to meet him at the Pop-A-Top next Friday after pay-day. We did and told this civilian, a few years younger than us, what we had for Mr. Big.

Before we even got our beers, he was out the door and then returned, telling us to follow him out back. There in the parking lot was Mr. Big, wedged into the passenger seat of a VW station wagon. We squatted as he had motioned for us to do, and Mr. Big informed us that we must be out of our military motherfucking minds if we called him down for some piddling-assed snapped-off belts of machine gun ammo. That we'd better get it right. Better have lots more for him when we called again and that better be soon. Dumb-asses, he called us. Then the civilian kid got in the driver's side and started up the car and took off without having to be told.

That night back on post, late, after the Hay and the IHOP, we pitched the ammo up high through the open hatchback of Ski's Gremlin. The short belts sending a few rounds loose and clinking out along the black hard top of Longstreet Road as they landed.

"Fuck 'em. That fat fuck."

Decided and said it many times that night.

And we did forget about him, or at least stopped talking about him. Even stopped telling stories about the guys who left him to us, Corporals Quinton and Collins. The cherry and newer scouts would have to hear them from the others.

There had been a big surprise send-off planned for Platoon Daddy.

The scouts had rented Mackeller's Lodge on post, and asked Sergeant Major if he'd come and please tell any of his other buddies from the 1/73rd. Sergeant Major said there was a bunch of times being planned for our Platoon Daddy, but he liked what we were doing and would try his best.

We'd given Platoon Daddy his plaque at the morning formation of his last day, and when he had accepted it in front of the platoon, he promised he'd be by that Saturday to say good-bye. He said this quiet and without looking up from the gun blue plaque that was inscribed with all our names, all his awards and places of duty, the 82nd and 173rd patches in the corners, combat infantryman's rifle and master jump wings dead center.

When he didn't show up back at the company later that day, we left word with the CQ that we were all at Mackellers Lodge. We had some of the beers and ate up some of the cookout, remembered him, and maybe were more of a platoon than ever.

When he had been with us, we worked at finding the small ways we were very much like him; we'd have been just like the Platoon Daddy if it weren't for those particular years he had on us. Now, it was his absence that showed up in the quiet of that day, by the picnic tables outside the big log cabin–style lodge. It gave us time to think of all the ways he was different than us. Mostly, it was that we were divided from him by everything unspoken that comes with a combat-side 173rd patch. Everything that made it perfectly okay to drive off somewhere, forgetting to say good-bye with full benefits, Ft. Bragg in the rearview.

The scouts were so quiet. Not soldier quiet, but more like civilian, regular people quiet, with not much to say. Awkward.

I see the guys around those picnic tables, the pine trees, and garbage cans of ice and beer, sitting and walking, ignoring the burgers and hot dogs burning up on the grills. I'm there, sniffing and breathing deep through the nose trying to keep all the smells separate: smoke, damp ground, trees, beer, each other, menthols, and regulars, jet fuel coming in faint waves from Pope Air Force Base. The way the Army smells on a Saturday off.

I didn't know then that it changes, that in time things bleed into each other, and I'm lucky when they don't once in a while so I can remember.

Dusk doesn't look the same as it did when I was a paratrooper.

We sent away the white girls who we'd hired to come to dance for Platoon Daddy. Frankie Meadows ran over to them before they got out of their two cars, paying them the flat rate through the window. They drove off with their radios loud, not waving, probably mad because they had already spent the money they'd thought they'd be collecting on tips and extras.

It was easy to just sit at that picnic table when the talk came back up, the guys remembering Platoon Daddy. I was offered a chance to say my own little bit, but I kept it to myself.

How, back when I'd been in the platoon for over two weeks, I had thought my own platoon sergeant didn't even know who I was.

My old-timers had told me plenty about him. That the top button of his fatigues didn't have to be secured cause of muscle, "and that shit's authorized, son." The story of how all the strength came from chopping his way out of the Louisiana woods to get to the recruiting station, about the jeep contests when Platoon Daddy would hold up the back end of one, competing against some fool holding up another, and every time he'd look over at his opponent and scratch his nose. I would come to see this enough to know that when he did this a thigh went where his hand had been in order to keep the jeep up, but it wasn't necessary for very long cause the other guy always dropped his jeep when Platoon Daddy was in mid-scratch.

The man was big, walked a little pigeon-toed, and those first weeks I was sure he didn't know me. The cherry who'd made all the fuss about wanting to hump. Maybe I was pouting over just this thing, trying to look like a paratrooper with a serious case of the ass, but probably also looking like a cherry pouting on duty at the CQ desk. He came out of the First Sergeant's office and went to the desk and said, "Private, give me a match." Still not used to being able to smoke just about whenever, I didn't have one, told him so, and he just said, "Drop."

I got in the push-up position and he went back into the First

Sergeant's office, slammed the door in my face and left me there in the front leaning rest.

I lay with my face on the floor, but every time I heard a noise for the office or someone coming, I'd pop back. While I was there people passing would stop and stare until I said, "Sergeant Timson," not yet allowed to call him Platoon Daddy, and they passed with happy glowing faces. He finally came out after an hour and forty-three minutes, walked over me, and out to his car in the parking lot. I heard him yell, "Young Soldier, Re-cover!" as he drove by the building. I felt cared for and included.

The scouts, wild as they were, had a minimum of official disciplinary actions. What we had was Platoon Daddy's heart punch, with little need for anything else short of the Correctional Confinement Facility. The heart punch came unannounced, and right where your heart is supposed to be. Anyone that got one went down on one or both knees and came up slowly, talking about how their heart stopped for a couple of seconds. "Swear to God man, it just stopped."

But in the weeks that followed, I went back to thinking that the man still doesn't know me. It seemed that way in formations, with him looking right through me. When he did speak at me, it was to tell me to chase my own self hard to some shit detail forming up in front of Brigade.

It went like that except when it got worse. One day on the way to afternoon chow, I was hanging back from the scouts trying to seem casual about fixing my beret cause the guys had been on me about looking like a pizza man. Platoon Daddy was at the end of laughing about something some scout had said, and stopped walking, letting the other scouts pass him while he marked time till I came right up to him. It was the first time he asked me where I was from, anyways. I barreled right into my answer, complete with the explaining about all the places I was from and all the nice people in them who always wanted to help and Platoon Daddy walked off, shaking his head before I was even half through.

There did come the day when the colonel got the ass about something—I don't even remember what—and he had the whole battalion out on a Saturday for a twelve-mile road march, regular duty day first call and everything. Half the battalion hadn't even been to bed yet, and no matter how hard the officers tried to motivate us, we kept the going slow and easy, everybody with a halfways blown-up air mattress in their rucks. After the road march, when guys were heading for bed, Platoon Daddy asked me to hang out, and so I got ready to face some kind of shit detail. Or maybe he was going to mess with me some more and ask me the question again about where I was from, so I started thinking up a shorter answer. But what he asked me was if I wanted to go play in a softball game.

I played for his team, which was sponsored by the Baby Doll Lounge over on Mercuson Road. When we got to the field, I went over into the back of his Buick to get his equipment like he said. Half sticking out from under the seats were two lady's shoes, two high heels. They were two different colors, two different sizes, one medium sized and the other smaller. Confident from our real good conversations during the ride over, I dangled each shoe by a trigger finger and turned to ask him what was up. Talking fast through a frozen smile, he said to get the other glove and greeted the pretty woman rapidly approaching wearing shorts and high heels of that I am sure were of yet another size.

I got on base each of my ups and turned a sweet double play. The women flirted with me, or were just really nice. I was a recon paratrooper in the 82nd Airborne Division and playing softball. Platoon Daddy's friends were all like him, talked southern and fast, walked with that one leg a little stiff, serving their twenty years in. And though they never said anything about it, they had all been in "the place." Could tell.

They called him "Tim" or "Timson" and all I could have wished for in the world that dusty afternoon on that side of Fayetteville was a pair of cleats.

We ate catfish sandwiches—there was seconds—and drank iced tea, and Platoon Daddy asked if I was ready for Recondo School anytime soon, his friends saying, "Shoot, that paratrooper was born ready," the ladies saying, "hmmm" and asking me to just be careful.

The game was ending, the food all eaten or packed away, everyone was going home for showers, naps, and to get ready for their night of dancing on the Merc, and to pay off all the bets that had been made that day. Seemed that there were so many Harveys Bristol Creams, Hennesey's, Courvosier and Cokes, Tanqueray's, and Pink Champales owed, that it probably all evened out and everybody could have just ordered their own. Platoon Daddy's friends all said good-bye to one another, formally, like it was going to be years before they saw each other again, not just a few hours, the place making all greetings and departures precise, particular. They had all spent years apart from each other after the place, rotated off jump status over to leg units in Korea and Germany, a year or two as Drill Sergeants, and there were those not present but talked about like they were just running late. But these men were paratroopers who'd gone to jump school in the sixties, stayed in, and always seemed to meet back up at Ft. Bragg, NC—Home Of The Airborne.

The ride back from the game and it had rained over by Main Post. The Buick slished along and Platoon Daddy hummed an old one, tapping on the wheel, Pall Mall held at the window, as he drove past the statue of Iron Mike. It was only the second time I'd seen it.

Platoon Daddy said, "Mike," and then, "Got a statue of the Buffalo Soldier going up in Ft. Huachuca. That's Arizona. Charles was down there—he was playing second base?—yeah, over to the 325 now, said it was going up just as he was leaving."

There was a cassette case at my feet and I could see the list of groups typed out in it. It'd be okay if one of the ladies with the shoes had made the tape for him, though, to me, still, a good thing to think about was Platoon Daddy late at night sitting up and making tapes and typing out the names, everything all perfect, maybe wiping down the records first, cueing, the order, and sometimes changing his mind and having to start all over. I couldn't see the names of the songs, just,

Spinners
O'Jay's
Delphonics
Major Lance
Bobby Womack
Stylistics
Harold Melvin and the Bluenotes
Johnny Taylor

And on one line by itself written in ink was,

Crystal Blue Persuasion

At a stop sign just past the Main Post PX and Commissary, a big girl—young and not fat—walked right in front of us. She took her time, her turquoise tube top moving wild in four directions all at once.

My eyes followed her the whole way across while Platoon Daddy's stayed to the front, and I thought: *that's how it's done.* That's how a senior NCO handles these things. With quiet and courage. Until, just as he eased down on the accelerator, he said softly, almost to himself,

"When those two puppies get done fighting, I'd like to have me one."

I didn't know what to say. Which was good cause he wasn't talking to me anyway.

"All right now" was what he said as he dropped me off. I tried to say it back, but it came out "Thank you."

He hadn't said where he was going, just that he was, and we knew what he meant. That he wouldn't be hanging around Fayetteville after his twenty. This assurance was all we needed, so we left him alone, no more questions. Any soldier still in Fayetteville, or even Southern Pines, after separating from the Army after a service of years Two to Twenty is maybe the most depressing thing. A sighting of one of these guys can send a whole barracks to bed early. So bad is this that when Frankie Meadows heard about the PFC from 1/305 who got chaptered out on a possession charge, being spotted working for Photomat in the little booth in the Peachtree Mall parking lot, he threw up coming from snack mess without breaking stride.

What we knew sitting around the picnic tables at Mackeller's Lodge was that Platoon Daddy was gone out of here. Some put him on his way back to Georgia to some property he had, others had him making the rounds of all the ladies he'd known till he found the right one to settle with. And always the fishing, cause some guys always got to say that after the twenty, there's going to be fishing. I didn't see Platoon Daddy getting all worked up over a fish, but maybe that's the point. Didn't see him as a deputy sheriff, or with a security company, owning a liquor store with a small parking lot. But I did see him, elbow resting through the open window, hand with a Pall Mall, other on the wheel, announcing at the beginning of each song, and again a little different at its end, "I like this record." If it was some dark road country, maybe Georgia, then he'd say, "This record's nice."

He'd never stop in the middle of a song, and I almost said that out loud, but stopped myself and saved myself from getting looked at hard again. The drinking that afternoon, with no chance of it going straight through, just made everyone feel uncomfortable. Soon the picnic area was policed, cans and butts in bags and the scouts—except for the few off to get in an hour of shooting at the clay pits, or to ride dirt bikes over by Area J—were back up the barracks stairs: Swift, Silent, and Napping.

The company remained on support cycle and in garrison. Trouble with troops usually comes with too much time in the barracks, and the scouts were without a platoon sergeant or a lieutenant. The First Sergeant and captain both took to standing around us before morning and close of business formations, just letting us know that there was only a small break in our chain of command. They never came right out and said what they were doing, but it was clear all around, especially when the two of them showed up at the company on a Saturday night while we were all getting ready to go out. Except for IG inspections, it was the only time anybody'd ever seen the CO and First Sergeant in the barracks. It was weird as hell having them in the hallway with us all standing around in towels. They asked whose stereo had been playing so loud, but didn't mention the beer bottles everywhere, only wondered what our plans were for the weekend and how were we scouts doing anyway?

Sergeant Walters from second squad was acting platoon sergeant, and everybody liked him. He'd been a Staff Sergeant twice already in his nine years in, and had been busted back to Sp/4 twice, always for drinking, which he didn't do much anymore. Only saw him the one time on Hay Street fighting happy. Old-timers said it had happened a lot before he got married—him picking a fight and smiling, sometimes swinging on more than one guy. Not a mean smile, just like it was really fun, and absolutely nothing personal. We'd have made his new job of acting platoon sergeant easy anyway, but he'd been having problems with his wife, who was an Army brat from Germany. She didn't like the bank she worked at, and Sergeant Walters had begun eating aspirins by the handful, mashing them up in his mouth like peanuts. Jencks said that was a sign of real craziness, that we'd have to cover for him.

For months, the Scouts dealt with Platoon Daddy's absence by trying to pretend that we'd just gotten back from Panama. Even so, everything about Ft. Bragg and soldiering was getting old. The new cherry didn't even catch much hell. We dropped the "Cherry" business and started calling him by his name way too early, and soon we were treating him regular and asking him about his home and his particular way with civilian clothes. He'd had some junior college, too. Once the guys found out about that, they asked him if he was going to try for officer. He said no time soon, but he'd consider it for his future. Everyone agreed that that was probably the right move when the time came, nobody messing with him about any of it, more like we were watching this guy, observing someone moving through us on the way to a different life. He wanted to be a lot of the things we didn't like very much and maybe it was his honest truthfulness about it that carried him.

We'd dropped hints early on about his clothes. That he looked like an officer or those college kids in Chapel Hill who danced a dance called The Shag to something that was Beach Music. College kids who looked like somebody's parents even when they were drunker than we were, and who invited us to their house after-hours cause they said they believed in soldiers. Me and Ski ruined it for all of us that time, when we started cutting into each other's palms with kitchen knives, seeing who could go deeper. A couple of the really drunk Chapel Hill girls seemed kind of impressed, shouting to each other about anthropology, till tiny red geysers of blood started up out of our palms and we got asked to leave.

This cherry from Boston didn't take the hint about his clothing or didn't care.

Then Sluguski got a letter from Quinton and I got one from Collins, and Togiola got postcards in thick envelopes from both of them. Me and Ski's letters said that all was good in the civilian world—girls, trade schools, three months worth of unemployment—and had we called to thank the uncle, meaning Mr. Big, for that dinner? Togiola's postcard said about the same thing—*Civilian–Be All You Can Be*—stuff and had he been polite and thanked the old soldier?

Richards and Limón started talking real fast and low as we told them about the mail. They spoke as if one mind working on the same sentence through two different mouths.

"I tell you something—"

"Motherfuckers better not—"
"Be sending me—"
"No—"
"Motherfucking—"
"Mail."

Being on post support, we had no choice but to try and ignore the mail. It kept coming steady from the two corporals gone civilian, enough that the mail clerk from headquarters told us in line at the mess hall that those corporals sure did miss us a lot. He wasn't being a wise-ass either. Before he lifted his tray off the metal runners in front of the steam table to join the other clerks and jerks at their table, he said that he guessed it was that way in the scouts. That we become solid friends, having to do with the good training, and being specialized and all.

That civilian kid of Mr. Big's shadowed us on Hay Street, started getting friendly with our dinks. Then he started bringing some of his civilian friends around with him, never saying anything to us, but making sure we saw him pointing us out to those guys whose short hair wasn't short enough for them to be serving on Ft. Bragg.

Mr. Big himself showed up at the company. We'd just come from drop zone duty and there he was in front of the barracks, by the CP, talking to the captain. He gave us the big hello and acted like he was Collin's uncle and had gotten to know Quinton, and us too. You could tell he'd been woofing the SF and combat shit with the Captain, who excused himself and he did it by saluting this fat bastard who took his time in returning it.

"Been waiting long time for y'all. Long time," he said and looked at his Rolex Star Sapphire.

"Gonna have to git. Now. But y'all stay in touch. Like to provide you with another dinner, drinks and beverages. Like I did before. On me, right?"

His eye was going all crazy, and over past his shoulder we could see the Captain was looking out the window of his office in the CP. Mr. Big looked and waved to the Captain and everybody was smiling. The Captain stayed in the window even after Mr. Big left across to the parking lot.

Everything was different now and this feeling was gaining on us.

I'd had all my pictures stolen. The letters from Paola had started coming and the guys let off teasing me about being whipped. I didn't write to her, and then I did, but by then the only letters I was getting from Panama were my own and returned.

The First Sergeant had left to go to the ANOC school and SFC Wright was acting in his place. Platoon Daddy gone. The scouts were even without a lieutenant, too. He'd been recycled again over at Jump Master school and then No-Go'd the JMPI section so he was gone from us and the division for always. The scout platoon had begun to feel more like a group home than a family.

We started hanging out at Mackeller's Lodge nights, and the lifers there were horrible. Word went round the battalion that the doper scouts were all going to re-up, going lifer, Hay Street Commandos no more.

That civilian kid was waiting for us in the Mackeller's Lodge parking lot one night when we had no car. It was going to be the usual, him just staring from the VW station wagon until Ski trotted over with Limón close behind. We heard them yelling, and there was no one else around under the grove of pines, by the picnic tables, in the parking lot. Our two guys were mad, they'd had it: we couldn't get them anything, okay? We were on support, didn't they get it? The civilian kid yelling back "Don't care! Don't care!" as the station wagon's tires threw up gravel with a small pinking sound from the undercarriage, leaving us to walk back quiet along the blacktop road.

Even our way of telling stories—or living something that would become a story—changed. Before, every day had been divided up into three separate parts all having to do with chow. Chow time was like a little holiday, and like kids with an eye on the calendar, soldiers are always very aware of the time. Especially when telling a story. But now everything was running all together into one smear of After. After the letters from Paola stopped, after Panama, after Platoon Daddy left, after my pictures were stolen, and after we couldn't pretend there had never been a Mr. Big. It was clear that the Before was perfect. Enough, that I wanted to close my eyes and return to it. Just for one minute when I could appreciate the shit out of it, cause it wasn't coming back.

Around this time I began to think about the platoon of Puerto Rican National Guard guys I went through Basic and AIT with. They'd kept them all together in the same platoon, as if they'd all come in on the Buddy System and would be together always.

I asked Limón about them, but he said I was making stuff up again in my own head.

They didn't have very good English. Lots of times you could hear them from the other side of the wooden barracks, or from behind the chow line, or from all over the training areas, the obstacle courses, and even late into the night and early morning from our bunks.

One Sargeen'—Two Sargeen'—Three Sargeen' . . .

Facedown knocking 'em out. Pushing Georgia.

Because they'd put their heads down when the drill sergeants were speaking to them. It was the respectful thing to do in their country with a person of authority. The more the drill sergeants yelled, the lower these guys' heads would go, even when the drill sergeants were yelling for them to look straight ahead. The Puerto Ricans and the drill sergeants were both told it was a culture thing, but still they couldn't get together on it.

No comprende? No comprende? You comprende 'chow,' right? Comprende 'payday'? Look at me! Look-At-Me!

Maybe me and the scouts had become like them. Putting our heads down when we knew we were supposed to be doing something else. Knew we could turn ourselves in about Mr. Big. Knew we could try and find Platoon Daddy and ask him what to do. Knew a lot of things, but we just wouldn't raise our heads.

Some nights we stayed in the barracks, with the beer from the machine downstairs, smoking up on the roof of the barracks. We hadn't made much of a dent in the red dope from Panama. Its smell too strong to risk inside. We took the cherry from Boston with us and listened to him tell about home.

He came from real bank-robbing people in Charlestown, Massachusetts, which he said was in Boston, right by Bunker Hill. There were white people projects there, and nobody believed him except Limón, who said they had them like that in New York, too. As he talked, the way he dressed came to make sense: it was the way somebody would if they had already left someplace kind of rough that they weren't going back to. Though he did say, when finally asked about it, that lots of hard guys wear it like that back home.

He said he wanted to get away quickly and stay away, not like the rest of the guys from Boston who always got sent home early. We all agreed that we'd known guys from Boston in basic, and even mentioned some we'd known around Division, all white guys—and it was true that they always got put out. The cherry said it wasn't

just the Army, but all branches of the service. He'd grown up thinking that guys just had to serve for a few months by the way they
came back to the neighborhood so fast.

All the scouts agreed this cherry was all right, and we had him
tell his story to guys from other companies and the brothers and
Mexicans and grits, Island Boys. Everybody fascinated by the stories
from an all-white northern project, generations of real bank rob-
bers, and we were puzzled about this information. It was like extra
money on Sunday, and don't know where to put it.

He'd done pretty good at the junior college. Had a warehouse
job, and even a little basement apartment to himself below a friend's
aunt in another neighborhood. The guys teased him and asked him
always to say that again—"Whose house was it?"—cause they'd
never heard them called that way, only Ants.

But he had to get out of there.

He had been to see his cousin, who was locked up, and from the
waiting room he could see through windows braced with steel mesh
into the room where the prisoners waited. There were all the same
kind of guy he'd always known, waiting and watching a television
chained up high, sitting slumped in chairs wearing long white boxer
shorts, three to a pack Fruit of the Loom sleeveless T's, their whole
bodies dusted in corn starch, and their feet bouncing in slippers
made of thick brown fake leather strips, tapping at their brows with
carefully folded white handkerchiefs. Some of them had been
friends of his sisters' who used to pick on him when he was little and
still did when they were around. The cherry had hated knowing that
there was going to be a fight soon about how the big standing fan
was facing. He told us that he hated knowing so much about prison.
Things you shouldn't have to know unless you've been there, like
how if you carved your name or wrote it anywhere in your cell, you
were sure to return. The fight did break out and visiting hours were
canceled and he and the fine girls all dressed up and missing teeth
had to go home without visiting anyone.

The next Monday the cherry was at the recruiting station.

Up on the roof of the barracks with the Panama weed, we
started finishing the cherry's stories for him and versions could later
be heard in the mess hall by all kinds of guys.

We wished he could have been in Panama with us and told him so.

———

One day, all around division, company commanders gave the same close of business poop to their assembled soldiers. There had been a series of incidents at all the major drop zones on post. Lone soldiers, who had either been dropped too early, or too late, or drifted towards the edges of the drop zones, were being set upon by men who came out of the wood line to relieve the soldiers of their weapons. This was, the company commanders said, no kind of preparedness exercise. This was a real world situation.

A stolen weapon, a lost or missing one, was a big deal. A few times a year you'd see homemade signs in the windows of different barracks reading DAY 37-C. COMPANY 2/324—HELD HOSTAGE—HELP!, just like Iran on the news, cause when a weapon is unaccounted for, the officers can put the whole company on restriction, meaning no one is allowed to leave post, and even the married personnel have to move back in.

But when weapons were being stolen by men who come up from behind with blackjacks, and garrotes—probably had their own guns, too—it was different. This was a very serious thing and embarrassing for the soldier who got taken. Jumpers were ordered to buddy up coming off the drop zones, and chem-lights were given to each jumper, a different color each jump, so if anyone approached without one you were supposed to alert the other troopers, sounding off in a good Airborne manner.

When the scouts pulled drop zone detail we were told to sign our night vision goggles and scopes out of the arms room. There were MPs strung out along the wood line of the big drop zone, Normandy, named after the battle where paratroopers were blown miles and miles off target and took more than half casualties.

In the dark sky above the trees, at the far end of the drop zone, came the C-130s at drop altitude, the scouts turning the night vision devices up to watch the aircraft in the washed out green of artificial light. We saw them make one pass over the long mini desert and then bank long and return for the drop. The doper scouts feared whoever was in charge of the men they were supposed to be sweeping the wood line for. They knew if it was that fat fuck Mr. Big, he wouldn't be trying anything tonight—not with the MPs out like they were—so they watched as first the jump masters leaned out the aircrafts checking the drop zone. Then the second pass when jumpers streamed out, all in that light green with black all around chutes fluttering, then popping open, and settling in a line like slowly descending hung wash.

On the ground the jumpers bent and cracked the seal to their chem-lights, getting the chemicals to mix and the finger-long plastic tubes to glow bright orange. They secured them under the green and cotton elastic helmet bands, so the whole black and sand drop zone was joggled by these lights. Men unseen to the naked eye appeared only as trails of orange which told their progress in the duties of rolling chutes, turn in, and assembly.

There was no trouble on the drop zone, not even a tree landing, or a twisted ankle. No sightings of bad men coming off the wood line.

It was a long night in support of this battalion, cause after the jump we still had to go provide range coverage for their live fire exercise, and we rode out in our gun jeeps to the big, huge firing range to wait on this battalion, who had to hump over.

Got high and waited some more, though the jumpers weren't long in assembling and coming by our area to collect ammo. We didn't have to do much but throw it down to them from a deuce-and-a-half until this supply guy from California, a Mexican, told us that he knew we were supposed to be helping, but we were not really helping, and so we went back to the jeeps and waited.

A battalion live fire was all in place now. The rifle companies strung out along the long sloping firing line. Scattered among the men with M-16s were the machine gunners, the Tow and Dragon missile teams, and the small Eighty-One Mike-Mike mortars. Each weapon aimed downrange at the targets of opportunity which littered the wide field. Old trucks and jeeps, armored personnel carriers, tanks, so bent and full of holes that the soldiers would have a hard time pretending that they were actually coming to get them.

We could tell by all the yelling that this battalion's Four Deuce mortar platoon, which was set in well behind the line, was having trouble computing their fire missions. They were tasked with lighting up the range and it was taking way too long for their illumination rounds to boom and then crack in the sky. And when they did, they were off enough that we felt sorry for them stepping on it like this in front of everyone. They had lit up sections of forest in all directions. A few rounds caught some wind in their little parachutes and drifted across a far corner of the range. It confused some of the soldiers along the firing line who squeezed off a few rounds.

The mortar crews were looking at leaves canceled and many, many nights of immediate action drills and hip shoots, many nights in the woods eating out of cans, sleeping in their holes.

They never really got it right, and the officers panicked. The general had arrivied in his jeep with the two stars mounted on a red background on the front and rear bumpers. His driver and aides, all wore heavily starched cammies and clean berets. The doper scouts wandered over by the general.

This was a game for us: who could get closest to the highest ranking officer while messed up. A big challenge was if you could be alone with one while all lit up and it was usually driving a lieutenant around while he checked on guard posts all night. They'd get bored and bum a dip of Copenhagen saying that "Skoal was for girls, right?" Then they'd want to tell that story about the girl in science class at West Point who raised her hand and asked if semen was mostly protein, why did it taste so salty? Same damn story, and they'd finish by looking out over the horizen like they were having a memory that used to be funny but now seemed sort of sad and then they'd say the same thing.

"Yeah, she put her hand down and then picked up her books and we never saw her again."

And it was difficult for the doper who'd heard the story many times before cause you'd have to nod your head and say, "Wow, sir. That's so fucked," and keep driving or whatever it was had you alone with an officer.

Dopers would work their way up. A captain and then a major and right on until they'd break bad like me and carry the colonel's radio for a whole night of rain in the woods on a half hit of the Malaysian's, the colonel saying that I was the most good-natured paratrooper he'd ever seen.

Airborne.

This whole battalion we were supporting were heavy trodding on richard, from full bird colonel on down. They stepped on their dicks big time after the bad mortar rounds, when, from the silent darkness, a whistle blew and this infantry battalion, on line along the terrain which was supposed to resemble a real battlefield, jumped alive. First the wire guided Dragon and TOW missiles sputtered downrange followed by hundreds of tracer rounds from M-16s and M-60s. Much of the fire was concentrated on the junked tank which was close enough to see by the half moon, and the tracer

rounds spun off it in all directions a goofy and wobbly red. Light
Anti-Tank rockets found the same mark punching holes in the metal
with a quick spray of sparks. Eighty-One mike-mike mortar rounds
and grenades fired from M-21s, blooped an assortment of ordnance
downrange and up the hill: White Phosphorous, anti-tank, anti-
personnel, high explosive. Some of this exploding in the air, the rest
on impact with the WP burning white hot.

The Four Deuce teams made another try but this time lit up the
whole battalion, the men looking up from their weapons to watch as
the little parachutes carried daytime overhead. Very, very, bad in a
real world situation.

The mortar guys probably got the order to just quit it, cause they
climbed out of their holes. From far away we could see them staring
towards the hundreds of soldiers they had lit up, the whole area
aglow like a parking lot seen off a highway at midnight. Jokester line
doggies from this battalion waved to their mortar crews in the final
seconds of falling illumination and yelled, "High Angle Hell! High
Angle Hell!" which was the Mortarmen's motto. The general jeep
had already left the area, and that's too bad, cause he missed it.

Short repeated blasts of the whistles blew again, and this battalion worked up to the mad minute, firing everything they had. Pour-
ing all that good stuff Mr. Big wanted through the night air and into
a big field, hoping to hit something even by accident.

All the bigger ordnance had been spent, leaving just the M-60s
and M-16s. These guys had loaded their last magazines and rigged
their last belts of ammo with straight tracer rounds, continuous dotted streams of red in 5.56 and 7.62 ball grain. They crossed their
glowing paths of fire at dozens of points all over this field. Interlock-
ing fire has its tactical purposes, but this was—and we knew it even
while high and sitting all over our jeeps—more like kids crowded in
a bathroom playing swords or aiming at the floating paper boat.

Other lights came on and off in the field. Little white ones here
and there, floating up and down around the tracer fire, some like
they were following a red tracer round which had gone wild, loop-
ing long and slow on ricochet. They were dumb fireflies seduced by
flaming bullets and for just this long a while, there we were, soldiers smoking from shared packs red and green, watching this
courtship played out under stars and the smeared and still half
bright Milky Way.

The fireflies got wise and finally stayed safely above their faster and more dangerous mates, appearing to tease them and the stars above and then it really was almost over.

With the last whistle—Cease Fire!—night fogs of cordite floated back towards us now, like that smell you enjoy and miss once in a while from an old gas station. *About that time, ain't it Recon?*—and we drove the gun jeeps too fast over the blacktop range road back to the company to check in, across the street and down the hills to the moter pool, locking the steering wheels down with chain and then walking back to the barracks with the keys jangling on tent pegs.

The support cycle was months long, with six weeks of being on call for Division Ready Force One wedged in the middle. Nobody said it'd be a good idea if we all stopped hanging together, we just did. Or they did, cause I got left by myself, and that doesn't go so good in the Army.

Payday Friday.

Going out the door of the barracks alone and slow, cause there was nothing I was late for, no plans to meet the guys somewhere. I felt many pounds light, like good weight I needed had gone missing.

I bought Ladies Drinks on the Hay. Took a cab to get there. Bought lots of those drinks and only a few girls asked why.

"Why now, after this time?"

"Why come now?"

"Where your friends?"

I'd been to the Re-Up NCO that day. I'd signed early—signed. Told him I needed to sign something binding that day, before I had time to make bad decisions for my future. He scrambled on the phone and through the paperwork, the neccessary waivers for early reenlistment. I took another four years, with the 1/75th Ranger Battalion, in Savannah, and got a seven thousand dollar signing bonus, which was two more thousand than standard for staying in the Infantry. Got a promotion to sergeant E-5 effective the day my original enlistment ended. The Re-Up NCO told me that I'd probably be an Acting Jack till then, and wearing the stripes early next week, no promotion board to face, and I'd already been to the NCO Academy.

Hard stripe with orders pending.

I knew how it would go. Get them pinned, three down on the collar, in front of the whole company, first formation front and center, the word "Lifer" whispered and even barked once and stealthy, but not from the scouts. Nothing from them, not even the way

Limón and Richards could talk to each other in formation through clenched teeth trying to make Togiola and Ski laugh. I'd watch and see them only tighten up to take it like it was personal. The Scout Reconnaissance platoon would stand fast, my pals at the position of attention like the rest, rigid, their knees locked by the betrayal. The other scouts confused because they too thought they knew me. And confused again because they weren't even sure they wanted me to join them among the ranks of the admitted lifers.

Went across Hay Street to the biker bars, watched the white girls on stage, got left alone.

Weeks before we'd even gotten some stuff for Mr. Big. Had to buy it from this guy in the 2/308 who was a new friend of Ski's. We pooled our money and put the stuff in a duffel bag that we handed over to the civilian kid in the parking lot of the mall a long time after closing.

We lost money on the thing. And Mr. Big still wasn't going to be happy, according to what the kid said, his arms through the car window bare to us for the first time, showing his fucked-up tattoos—bad copies of Molly Hatchett album covers, vikings with swords—that didn't go with his car. But at least we'd gotten the fat fuck something.

Back from across the street I'm sitting at the bar of the Kim Chi Chib about to buy a dink her second twenty-dollar Special Ladies Drink. I'd reenlisted this day and then been to see about the black Corvette Stingray. It had sat out in front of one of the smaller used-car lots on Yatkin Road for months, and lots of guys had made noise about it, but the guy wanted too much for it. Everybody said he was waiting for some dipshit bonus baby to come by and I just knew that it would be me.

My bonus money was going to get me that car, and that black Corvette Stingray would be where I was from.

I was going to finish my time at Bragg. Keep a couple of weeks' leave time and still have a lot to cash in cause I'd never taken a leave. Drive around seeing different places, staying in motels, and arrive at the 1/75th Ranger Battalion just outside of Savannah, Georgia, in the Corvette wearing clothes like the cherry from Boston. Guys there would know where I was from without a whole lot of talk.

They'd figure a whole lot of everything about a sergeant with a car like that, and it'd be things like playing varsity ball, having big brothers and little sisters, maybe having gone to junior college—folks would've paid for it, but really did want to serve his country and be with the best. I'd settle in there without a nickname, maybe live off-post, and when the nickname would come it would be behind my back like it's supposed to for an NCO on his second hitch. Ranger School would be no problem for me, the months-long school in three different states, nobody would expect it to be a problem coming from such a place like where I was from, and the navigating would make sense then cause I'd have been making decisions and sticking with them all along. I'd be an Airborne Ranger, like they sing about with the tab on my shoulder. I would have friends who were sergeants too, and who would have me over to eat their wives' cooking and there would be a civilian woman there who wanted to meet me she'd heard so much, and not just about the Corvette, which would have the handle to a reserve chute hanging from the mirror, I'd have long ago scraped away that white paint along the top of the rear window spelling out *The Most Toys* . . . , but if she took a ride with me, I'd tell her about it and we'd both have a laugh about how lame and tacky other people can be. Then she'd pick out a tape to play from the wide assortment I kept in a case for people to pick from, cassettes definitely.

That's the way it was going to go.

If it were true, then it wouldn't be so bad in the Kim Chi Chib at a back table with the long tablecloth getting jerked off under the table by the two I'd been buying the Special Ladies Drinks for and I'd had plenty beers right with them. Not so bad that it was two Hay Street dinks trading me off under a table talking that yang when their hand got tired, the heavy and sharp smell of their food, waiting and covered, right in front of me making it very difficult to finish. No, I was feeling awful about it being their hands under the table, which were not Paola's hands, and because I'd forgotten her real name, couldn't remember it. Paola, who I hadn't written back in time, whose picture I let get stolen.

I did finish, just so they could eat, and in the bathroom of the Kim Chi Chib, where I went to clean myself off, there was a thick young Korean guy, tall for them, taking bets if someone could block his kick. He was drunk and mad, and you never saw young Korean guys down on Hay Street, just the girls. This guy was yelling at these two other guys who weren't cherries but who were drunk too, and trying not to be, smiling.

"You block kick? You block kick? You block? You say something you know! You block kick?"

The Korean peeked a knot of cash out of his pocket, and motioned for one guy to get ready. The bathroom was so small, the guy really had no choice and maybe should have quit smiling while he raised his arms to block. But it didn't matter, cause the Korean had chambered his leg in high, the knee almost reaching across his chest, and then with a half skip unloaded on the guy who on impact seemed to get sucked into the outside corner of the stall and then deflated.

The Korean standing like he'd never moved starting on the other guy now.

"You block kick now! Can you block?"

I decided to stay sticky and backed out letting the door, which I'd still been holding, close slowly, thinking this Korean was probably good at magic, too.

If the man at the used-car lot would've sold me the Corvette after I signed the reenlistment papers, everything would have gone the way I said. But he wouldn't hold it for me until my reenlistment money came in. Said there were too many other guys coming by serious about it, car like that.

From the used-car lot on Yatkin Road I took a cab back to post and found Ski's new buddy from the 2/308, who sold me one hand grenade. I told him I was bringing it home on leave to give to my pals for 4th of July, been promising ever since I came in.

I went back to the company, took the back stairs and got a nap, waking up at 9:45, in time for snack mess. Then, hours after everyone—except the cherry on CQ—had gone for the night, I called for a cab out to Hay Street.

So on this night of the day I reenlisted, I had taken a cab and bought drinks on The Hay, had been across to the biker bars, took a cab and got a nap back on post and some chow and I still had two cab rides to go.

Back on Hay Street I hid the grenade and had more beers with the dinks at the regular places.

When I was ready, it took me some time to find the grenade where I'd hid it over between two buildings at the back end of Hay Street.

I had to go down that street a good ways, far enough that it turned into a regular-looking downtown, with normal type stores that were only open during the daytime. Past the monument in the center of the street, which was an old wooden platform where they used to auction slaves. There was a bronze plaque that told all about it.

The grenade was in the inside pocket of my brown Levi's corduroy jacket. It was heavy enough that it had the jacket riding down to one side.

Back to my part of Hay Street and to the cab stand where the gypsies were lining up to take the early drunks—cherries—back to post. And there they were, outside the Bunny Club, in Airborne T-shirts, all brands of jeans tucked into Daniel Boone boots. They were trying to get one of their own inside the goddamn cab, cause *She doesn't really like you, man,* and one was bent down on one knee cleaning something off his boot with beer from a bottle snuck out of the last place.

This scene was what should be frozen in a statue with a plaque, the railway station behind, glimmer city in front, and cherries around a cab looking after each other and tending to their knee-high, rawhide fringe, suede Daniel Fucking Boone boots. They'd have their mouths open wide, and the plaque would tell you they were yelling *Airborne!* and *Paratrooper!* Which on Hay Street, Corporal Marty Jencks once said, made as much sense as walking his town's square on Sunday morning yelling "Yeah, Baptist, baby!"

During the cab ride to Yatkin Road, the grenade—perfectly round except for pin and spoon, weight like a peach-sized ball bearing—stayed on my hip in the jacket. The worry was of Mr. Big appearing alongside me in the window of the VW station wagon, the kid driving, and them knowing I had something that blowed up real good which belonged to them.

I had the driver drop me off in the parking lot of Saigon East, the restaurant where I told him I was meeting friends, hoping he thought I was SF like the guys who ate there. But I headed across the big busy street before he'd even pulled away.

There was no fence or dog to keep people off the lot, which was maybe twenty cars in short rows. Next to them was the miniature house that served as the office, where the man had told me that he wasn't saving that black Corvette for anyone who wasn't handing over fifty percent of the price soaped on the front window. I sat on a rusted-out race car in the dark under the peaked roof of the tiny house, and smoked a couple of cigarettes, one Kool, one Marlboro, as I'd taken to fixing my packs half and half. I wasn't questioning what I was going to do, but as if it were someone else's idea, I was going to take my time about it.

Field stripped the butt of the last one, the Kool, funny about what you get careful about, pushed off the fender of the race car, taking some rust and flaked up paint with me, and walked to the front of the lot till I was right next to the Corvette. I looked inside: under the powerful lights, it was like a fighter jet cockpit, except room for one more, that girl. Stepped back and could see my reflection in the layers and layers of black paint and the wax over it had been rubbed and buffed, rubbed and buffed by hand, which was the only way to get it right like that, the man had told me.

I pulled the pin elbows high, and let it fall, let it land on the ground with no noise, feeling awkward handling ordnance in civilian clothes in front of the busy street. When I released the four fingers which held the spoon it jumped from my hand and tinkled onto the pavement.

Not counting, I went to one knee and then the other. Stuck my hand under and as far to the middle of the low-riding Corvette as I could reach, and placed it down on the ground. When I was sure it wouldn't roll, I got up, backing out of the rows towards the race car, slapping the pebbles off my hands on the sides of my pants.

When we'd got to throw hand grenades in basic training I was so disappointed when all they did was scatter dirt around and I got in trouble for sticking my head up.

This one did bang whomp and the Corvette lifted off the ground about a foot. A nice feeling of warmth came across my face, little pieces of Corvette coming down on the hoods of the other cars and I sat back up on the race car and watched as the fiberglass twisted and wormed around in the fire, falling away fast from all the metal.

I took my time in leaving. Guys were out into the parking lot of Saigon East pointing, one walking back in to call. Cars started to go up on the median and pull over on both sides, while I had me a nice sit hidden by the flames and the dark by the tiny house, wanting to stay longer while the colored plastic triangle flags strung up above and around the lot continued to hang and burn like a fuse, trail of gunpowder.

Easy over a wooden fence behind the race car and perfect came the sirens from far away. Voices yelled, "Hey!" closer, and another fence, this one wobbly, more like grown up sloppy from the ground than put in proper, and then a street I'm running right down the center of it, and on both sides of me are homes and lawns, driveways, lights coming on, front doors still holding shut except for one or two opening as I run past. The temptation to hide under a car is faint, getting caught like that twice before I wore a uniform had taught me something and I would make it into the woods at the end of this street, probably called a lane.

The woods would keep me.

I wasn't going to climb more fences, rattling over metal or climbing creaky wood into a backyard owned by some dangerous career man retired out of Ft. Bragg who probably missed the old days and would love to draw a bead on something moving in their home perimeter.

I heard men off and away and promised myself I wouldn't panic until I saw flashlights. The fences, when they came up again, pushed me in the directions I needed to go. It was like when my squad got chased by the 101st in Florida, with me as patrol leader: nobody wasn't ever going to catch me cause like the guys said, I had no idea where I was going my damn self. I'd lose them by getting lost.

E and E—Escape and Evade. I could do it right, had to in order to graduate Recondo School, and the NCO Academy; besides, the scouts wouldn't have kept me if I couldn't pull it together by really trying. The navigation just didn't come natural is all. Got in the way of everything that was good about the Army—jumping in someplace and walking outside in your uniform with a weapon and pals cause it was your job, not just some camping hike you had a choice about, and letting your thoughts go wherever they wanted. Which lots of times for me was imagining that I was a civilian living in an apartment complex and I had a car with a place to park it, and girl troubles. Mostly having to do with two girls living in the same apartment complex, but always these girls wanted to know more about the Army, and would like to see the pictures and hear the stories until they'd say they felt like they knew the guys too.

In the woods, being wanted was making me weird. I hid in a thicket crouching down and saying "Shhhh" to myself, then on a thick branch in a tree it took me three times to climb up, hanging my legs, swinging them and listening to the imaginary police walk under, and saying to myself again, "That must be some MPs and C.I.D—must have found the spoon and pin." I spit a few times after they'd gone to see how far I'd climbed, but couldn't hear, and it wasn't so dark that I couldn't see a little ways from the tree, just not right underneath it.

I could be the raggedy man and haunt the woods if I stayed just like I was, already fed and already drunk and with cigarettes.

Still letting the fences navigate for me as I skirted them, I crossed one civilian road. Then many minutes—maybe hours—later cause of all the thoughts, I came to a small path which grew wider, the width of a jeep and twice, the wind blew a little colder. It was a fire break that led into and across blacktop, the marker there saying it was FB 31. I knew it to be a very long twisting one, telling me I was for sure back on post.

On the shoulder of the blacktop I stayed walking and from the Big Dipper found the North Star, all of this clear with a strong moon, and I fixed them so that even when the clouds took them I knew where they were. Except what good would it do me to walk east or west or any way, if I didn't know where I was on the base in the first place. This was what always got me confused, before I got lost, even when I had a map and compass.

Scrub oak and pines lined right up against the blacktop and set in aways I heard the first bunch of soldiers, their music, before I came around the bend and saw the lights, floodlights rigged to the roll bars. Country boys been boonying in their trucks making like it was home, coolers in the back, maybe a bottle passed, Waylon and Willie coming from a decent stereo. I crossed the road and went by unnoticed, not recognizing any of the voices.

I did notice the stickiness under my pants, and there was still the smell of burnt up model airplanes stuck in my nose to remind me of the burning Corvette. Those guys in the woods had probably finished building their model airplanes and cars before they torched them, stuffed them with firecrackers and plastic soldiers. I'd tried, but never managed to get them painted and with the stickers they come with.

If there were more of them in the woods along this road, I'd know pretty much where I was and if cars full of GIs came later, driving slow—some with the headlights off—I'd be sure I was on the way soldiers took back on to post from Southern Pines when it was a payday weekend and the word had gone round that MPs had road-blocks going up along the normal ways. Damn turkey shoot was what soldiers called it, giving the field sobriety test on payday week-ends to every car coming on post.

The ride out to Southern Pines from Hay Street and other of the more normal taverns, the Western dancing clubs, the brother's spots on Mercuson, was over a half hour out of the way, but worth it now that the Army was cracking down with the DUIs. There were even rumors about piss testing for drugs, which for some was like hearing that the world was going to end. Guys coming back from first enlistments in leg units over in Germany saying that there was a black general over there in charge of all of the U.S. forces in Europe who piss tested the hell out of them, court-martialing all the heroin addicts serving proudly and driving the rest to reenlist stateside, going Airborne even, just to keep their get-high.

There were needle jockeys over in Alpha Company that everybody knew about and even four guys from the TOW missile platoon in our company who'd taken a trailer off-post and were tieing off. A little elite unit going on with their own kind of glory badges. Secret shit.

We'd partied with them once and they offered, but we stayed with the Malaysian's and they went into the bedrooms to do their buisness in private. My guys made pacts that we wouldn't cross that line without everybody else going along and so far we hadn't wanted to do it all at once. I never told about it, but I'd done it once already, as a kid and in a way stupid enough to keep me away from it forever and ever, those genuises at the home palming needles from the clinic during checkups and then cooking down PCP and driving it home without even dragging it through cotton. The half dozen of us who'd done it after lights-out all left out of the home and were found out in emergency rooms, up in trees, and the strongest wandering and fighting off the chemicals telling the sad story of what was being done to their brain out loud. The last time we'd see any of each other again before we were separated was days later with a counseler and a real doctor, who brought popsicles, asking us in the common area used for rap sessions *what the hell were we thinking? What was wrong with us* and the counseler giving us the parting advice to get some help about the drugs one way or the other.

On the blacktop road through the woods of pines and scrub oak, I remembered that I'd had a very early start that night, and I had no idea when it would get light out. Soon a drop zone, one of the smaller ones—maybe St. Mere Eglise—came up on the right. It was open and quiet, with one patch of grass to cross over before the sand that was squiggled all over with jeep and deuce-and-a-half tracks you could see from the strong moon. Didn't walk to the middle, but stood and smoked where I was. I knew not to hope for 1–30s or 141s to come banking, low and slow at the far end, flattening over the last trees to put jumpers out center line of the DZ. So I took a seat instead, and made the noises of the planes myself and watched the sky.

Back on the road the ground began to gradually rise up next to it and I took a left at the intersection and walked past the next bunch in the woods who spotted me and yelled out to join them, then "Leg!" and "Lost Cherry Motherfucker" when I didn't.

Cars started coming by and so I walked off the road and just into the wood line. In the thin forest, I saw sets of floodlights off in the distance. They were shining on guys and their trucks set down on a small clearing, and I didn't recognize the voices or the vehicles as I walked closer. Further on, in another clearing, I did and approached them straight ahead and noisy. I answered the "Halt—who goes there?" and got asked to join the recon dogs from the oh-nine. Grits, and their music, "Green Grass and High Tides Forever," had already been turned down and back up and down again when I told right away about my reenlisting and how that got me out walking alone at night separated from my guys and thinking about my future. This bunch were all looking at re-upping soon—some holding out for the best packages—but all lifers with nothing but congratulations and one of their last beers for me.

I asked how far it was back to post, my barracks, and they said, "God damn, Recon" and then told me it wasn't far at all if I took the third fire break running across the blacktop. That one would leave me out in Area J, which led through the woods right into my company street.

They offered to carry me back if I could wait a bit, but I said about being reenlisted now and still a grunt so's I'd just keep walking. Thanks for the beer. They handed me a green label bottle of Jack Daniel's, saying to take one slug for the road. I heard them put another tape in as I let the short slope back down onto the road get me running. After my feet slapped down hard on the blacktop one said, "Damn, out humping on a Friday night. That's hard core" and another saying, "That's what they call him over in the oh-four." I waited to hear some laughter, but there wasn't any. So I moved out.

No white guy on Ft. Bragg ever seemed to get tired of "Sweet Home Alabama."

Twice when cars came I jumped back into the woods and stayed prone, low crawling into some cover and concealment like I was wanted.

Finally the night sky of gray-green was fading, and over by the ranges the in-between blue of the hour was spreading. When I came out of Area J, the streetlights across from the company and the lights around the moter pool were still burning. From the wires connecting them wooden pole to pole hung the boots tossed up by short-timers most already processed out, gone. I wished for them all maybe just one memory of this Army fort in the morning alone before all the rest.

There was a cherry from one of the anti-tank platoons standing to the side of the CQ desk. He had his hands wrapped around the top of a mop, his head resting on his hands, eyes closed, almost getting it right—how to sleep on guard duty. From the walkway straight across, I took the front stairs up to the scouts' end of the third floor of the barracks, where there was a small smear of blood across the floor from the roughhousing. Beer cans had been kicked to the sides and corners under the airbrushed murals of old and present Airborne patches, mottos, creeds:

Danger's No Stranger To A Recon Ranger
U.S. Paratroopers Give The Enemy The Maximum
    Opportunity To Give His Life For His Country
If You Ain't Airborne You Ain't . . .
I'm The 82nd Airborne And This Is As Far As The Bastards
    Are Going
Ours Is Just To Jump And Die

There was a bumper sticker on my wall locker that had been rigged to read

CIVILIAN—Be All You Can Be,

and I peeled it off and tore the hundred mile an hour tape down from around my door. Then I fell to a deep sleep in my clothes on a bunk, with a camouflaged poncho liner for a spread, and I was the first to know that payday week smell of the barracks on Saturday morning.

The MPs and two guys in suits, short hair, pulled me out of first formation Monday morning. The plastic handcuffs like twist ties, tight, hurting like an all-day Indian rub burn. The captain stayed in the window of his office, leaning on the sill and watched them come and take me till the curtain fell, and behind it I could see him move to sit at his desk in the chair with all the plaques hung above his head. I was worried he'd come out and say something to me, final and mean.

Behind the company in ranks—dress right dress—they walked me, and from Headquarters platoon, the two Anti-Tank platoons, and the Four Deuce Mortar platoon came the hissed loud whispers.

"Garwood."

"Fucking Garwood, man."

"Garwood."

"Garwood."

They were calling me like the traitor from Viet Nam.

Garwood.

Who'd gone to the other side and caused his own guys to get killed. Who had just been tried under the Uniform Code of Military Justice all these years later. And whose name was used around Ft. Bragg mostly when someone wouldn't do you a favor or loan you money or give you a ride, and once or twice serious for guys who cracked and buddy fucked the whole training company in the POW phase of Reconnaissance Commando school and got told on, so the whole division knew.

If I had thought about getting caught since Friday, I didn't ever think guys would call me that. Not for a bought hand grenade and a black Corvette. I would have liked for it to become a legend about not reenlisting when you're not the type, no matter who you miss or how bad things got. Guys would talk about how nothing's so bad that reenlisting won't make worse, but I was a Garwood now.

In a green car, the MPs in the back with me, and the guys in the suits up front. I figured it was part of their training not to talk to me.

Don't think I'd ever slept so much. Did it in all different cells—and there were so many—till I saw a lawyer, a lieutenant. I stayed in that one for a while, which was the stockade for the whole post, and there were soldiers there who weren't even paratroopers and mostly not paratroopers was what I found out when the questions from the cells began at night and they were always, "What unit you from?" They were from Finance units, and Transportation, Supply, Commo, and a lot of them were Spoons. Every night when there was some-body new, they'd get to me when they'd say how anybody stupid enough to volunteer for the Infantry and jumping out of planes needed to be in jail. Who were these guys? I'd call them Nasty Fuck-ing Non-Jumping Puke Legs, and some of them didn't even know their own nicknames, even when the post they served on was offi-cialy called, The Home Of The Airborne.

Told them about the Corvette once. I didn't see what was so funny, so much funnier than selling dime bags at the main post enlisted men's club or assaulting an NCO and an officer, stealing from wall lockers, going AWOL.

My lawyer, the lieutenant, said he didn't want to hear about the Corvette. He even plugged his ears with his fingers when I went on about it, and he did it again just when I was finally getting to ask somebody about why did he think the guys back at the company called me a Garwood?

He said he wanted to focus on Mr. Alfred Prymsilat. I didn't know what he was talking about till after it had sunk in that he meant the Malaysian.

The lieutenant said he was going to build the defense on the Malaysian's mescaline. He was going to argue that it messed me up so much in my thinking that I really hadn't known what I was doing when I conspired with Mr. Jimmy Deeks, and him, immediately, I knew was Mr. Big.

That would tie in with why I had been acting so strange the last few months around the company, which was how they got me to begin with, he said. He added that it's not good for soldiers to go around talking to themselves, having whole conversations. And then there was CID, who'd been seeing me repeatedly with a Peter Hubbel, which was the civilian kid.

The lieutenant told me during the trial to shut up, that I had to be quiet. Talking to myself wasn't helping, no matter that no one could hear. And that no, I couldn't draw.

My prints were all over that little bit we'd sold to Mr. Big, and they had only my voice on the phone recordings from the times I placed the calls to him. It all made sense, cause towards the end, it had been always me doing the calling, so's there was nothing this lieutenant could do for me except bring up all the good ways I'd served until the Malaysian started to disrupt my ability to think straight. He said to me that it was an insanity defense without really stating as much. He said it was a smooth move on his part, which got me worried for some reason, and I wanted to get up and tell all about the Red Lobster and just extra money and the Old-Timers, and Panama, and the Corvette and about not having my pictures.

Before the last day of the trial, which was only two days long, the lieutenant told me he was trying to help me. He brought another lieutenant to help him talk to me and who told me about how his sources told him that the grenade I used to blow up the Corvette had come from Ft. Sam Houston—they knew this from the lot numbers found on a piece of the grenade, which can always be found after detonation. It was his strong opinion that it wasn't going to be traced back to me, and again the best thing I could do was let them continue to plead me guilty about the Mr. Big stuff and to be quiet about the other thing.

All I remember is having a sour stomach the whole time, like I was carsick. I tried not to make the lieutenant's job any harder than it already was and did notice that out of all those uniforms in the courtroom, nobody had jump wings. At the end, a colonel, who was like the judge, made me stand, adding his personal comments to my sentence of fifteen years at hard labor.

He said that I had come in his Army through a courtroom and that I was headed out the same way. For the life of him, he could not understand why a man like me would consort with men whose ideologies were dead set against my very existence. That my pursuit of the almighty dollar had finally landed me in a place where I would have plenty of time to think about my own value system. That is all.

I knew I had done some wrong things, but not necessarily the ones he meant, cause I really had no idea what he was talking about. I mean, I do, and I did, but he was off about three notches, three turns, three clicks, and my stomach was awful and I could sleep forever.

Between the two trial days, the lieutenant told me—him being the second one to do so—that just because someone went to college, it doesn't automatically mean they're an asshole.

12

The Castle–A Package–Human Beings Can Be Awful Cruel

You don't get to know it all at once, especially if you weren't awake on the bus till it was time, but there are two other prisons there in Leavenworth. From hearing the guards talk every day, it gets like you're part of a colony banged into the side of the moon.

The castle looks so orderly through the windows of the bus, which are covered by a black metal mesh. Sitting there in that bus, which was chunked up into sections of new prisoners by more black metal, you hope that all things here are like that. Orderly. And handled, like the way the driver swung through curves and fast down straightaways. It wouldn't be like all the stories.

That bus was so hot with the heaters blowing full and humming. Wishing I was sitting up front, as a guard or the driver, next to the open window. Wished I was still in the Army and not wondering about so much, nothing to talk about cause they were sitting silent much as I saw. Not much to talk about when it was nothing new.

Yes. Yes. Right off the new river train.

It's how they called us when we entered the castle to be processed in.

They're all in the Army—the guards—and it's one of those jobs you have to want in order to get.

About a thousand in the castle. Supposed to be from all branches of the service, but I never met one from the Coast Guard. Heard there was one over with the females.

Half of them in those stacked tiers are sex offenders. Five hundred of them. Half of those five hundred are child ones.

There are more than two hundred and fifty murderers in the castle.

You have to keep a brown uniform standing tall, observe military courtesy, and have a regulation haircut.

224

Most were there for crimes committed against a person.

Most were on their second enlistment when the crime was committed.

There's guys to tell you this stuff who know all about Ft. Leavenworth, but they've been there awhile and made minimum security or at least medium.

Like everybody else, when I got there I was put on Six, which is the top tier and maximum. There they keep you all chained up for any kind of moving around. They gave out an *Army Times* article on ditto paper all about the castle, along with the manual: the U.S. Disciplinary Barracks Manual for the Guidance of Inmates.

Alone in the cell, and so far that much of what I'd heard before was true.

Maybe I'd have wished that it'd taken me some time to learn what the *Army Times* article told. At least I could have found out by a person, so I could ask questions.

That it was a three-quarters chance the man belonging to any of the voices speaking their minds at the dark, around and below me, came from military sex crimes guys or military murderers—many voices. Echoing all at once as if from inside one of those stories-high oil tanks off the side of the highway, on the way into any city drained of oil.

Locks with motors.

There were the Heavys. That's how they called the gangs. The white Heavys were in charge of the stealing and the black Heavys were in charge of the beatings. The Hispanic guys were all fucked-up amongst themselves: the Mexicans and the Puerto Ricans having serious problems with one another, so they did some stealing and some ass kicking, but were not very organized.

Getting moved from place to place, I'd seen the Hispanics sniffing me out, confused by how the guards called me.

I have always been lucky. I say this as a prayer of thanks. It is a prayer, and the best one I know.

It had been a couple of weeks and I hadn't heard from any of the guys, but there was this big man, even for a Samoan, with long arms and a dented head. He found me the first day I was unchained to use the gym.

Said he was Togiola's cousin. Said everything was going to be very okay, brah. There were two Guamanian brothers at the castle with him. "With us," he said.

His name was Tatopou Tatopou, was called Repeat, and said it was easy, brah. Just lift the weights, get a bunch of fucking tattoos, go crazy once in a while, and special, just for me, I'd have to box him.

Been there a while and a package did come. A large manila envelope wrapped in green hundred mile an hour tape, with little windows for the address of the U.S. Disciplinary Barracks. The return one which was from The 2/304 Scout Reconnaissance Platoon. It had already been opened. In it was my book of *Huckleberry Finn,* and inside the book was folded my letter from Paola. I thought that was it, but something stiff didn't give right when I balled up the taped envelope. It was another letter, from Frankie "Country" Meadows, written on the back of a torn box of c-rations.

He said, "Hey, Bud. Thought you might be wanting these."

And that there had been a quick detail formed up, with an MP in charge to bag up all my stuff in the barracks after they pulled me out of formation. He'd only had the chance to grab these two things. Took him a while to find out where I was at.

He said right after I was gone Grenada happened and all. When they got back the captain got transferred and most of our guys in the scouts got reassigned to other units except for him, Jencks and Hightower. Oh, yeah, and the cherry turned out to be a real good guy. He had heard something about a whole bunch getting chaptered out over in the 324 for some White Power bullshit. Even officers. Lots of rumors going around.

He hadn't seen that ol' kinda overweight girl I used to like over at Nashville Station.

He said that the scouts had had a plan to bust me out when the word came down about Grenada, if they'd known where I was they'd a tried it. "Ha Ha," he wrote next to this, which was probably good. They were going to hide me in the wood line off the tarmac, all cammied up with a chute and a weapon and I'd just fall into the stick. It'd be like I was coming back from a piss as they boarded up the dropped tailgate of the bird, and what could they do if they found out on the way to an invasion? But they didn't know where I was at, he said, and again he wrote "Ha Ha."

He wrote me about a Jamaican cherry from Brooklyn who had that music and still talked like that and I would like him.

He said that he hoped I liked that he wrote on a c-rat box like a real para, and that the girls on Hay Street all said, "Hello, baby."

In a corner of the weight room I faced that Samoan six days a week. They were all the time changing their mind about boxing in the castle and now it was officially forbidden but we were allowed to slap box over in this small corner. The large Samoan called Repeat said I couldn't make noise even when it really hurt.

If you follow the thumb down the inside of your open hand you will find there is a hard spot.

Repeat wore garbage bags when we boxed, big, heavy, prison garbage bags which kept him sweating and made noise especially when he went to the body.

At night, when I'm out walking I sometimes rustle on a garbage bag working up a good noise from it and remember when I was a boxer.

The latticework of scars which framed the Samoan's head, and the way his elbows always tipped up just before hooks I could neither slip nor block. In a flurry this hand, then that would close, land and open again. I once tasted urine in the back of my throat from a shot to the kidneys, and there was the way getting hit in the head made my head ring and vision alternate between blurry and the most intense focus with the odd knowledge that this was just for me.

Repeat liked to think he had a pogo stick jab like Tommy Hearns and I can't really say if that's true or not. But he'd found a rhythm in the way he got me to drop my left, and with the very bored guard on duty in the weight room, he'd peppered me good, causing this small mouse to rise up over my eye and the mouse became tight and permanent until one day it busted open and oatmeal blew out of it like a sneeze, just nicking Repeat's shoulder. I went to the infirmary where two brothers waiting to see the doctor ahead of me discussed how they would get me, tear my insides up. They called Samoans the same thing in the castle as they did at Bragg, cause they were saying what they'd do for me if only it wasn't for that "Big Chinese Nigger you got minding you."

At night when I couldn't sleep I would sometimes whisper, "Big Chinese Nigger" into the crook of my arm until drool and sleep warmed my pillow.

I boxed every day except Sunday and never hit anybody. But you should have seen me pivot on the front foot to take the sting off a whistling right. Sweet.

My face has never stopped hurting like a bruised rib.

Not bad like you think, military prison. Not as bad as the Fed

Pen at Leavenworth, which you heard spoken about like it was an elite unit, they had it so bad. But there'd been riots in the Castle years past and prisoners did get taken by one another and when you heard them, the sounds usually from the places hidden and dark of the middle tiers—Medium—swirling up and around and if the men are with each other then their noises, their cries sound like men. If one or more men are taking another, then the man who is being taken against his will he does not sound like a man.

So with the sound of the whooping horn, fast followed by the siren and the barking guards, I could leave that corner of the gym trailing the fierce brown men of Guam and Samoa and return to my cell, where I would remain, like a man, to read one book and one letter.

Repeat and the two Guamainians had been down to Medium and almost made Minimum, but there'd been this problem with the guard named Time Bomb. He liked to watch me and Repeat box and we didn't have to be careful around him about me getting hurt.

When things happened at the U.S. Disciplinary Barracks, big or small, it most always had something to do with an insult. What you'd find if you listened to the explaining and telling of it after— you didn't take a side—was that somebody some way had been insulted.

I did then what I still do when I see something, and that's to go to the book as soon as I can, and read the part that says the plain truth of it. I've known it by heart for a very long time, but it's the reading of it that makes it work right, settles the stomach. Says there in a book just what your own self is thinking, what everybody knows but can't do a thing about.

If you read the whole book you'll find out that the most horrible people can have bad things done to them too. You could say that these things had been happening to them long before they became horrible, but that part's not in the book.

Especially there, in that military prison place, to read it out loud pretending to be joined in by others made me like one among many pledging an allegiance of the witnesses. A way to see it and not alone.

Well, it made me sick to see it; and I was sorry for them poor pitiful rascals, it seemed like I couldn't ever feel any hardness against them anymore in the world. It was a dreadful thing to see. Human beings can be awful cruel to one another.

Might be that you could hang that last part over the entrance to a lot of places.

I talk to the captain of my tug about things sometimes, and he calls this—and most opinions I have about what goes on in books—"A gross misreading of the text."

I ask him only not to call the book I keep my letter in "a text." Then I say about how if college is a place where books get turned into texts, then I won't be wanting to hear more of that anytime real soon. Then he says a lot of the same mess the lawyer said to me about just cause someone went to college doesn't mean they're an asshole.

Then it's quiet between us two—just the powerful engine of the slow moving boat—and it's always okay.

I had taken my book to Egypt, and that was the first time I used that part of it to comfort myself where it was in a book that was a story and written official.

Human beings can be awful cruel to one another.

Used it so much at the Castle, but always remembering Egypt and the first time.

Anwar Sadat had been killed by his own guys during a parade, pass and review, so we got alerted and flew eighteen hours straight, got refueled in midair, escorted over Libya's airspace by French Mirage fighter jets, and parachuted in, a couple of thousand of us. My first look at Egypt was from just off to the side of the open door like you do it in the C-141s and after all those hours in the air and the confusion of an In Flight Rig, I was rocking, wanting to get out in some of that air. All around everything was pink, and rocky desert, and foreign, a sun that had to be a different one.

We were there a month and bought hash, fucked around a lot yelling "International Incident! International Incident!" and made friends with our counterparts, Egyptian Paratrooper Scouts. We'd sneak over to their tent city at night to drink their tea, which they made with heat tabs that burned bright orange, and to put on shows of imitations. They liked to do Charlie Chaplin and would beg Limón to show the moves from martial arts movies they'd never seen: Drunken Monkey, Shaolin Temple. They told us about their men holding hands with each other and what that was and wasn't, but then presented two of them off in a corner who they called "Rosalyn and Jimmy Carter," and making a big deal about how they had only one sleeping bag unzipped and spread out for the two of them. The one they called Jimmy Carter did look like Jimmy Carter so much, even when he wasn't smiling. But when he smiled and spoke their yang and cuddled on his Rosalyn who had little bitsy eyes, it could make you scared. Especially when they weren't sure we were understanding their relationship and they lay down together like they were sleeping and making loud snoring noises.

Late one night and just back from night exercises, I was serving out one of my brief exiles from the guys for trying to make a point about officers, ours and the Egyptians, how the Egyptians were so much worse than ours because they had to be born into an officer family and that it was making our officers jealous cause that's how they really wished it was in our country and that our officers were getting ideas about how they should be treated, and about the desert how it made everything in the sky different, that there had to be a different sun and moon, but not really cause it was impossible, but it would make sense if it were true cause that might explain why people were so different here and people are made up of mostly water, which is what the moon controls and I wouldn't shut up till I got banished. Which was the word they yelled at me when it got too much for them.

The guys went out the back flap of the tent—a GP Large—to smoke bowls under the cover of Kools and Marlboros without me. I rolled over and got right into my book like I said I was going to— even though I hadn't been invited—with no trips out the back flap that night cause it made the reading bad. Like opening the book and having to read the same mess of words over and over, trying to make it a particular story that's not just about anyone.

Shattuck could do it. Read his Casca the Eternal Mercenary books while all lit up and quiet going on for pages and pages. He said it made it easy to get into the story of the Eternal Mercenary. Casca, who was from history, had been the soldier who poked Jesus on the cross with a spear and God punished Casca by making him a mercenary for all eternity. Shattuck said that maybe it was good with the smoke cause in the Casca books you had to go so many different places like when Casca got killed in World War II as a German he'd come to life again in the middle of some battle on the side of Napoleon and Shattuck would go "Whoa," really would say it out loud and being high could help emphasize how messed up that must have been for Casca over and over, the eternity part.

When guys came back into the tent they said they'd seen the dogs again. Then there they were, right at the front of the tent, sniffing around, little pink and black and fat and pointy noses, poking under the canvas, actually even starting to dig their way under they were so bold. We threw stuff at them and yelled, and when they growled back and jumped at the tent we could see their outline agianst the canvas daring us to come out. We jammed rifle butts at the sides of the tent and finally the dogs left off. It'd been hard to tell any scout that these weren't the same dogs from Bragg, California, Smokey Mountains, Florida, and all over the world, wherever we went. And if you could've gotten us to see how it made no sense that these were the same dogs we'd of demanded that they all at least knew each other.

The inside of the tent had a long piece of parachute cord strung out along the length of each side, and issued flashlights dangling so you could read or whatever at night almost private, like on a civilian long bus trip. The dopers were playing Tonk without me and some guys were already asleep, and others were trying for it after arguing about the flashlights being on. I was with the book getting towards the end, and it's not a very good part. Most of the best ones are already pages past, but it's always been a thing with me to keep reading even after Tom Sawyer shows up. Which is harder and harder to do once you realize that if Tom Sawyer joined the Army, he would have definitely become an officer and make Huckleberry call him Sir.

I wasn't expecting the book to work for me like it did that night. Wasn't expecting any of it when the Egyptian officer, a captain, opened the front flap of the tent and stood right there holding it while looking at our sign. We'd drawn it on cardboard from a case of c-rations with a grease pencil. It showed a skull wearing a beret with crossed sniper rifles over parachute wings. Written across the top Recon 2/304 and below everything, it said "Bum Fuck Egypt."

The Egyptian captain stood in the entrance to our tent looking at the sign. Then he folded back the flap and stepped inside, saying, "Yes, I have heard of this expresssion." His eyes swept over us till they found me, and he signaled for me to come outside the tent. Some of the guys looked up and said, "Ohhh, shit" and from the Tonk game they yelled, "International Incident! International Incident!" and stuff about that's what I get for thinking dumb stuff and asking stupid questions all the time, bugging the shit out of people, and they hoped I got some extra duty that was really interesting.

The Egyptian captain was standing in the middle of the road which ran through our tent city, standing like officers are supposed to with his hands behind his back, looking away. I said "Sorry, sir" even though it hadn't taken me a minute to put my boots and cammie shirt on, find my beret, ask the guys to watch my weapon.

We walked out of tent city. Him not saying anything, not even when two soldiers were double timing across the dark open piece of desert towards the rows of latrines, not even when one of them started to hop. I thought he'd maybe laugh or lighten up a little about seeing our sign on the tent cause maybe these soldiers visiting his country, so many with stomach difficulties, stuff leaving them unannounced from both ends, would make things even-steven tonight. But none of this showed up on his face, so I just followed him knowing soon that we were headed for our counterpart's tents. The doper scouts had been sneaking over here to hang out on a lot of nights like this one, where walking out in the open, if you weren't calm and sort of happy right where you were, looking around at everything so different, you felt like later you'd have to ask for forgiveness or at least be mad for using up good parts of your whole existence without proper appreciation.

I couldn't be in too much trouble: one of our officers would be there if I was. Going visiting meant we'd been off-limits, but we hadn't done anything really bad, unless he knew about the hash. And if that was it, why only me? And where were my officers, my Platoon Daddy?

It wasn't me in trouble. Once over the last mound of raised geography I could see the counterparts along with the rest of their company in formation outside the tents. They were locked in at attention and the captain stopped, me beside him, facing the company. There wasn't much moon, few stars. Still when I looked over at the soldiers, my Egypt buddies, their faces in the front two ranks were easy to see. Could tell this one from that. Blue silver night like it gets there, and my friends were wearing soldier faces at attention, telling me I understood nothing.

The captain handed me my Mini Maglite, the flashlight I had bought at Ranger Joe's with the nice heft to it, small enough to hide in a fist. It threw a potent beam, solid, right through where ever it was dark. The Egyptians had liked it a lot and I'd let them mess with it when we had been out training. Even their officers had been impressed with it, especially the plastic disks to use as filters during tactical situations that were stored in a stack at the butt end. I hadn't known I was missing it but told the captain,"Thanks, sir," and got myself back into attention, after almost walking away.

"You may be at ease," the captain told me. He signaled with a nod to an officer at the front of the formation closest to us, who then spun and nodded to another and he to an NCO. Back through the ranks this nod went until two soldiers I did not know carried out another soldier under his arms. This soldier had his hands tied behind his back and his feet tied to his hands and his knees bent up so much to accomplish this that he looked like a mostly dead out of water fish, stuck in the arch of its next to last desperate flip.

The bound soldier was brought towards me and the Egyptian captain, his body skimming above the sand, which was fine and smooth. He was dropped in front of the captain. The two soldiers who had carried him came to attention, saluted, and after the salute was returned they spun and joined the rest of the formation. The soldier down in the sand kept his chin tight to his chest. From where the captain brought it out of I do not know, but he handed me a black metal stick no longer than a foot and said that this man had stolen my fine flash torch and that I may punish him.

I responded quickly—which I thought was good—and I was firm to this foriegn officer. I said that, No, it was just a flashlight, and I'm sure I called him "Sir" six times while saying it. I really did not know how he would want me to begin punishing this man with a metal stick only a foot long. He explained about his country, laws and theft and honor and I still said, "No, sir," feeling more like an American than I'd ever had. There was no way this guy could make me do this, and I was in no danger at all by disobeying this officer and, he, unlike his men, probably had big problems with Americans being in his country, and all this had more to do with that than anything else.

The captain tilted his chin and looked over the top of everything in front of him, the man on the ground, the officers at the front of the formation, the NCOs, and all the men. Over the tents and into the sky, maybe the night clouds moving quickly, the stars, and he said, "This is . . . This is . . . Well. This is this."

And in one motion he took the metal stick from my hand and shot his arm straight out to his side away from me. The metal stick grew, and clicked as it grew, so fast did the captain then have a metal whip three times the size it had been when I held it just before. A thicker car antenna. The captain spoke Egyptian to the soldier tied at his feet, and half circled him this way and that as if the soldier was a barn animal avoiding an inevitable capture. But the soldier didn't move and did not even lift his head so that I could see that he was Rosalyn Carter until maybe three or four times after the captain brought this metal down upon his back. Those whip blows came from up high, where the captain seemed to stab the sky with the metal before bringing it down again, and again. And the captain beat Rosalyn Carter long and bad. Rosalyn Carter looked at me during the beating in which I did and said nothing, telling me with eyes that this was not the first time and that there was an understanding between us about the flashlight. That it was okay he stole it just between us two, and it was just a flashlight I'd of given him—from one Para to another—if the guy had asked. That was the only thing, when he looked up at me, that he'd forgotten to ask.

The captain didn't stop when the whip blows made wet sounds on the back of Rosalyn Carter, his fatigues soaked right through. It took too long for him to finish the up down of the metal whip, talking Egyptian, and making sounds like he was the one getting the beating.

Rosalyn Carter put his forehead to the sand. The captain gave an order to the officers and the officers to the NCOs and to the soldiers who were released back to their tents. The captain said nothing to me and walked away and I did the same back towards our tent city. I looked back and Rosalyn Carter was still there. All three times I turned around to see. Still there alone, forehead in the ground, from the distances I looked, down in the sand like they pray and the flashlight miniature was heavy, tight, in my palm. Only kept on walking and didn't turn again, only walked. When I'd come far enough to see again an American soldier booking across the open desert between tent city and the latrines, I clicked the flashlight on and off, on and off, in step, left right, on off, on off.

The tent was dark, except for the tip of Richard's Kool, flaring up bright enough for rings to appear around it as he pulled the drag in deep.

"What was that shit about?" he asked low-voiced, followed by an exhale, as I stepped over bodies wrapped in poncho liners.

"Some shit," I said, "about a flashlight."

I smoothed out my sleeping spot and turned on my knees to face

Richards, the cigarette coming on again more, like a slow beacon, and I spoke to it.

"Man, R. Those Egyptian officers just fucking suck. You know. Royalty and shit."

He must have had a little c-rat can ashtray resting on his chest like he did it all the time lying down cause that little bit of orange hardly moved at all in the black of the large tent.

Didn't say anything to me. The orange tip glowed twice more and was gone.

This happened. Some times before. The guys just got a little sick of me with the questions and Too Easy stuff, and would let me alone for a day or two till I stopped trying so hard about everything and did good paying only the right amount of attention to stuff, not drifting off and coming back too much and fucking up.

I rolled over and put a red filter on my Mini Maglite and turned it on. Keeping it down close to the page of book where I'd left off and it was only a few sentences till I read, *"Human beings can be awful cruel to one another."*

And that was the first time I used it. That part of the book. Would again, so many times, take comfort, cause it was written official and in a book.

Cause it said it in a book like everybody else was born knowing it, and I had to catch up right there and then when the book worked for me, giving help, and a place in a book to read whenever there was awfulness around and a book was the way to face it, so that imagining wasn't wasted on changing around real things.

13

Had to Have a Thing at the Castle–Portugal Story from a

Major That Was a Chaplain

There was this big white guy in Medium at the Castle. Silly, happy, countrified and named Pete, said he was serving cause, " Back at Ft. Sam, maybe this girl said I was in her house off-post." Whenever a new batch came down from Maximum it'd be a thing during lunch that one of them would go at Pete. Cause if they hadn't heard it as a kid or later, then somewhere along the way to the Disciplinary Barracks somebody'd pull their coat to the fact that once in the general prison population, it's good to go after the biggest guy you see right as soon as you get there. Let everybody know you ain't a punk and sometimes it was even the guards up in Maximum who would tell this if nothing had happened for a while.

But Pete—Big Pete—called his own self a "Shy Guy." Always been that way, didn't want trouble, just wanted to do quiet time and go home, where he said you had to plan it and work real hard at getting in any kind of trouble. Sometimes Pete would be warned about the new guys, and he'd eat with his head up, looking around, ready to swing a tray and yell, "Oh, no you don't! You take your difficulties somewheres else," just like his once a week counselor told him to. Even when nobody warned him he'd say the same thing. Even when a punch went off the side of his head when it was down close to his food. Only then he'd yell, "Goddammit!" before the rest of it and everybody laughed the same way, Black and White, and Latins, cause that was Pete's thing, and you had to have a thing at the Castle.

Like the two guys who walked on their hands a lot, and mine was slap boxing with the Samoan and having one letter and one book.

My counselor, who was also the chaplain and a major in the

Army, spent a lot of the time in our sessions asking me to talk about the book and the letter, and what they represented for me. Even though the book was easy to talk about, I didn't like doing it. One week I told him that it was ruining it for me, especially writing down answers to the questions that he gave me for weekly homework like they were tests.

The letter. He asked if I would share it with him. I copied it out and gave it to him, a copy of my letter, and the next week he read it back to me. All I could do was smile, it was so good to hear it come in another's voice. It was like me and Paola were now a part of history, just by someone else reading it out loud.

"That's quite a letter," he said.

"Yes, sir."

And then he found his thing with me, which was that I could find this again. That a person doesn't only get this once, that good things can happen many times in a person's life, over and over.

He made a fist, and held it up and said, "See, it is hard to accept new things when you're holding on tight to something else. Hard to grab that new thing. But . . ." and he opened the fist and made a catching motion with the fingers saying, "See? See?" Opening and closing his hand, putting the letter in his fist and letting it fall to his desk, over and over.

"See? See?"

Like I was a whole lot dumber than I am, and me still smiling and happy about the part when he read out loud and I was thinking "Fuck you, man. Give me back my letter," but actually saying it without the swearing, only smiling.

Because he knew from the other guys who he saw once a week that they wished they had a thing like that to keep them for all the hours like I was with one letter and one book. I could just go and go, and they liked me for it, those guys. And from me he knew that I didn't need much else and people will like you for that, being content, maybe cause they weren't such big things and that they too might find a thing just like that, either one. My counselor, who was the chaplain and a major, liked to go over the letter with me starting from the beginning.

Dear Sergeant Cara Bebe

"I see she promoted you," he said, and I would explain that that was very embarrassing and awful and she didn't mean anything by it. She couldn't know how bad that was, it wasn't her fault but mine.

When I'd told her that I'd be promoted soon, I was sure . . . and he stopped me.

"She obviously has faith in you."

And he'd grin like we were both just guys and knew all the same things and then he'd ask me about the . . .

Cara Bebe.

I translated it for him though he knew, and I said that I liked her calling me Baby Face the way she did. He asked why.

Cause the guys at Bragg were all the time saying that I looked like I never quite healed up from some long ago beatings and enough of that would make you appreciate a name like Baby Face in a foreign language.

He said that messing with that Samoan would ensure nobody'd call me that Cara Bebe again. But that was part of my thing, and everybody had to have things at the Castle, he understood.

I did say this to him about the letter: that Paola had said right from the very beginning of it that she'd—

begin this letter many times

—and I told him that even somedays just reading that part was enough. I'd get a mental picture in my own head about her trying more than once to write me a letter.

"Yes. Yes. I see now, " he said, and he was so excited about what I had just told him that I forgot about being at the Castle for a long second or two.

He was really on to something mentally and wanted to do the whole letter the same way.

"Yes. Yes. She had to take risks to use the typewriter. And her friend. Yes, she got help in order to write you this letter and risked both of them getting in trouble from their boss, you see. This must make you feel good, no?"

We must steal bar office

He wanted to go over all the words and I didn't like him using up my letter, opening it up and using it like it was his own. It was awful when he said, "Let's just think about some of the words here" and said out loud about

missing from me you
all word
want you only remember me
up of stairs
stay only

I only happy and hurt
I want and happy
come Panama
what.
baby face.
I make i kiss you
what to happen

They didn't send me back up to maximum cause I really didn't go after him. He told them that, too. It did feel like I went after something, which I guess was myself. I had to stay in my cell for a few days. No exercise. No radio. The Army doctor came to look at me, and the bruises on my ankles and elbows wern't bad at all, but the guards had told about my ear which they swear they hadn't done and everybody, me included, believed them. The doctor checked me out and said everyone could relax, cause the dripping blood was not from the billy club blows but from something else. He wasn't sure what—maybe pressing the wrong way on the inside of my head—he'd have to make some calls.

It stopped after three days and never got worse than drips, except when I slept. After it stopped for good, the doctor said if it started again they'd do something with a specialist.

When my ear was still dripping, a guard gave me a plastic bag with a book and a note from the chaplain major. It said that he'd been to the Castle's library to find me a book and came up with nothing, the selection being so poor. So he brought me a book from his home that he thought I might like.

Then in a whole new section of his notes, he said that it would be good to try and give the Huck book and letter a break. He looked forward to seeing me.

It became a thing just for that day. This new book fitting perfect, on the floor and placed into a corner of the cell. One of two corners that meet wall to wall. Hardcover book. Me sitting up in my rack staring at it. Making a big deal. Staring at it. Wiping my neck.

I read it. Stayed with it even for a while. It was from Portugal, this book, but there had been a translation.

The book had a lot to do with shadows and that was easy to know in the beginning parts, but later it got very imaginary when the main guy left the city which was old and Lisbon. He had to send postcards to somebody who was his boss, and maybe the boss owned the places he was sending the postcards from. It was easy to get lost and confused in this book, when you weren't sure if anybody really existed, not like the Huck book at all.

Staying with that book in the Castle, I was doing just what the chaplain said and still do it sometimes, giving the Huck book and the letter a break. I did have to give it back, but know the best parts almost perfect and can even feel my face change when I tell it. I used to laugh a little when it gets so fancy and the way I would jiggle my head with the telling all to myself.

It works for you, this book. It can work for you if you time it right, use the part when the main guy moves along the coast to a place called Oriundia, and the land and sky and sea change like the thoughts of the weary. When he starts to tell about how the women of Oriundia have wrists as thick as oars from working their curved fish knives like whips, from sunup to sundown. That during the day, there are only women and the racks of drying fish along the beach of Oriundia. The men with the plaid flannel pants and the long stocking caps will be at sea until their many brightly colored boats float under the same constellations their forebears followed in pursuit of the new lands they would give the wrong names. The boats now only hug the coast in search of Merluza and Chocos. The sextant—and maps drawn from imagination—long placed under glass in the Fishermen's Hall.

The picture postcard that he sends to his boss is of the beach on Sunday, the boats pulled up into a long neat row along the shore. Each small boat has been painted by its owner in the fashion of a famous navigator's grand vessel. Every man claims a navigator as his ancesctor in Oriundia, and many fights with knives borrowed from the women have been fought on this shore over the rights to a certain swirl of purple, dash of red. As the boats became smaller, the painting of them became more elaborate, as if strokes of the brush could replace strokes of the oar and full sails.

In the postcard the man tells his boss that the people of Oriundia are his saddest. That the songs they sing are painful more for the angry thoughts that cause such songs, than the sad words themselves. As they sing, they heave green wine from their guts into the ocean from the cliffs. The bottles have labels which resemble the old maps, except the burnt edges are fake and sad. The man wanted to leave immediately, even before he heard the songs from the cliffs at night.

With the first meal he ate with the women, the thought came that he should leave this place. By the time the day's last meal was done and the single-file line for the was cliffs formed and moving, the bottles swaying slightly, carried below the hips, the voices warm, he knew he'd stayed too long. He questioned why he'd stayed at all.

The women sing of the pain in their wrists and of a time when men used to leave for years, who used to return with dolls and spice and knives of their own. They sing of men who would sail out of sight and return to hold their wives close, not leaving the bed for days. They sing of men who now hold close only to the shore and lay down on the cliffs to spill tears, wine, and this only with other men.

The men sing that they need the kind of glasses not yet invented, that their form of nearsightedness has no remedy. They sing about Mindelo, who rowed out to find a land where this glass could be found and whose boat returned without him, but filled with empty bottles floating in seawater pink with blood. They sing about women who they fear. Who they must ask before borrowing their knives to fight on the beach. They sing of a time when paint grew dull at sea and men's minds were alive and bright, and they'd sing to the men who sang and drank at the sight of new lands, all the while standing on the same stupid cliff. They sing to women in lands they will never see, with names they cannot pronounce, and to women weaker than themselves.

It is this way with the children of Oriundia: they live alone in the white brick homes south of the cliffs. They never look towards the sea when they play. When they can work a boat or cut a fish they must move down to face the sea, never to return to the white brick houses. When children grow old in Oriundia, they will fall asleep singing, either with the women on the beach or the drunk men on the cliffs. It is the children who told the man not to look at the sea, but to stay with them, south of the cliffs, and play a game, Palace In The Forest. It is only the children in Oriundia who never sing.

That all of this is just a song is what you're supposed to think about the whole book. I had to give it back, but did stay with it long enough to still be able to use it when I want.

I did have a job at the Disciplinary Barracks. I had enough to do just trying not to get fired from this prison job in the wood shop. My nickname there was Picasso. And my mind did wander.

14

New York–Panama–New York

Inland. Mexicans cleaning restaurants, sneaking beers.

There are men out walking. Most up to no good. But there are others who aren't used to it. Can tell.

They have homes and jobs, though too much of this could lead to their loss.

Men out walking this hour.

In every part of the city. Something on their mind that's old and good forces them out walking. Some of them aren't sure if it's okay to sit, and they worry about the next day with no sleep. A few have given in long ago. They know that sitting for a while is perfectly good and helps.

Southbound on the Broadway Local. Safe on the subway. I've learned how. Around my neck is a beaded Puerto Rican flag, and the long rosary beads with a cross at the end that you can only get from treatment facilities. In my hands I hold a white plastic bag that says Patient's Belongings and Name_____. These bags are found in garbage cans outside any public hospital, usually stuffed with clothes, the names never filled in.

I'd like to give up the story now and head home.

To sit by my apartment window, so far west that in some good hours and in the same minute can be heard the horns of big ships leaving the piers, the whistle of trains continuing on, and horses' hooves, the clip-clop so slow as they return to the stables on Eleventh.

Instead, I sit with Platoon Daddy across from me smiling and asking, *Was is los?*

Many of the brothers who had done tours in Germany said it. But Platoon Daddy the best when we were in the field and he came upon white boys—country white boys from Alpha Company—playing June Bug on a String. And it was a long string, slipknotted around the fat buzzing bug, way up high as the trees and Platoon Daddy smiling like only Combat that's still around can.

"Yo, man. Was is los."

Get off the subway last stop in Manhattan. To walk the bridge. See a fighter running across in boots, garbage bag, old-timer, and hope he fought pro.

I pick up speed at the middle of the bridge, no use pretending it's the first time that I've seen everything from here. It's all sky and lights, no ships, boats, this night. Can't pretend to be a sad Portuguese Foreign Legion guy either. With his gutter French how he says it.

There is no time to change my mind about where I'm going. It can't be the park, where there are benches under trees like Europe from pictures, where Sheep's Meadow's as wide and open as a lake, nor can it be the grass by the drive all the way west. It will be the Promenade facing black water, open air, the city and the dawn as it comes.

First, a little out of the way, to the corner store in the middle of the block where you can still get Loosies—for me two menthol, two regular from packs red and green—and a small bottle of sweet wine. Anytime, all mornings.

Into Brooklyn Heights at this hour brings the desire to creep. Old houses, shadows, water.

For now, there is not one person along the promenade, and any bench is where I could sit. But at the edge is where I have come to hang and bounce my feet.

Flat barge coming across in front, man coiling rope aft.

I have to relearn the knots, and how ropes go around poles, about four times a year. The same ones from a book and practicing in front of the captain till they are all perfect again every time, for now. They don't call me Too Easy on the boat. Just implied.

There's a guy works my boat has a truck with Jack & Diane written on the back window in script.

Hanging feet, light a menthol, the bottle full beside me. It made a heavy glass sound when I set it there.

I had some sweet wine years back, one night, when I tried to go all the way through. I was serious then, only didn't get very far. Didn't get much off the wine either, I was so careful.

Years before that I'd embarrassed myself into not drinking or anything anymore.

Was staying at the three-quarter house run by the retired social worker couple over on the East Side, Yorkville, and they got some State money for it too.

This kid at the house had a grandmother who had stomach cancer and he got a pass to be there when she died and when she did, and everybody was doing the mourning and distracted, he pocketed what was left of her Dilauded suppositories.

The next night, me and this kid broke the trust contract and snuck out of the house. We were going to do them, and have some beers, too, which we did in the park. Only the kid had such a time with the suppository and it broke in half. I was really high, really fast, and he got mad at me for not waiting and the cops were coming around patrolling in their little three-wheel Cushmans, and we ran for it, the kid with his hands down his pants, running, and trying to find that other half.

We got separated.

I don't remember going back to the house and in through a window, don't remember talking to a girl on the phone. But know by how they found me that I had passed out with the phone under my chin, eating a cookie with one hand and jerking off with the other.

Got thrown out of the three-quarter house. A guy told me at the church on Thanksgiving dinner that the phone bill was over a thousand dollars, and that because of me there was now a law that you can get the phone company to block the line so that you can't call those numbers.

It was the embarrassing part that made me quit. And maybe that that stuff didn't go so good anymore. I used to think that the perfect mix would help make the story better, that I'd be able to just touch a part of Panama. But then it started taking pieces of the story, dulling it, and so's that I couldn't pull in any part slow, it just came in big chunks all at once, not special. Not like my story at all. Worse was the smells were gone.

Tug going by now. Not one of ours, but Moran. Know it easy by the smokestack.

Like to think that there's one person watching from the shore when we go by, watching and thinking about things.

Winter's coming and we'll really earn our money. Know it's coming by what's hanging down the building I see out my apartment window past the fire escape. String, twine, and rope, knotted around sodas, milk, little tubs of ice cream later.

All the girls I've paid and what I am, more than anything else, is a good and kind customer.

I'm marked for all those working girls to see. By the money.

When I took it on that road, hitchhiking from St. Jerome's School for Boys into St. Louis, so I could have money to get a girl-friend. Then by Paola—how I paid it, and fell so bad. These girls can see it, even if no one else does. They know you've been paid and that you pay. Taken. Given.

They're nice about it, too.

Long, it sticks on you long.

Paola had told me. With Limón translating she said, "Dangerous the way you look at me. For you. Not for me."

Light a regular one, Pall Mall like Platoon Daddy, and twist the cap on the wine how it cracks.

A sip for almost getting there, and I leave my mouth wet by it.

Sips and Pall Mall. Together, so good.

The next weekend in Colon and we were buying drinks for all the girls. The other guys going up of stairs—sometimes twice—but always with the same girl. Paola and me on her stage and she's pointing to the red on my pack of cigarettes and then pointing between her legs and I really and truly don't understand. She doesn't like having to do this—having to keep pointing to the red on my pack of cigarettes, tapping on it, and then pointing to between her legs. Limón saw our communication problem all the way across the Bar Le Fleur, and he told me she was sick down there. Caught some-thing that showed up on their monthly tests from the government.

So me and Paola stayed by each other in the Bar Le Fleur, sitting at the edge of her little stage. Downstairs, while our friends went up. Both nights.

Another week of patrolling in the jungle. We hated it now, having to run missions for battalion and being pestered by those skinny per-manent party soldiers, so fast and stealthy.

By the third weekend, Paola was ready, everything cleared up. But I wouldn't go upstairs with her. I didn't want to, now, the way it was between us. Not that she had had the sickness, not that at all, but her working was what it was, and how we'd spent those nights the weekend before just sitting, and it didn't seem right to go up of stairs.

Big confusion in the Bar Le Fleur—girl trouble—and Limón in the middle of it trying to fix everybody's feelings. Paola was ashamed, cause no matter what she was told she thought it had to do with her sickness. She told Limón, who told me that this thing happens here, she was sorry, but it happens, and then with some time and medicine it goes away. She stayed with her friends on her stage and I stayed by myself or with the man from the northern countries at the bar who thought the whole thing funny and so much like life, he said.

I drank a lot of Balboas and listened for the song when it came on how the music and singing was too fast to be sad. I didn't remember hearing it the weekend before.

Those guys came in. The former soldiers from our Army with the grown-out hair, those tropical straw hats cut up how they liked, and the legs of their pants high-watered and fringed. If Paola was an American girl, she'd of gone up the stairs with them, made them want to, maybe for free, to punish me for my feelings. So upset I was that I didn't even get scared when they came over to me and said, "Hey," and told me about how there were "lots of opportunities for soldiers here." Togiola came over fast and put himself between me and them and did all the talking for us. They asked if he was Samoan and when they heard yes started to leave friendly, making sure when they said good-bye that they stuck their faces in mine and then were gone.

From the bar and from the stage we would look at each other, me and Paola, and finally on that Saturday night so late, when we were again betting on the drawbridge being down, she sent Limón over to me. "Look, man," he said. "She says she believes you, okay shit? Just stop with your face, man. Your fucked-up baby face is killing her, okay?"

"Tell her okay" is what I said, and it was so late now. Limón went back up of stairs and so did Ski and Togiola.

Like it had been the nights before, first the owner of Bar Le Fleur told me it was close to the time, and after a few minutes later, he called out to men according to their country or ship when it was their time, four or five different ones and all from his mind nothing written down. Then the man from the northern countries told me it was time and I went up of stairs, the man in the banker's cage told me "okay," and down the hall with nice carpet I yelled, "Recon! Recon! 'Bout that time, Recon! Let's go, scouts!" Doors opened on different sides of the hall, staggered. At each one, the face of one of my pals appeared and they all said very quiet, serious, that they would be out soon.

I went back down to the bar and now it was the bartender woman who said it was time, and the woman who belonged to the green and red bird said it too as she stroked the hair of the man from the northern countries, his nose making circles on the bar. I told the bar woman "quatro" and the please and thank you, paid for the beers and went back up of stairs, taking them three at a time to the top where the three scouts were already assembled, tucking in shirts, fastening belts, and talking low. They looked at me like I was early first call.

We picked the Balboas off the bar like they were being issued. Nobody said "good thinking" or anything. Paola wasn't at her little stage, and we missed bed check.

The bridge was split and sticking straight up like something exploded from the water and right through the middle. We got out of the cab and slammed the doors, pacing. The La Guardia laughed at us and the cab driver took out his newspaper. Worse cause we all had more of the girl's speed on us and long bumpy joints, bought one apiece from the men who sold the violet Chiclets, stuffed animals, meat on a stick. One of the La Guardia came over for a light, but that was it. We must have been too pissed off, quiet, and Depresso, to seem guilty.

Back in the cab and over the bridge is when it started. The guys saying that, "You don't fucking understand—I fucking love her, all right?" All of them on the ride said something like it. And now we were going to miss bed check and never see them girls again and the "I don't fucking care" started and so did the yelling out the windows, "Fuck it! AWOL-A-W-O-LOOSE," and "Failure to Motherfucking Repair—and I don't care!"

Lots of guys didn't make it back that night, including Staff Sergeant Clenton Macovey from Headquarters Company, who was last spotted walking down a side street with two girls and two bottles of rum, never to be seen or heard from again.

Platoon Daddy couldn't help us. Said we were lucky to only lose the next weekend's privileges; said they could've taken rank and some money. We told him all about the girls and he listened and asked about how "The Lover" was doing, meaning me. So that part got told too, about last weekend and this one, how Sensitivo me and my girl were being.

Back out to the jungle, a jump with the Panamanians, and then a beach assault like World War Two. We used those boats again, only we were going straight in, so there wasn't much sickness. Slept on the beach and the dogs found us there. Whole battalion remaining overnight, all laid out on the beach and the dogs came to us, one or two at a time, noses down, snaking into our position and then all of them circling and dragging out rucks across the sand. The whole battalion stood to watch, getting a good laugh at all the recon dogs.

Went to the barracks the next day to clean weapons and sleep in the cots before going back out to the jungle again.

We all talked about it, me, Ski, Togi, and Limón. How we could sneak down the long stairs that run outside the white barracks that face the sea, and through the unmanned entrance to the post, then get a cab or hitch a ride into Colon. Fuck it.

See our girls.

I was barely in the conversation, cause they were the ones who really had experienced the whole deal. But it was me who really went, saying I was going for the beer machine—*I fly you buy*—leaving those guys to burn the long bumpy ones and stare out so sad across the water at the place that was for us.

Got as far as the entrance, too. About to step off-post, past the flagpole, when the voice came from the dark by the stone wall.

"Come here, young soldier."

He took a step out into the streetlight, and I many more to meet him. He was holding a can of Mountain Dew with the top cut off when I came up to him and looked him in the eye. Looked up, looked him in the eye. Over his shoulder, back in the dark, I could now see the glow and fade of Sergeant Major's pipe and the shine from his can of Mountain Dew.

"Before you was here there was a battalion from the 101st and she was with them. And after you leave there's going to be some from the Rangers at Ft. Lewis, and after them some honest to God legs from the Big Red One. And she going to be with all them, too. Now you're looking at me like you want to do something, and go ahead, now. Ain't nobody going to bust you. Could bust you anyway.

But you know I'm right. So go on back to your buddies. We'll be here. You ain't going to be the only one tonight."

The guys were talking about love, watching the city across the water, and didn't even notice I'd come back. I handed out the beers, which seemed to be my new job. The guys had their minds on the girls and love, and a very important decision had been made: nobody wanted to smoke the red stuff anymore, saying it made them hurt more.

In the jungle again and for the last time.

Limón caught a scorpion and some red ants and this time kept them separate and alive, having gotten some foil from the spoons to cover the c-rat cans and poked enough breathing holes. Only had a few days left and the guys tried to cheer up cause it was maybe some of the last bits of time with Platoon Daddy, and because there's nothing worse than being in the field with a bunch of depresso Airborne scouts.

Even if you're just looking for a place to ghost, fuck off, you've got to be motivated about it unless you're ready for bad things to happen, get on people's lists. Basic knowledge for the soldier. Like even if it's okay to lay out, after a long mission or something, you shouldn't ever look truly comfortable around officers or any non-com above E-7. Lay there, but with a face like there's a little rock sticking in your lower back, but you're too tired from all the good soldiering to fix it out.

I talk to the captain of my tug about this. How working the boats is some ways like the Army, the hurry up and wait. On land and traveling the waters too.

He said the same thing enough times that I actually go in the stores and read it sometimes, though not more than the section from the book, and I know more of it by heart than he does by now.

The Bible legend says that the absence of toil—idleness—was a circumstance of the first man's blessed state before the Fall. Fallen man, too, has retained a love of idleness but the curse still lies heavy on the human race, and not only because we have to earn our bread by the sweat of our brow but because our moral nature is such that we are unable to be idle and at peace. A secret voice warns that for us idleness is a sin. If it were possible for a man to discover a mode of existence in which he could feel that, though idle, he was of use to the world and fulfilling his duty, he would have attained to one facet of primeval bliss. And such a state of obligatory and unimpeachable idleness is enjoyed by a whole section of society—the military class. It is just this compulsory and irreproachable idleness which has always constituted, and will constitute, the chief attraction of military service.

Guess I have my own way of pronouncing the words I've only read, never heard spoken, and I'm not buying that big book to make myself crazy with, *War and Peace,* only put it back after checking to see I've still got it right, not adding things my own. The Huck book tells plenty about idleness anyway.

I do keep that part of the book, *War and Peace,* and said to Captain that maybe that wasn't right to keep a part of a book when you haven't read the whole thing and that it was a good section, I liked it, but maybe it was combat guys who it was meant for. He said it was still okay that I enjoyed it and could keep the part like I'd been. We talk about idleness and time to think, and I tell him some about the Army, but not about the Castle, and he does know about the Castle, it's only that the Castle wouldn't make for good talking on the water, up at the bow, out in the open.

Maybe it's not good to leave the military after enjoying what the section in the book says. I tell this to the captain, who tells me, all the time cause it's like a routine between us two, "I don't know. You can always get a job on a tugboat."

He says, it's not only the military but jobs he's known for himself that can provide idleness as part of the job: rock and roll guy, college professor, and tugboat captain with the two on, two off work cycle.

Captain tried to get me to read some Ernest Hemingway, seeing that Ernest Hemingway said such grand things about Huck and that all great American literature comes from Huck is what Ernest Hemingway said, and I tried to read some, but I think maybe he got confused between Huck and Tom cause if there were ever two people needing to be officers it's Tom Sawyer and that Ernest Hemingway. Give me fits.

Another tug passes, pushing a garbage scowl, it's Moran again, a flat barge not far behind it. The sky's not pink at the edges.

Don't need the wine, but take sips anyway.

Wale is a mark made on the skin by a whip or rod.

Weir—a small dam in a river or a stream.

Blood tastes like iron.

"Pop a bleach balloon in this motherfucker's face."

If I sat long enough on the train tracks between Tenth and Eleventh, I could make a train come right at me.

If you stare at someone while they are sleeping, you can make them wake up if you are thinking quiet and hard on the right things.

You can find a way to remain idle, with a purpose, and wind-blown.

Benevolent is the name of a street in a city in New England.

Back in the barracks and restricted that Friday night. Lots of guys around restricted, or lured in by Limón's game enough that they'll miss the trucks into town.

From all over battalion they're crowded up to and all over Limón's cot, where Limón sits holding a huge glass jar with a white lid torn up with puncture holes for air. He's taken all the bets, and told us it's a sure thing, but his pals aren't betting, us being content that he didn't ask us to cover him, he's so sure.

First, from one c-rat can, he pours and shakes the fat red ants into the huge glass jar. As they scramble up the sides, the other c-rat can appears in his hand. Not even careful at all, he begins to talk Spanish into the can, his face close to it and then the can is tapped on the edge of the jar and the scorpion free-falls down to the bottom of the glass. I recoil from the sound it makes, brittle wings, trapped bird. Not still for a moment the scorpion goes round and round and up the sides of the jar like the motorcycle guy with gravity on the Wall of Death. Paratroopers yelling and they're for the scorpion, having all bet that way a few dollars. The ants begin to sprint across the back of the scorpion, who is moving right and left on the bottom now and his stinger, up high, curled only at the tip, wavers: it's too tall. The stinger, a thing of its own, is fast, but not like you'd think; you can see it strike, which it does so many times in the same spot. The ants flung, maybe not hit, and they're all over him now. The stinger quivering up high, so awful, and down it comes, more slowly like aiming, except when he's rolled over and covered, done for, stung himself is how they told me.

That, and not to think too much about it, cause it just stung its own self, that's all it did. And they weren't wanting to hear any wondering about it.

"Yeah, but martial arts and stuff, " I muttered, pushing my luck. Guys who weren't restricted were taking off, cause word went that there was still trucks leaving for town and they all said it was pretty cool to Limón, and nobody was pissed cause it was only for a few

dollars and everybody knows not to trust Limón in that way especially when he's from the place where the scorpions are.

There was a small group of other guys around us asking what all
the scouts were going to do on restriction and through them came
Ski, saying we could go. Smiling like the unsuspected and saying we
could go. Tomorrow night we could go.

He'd fixed it. Nobody had wanted to help him, saying it was no
use. So he'd done it for us all on his own. He worked the captain
over. Ski had stayed on the captain since before the beach assault,
whenever he was around the scouts Ski was going right up to him
and working. Hard. The captain liked Ski, thought maybe he could
bring him round, probably even knew he was a doper, but the two of
them had this thing. Since anyone could remember, the captain
would ask Ski questions like "How's it going" and "When are you
going to reenlist? Ski would turn into the super-duper paratrooper
and put on this voice, "Ahhh. Yeah, Sir. Great day to be Airborne,
Gotta love it, sir" and "I'm going to reenlist as soon as we get back
in, sir . . . For anywhere you can lead me, sir. Airborne."

I used to wonder to the guys if the captain didn't used to be like
Ski, and got reformed—maybe that was it—but everybody said in
unison, "Nah."

Ski told us what he'd been saying to the captain, cause we hadn't
cared before when it was impossible. Said he'd told the captain that
we'd met the girls on a bus in Panama City and had dinner with
them in a restaurant outside and how they were real good girls, and
that we were late for bed check cause after we'd dropped them off at
a decent time, we'd stayed up the whole night talking about how
great it was to be paratroopers and in a foriegn country and meet
nice girls. He told the captain about the train from Panama City, and
that one of the girls—the one he liked, and she kind of likes him, he
thinks, maybe—was wearing a yellow dress with all different kinds
of dogs on it. He told him we're supposed to meet them tomorrow
for a picnic at a place that only good families from Panama can go.

Ski had to promise to go to church with the captain and his wife
when we went back to Bragg.

Everything was changed now and good thing, too, cause we
hadn't known what we were going to do for the next two nights. We
were afraid it would be too much like regular times only much
worse, when we couldn't smoke cause it made a guy so sad having to
look across the water all the time seeing the city where we couldn't

go. But now it was a Friday night before the Saturday when we could go, and it would be like a full pass from the old Army days. We wouldn't have to be back until Sunday, getting ready to leave back to Bragg on Monday. The Bar Le Fleur doper scouts followed Limón to get change for the beer machine, his treat, singing the Limón song.

"AOAOA-Eight-thurty? Eight-thurty! My lady! The Disco! AOAOA! Eight-thurty!"

With everything different now, we stayed on the rocks that make the road out into the water, our spot. We made many trips to the machine, and the long bumpy ones, with lots of cigarettes. Didn't think about what the girls were doing across the water, past the ships, in the city, only that we'd be there tomorrow. I was back to being included in everything, cause I was definitely going up the stairs tomorrow, it was decided.

Platoon Daddy was real impressed with Ski. The way he had worked the Old Man, worked the hell out of him he said. But he couldn't be *too* happy for us, getting the one night back, cause we'd gotten caught in the first place. Thought he'd taught us better.

If I left the promenade now I could be back on Ninth Ave in time to see the sanitation guy doing pull-ups off the WALK/DON'T WALK sign. Feel like I should know him and the other one I see sometimes when I head for home.

That square thin bottle of sweet wine can just stay there by me. It's okay, the wine. Every few years for the attempts at telling, and now not needed except to sit by me, some sips to mix up the taste of cigarettes in the mouth. Coffee'd do the same thing.

Bottle of wine would like for me to get sidetracked, tell so many other stories according to it, and ones that are dumb.

It would like to have me back down low and talking to myself out loud. Fascinated by the stink on me cause it meant I was alive, and proud of it too cause I made something. So interesting that I had pus on me that got pushed up out of a wound that can't even be seen.

But now I'm a working man. Have been for years. Work the tugs out of Staten Island, Macalister Nautical Towing.

It was on guard duty, a warehouse with nothing else around, way at the back end of Ft. Bragg. I had walked that post with a shotgun pulled from the arms room, four shells in the pocket, and I didn't even jump when he came up behind me, ghosting out on a loading ramp shotgun across my lap. I didn't jump, maybe cause I knew the voice.

"You out here splitting stars, young soldier? Better serve right."

He should've never stopped catching me.

Knowledge of appropriate times and places for doing certain things.

I will have to tell you what it is like.

It's our last ride in deuce-and-a-half trucks under palm tree tunnels. The guys are quiet, so healthy from a day on post, on the beach. The girls in tube tops, short shorts, and heels outside Ft. Sherman give us a shimmy, and we salute them.

We're dropped off where the good road ends and the cracked pavement begins. Wait for the Chiba-Chiba bus, decorated Spanish psychedelic, and inside we're rocking along with the people, the music loud and cracking from the speakers everywhere.

We go to another bar first, on a main street, and big and bright. Stayed there for longer cause of the fun when we redirected the flow of girls over to the table of lieutenants from Alpha Company. They'd been ignoring us, so we sicced these girls on them, whispering in their ears "Go get *him*! El Capitains—Mucho Dineros." Then saying to ourselves, before the laughing, "Goddamn" about the swarm.

Collected packs off the bar—green ones and red ones—tipped like good guys, and walked over to ours.

The entrance into the Bar Le Fleur.

It must be that.

We walked into the Bar Le Fleur and girls we knew squealed, screamed a little, and shouted out our names.

Guys from all over battalion were there and they came to us, too, greeting us like it was a surprise party in our own home.

The girls had been told about our restriction the night before, but the guys said,"Didn't tell them y'all gotten off it for tonight."

Anti-Tank Platoon gunner Makuski, from Pennsylvania—managed to keep country hair that fell down over his almost chinese eyes when he didn't wear his beret—was dancing up on Paola's stage. It was okay. We knew him and from his stories. We was an erratic and dangerous boy from such same place who stood each day in wonder that the rest of his live long days had not been ended for him. Exaggerate, I do not, for this final day had come early for his father, two brothers, a great uncle, and one pugnacious and excitable bitch of a sister.

Paola was at the bar with the woman who belonged to the green and red bird and the man from the northern countries. She was wearing the yellow dress that had all different kinds of dogs on it. The same one Sluguski's girl had been wearing before; he hadn't made that up just for the captain. Makuski unsnapped his shirt and was pulling up on his T-shirt. It was Creedence turning round the big tape machine, music we all kept cause it was so big in The Place, even with the brothers and everything. He went down to his haunches and side to side. Back up for a spin like an about-face, and the whole Bar Le Fleur was clapping and telling him to go on.

And during just the instruments parts guys from his own platoon starting singing, changing the words.

Born on a pig farm/ Born on a piiiiggg faarrmm

And Makuski—the good guy with stories about dusting Amish kids in a Valiant with no hood until they caught him one time and beat the shit out of him and him saying that one Amish kid was so big he hid the moon—kept dancing from Paola's stage, yelling back to his pals.

Goddamn right!

I bought a blow-up wading pool from the guy. Made him sell me the one that was already blown up and for show, and a stuffed monkey on a stick from the other guy, and from his friend a handful of violet Chiclets, two gums to a box. Brought them over to Paola and gave them to her over at the bar, saying, "Here." The woman who belonged to the green and red bird gave a look to the man from the northern countries, like "boy what a charmer he is" and "we should let them be alone."

We waited, and the music was changed, and Makuski came down from Paola's stage. The people who knew, my guys and the girls, saved our spot so me and Paola could come over and hang feet, hook and bounce our legs.

The woman who belonged to the green and red bird left early for up of stairs with the man from the northern countries who had only said those words, "Cunning, Exile, Silence," to us before he went.

But first, the woman came over and took the bright blue blow-up wading pool and the stuffed animal monkey on a stick from

Paola. They had some words like "I'll put this in your room for you" and then some about the monkey like Paola was being teased and didn't like it, something about the monkey. All the girls laughed.

The man from the northern countries stumbled and fell when finally free from navigating between the chairs and tables—the crush of soldiers, and sailors from around the world. He lost the hand of the woman who belonged to the green and red bird, and when he got to his feet, he wanted to dance and speak to the bird that only slept these last times, until he was led away past the man in the wooden banker's cage, and we wouldn't see him again. Or find out the new name for his family's ship.

Paola was holding up five fingers to her friends and saying that I was superman and it would be this many times, you wait and see. It was Limón translating, and her friends went crazy with their laughing even more when she was so embarrassed. She squeezed my arm, which told me she had to say those kinds of things once and a while to be included, and I hooked our legs tighter to say I understood.

It was time, and I would have to go with her in front of everybody. I would try to go elegant like the man from the northern countries had gone those first times. I had watched so careful. I quit trying to identify all the dogs on Paola's yellow dress, and her eyes were down almost all the time looking at her little white sandals with the small heel, my boot in between the two of them, hanging, bouncing. And when she'd give me a look right in my face, it was that of a girl in open-eyed prayer, and I'd felt like I received something, just before her eyes were downcast soon and again.

I needed Limón to tell me he would help with the words when there were misunderstandings, even if I had to run back down to find him. I wanted to know that I was a priority. Then I could go. He was at a table and his girl was next to him and other guys had their girls and it was the whole battalion it seemed. Limón, cause it was the last night, promised not to get pissed from all the translating, and it was mostly the same kinds except for my guys, who were now all very sensitivo.

"Limón. Okay. Limón. What the fuck is she saying to me? All right. Alright. She knows I love her, right? The real kind like back home."

I don't know how we crossed the Bar Le Fleur, me and Paola. But when we did, there was a soldier's voice, one who had just returned from up of stairs saying, "Sarge, man, she did things to me they ain't even got names for."

And I was left with Paola in front of the man in his banker's cage. And afraid, maybe like the first time your ticket's been paid and you face a platform that's wooden and it's one step up to the best thick painted horses, iron stirrups, and real leather reins. You'd seen them rounding fast, but now were stopped and waiting.

Left standing at the banker's cage holding out money to the man, who took out the right amount. Paola gave him more from out of my hand, for extra time, which I had heard all about.

My hand on the banister rail and going up it slid across gouged wood both deep and worn. It said, DENY ALL SHORES.

Inside her room the bed was old-fashioned, and everything was old, which made it nice, not like you'd think. Leaning against her bed was the blue blow-up wading pool, and in the center of the bed was the stuffed animal monkey on a stick.

Paola gestured to my gifts and said thank you again. Then I saw that the ceiling was filled with dozens of stuffed animals removed from their sticks, suspended by pushpins through the ears and feet, all kinds, crazy colors when all together. So many more than the prize wall at carnival games, no room left for the monkey I had given her, and in a corner of the room there were blown-up wading pools leaning, two or three, and next to the stack there was a pile of them deflated and folded neatly. I wanted to leave.

She must of seen that or that I moved that way cause she grabbed my face and said, "Por favor, Cara Bebe, Por favor," and a lot of "No." She said "No" a lot, like I was doing something to her and she was smiling and pulling me around in almost a circle. She picked up the monkey off the bed and said "Especial" and propped it up next to a pillow and said the same when leaning the blue wading pool on top of the others. I thought, "Kinged You."

By the bed there was a window with dirty and rain-stained lace curtains gone rusty at the bottoms, the attempts to clean recent and obvious. The curtains made patterns on the wooden floor from the lights outside, what was left of the moon. Next to the window was a bureau with perfume boxes all over it, except in the center, where there was a glass bowl filled with little boxes of violet Chiclets. Paola moved behind me and reached up and dropped a handful in, almost overfilling the bowl and she wanted me to come with her away, but I stayed and looked at a picture which was taped to the bureau's mirror. It was a Golden Knight from the Army's Golden Knight Parachute Team in free fall and waving at me. He was a Staff Sergeant, the picture was signed.

Under each perfume box, when you looked close, there was scotch tape and the boxes were empty and only for show, you could tell. There were pictures of guys from every branch of the service and foreign, too, taped and tucked in one over the other, all smiling. There was headgear piled on the wooden points that rose above the mirror, sailor hats from all over and Marine garrison caps, and berets: all three, Airborne maroon, Ranger black, and SF green.

We could have had a real fight. We could have, guy and girl, right there in her room up of stairs at the Bar Le Fleur, me standing at the bureau and Paola sitting on her bed holding the stuffed animal monkey, staring down at it and saying *Especial*, wearing a yellow dress with all different kinds of dogs on it, and I'd of done something stupid like take the monkey back or something, and I'm just going to say it now so I don't have to keep saying it but she said *Especial* so many times that whole night.

It's just like they teach you in the POW phase of Reconnaissance Commando School: if you say something to someone long enough, they will believe you. They just don't tell you for how long.

From under the bed she pulled out a shoe box and was holding up to me a wooden animal which she called exactly this, "Es Sleeping Monkey." I came to her now and sat and said that no, it was a sloth, and she made such a face and said, again, "Es sleeping monkey" and I said, "Sloth," kind of mean. And this is what we fought about, something stupid that didn't really matter like a real guy and his girl who don't want to fight about what really does.

She taught me to slow down, and before that, we kissed before we kissed. I dropped my head to her but didn't. I went forward, my face, and came back; my lips felt as if they'd been touched, I swear, though we hadn't moved those last inches. It was being able to see her so close, with her not looking down, and we looked and that was a kiss. When we did for real, I drew her lips into mine and back a little and again like gentle drinking. I hadn't meant to, so she laughed, and we kissed longer, so much, maybe cause we couldn't really talk and somewhere in the kissing I said, "I give," said "Uncle," and couldn't take it back. The smell on her neck was smashed ripe melons and a way to stay in that second when by the open jump door the red light goes off and the green light comes on—the seconds between leaving the plane and the open chute's first sweet tug at your shoulders and you could live there. To draw back inches and feel like it was already too much like leaving. To look away through the space between the dirty lace curtains and see down into the streets of Colon wild with men at liberty, and over the tops of buildings easing away to calmer parts of the city, and feel the water close, unseen through that window.

She sent me to the back of her knee.

It was when we were holding each other after so much time that the man from the banker's cage first came and knocked on the door. Paola had to show me how much money to slide under to him. Then me holding her again, exploring what I actually got to do and it was what I had wanted when we sat on her stage with our feet hooked. It came on so slowly, all the pleasure, the more and more of it circling around us, close and held, even when she had to teach me to slow down it was what I felt in my arms and being able to look as much as I wanted that had spurred me on so, and needing a lesson.

So many times within that time up of stairs. When we did it different, and Paola wasn't making me slow down, she said some words over and over sounding like "Metay Mello" and other ones I don't remember, over and over. When Paola fell asleep, I put my clothes on and went downstairs and gave the man in the banker's cage more money and got beers and a ladies drink for Paola. I found Limón and yelled the words, "Metay Mello" to him, and he told me that means to "Put it hard, baby." I yelled the ones I don't remember anymore and his girl covered her ears and Limón said it means, "To take it." She is saying, that "You're supposed to be the man, so take it. Take it." He was very enthusiastic about translating this, and said I'm doing good.

Back to up of stairs. I tried to give the man in the banker's cage more money and DENY ALL SHORES. Paola's still sleeping and my hands, I know why Hightower's girl says he feels like warm mocha ice cream when they do it.

She's sleeping like maybe only these girls do. I take out the other wooden animals from the shoe box and have to make myself only look at them, not let them run over her body. I want them to stand on her butt, the giraffe dipping his nose to take a drink from the small depression where her back begins and it's a little darker there. She moves, shifts on top of the clean white bedspread with bumpy designs in it, and she's been here so long that the designs are pressed into her skin. Across the room there are three pairs of pastel-colored high heels which your hand couldn't fit in. Garfield slippers.

In a frame on the bureau is a photograph I hadn't seen before and it's three children with strong Indian features and a priest standing behind them.

Five prayer cards, all with Jesus looking skyward.

Sounds from downstairs—raucous out there—but now faint in the room like when you're supposed to be asleep.

The patterns on the floor from through the curtains, how I looked and each time they were different. The repetition of looking dividing time in up of stairs and so did the man when he knocked. I slid money again and again.

When Paola woke up she blinked and looked at me like "you're still here?" I thought it was time to leave and she said no and shook her head, and blinked more like she was only waking up, that was it. She made me come toward her and she opened my mouth and felt my teeth, the top and bottom front pointy ones, and tapped one of them and pulled my face to between her legs and the soft skins there. I had been to this place before, but not for very long and I know she meant something specific so I stayed only inches away. That was good, I thought, when she didn't pull me any closer, just stroked my head and the smell which was some of me and her and some like maybe the earth. I looked up at her and she tapped her own pointy tooth and then I followed her fingers so carefully as she parted her soft skins and I drew my tongue up slowly, which I knew she liked cause I'm not stupid, and now she tapped her finger on a place I did know about, but won't use the word. I understood even more when my bottom pointy tooth slid in under the cover of this place and it was the hard wet surfaces of my tooth over her place, hard, wet, and fattened where she wanted me. Sliding across each other was what she wanted, and good still with both pointy teeth only meeting and with the tongue how she wanted, and she was good at showing. Her noises were maybe why her friends had laughed when I gave her the stuffed animal monkey, and I stayed right with her as she moved, more like quivered.

More again with the holding and making me slow down and she made me notice as I went and where I went was someplace difficult to stay, easy to go, leave, go, come, left, right, left, and "please" I said, when she started that talking and I made up things in English to go with what she was saying in Spanish. That I am like a great animal, and to Go! Go! you great god animal me the monkey god.

And we stayed, the bones of our foreheads together, the skin shifting back and forth as she rolled her forehead on top of mine.

So many times within the time up of stairs and when she slept again I heard the woman who belonged to the green and red bird help the man from the northern countries down the hall. He sounded bad, like he needed more help, but I stayed and drank the warm Balboa, another one full on the windowsill next to Paola's ladies drink, untouched, and both the glass and the bottle condensating so the curtains stuck. And I slept, not meaning to, and I awoke to her holding a torn-up magazine that was like a book as well, thick cover, and the pages were shiny. She said, "Oh, my God, baby," and that she had figured out something.

Without Limón, it took a long time, with lots of pointing and acting like in charades, for me to understand that I was like someone in this magazine, in a story, and maybe the person who wrote it, or who it was about, was a friend of her mother's, and his name was Maqroll. He had another name, which was for Lookouts on a ship, and it was The Gaviero—The Lookout. About this I'm sure because I remembered the word, and later Limón helped me.

I also was to understand that this was not such a good thing that she compared me to, but not bad either. She let me know that she couldn't tell me any more unless Limón was right there with us. She let me hold it, and I did, cause I know how to hold someone's book.

We both slept together and then she went between my legs and took me in her mouth. I asked her not to, and then serious asked her not to when it didn't feel right—that if there was going to be another time, I wanted to see her, and it didn't feel right when she kept going anyway, and when the man from the banker's cage afterwards came knocking again, I knew this money was only for the room. I would have to pay Paola separate for all these times within the time.

I was making the face again. I could tell from seeing hers and everything was quiet, nothing coming from downstairs or the street, and maybe too quiet, so Paola went under her bed and came out with a record and a record player that was like a Close and Play, a big Close and Play. The record's jacket had a photo of a black woman with a short afro who sang in English, from England.

The first words she sang were, *I'm not in love/but I'm open to persuasion,* and in some places throughout the song, the singing went, *Oh ho/hee hee,* making it not sad, and then notes nice, low, and repeated, like classical.

I immediately wished I hadn't wondered who gave her the record, when what I came up with was that it was probably the pilot standing next to his C-130 in the photo below the one of the Golden Knights guy.

When she gave me her picture she said, "Please."

And made me understand that these kind of pictures are only done twice, once for their confirmation and again for something else. The white borders of that small photo were almost like cloth, and inside them she was younger. Maybe not that much, but it is enough to say about that photo that she had a different name when it was taken. I don't remember how it was written on the back above an address that was real and in Colombia and good for always.

Her hands flew up in the air after she handed it to me and came down in her lap—she had no more photos.

I talked. Said about being a sergeant soon and re-upping for SF in Panama. I said that, and more, and when it was morning and the knock came, I got up to slide the money under the door, and now in the light like I could do this forever. But it was the guys behind the door, could tell by their whispers, and they said to come on, we had to go.

I made them knock three more times and their voices rose, and during that time I said things to Paola who was pretending to be asleep. I dressed and left my name and the address for the company and all the money I had in the world on her bureau. She stayed pretending when I kissed her.

It was one of those rides when guys don't talk, a thing itself the taxi ride in the sun back to post, marking the end of a time. The not talking went on until we were outside the entrance to the post, and found that we'd all left all the money we had in the world in rooms up of stairs at the Bar Le Fleur. Played hell trying to find somebody in the barracks who hadn't done the same somewheres else.

They think I don't know about why I was the only one to go to the Castle.

Last couple of years I've talked to all of them that went to Red Lobster. They all stayed in except for Sluguski, who became a cop in Florida and who probably found me, but that couldn't have been too hard, cause I've always stayed an active member of the 82nd Airborne Association.

And Frankie Meadows stayed in, too, and didn't marry that girl. They all went to Germany and Korea. Had to. They became Drill Sergeants and Black Hats at Jump School, but mostly stayed Paras back at Ft. Bragg.

All of them are getting ready to retire now.

I'm older than Platoon Daddy was when I knew him.

"All right now."

Still try to say it. Never comes out right.

Those guys, how they call me now once in a while.

They think I don't know.

I know.

I just wouldn't let it get in the way of a good story.

There's a photograph that should have been taken, and I should have it. It's of a young man and a girl at the beach and she is wearing his maroon beret and has her arms around his waist. He has a cigarette in his mouth and his hands folded over hers. Behind her face would be balconies and banister rails, violet Chiclets, jungle and birds, and water, light through dirty lace on a clean floor. A time well liked, and guys who saw no reason why it shouldn't continue. Behind the face a room and downstairs of it a bar, and either in the rooms or at the bar, pals who would see you back okay.

Got a whole bunch of days left before I report back to the Macalister shack off the Staten Island Pier. See if I still have my good thing on land, and then the water. If I used it up.

I didn't. I just told a bunch of other good things on the way to the best thing that will always be there. Maybe the people who have told me so are right. There can be more good things. That they repeat.

The expensive girls who like the pointy tooth—and not all of them do—like it a lot.

I only talked to Frankie Meadows the one time. After he told me about Platoon Daddy's accident and how Sergeant Major passed, he asked me if I saw the dogs up there in New York City and we had a laugh. I asked him if he still saw them around Bragg. He said, "Nah, not like before. Dogs must have liked the 2/304 Scouts all together." And then some quiet before he says, "Shoot, those dogs just like us. Barking at a moon they think is a girl."